the Secret Hamlet

Brian Barnes

Judith Briles

Book 2: The Secret Hamlet
The Harmonie Books Series
© 2024 Brian Barnes and Judith Briles.

DO NOT TRAIN
Created by Human Intelligence

MileHigh Press

Published by Mile High Press

Editor: Barb Wilson, EditPartner.com
Proofreader: Peggie Ireland
Cover and Interior Design: Rebecca Finkel, F + P Graphic Design, FPGD.com
Book Publishing Expert: Judith Briles, TheBookShepherd.com

Books may be purchased in quantity by contacting the publisher
through the author's website: www.HarmonieBooks.com

Library of Congress Control Number: 2023923629
ISBN trade paper: 978-1-959737-93-3
ISBN eBook: 978-1-959737-00-1
ISBN audiobook: 978-1-959737-01-8

Historical–Medieval Fiction | Women's Fiction | France | Paranormal | Mystery

First Edition
Printed in the USA

For the fans of historical fiction ...

The Harmonie Book Series weaves a tapestry

of the 11th century—its truths, myths, and wrongs.

And to share a story of "what if" ….

Also by Dr. Judith Briles

When God Says NO: Revealing the YES

How to Create a Million Dollar Speech

How to Create Snappy Sassy Salty Success for Authors and Writers

How to Avoid Book Publishing Blunders

How to Create a Crowdfunding Campaign for Authors and Writers

AuthorYOU

Show Me About Book Publishing

Stabotage

Zapping Conflict in the Health Care Workplace

Stop Stabbing Yourself in the Back

The Confidence Factor—Cosmic Gooses Lay Golden Eggs

Woman to Woman 2000—Becoming Sabotage Savvy in the New Millennium

Woman to Woman: From Sabotage to Support

Smart Money Moves for Kids

The Briles Report on Women in Healthcare

10 Smart Money Moves for Women

The Dollars and Sense of Divorce

GenderTraps

The Confidence Factor—How Self-Esteem Can Change Your Life

Money Sense

The Money $ense Guidebook

Raising Money-Wise Kids

Judith Briles' Money Book

The Workplace

When God Says NO

Faith & $avvy Too!

Money Phases

The Woman's Guide to Financial Savvy

Self-Confidence and Peak Performance

Contents

Nichol's Secret Journey

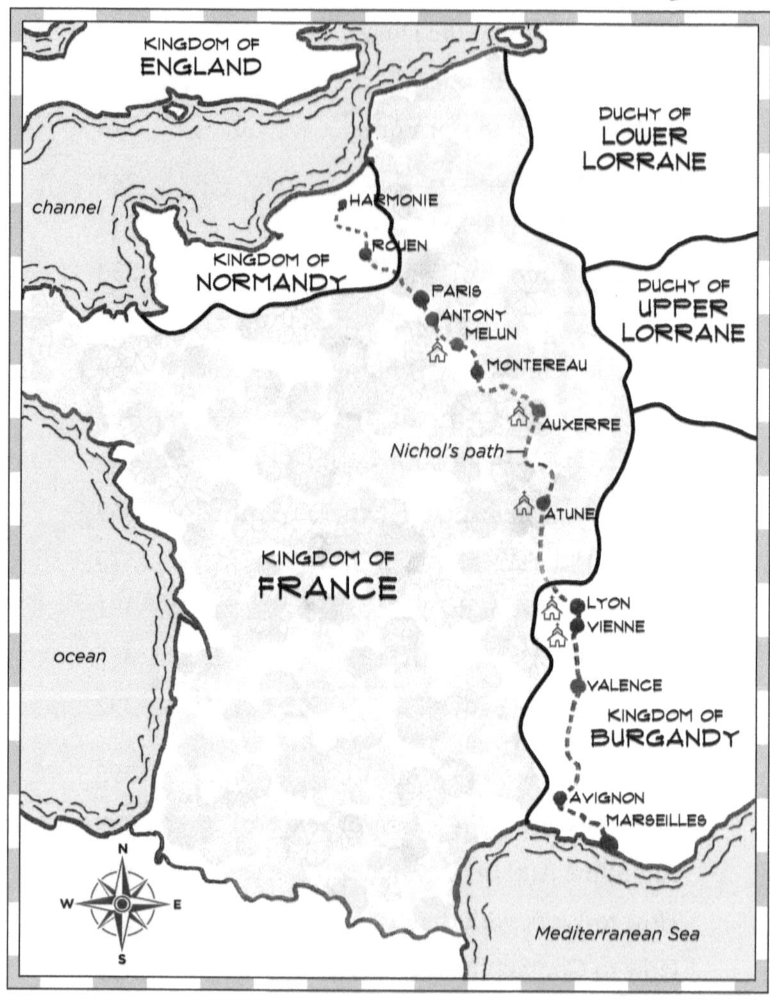

The Secret Hamlet

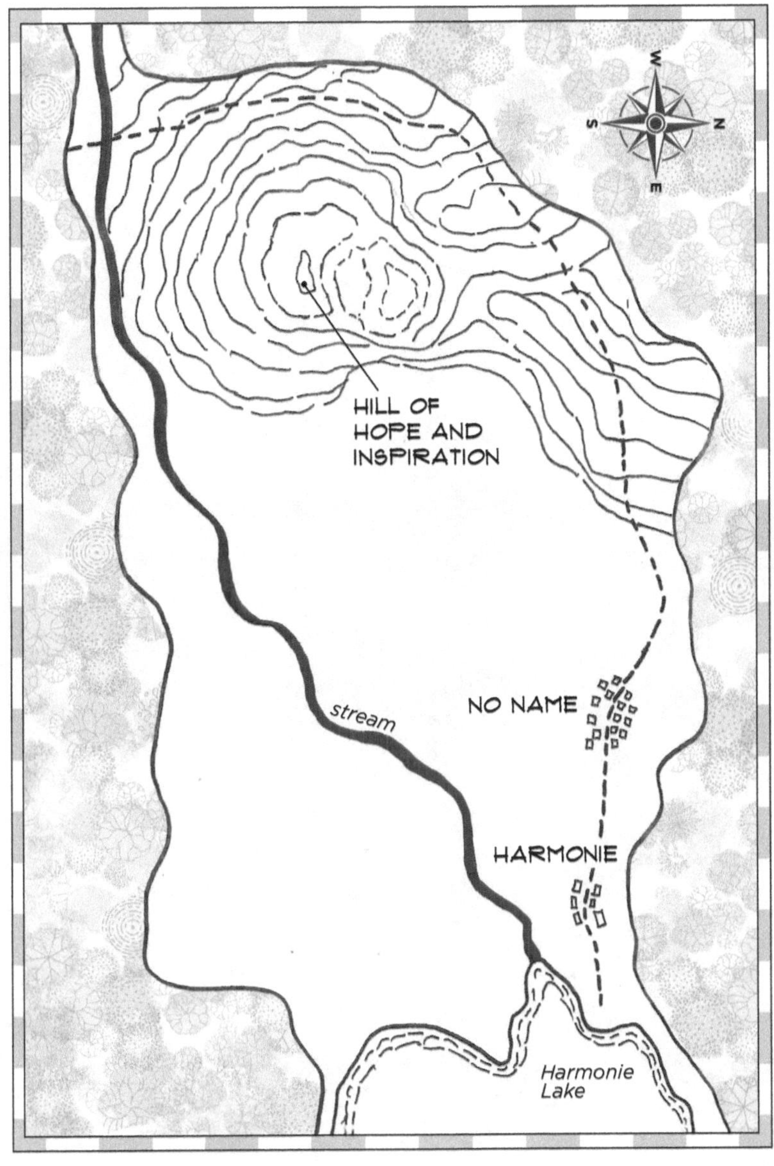

Winter Solstice

in the Year 1000 AD

A Daughter Is Born

You had to be in the room to understand.

By late December, Nichol was having a difficult time getting around. She was uncomfortable, but she felt the need to keep moving. Now fully grown, Shadow stayed close by.

The day was sunny, with a brisk wind outside. She and Robert had spent the day walking up and down the cobblestone street in front of Ezra's home.

"Shadow seems to be more protective of you. Do you think she knows that a baby is coming and she will have someone else to watch over, too?" Robert asked on one of their walks.

Nichol tensed up, then relaxed. *He does not know yet just how important Shadow will be in protecting our daughter.* "I am sure she is aware of how my body has changed and that I am not running with her right now."

Returning to the house, the extra weight and how the baby was positioned in her body tired her. As slim as she was, her belly jutted almost straight out, putting her off-balance. As she climbed the short stairway to their bedchamber, she told Helene, "I will rest before supper."

A light meal was eaten later and Nichol began helping Helene with the supper cleanup. As she moved the porridge bowls from the table to the kitchen, a horrible pain shot through her back and stomach, one that she had never felt before.

Nichol knew the baby's arrival was close. Shadow would not leave her side; ears alert every time she moaned from the discomfort her body generated.

Helene was now alert, too, and led Nichol to her bed, settling her in the dimly lit room. "I will have Robert get Sacha," she said excitedly, and she went to find Robert and Ezra in the lower great room.

Helene's demeanor told Robert why she was there. As if she could read his thoughts, she said, "Robert, our baby is on the way. It is time to bring the midwife, Sacha. Go to her home and tell her we need her now."

Helene gave Robert directions to where Sacha lived and sent him on his way to retrieve her. After he left, Helene started assigning tasks to Ezra. She remembered that Sacha said it would help the birth if Nichol drank warm water when she was laboring. "Ezra, we will need plenty of hot water. Fill the containers so they can be heated. We will need wood to keep the fires going and more soft linens for both Nichol and the baby." Her needs list grew for all the things she wanted him to gather.

Ezra could feel the excitement building under his roof. He collected everything that was needed and distributed it to where it would be used. As he gave Helene the linens, his hand lingered on hers. "We will have a baby in our home at last," he murmured.

Leaving, he turned and added, "Give this to Nichol and tell her to bite down on it when the pain is great." He handed Helene a piece of leather. Touching his wife's cheek gently, he smiled and headed down to the great room.

Robert burst through the great room door with the midwife, leading her to Nichol's bedchamber. Helene sensed that Nichol's time was close. Putting a hand on both men's shoulders, she shooed them out of the room.

It was not long before she heard Robert and Ezra laughing and telling stories, and consuming ale.

Sacha knelt by Nichol's side and conducted her first examination. "Your baby is close to birth." As dawn approached, the one narrow window in the bedchamber began to deliver the first of the morning's rays, bathing the room with a gentle light.

Once again, Sacha knelt by Nichol to check her progress. "Your baby is ready to come."

It is time. My daughter will be here soon.

Biting the piece of leather that Ezra gave Helene, Nichol let out a deep, protracted moan. At that moment, a baby girl entered the world with a gentle cry that brought joy to those in the room. While Sacha tended to Nichol, Helene cleaned the baby with warm water and wrapped her in the soft linens Ezra had delivered earlier.

The men slumbered in the lower room, waking when they no longer heard Nichol's moaning. They listened to the soft noises of the women murmuring above. They heard another sound … soft mewling, like that of a kitten. They knew it had happened.

Leaping up, they headed to the stairs. As they approached the door, Helene met them, cracking it just a few inches, holding the infant in her hidden arm.

"Go away … we are not quite ready. I will call out to you where we are." Helene turned back into the room, closing the door.

Moving toward the bed, Helene placed the baby girl in Nichol's waiting arms. Taking her daughter, she propped up her knees to create a backrest to lean her daughter on as she took in what was no longer in her but now in front of her. A loving expression spread across her face.

Nichol touched her daughter's face with gentle strokes and marveled at the tiny hand and fingers that reached out to her. Sinking into the blankets that had been built up behind her so she could sit, a huge smile spread across Nichol's face as she embraced her motherhood … and her daughter.

As she gently spoke to her daughter, she looked up at Helene. "It is time for Robert to come and meet his daughter. Would you please bring him?"

Turning to get the men, Helene felt a strange energy and motion behind her. She turned back to see a bright light dancing about the room, finally settling over Nichol. At the same time, Nichol raised her daughter up as if she were offering her to the light. Silence filled the room, and all three women watched as the baby responded to the light … as if something was physically present in the room that only the mother and newborn child could see.

Nichol smiled at her daughter's reaction, pulling her closer to her chest and kissing the top of her head.

Helene stood in awe. She knew … she had a feeling that the Lady who visited Nichol in her dreams was present. *The Lady is real.*

Helene glanced at the midwife to gauge her reaction.

The frozen stare on Sacha's face alarmed her.

Suddenly, Sacha looked at Helene, then back to the baby and Nichol, both surrounded by light. She backed away, flattening herself against the wall until she could go no further.

Her face contorted with fear and a howl came from her quivering lips. "The child and mother are cursed!" As she said this, her right hand made the sign of the cross.

Shivers spread down Helene's back when she heard Sacha's words.

Nichol caressed her daughter, oblivious to the midwife.

The light danced around the room one last time and disappeared.

two

Meet Your Daughter

She shall be called Lucette … Little Light.

The midwife's panic was apparent to Helene. Sacha shoved Helene aside with force as she dashed past, rushing through the door, down the narrow stairs, almost colliding with Robert and Ezra as she fled from the house.

Shivers slid down Helene's back once again.

Still, as she watched the gentleness between Nichol and the baby, calmness returned to her. *She will be a good mother,* she thought, drawing in a deep breath.

Helene stood to one side and invited the men into the room. Grinning, she told Robert, "You have a beautiful baby girl. Come in and see your daughter and her mama."

Robert was excited and nervous all at once. Forgetting to ask why the midwife Sacha fled, he smiled from ear to ear. Nichol was lying back, cradling her daughter to her breast; her joy was apparent to all. Taking Nichol's hand, Robert bent to kiss his wife.

Nichol looked from him to their baby. She handed the baby to him and all he could do was gaze at her in wonder.

"Robert, look at this beautiful little girl we made!"

So tiny ….

He admired his gorgeous daughter, with her rosy cheeks and perfect little features. As his smile widened and he looked at her face, her eyes locked on his. Overcome with emotion, he could not even speak.

Nichol looked at Robert and whispered, "You look like you have done this before." She was happy to see how at ease he was. He had always been gentle and loving with her, and the playfulness he displayed with his little sister, Raisa. Now, she could see his kindness and the tender way he acted with their daughter.

"The only thing close to this experience was holding my sister Raisa when she was a baby. This is very different. This little baby is ours."

"Robert, do you remember the most recent dream I told you about?"

He nodded in response.

"This is what the Lady told me in the dream. She said, 'She shall be called Lucette … Little Light.' When you and I discussed the dream, we were not sure who the Lady was referring to. Now that we have a baby girl, how would you feel about naming her Lucette?"

Looking at the baby snuggled in his arms, he murmured, "It is a beautiful name. Lucette. Yes." The baby stirred when he said her name. Robert chuckled. "She is already responding to it. Lucette it is."

Helene and Ezra were standing close to the door. Ezra whispered to Helene, "Why did Sacha leave so fast? She had a look of fright on her face."

"I will tell you later. I fear Sacha will become our enemy. She is dangerous."

Nichol gestured, inviting them to come closer.

Helene took Ezra's hand as they both moved to Nichol's bed.

Robert knew Helene could hardly wait to hold the baby again. Turning, he offered his tiny bundle to her. She took Lucette and cradled her in the crook of her arm.

Her face said it all … Helene was in love.

After a few minutes, she offered the baby to Ezra. He backed away, held his hands up, and said, "Not yet. She is too little. Maybe when she is bigger, I will hold her."

Everyone laughed at his reaction. This tiny girl had already unsettled him.

"Ezra, I predict that she will have you wrapped around her finger before long," teased Robert. Ezra shivered in response to Robert's words.

Helene saw Nichol's energy was fading and announced, "I think this new mother could use some rest. She has worked hard for the last several hours. Come to think of it, she has worked hard for many months to arrive at this moment."

The men left, patting each other on the back … as if they had done all the work.

Still cradling Lucette, Helene carried her to Nichol. Nichol held her to her breast as Sacha had shown her. Lucette latched on and began to suckle. Nichol's milk had not yet come in, but with Lucette's help, it would not take long.

Mother and baby quickly adopted the correct nursing technique and bonded peacefully. Before long, both were asleep, and Helene tiptoed from the room.

Finding Robert and Ezra in the kitchen, Ezra began to speak as Helene entered.

She held up a hand to quiet him and said, "We must discuss what I just witnessed in the birthing room. It confirms what Nichol has told me. Not only is the Lady's voice real, but I am also sure she was present during Lucette's birth. I saw a bright light settle above Nichol and Lucette, and they responded silently to the light. I believe the light was the Lady."

"How could a newborn communicate with anyone, let alone a mysterious unseen voice and a light that suddenly appeared?" asked Ezra with doubt.

"You had to be in the room to understand," said Helene. "Nichol has come into our lives not by chance but for a good reason. I believe it is our duty to protect and nurture this special mother and daughter. Their welfare depends on us doing that.

"The midwife also saw what I saw. She saw Nichol offer up the baby to the light that hovered over the bed, and she saw how Lucette cooed when embraced by the light. Not only did Sacha witness all that I did, but she turned pale with fear, making the sign of the cross and proclaiming the child and mother are cursed."

Robert's and Ezra's eyes locked across the table. Robert was the first to burst out, "No person could see what we saw when Nichol was holding Lucette and then say they are cursed!"

Turning to Ezra, Robert pleaded, "What should we do?"

Before he could respond, Helene quietly said, "Robert, I do not have a good feeling about this. I am afraid she will bring trouble down on us." Then she turned to Ezra. "You must go to the midwife tomorrow and buy her silence."

Looking at his wife and now sensing her fear, he nodded, saying, "I have never seen you so distraught, Helene. Of course, I will do as you suggest."

three

A New Role

I know that Nichol and Lucette must be protected.

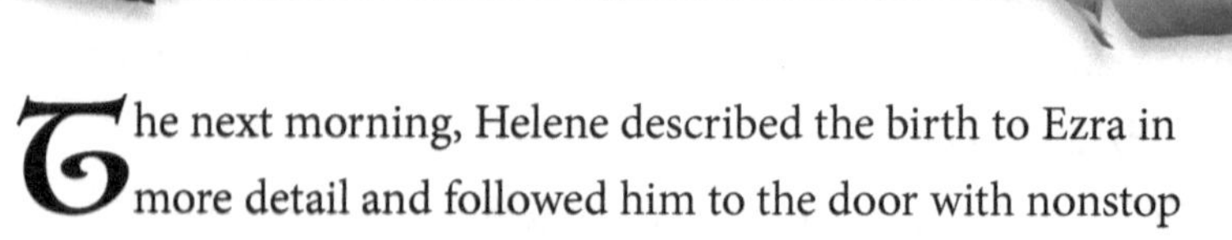

The next morning, Helene described the birth to Ezra in more detail and followed him to the door with nonstop requests: "When you talk to her, I want to hear exactly what she has to say and how she says it."

Ezra turned to Helene and kissed her on the lips. "I will do as you say, my love." Waving, he turned and walked toward the midwife's house.

There is more to what happened in that room than she has words to describe. I must buy Sacha's silence, he thought. *This is an important mission. I need to be persuasive.*

Approaching the door, he lifted his hand, knocking … dread vibrating through his body. Again and again, Ezra knocked on her door, and still no one answered. Hearing children talking and laughing inside, he knocked again, this time louder. At the same time, he shouted, "Please, someone open the door! It is me, Ezra."

Finally, the door cracked open revealing the partial face of a man. "Is Sacha here?"

The man glared at him. "Yes." Then he abruptly closed the door.

Moments later, the door opened, but this time Sacha appeared. "What do you want?" she snapped, a scowl on her face.

"I wanted to pay you for your services. Yesterday you left before I could do so." Ezra handed her a hefty purse of coins. "Thank you for your help with the delivery. Nichol and her baby are doing well."

"The devil is in that woman and her child!" she shouted and slammed the door in Ezra's face.

Stunned, he stared at the door. Alarmed by what she said and by her behavior, Ezra knew he must return to his family immediately and tell them what had happened.

This woman is dangerous. For Nichol. And for all of us.

As Ezra returned to his house, Helene pounced upon him before he removed his cloak. "Tell me what she said. Did she take your coin?"

In a lowered voice, he began to speak. "As I approached the house, I could barely reach the door before foul odors hit me. I could see dead rats in the pile of filth by the door. It was over-whelming. No one had pushed the mud from the entrance. It was not welcoming.

"No one answered the door at first. I could hear voices behind it, and I knocked again and again. Finally, a man barely opened the door and peered out at me. I asked for Sacha. He shut the door, and then Sacha appeared. Handing her a bag of coins, I thanked her for her services and told her that Nichol and the baby were doing well. She snatched the coins from my hands and then spit out, 'The devil is in that woman and her child!' Then she slammed the door in my face."

Helene took in his words, then reached for his hand and guided him to a chair at the table. "Ezra, Lucette is special. Evil does not bring a gentle light. Nichol and Lucette have a great purpose, of that I am certain. And we need to be part of their lives."

"I am aware that both are special, Helene. Until now, I have been careful not to judge Nichol because of what she has been … through. When we arrived in Marseilles, I first went to Rose to share news of Nichol and thank her for helping her escape. She was happy to hear of her safety and arrival to Paris. and of Robert and Lucette. I next went to Nichol's villa where Alexander was killed and met with the housekeeper Margaux who confirmed everything Nichol had told us.

"On the way home, I thought of how Nichol's papa forewarned me why he had to protect Nichol. Alexander told me about hearing a woman's voice warning him to protect his daughter and telling him repeatedly that she was in danger. He must have been referring to the Lady you and Nichol talk about. I know that Nichol and Lucette must be protected, and I promise you that I will protect them. I will be their defender. It was in Alexander's plan."

The Visit

Their bond was immediate.

It was time to celebrate Lucette's arrival.

Lucette was a good-natured baby who held everyone's attention from the moment of her birth. She nursed from her mother's breast with ease and slept well between feedings.

After her arrival, the house took on a new air—a welcome one woven through with happiness and warmth.

Lucette loved being held and was content in any family member's arms. Shadow would nuzzle her when Lucette was at Shadow's level. Robert and Nichol were amused that Shadow stayed close to the bed Lucette shared with her parents—almost as if Shadow thought she could stop baby from falling if she rolled too close to the edge of the bed.

Even Ezra coddled her. After much ado about a baby being so tiny, he realized this little baby was not as fragile as he had imagined. He held her and whispered to her as if there were secrets between the two of them.

Helene smiled when she overheard him telling Lucette stories about his travels and promising he would teach her how to be a merchant when she grew up. Chuckling to herself, Helene turned back to her tasks.

Helene's contentment was evident to everyone. Having an infant under her roof for the first time was a joyful experience she never dreamed she would be able to enjoy, never having been able to bear a child. Each day was one that she embraced.

Within a month, each adult developed a special bond with Lucette. Helene was proud of Nichol and Robert for adapting to parenthood as they had. They were both loving and gentle with their daughter, treating her as the special light she was in their lives.

One morning, Helene asked Robert if he would like his family to come and meet Lucette. Looking at his aunt, he smiled. "I would love that. Thank you."

"I know your sister and brother will be excited to meet your new daughter. I will send a message and invite them to come to Paris as soon as possible."

Surprised and delighted to hear of Lucette's birth, they could hardly wait to meet her once the cold was not so bitter for travel.

Arriving within a few weeks, with Raisa asking every hour if they were there, they finally crossed the bridge that led to Ezra's home.

Raisa ran to the door, shouting, "We are here; we are here!"

Pulling a cradle off the pack animal that carried their belongs, both Achim and Dinah laughed at their daughter's excitement. Robert was the first to get to the door, hugging his mother and father, followed by Helene and Ezra.

Once the greetings were over, he offered, "I'll unload the horse and take him to the stable." As he said it, Raisa had already rushed through the door and into the house. "Where is the baby?"

Achim carried in the cradle. "We thought you could use this."

Looking it over, Helene marveled at the craftsmanship. "This is ideal, Achim. I know that Nichol will be grateful to have it. Let's take it up to the bedchamber."

As if called to duty, Shadow followed closely as the cradle was moved, with both Dinah and Helene following. Nichol had just finished nursing Lucette and had lain her on their bed to sleep. She was happy to see Robert's parents but even happier to see the gift they had brought.

Directing the men where to place the cradle, Dinah immediately added straw, packing it down and then covering it tightly with linen to smooth Lucette's new bed. Nichol added some of the baby's blankets and Shadow sniffed all around it as if she needed to approve the addition.

Nichol gently lifted the sleeping Lucette, moving her to her new bed. Amusing the women, Shadow lay next to it, ready to do her overseeing task.

Upon seeing her niece, Raisa could hardly contain herself. She wanted to wake Lucette.

Nichol took her hand and promised she would be the first to hold her as soon as she woke. At the same time, she urged everyone to leave and go downstairs to talk and eat.

In the evening, everyone watched in amazement as Raisa held Lucette and explained to the baby that she was Auntie Raisa, and she would take loving care of her and teach her all that she knew. Then, she added that her brother, Uncle Gideon, would teach her skills, too.

Lucette turned her head when Raisa talked to her and waved her little hands, as if she understood every word. Their bond was immediate.

Gideon had no interest in the baby. His interests were directed toward Shadow. He wanted a dog like her. When Shadow wasn't carrying out her Lucette duties, the dog found that walking and running with Gideon was more fun than just being in the front room of Ezra's house.

The visit was short. Achim needed to return to Antony for his work. He was pleased with the acceptance of Robert's goldsmithing and the commissions he was receiving. Over supper the last night, Ezra talked about his concerns. He discussed the unending greed of the church and the threats he was hearing from those who were also Jews in Paris. He was careful to warn his brother Achim to be alert for any acts of hostility that could be directed at him.

Before Achim and his family left, Raisa took the blanket she always carried and handed it to Nichol, who was rocking Lucette in her arms.

"This is for Lucette. It is my favorite blanket and I want her to have it now."

Nichol took the blanket and kissed both of Raisa's cheeks. "What a thoughtful gift. I will wrap her in it and when she is old enough to understand, I will tell her it was a special gift from her Auntie Raisa." Raisa was very pleased that her gift was appreciated.

As Gideon said goodbye to Shadow, he nuzzled her neck. "I'm going to make you a special collar when I get home. No other dog will have anything like it. I'll bring it the next time we come."

Goodbyes were said, and the farewell waves seemed to last forever as Achim, Dinah, and Gideon walked, with Raisa carried on the horse for the long walk back.

five

Timo's Warning

*Now we'll be threatened because someone thinks
our daughter is the devil's child.*

Each day flowed into the next as the house settled in. Lucette had taken to the voices around her with little interruption to her peaceful sleep. Nichol's ear listened for her child's first whimper, waking at the slightest stirring from the cradle.

The house activities now revolved around Nichol and Lucette.

Late one night, there was a loud and persistent knock on the door. Ezra awoke, went to the bedroom window, and opened the shutter on the floor over the doorway.

"Who's there? And what do you want at this hour?" he growled. He could only see a dark shape outside.

"I am Timo, the monk who traveled with Nichol to Paris. I have urgent information for you."

Instantly recognizing the name, Ezra knew it had to be news about Nichol. "I will be right down."

As soon as Ezra spoke, Helene was on alert. When she heard the voice outside, her thoughts raced. *Timo? This must be Nichol's Timo.*

Lighting a candle before descending the stairway, Ezra headed to the door. Moving the rabbit skin and peering out, he could see the outline of just one person. Lifting the door brace, he opened the door and beckoned Timo inside. Helene had followed Ezra and lit candles around the great room. Inviting Timo to sit, she asked if he wanted something to drink. Timo declined.

Hearing noises below, Robert woke Nichol. "Someone is at the door. Stay here." He heard Ezra talking, but he did not recognize the other voice. Looking at Shadow, he wondered why she was wagging her tail.

Wide awake, Nichol said, "I know that voice, Robert," as she quickly rose from their bed.

Lucette stirred and Robert picked her up. The three of them moved down to the great room with Shadow at Nichol's heels.

Upon seeing Timo, Nichol raced to embrace him, as did Shadow, with her tail wagging uncontrollably. Turning to face the others, she said, "I see you have met Ezra and Helene. This sleepy man holding our baby is Robert."

Walking to Robert, she proudly took Lucette and held her up for Timo to see. "This is Lucette."

Smiling, Timo declared, "She is indeed a special baby. I have heard a lot about her."

Nichol looked at him, knowing why he had come in the middle of the night. His silence filled her thoughts with concern that now spread across her face. Instinctively, she pulled Lucette close.

Ezra watched Nichol with a keen eye. Tired and not one to mince words, he asked without hesitation, "What brings you to our home at this late hour?"

Everyone remained silent. Breathing deeply, Timo relayed his message.

"I had to come late so no one would see me at your home. I fear there is danger for you—for all of you. A woman is spreading rumors about Nichol and Lucette. She is the midwife and is going about proclaiming that Lucette is the devil's child because of an unusual happening during the birth that frightened her.

"This woman talked with a local priest and told him that evil things were happening in a house owned by a man named Ezra. I was told that she said that suddenly there was a bright light in the room. Nichol lifted the baby toward it as she lay her head back. And that there were mysterious demon noises and happenings that occurred.

"The midwife saw something unexplainable and immediately thought it was evil. If there's one thing I have learned about Nichol, I know whatever it was, it would not be evil. If there was any unusual presence in the birth room, it was not the devil—but quite the opposite.

"I recently arrived at the Paris monastery and planned to seek out Ezra and confirm that Nichol was safe. Then, I heard the rumor this woman was spreading many times from others. I do not know what action the priest will take or how soon he might investigate the midwife's claims, but I think you must take this situation seriously. You are in danger and Nichol will be discovered.

"I knew I had to get to you immediately. How to find the moneylender Ezra was not difficult. As soon as I learned his location, I waited until dark to alert and warn you."

Everyone was now fully awake and alarmed with what Timo had revealed.

He continued, "A new priest recently arrived in Paris. He demands complete loyalty and those questioning his authority soon learn that his word on all matters is absolute. I have heard that when he walks into a room, you can see immediate fear on the faces of those present. Knowing these things, I expect that he or another priest will investigate the midwife's story very soon."

"I have heard of this new priest. What is his name?" Ezra asked.

"Loupe."

Nichol gasped and her fears exploded. *Little one, we must run soon.*

All eyes turned to her. A look of dread now covered her face. "This priest's name wouldn't happen to be Kilian Loupe, would it?"

Timo answered, "Yes, it is. Why do you ask?"

Nichol lowered her head. *When will it end?*

She paused, and then lifted her head and began to explain.

"There was a young priest in Marseilles named Kilian Loupe, who visited Papa on several occasions. He was quite charming while soliciting tithes for his church, but the last time he visited the villa, he came alone. There was nothing pleasant about him then. He was threatening and demanding far more than tithes.

"Papa denied his request, and Loupe became outraged. He began swearing and hurling threats, and Papa told him to leave. Because I was hiding in my niche in the solar, I witnessed his demands, which had nothing to do with the church. He wanted a part of Papa's business.

"Loupe reminded me of my half-brother Fredric, who tried to kill me—his mannerisms, his body language, even his looks. I felt that they were two of a kind. Both bad and to be avoided."

Helene was watching Nichol. Moving to her side, she guided her toward two chairs, gently pulling on her elbow to sit down. Leaning to Nichol's ear, she murmured, "Keep Lucette very close; I feel more bad news is coming."

Nichol did what Helene told her without protest despite being deeply alarmed. Looking up at Robert, she asked, "Now we'll be threatened because someone thinks our daughter is the devil's child?"

Wincing, Timo interrupted. "Nichol, I am afraid there's more. Priest Loupe has made it known that he has taken up the search for Astrid's daughter."

When Timo mentioned her venomous mother, all Nichol could think about was Astrid poisoning her papa. Refocusing on Timo's words, she heard him say, "Somehow, Astrid was convinced that you were making your way to Ezra's because he was your papa's partner in Paris."

Ezra jumped to his feet and began pacing.

"Nichol, I did not want to tell you this because I thought it served no useful purpose, but now that all this has become known, there's too much in the way of coincidence not to share it. When I was in Marseilles at the villa where you lived, the housekeeper Margaux greeted me and said, 'Hello, Ezra … I remember when you visited Alexander, and I brought you wine in the solar as you concluded your business with him.' Then she told me that after Alexander died, a priest named Loupe visited Astrid often. His visits lasted for hours and always took place in your mother's private chambers."

Nichol interrupted Timo. "Loupe slept with her in Papa's house. Astrid is cunning and she would have recognized that same thing in him. I suspect that she lured him into her bedchamber and plotted with him to track me down. If power and fortune are that important to him, doesn't it make sense that he would do her bidding? She is a whore, just like the women Fredric favors. I wonder … I wonder if Loupe is connected to him somehow."

"The danger we all face is apparent and coming fast. I want all of you to prepare now to leave Paris." Ezra stopped pacing. "If Priest Loupe rules with an iron cross, Timo is correct. He will force someone to investigate the midwife's claims soon. I want all of you to prepare to leave for Paris before the light and go to our cottage. Take everything you need and make certain you leave no trace of Robert, Nichol, or Lucette behind. There can be no items under our roof that would suggest a baby has been here. And nothing else that could relate to Nichol as well."

Helene gave her husband a questioning look. "Yes, Helene. I am asking you to go with them. We have only a few hours to get all of you packed and on the road."

"But, Ezra, how will we transport all our things on such short notice?"

Fear and anger filled the room.

And during the tension, Timo smiled. "I have the answer waiting right outside. Nichol knows how I travel."

At those words, Nichol rose from where she was sitting, went to the door and threw it open. "Oh, can it be?" she said aloud, more to herself than to anyone.

Nichol's friend Moki stood at the edge of the road—Timo's donkey and four-legged road companion.

Nichol turned to them, "Meet my friend Moki. He carried more than his share of seeds and tools all the way from Vienne. I am sure he can get our things to the cottage."

Ezra waved Nichol back inside. "Nichol, step back. You must not be seen … not by anyone but us. We must move quickly. And we must all keep our voices down and move about quietly."

He turned. "Robert, you and Nichol must pack your belongings and Lucette's items as well. Helene, collect all the valuables you can safely carry and gather some clothes. Timo and I will pack enough food for you to eat when you get to the cottage. Each of you can carry a food pack on your back and we'll load the rest on Moki. We have little time. Now, let us move!"

Everyone did exactly what Ezra had instructed. Before long, they had Moki packed with their possessions and ready to go. The reality that they were fleeing their home settled in on everyone.

Helene began crying and hugged Ezra tightly. "Ezra, why the hurry? What are you not telling us? I do not want you to stay here alone."

Kissing her goodbye, Ezra led her to the door. "There is no time for explanations. I promise to meet you soon. And at that time I will reveal more. Depart before daylight. I will stay behind to see who shows up and listen to the lies they spread. In turn, I will spin my own tales to confuse them and send them searching in other directions.

"What I have not told any of you is that I have been insulted and threatened by the likes of this new priest before, and I ignored all of it. The Catholics are determined to rid France of the Jews who live here. If they cannot manage to steal our wealth with their demands and threats, they will find other ways."

He shook his head. "How could I have let it go on for so long? No more. There is something happening here that is greater than you and me.

"Robert, lead our family to the cottage. I will follow in a few days. I will send my protectors a message to get ready to move forward tonight. One will be with me. The other will head to the cottage to make sure it is safe before you arrive. Now, be on your way at once."

Ezra pulled Nichol aside. "Nichol, we now know that Loupe was responsible for the attack on you at our cottage outside of

Paris. When morning comes, I will send John there. Expect him to arrive at midday.

"You know how to protect yourself; you are the only one trained with knives and swords. Take mine. Make sure you have your dagger on you. With what you already have, place the weapons on your body and on Moki, where you can access them quickly. And, if you have not told Robert what happened at the cottage, you must do that now so he understands the high level of danger you are in … that we all are in."

Hugging Ezra, she whispered to him, "I will. I taught Timo how to fight with swords as we traveled together. I will be on alert and so will Shadow."

As she moved away, Ezra nodded and turned toward the others. Farewells were said and the unexpected journey began.

Ezra shut the door and put the wooden beam into the brackets. He sat at the kitchen table, and thought *I knew this would happen someday. Not how or why, but I knew ….*

Then he slammed his fist on the table.

And I am prepared for the bastards.

Midnight Escape

I have seen the land ... our next destination.

They traveled slowly, moving quietly and deliberately throughout the night. Morning broke into a gray, overcast day but their spirits were not dampened.

Each of them had spent time carrying Lucette and now she began to fuss. She was hungry.

"Can we stop for a brief time so I can feed her?" Nichol asked. "As soon as she settles in, I can continue walking." She turned to Helene. "Helene, I thought of a way to use the small blanket Raisa gave me. With Timo's help, we can stitch a holder for Lucette that wraps around my back and neck, allowing her to be carried close to my breast and feed at the same time. With the holder in place, my arms will be free and no one else will need to carry her."

Timo was intrigued by what Nichol had described. "When we get to the cottage, let us make your carrying sling."

Robert pointed to a stand of trees a short distance from the road, and they made their way there. As Lucette settled into the offering of milk, Helene helped Timo pull food from a bag on Moki. Everyone was exhausted and huddled close together to stay warm as they ate.

After her feeding, Lucette fell asleep. Their journey resumed and conversations flowed back and forth as they made their way to the cottage. It was late morning when they arrived.

Timo found a suitable spot for Moki. He chose to stay outside to keep an eye on his friend. Unpacking the many bags that had been piled on him, straw and water were set out. And Helene prepared the sleeping arrangements for those staying inside.

As promised, Ezra sent John to help protect them. Arriving in the early afternoon, he tied his horse to a post and entered the cottage. He did not say much; he did not need to. Very few would challenge a man of his size.

All were relieved to have his presence nearby.

A fire was started and Helene prepared a warm meal, gathering all around the small table to eat. Shadow stayed at Nichol's feet, waiting for her share. Nichol scratched her head and murmured to the dog, "You will have a big meal tomorrow. I know you did not get all the rabbits."

Nichol's and Helene's eyes met. Helene looked troubled as she turned her head slightly and looked at Robert, then back to Nichol, raising her eyebrows as if to say *it is time to tell him*. This interaction caught the attention of all sitting there.

Robert and Timo stopped eating; all eyes focused on Nichol. Nichol looked down to collect her thoughts and then looked directly at Robert. "Robert, remember when Helene and I came here when you were in school? We did not want to tell you because—"

Abruptly, she stopped. "Helene, please tell him."

With Lucette in her arms, Nichol stood and went outside, with Shadow following.

Leaving the door open, she paced back and forth in the front of the cottage. Shadow settled down and watched her move back and forth, eyes shifting.

Everyone looked at Helene.

"Tell me what?" Robert asked.

She took a deep breath and as the air escaped from between her lips, she began.

"When Nichol and I were here last, we had just sat at this table to enjoy lamb stew. Not one bite was taken when Shadow leaped up, looking at the door. A deep growl erupted from her. Immediately, Nichol pulled out her dagger.

"Suddenly, the door was kicked open, and a huge man stood there with a knife. At the same time, Shadow lunged and grabbed his hand that held the dagger, jaws gripping him tight, like the tongs a blacksmith would use.

"With Shadow protecting Nichol, she jumped from her chair and plunged her dagger into the man's belly. The man hit Nichol across her face. She fell to the ground, still holding the dagger. As she fell, she ripped his gut open. On his knees, he screamed in pain. Shadow did not stop, shaking his limp arm from side to side, dragging him to the ground."

Helene stopped to catch her breath. It was complete silence. No one's eyes moved from her face as she took a drink from the cup before her.

"Immediately, another man appeared at the doorway. Moving faster than anyone that I have ever seen, Nichol was on her feet and repeated what she had just done, plunging her dagger into the second man's throat. He fell to the ground, holding his neck as blood spurted through his fingers. I could hear gasping and choking sounds and knew that he would soon be dead.

"All this time, I sat motionless at the table, watching something that I could never imagine … just as you are doing while you hear my words now. At the same time, I marveled at what Nichol did next. She cleared the door, pulling both men out quickly, then stood outside, covered with blood.

"When her eyes met mine, I saw anger in them and then a sense of her telling me silently, *I am sorry, Helene.* Shadow was at her side and Nichol dropped down and pulled her close. At the same time, she turned to look across the countryside, like she was watching for more attackers."

Helene scanned each of their faces. The room was heavy with shock and awe—and pain. Once more, she spoke.

"There is more. I willingly became part of this. I helped her and together, we made plans to bury the bodies. Nichol had noticed two riderless horses not far from the cottage and she felt they belonged to the men. She retrieved them, bringing them to the side of the cottage where they were tied. With the two shovels we had, we dug a large hole and buried the men. They are now where our garden was.

"Exhausted, we washed the dirt and blood off, ate the dinner we had begun hours earlier, and slept a little. As the sun rose, Nichol went to Jacob's house early with Shadow to hunt rabbits as promised. Then she lied, saying we had received news that Ezra was ill, and I wanted to return to Paris. We rode the horses back to Joshua's house. We thought the horses would return to their owner, and Joshua would feed and release the strays for us."

Abruptly, Robert stood, pushing away from the table. He rushed out the door and embraced Nichol, nuzzling her neck and gently stroking Lucette's head. Neither said a word and neither let go.

Lucette started to cry. Gazing deeply into Nichol's eyes, Robert murmured, "Let us go inside. Our daughter is hungry and you need to eat. And I now understand why you did not tell me what happened at the cottage when I was at school."

Nichol was relieved that Robert finally knew. The attack and killings had followed her like a blackened storm cloud. Now, it was out.

Once Lucette was fed, Robert held her as they sat at the table. Nichol and Helene finished the rest of the story together, but Helene did most of the talking.

"There is more. Joshua spurred the horses toward Paris. He dropped their reins and followed them to their destination. When they stopped at a stable owned by a bishop, he learned from the priest Loupe who emerged from the stable that those horses belonged to the bishop. The bishop allowed the priest to use the horses for his own purposes. It was then that we learned of Loupe's connection to the attack …."

As Helene was in mid-sentence, Timo buried his hands in his face. "Betrayed … I have been betrayed …."

Nichol stood and moved behind him. She put her hands on his shoulders, leaned in, and softly said, "You will always be part of our family, Timo. We will never betray you as the church has."

"It is only a matter of time before someone looks for us here," Helene added. "I would like to wait for Ezra to join us and then we must all move on together."

Gazing at Lucette, Nichol said with absolute certainty, "I know where we are headed. I have seen the land; it is our final destination. The Lady showed it to me."

No one was surprised by what Nichol had just said. Instead, they wanted to hear more.

"We will travel to a town and stay until spring. From that town, we will continue north. After many days, we will walk through a small forest, and a hill will come into view as we exit the forest. After we cross a strong flowing creek, we will find a road that follows the base of the hill until a hamlet becomes visible.

"The homes there are built next to a great forest that extends as far as the eye can see. We do not stop here. Instead, we will move further until we find a lake surrounded by another forest. The hills have gentle slopes that are vibrant with colors of many shades. The soil is rich and will grow vast quantities of food.

"Close to the lake is where we must build our homes. That is where we will raise our children and other children of the families that will join us. Timo taught me about planting and now that he is with us, the rich fields and gardens that I saw are the ones that he will oversee. There will be a large stable for our animals— and eventually, a large common house for the women to gather. There, we will be safe."

Stillness enveloped the group as Nichol revealed this. The eyes of all present followed her as she got up and lay Lucette down to sleep. Shadow trailed behind her and lay next to Lucette.

Returning to the table, Nichol began to speak again. Everyone's attention was entirely focused on what she would say next.

"When I left Marseilles, I was all alone and had only the map Papa had given me to guide me to Paris. I had not traveled far when I began hearing the same Lady's voice I had heard since childhood. It normally spoke at night when things were quiet and still. I also heard the voice as I slept. When I was traveling and before I met Timo, she would come to me as I settled into the trees to sleep at night, always offering words of assurance and comfort and telling me that I would get to Paris. And find Ezra."

Looking at Robert, she smiled. "She did not tell me about you," she added.

"It was always a soft, reassuring voice. I questioned her and wanted her to tell me what I should do. She would not. She would often respond to my questions with her own questions. I now know that her questions guided me to consider and follow what I thought was best. The Lady made me think and trust my judgment and skills, just as Papa did."

Smiling as she folded her hands to her chest, Nichol continued.

"Before I reached Paris, Timo was the only one who witnessed my nightly conversations with the Lady. True to his good nature, he never ridiculed me for it. We had many discussions about what she told me, and he encouraged me to talk about her messages."

Timo nodded his head in agreement.

"I finally realized the Lady was guiding and protecting me at the same time because I would go places and do things that seemed uncharacteristic of me. Now I am confident that everyone in this room is here because of her guidance since I left Marseilles."

Looks were exchanged around the table. At first, no one said a word. Each of them had witnessed Nichol's nightly exchanges. None of them doubted what was being said. Then Robert spoke.

"We cannot travel there without the proper provisions to build a home. I need to go to Antony to purchase a horse and wagon; then I will go to see my family. I am sure my father will provide the tools we need. If Timo tells me what tools we need to prepare farmlands for planting, I will bring those as well. I will leave in the morning to get the things we'll need. It will take at least three days for me to accomplish everything."

As tired as she was, Helene was energized. She began organizing their efforts like a commander would direct his troops.

"Robert, I have sufficient coin for your purchase of the horse and wagon, and the tools required to build our homes and develop our fields."

"We can use all the coins you can spare, Helene. But here's what we need to do right now. We are all exhausted from our trek. I am sure we are safe for at least a few days here—but only a few. Let us rest and we will make final plans at daybreak. I have been thinking … I may be able to get a horse here that will eliminate my need to walk all the way and save a day of travel."

As Helene slipped into her bed, her mind was full. So much had been said, so many questions to be answered, and so much uncertainty remained … even as her eyelids closed.

As Nichol settled by the fire in the kitchen with Lucette lying on top of her, Robert eased down beside them. Shadow nestled next to Nichol and put her head on her lap.

It is too bad that none of them can run the way I can. We could move much faster.

John lay down in front of the door. Before the candles were extinguished, he gave Nichol a wink, a nod, and a smile from one warrior to another.

Nichol nodded and returned the smile.

Timo went outside to sleep, lay down next to Moki, and said a prayer. Then he had a thought.

I will not return to the monastic life. I learned from our journey that I can teach people farming skills to improve their lives and to better feed their families. That would be my service to God and to them.

seven

Discoveries in Antony

Turning back, he waved goodbye.

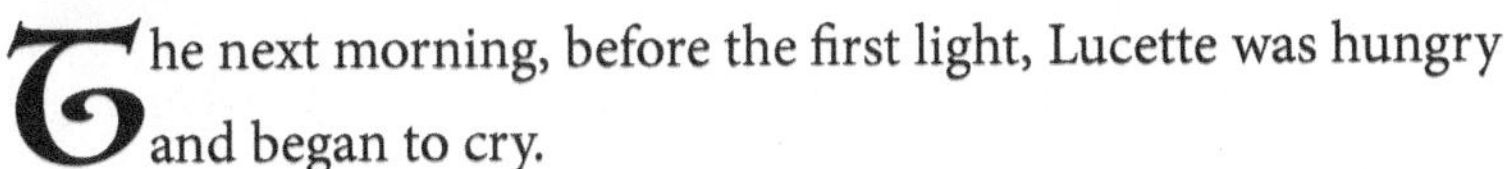

The next morning, before the first light, Lucette was hungry and began to cry.

Her wails did not wake anyone, as the household was already moving. Thoughts of events to come were on everyone's mind. Helene gave Robert some of her coins as she prepared the meal. After eating, he told Nichol and Helene he was heading to Jacob's to see if he knew anyone willing to sell him a horse.

Nichol glanced down at Shadow. "I did promise you a rabbit, did I not?

"Robert, you will win favor with Jacob if you take Shadow with you. She will rid his gardens of several rabbits quickly. Jacob will keep some to make a stew and probably offer you some of them, too. We could cook them as well. Shadow will want to carry one home as her reward."

Laughing, he reached down and scratched behind Shadow's ear. "Let us go, Shadow. We have work to do."

Shadow was at the door when she heard the word *go*, her tail thudding against the door as she waited for Robert to open it. Turning back to Nichol as he exited, Robert chuckled. "She knows where we are going."

When Robert reached Jacob's, Shadow was ready to do her part.

Before Jacob came to meet him, Shadow had already caught a rabbit, brought it to Robert's side and dropped it on the ground. Robert fell to his knee and petted Shadow as he lavished praise on her.

"Now go for the rest," he told the dog.

Hearing Robert, Jacob had come out of his barn and was delighted to see Shadow in his garden. Seeing him approach, Robert greeted him.

"I remember you … I was at Aunt Helene's cottage when I was a child. I am Robert, Nichol's husband. We are here for three days before we travel again. Nichol promised Shadow a rabbit and did not think you would mind her ridding your garden of them."

As Robert spoke, Jacob said, "I wish Shadow were my dog. She is welcome here at any time."

Robert then told him what he sought. "I would like to get a horse I can use when I travel from Paris to fairs to sell the jewelry I make."

"There's a man on your way back to Paris that might have one for sale, Robert. His farm is just outside Paris. Tell him I sent you."

Thanking him, Robert headed back to the cottage with Shadow proudly carrying a rabbit in her mouth and Robert carrying another for their evening meal.

As they approached, Nichol was outside the cottage, and Robert paused to speak to her.

"Jacob thinks there's a horse available close to Paris. I am going there now and then heading to my family's home for more tools. I will be gone for no more than three days."

Robert set out for the farm Jacob had told him about. Reaching it, he shouted out, "Is anyone here?"

Out of the barn came an old man. "I am here and this is my farm. Who are you?"

"I am in need of a horse, and Jacob told me you had one you wanted to sell."

The owner looked him over and huffed, "You do not have enough coin." Then he returned to the barn and shut the door.

Standing firm, Robert spoke loudly to the closed door. "I have enough for two horses."

Slowly, the door opened. "Show me your coin."

"Show me the horse first," Robert replied. *That was easy. If he has one good horse, I will ride away from here.*

The man took Robert to where four horses were pastured. As they walked into the pasture, Robert watched the animals move.

"You have only two horses that can be ridden." Pointing to one, he asked, "How much for that one?"

The man responded with double what the animal was worth.

"I will give you half that amount for that horse and bridle."

"That is not enough."

Robert turned and walked away.

"Show me your coin!" the man yelled.

Robert smiled and counted out the amount, then he turned around, walked back, and gave him the coin. "Count it. I will take the horse."

I miss the haggling I did at the fairs; the horse is worth double what I gave him.

Robert took the bridle from him. As if the horse knew it was for him, it presented its head for the bridle to be fitted. The animal seemed to be almost welcoming it.

Does he want to leave this farm, Robert wondered.

He patted the horse on the side of its face, moving to the neck and talking to the animal as he did. Then he grabbed part of the mane and quickly mounted it. As he leaned forward, his arms rubbed both sides of the horse's neck and they rode back to where the old man stood and nodded, and Robert turned and left.

It was early afternoon when he arrived in Paris. He stopped where he could see the entrance to Ezra's home. Not much had changed from the outside. A few people were walking in the street. Some were carrying bread under their arms. The hoofs of the horse echoed on the narrow cobblestone street. He looked around to see if there was anyone he recognized. There was no one. He then guided the horse slowly toward the door.

Robert's knock on the door was met with silence. He knocked again, and the door opened slightly. A strange man peered out. After he saw Robert was alone, he fully opened the door and stepped forward, giving Robert a threatening look.

What Robert saw as the door opened shocked and alarmed him. Furniture was broken and tossed about; everything was in great disarray.

Robert craned his neck as he attempted to peer into the once-beautiful home. "I want to talk with Ezra."

"He is not here!" the man growled.

"Do you know where he is or when he will return?"

"No!" the man shouted at him and slammed the door.

Turning away, Robert noticed the old woman who lived across from Ezra, frantically waving for him to approach.

When he was close to her, she blurted out, "There is trouble! Early this morning I saw a priest and two armed men enter Ezra's home. They were inside a long time. Then I saw Ezra leave in a hurry out the front door. As soon as he was gone, the men started carrying things out of his house, putting all of the items into a cart and left."

"Thank you for telling me. You need to be careful as they are all bad men," Robert responded, quickly walking toward his tethered horse.

As he rode away, all Robert could think about was his family. They depended on getting the supplies needed for their journey forward and he had to get the task done quickly and return to them. He was alarmed at Ezra's sudden disappearance.

After finding the stranger in Ezra's home and talking to the old woman, he realized the danger they were all in. *Timo was right to warn us. I must always be on alert.*

With renewed vigor, he said out loud, "I need to get to Papa's at once."

Riding through the night on his way to his family home in Antony, Robert thought of Nichol and what she had encountered since the murder of her father. He realized the energy and cleverness she displayed on her long journey to Paris, and that she never gave up.

How did she do it?

Now, his only concern was getting to his parents before the following day dawned and then quickly returning to Nichol and Lucette.

I need to reach my parents' home and I must get there before the sun rises.

Arriving before the first rays of light were visible, he saw no light coming from any of the homes or merchants that were close by. Picking up a stone, he started rapping with it on the heavy front door. At the same time, he spoke loudly at the closed door: "Papa, it is me, Robert."

He repeated his words several times, and then he heard the door being unbarred.

Achim and Dinah stood before him as if they were expecting him. After Ezra's visit the previous day, both were troubled and worried.

"What has happened that you have come home in the dark? Where are Nichol and the baby?"

"I have much to tell you," Robert said as he entered the room. "But first, you must know that Nichol, Lucette, and Helene are safe at Ezra's cottage. One of his protectors, John, and Timo, the monk, are with them. I stopped at Ezra's home before coming here. Once there, I learned from a neighbor that Ezra was gone. Items were taken from the house and an armed man was left behind."

Dinah handed Robert a cup of ale and motioned for him to sit in a chair close to her as Achim started a fire in the kitchen hearth. "Son, drink this and rest. As you gather your strength, we'll tell you what we know about Ezra's disappearance and what he told us when he was here yesterday."

Leaning close to him, Dinah lowered her voice so she would not wake Gideon and Raisa.

"Ezra stopped here and told us what happened. He described the events of Lucette's birth and told us how the midwife panicked and repeated her embellished story of a devil's child to a priest. That is why a priest and armed men showed up at Ezra's home on the pretext of looking for the infant and wanting to baptize her. The priest asked where the mother and baby were.

"Ezra told him both had left, and he did not know their whereabouts. The priest asked about the mother's unusual behavior at the birth. Ezra told him there was nothing unusual about the birth, or the mother's behavior. He explained that the midwife was known to make up stories about all sorts of things. Even so, the priest continued to question and threaten him."

The details Dinah relayed to Robert fit with what the old lady had also told him.

"But how did Ezra get here so fast?"

"He is traveling on horseback with Roger, his own protector," Achim replied.

"Achim, tell Robert the rest of Ezra's story."

Taking a deep breath and exhaling, Achim revealed what had happened.

"When you are as successful as Ezra, some people become envious of your wealth. They see it as an insult to their power. Ezra was not physically harmed, but the priest's men were common thieves, stealing everything they could carry out. Then they destroyed whatever was left in the home. They confiscated a bag of coins Ezra had deliberately left in plain sight and he watched the priest direct his men to take their knives to his cherished paintings.

"The priest was trying to provoke him, but Ezra stayed calm, knowing the danger he would be in if he tried to stop them.

Finally, Ezra told the priest he had business matters to deal with and left the house abruptly."

Robert was stunned by all that had happened in the last few days. He needed to tell them the rest of what was occuring.

"When Nichol first started on her way to Paris, she met a monk called Timo. Several nights ago, he came to Ezra's home and told us the rumor the midwife had spread. He also told us about a priest named Loupe, who has quickly risen to power in the Paris clergy.

"Thinking that the priest would have someone investigate the rumor quickly, Ezra had us pack our things and leave for the cottage immediately. Had it not been for Timo's forewarning and Ezra's quick thinking, there's no telling what could have happened. Nichol knows who this priest is. She says he is dangerous and is suspected of bedding the woman who is her mother. She believes —as we all do—that this priest was behind the attack on her and Helene before Lucette was born."

"What attack?" Achim and Dinah said in unison.

Briefly as he could, Robert told them what happened at the cottage. How Nichol protected both herself and Helene and killed the attackers. They listened closely, knowing their son was telling the truth. Tears flowed down Dinah's face as she listened.

Finally, Robert asked, "What else did Ezra say?"

Achim sighed. "Ezra came here to warn us that Loupe is now searching for the baby … your daughter … the 'devil's child,' born into a Jewish family."

Dinah continued the conversation. "Ezra feels that he will be satisfied for the time being since he left a purse full of coins for the priest to find. Ezra has connections with many wealthy Jewish people, and he is spreading the word that Loupe is a power-hungry zealot and a threat to be feared."

"I need your help. We are all focused on escaping the priest and his men now. I must gather supplies to move Ezra, Helene, and the three of us. I need a large wagon, tools to build a new home, and start a small farm," Robert told his parents.

"Of course, we will help. You need to rest, Robert. We will continue to talk later," Dinah added.

Robert folded his arms on the table, leaned forward, and fell asleep. He woke when Gideon came in with an armload of firewood, followed by Raisa, who carried a small twig. Seeing Robert, she dropped the twig and leaped onto his lap.

Cupping his face, she said, "I missed you! Where are Nichol and Lucette?"

Struggling for the correct answer, Robert said, "You will see them soon, I hope."

After supper, Dinah lit candles. Then she and Achim took Robert to the forge shop to talk. They were barely settled inside when Achim started.

"Ezra made a brief stop here and told us his story. Is there more that we should understand?"

"As I said last night, this priest Loupe is looking for us. What you do not know is that Nichol's mother, Astrid, poisoned her father and now actively pursues Nichol. Nichol has proof of this murder. Astrid is also believed to have bedded Loupe and is looking for Nichol because she believes Nichol knows where her papa hid his fortune.

"I came here with coin supplied by Ezra and Helene to buy tools from you and to purchase another horse and large cart. We plan to move further north of where the cottage is. I do not know where, but Nichol has said she has a vision and will know it when she sees it. Now, we will need more tools to carry with us as we travel to our journey's end. You need to be alert, too. These men are vindictive and will harm anyone in their way."

"Go to the farm and stables at the end of the road. Marcel knows us and he knows you, too. I think they have a cart and horse to purchase. Tell them I will settle with them later." Achim's tone was firm.

That afternoon, Achim saw Robert riding the lead horse-drawn cart down the path while holding the reins to another. He went to meet him. As they walked back to the forge, Robert voiced his concern.

"Papa, what if they come for you, too?"

"Dinah and I will be all right. We are outside of the priest's realm, but we'll keep a watchful eye. Ezra has warned us that this priest is making demands of all the Jews. Now, pull over to the forge with your cart. I have gathered the tools you requested. Take what you want. As for spending Ezra's coin, keep it. You will need it. I will gladly supply the tools to start your new life."

Dinah appeared and stood between the two men. Knowing this was the last time she'd see her son for a long while, she took his hands in hers.

"Robert, we wish only the best for you, Nichol, and Lucette. We want you to be safe and establish a life for yourselves, and we're relieved that Helene and Ezra have decided to go with you. Come back to the house and get the food I packed for you while you say goodbye to Gideon and Raisa."

Robert was in a hurry to be on his way, but he did as his mother wished. He said his goodbyes, picked up the bag Dinah had prepared and headed back to the forge. Achim pointed to an old forge and anvil on which he had trained Robert.

"Those are yours now. Every tool you need to build a home or plow a field is here. Now, let us load all of this up."

"Papa, I cannot take—"

Achim stopped him in mid-sentence. "You may or may not need any of this, but I want you to have it. And Robert … Dinah and I were talking about what you and Nichol will create. And with my brother joining you, we think we may want to be with you soon as well. I want you to take as much as you can carry. No more talking. Load up!"

Robert felt a burst of joy at Achim's words.

The last of the tools were packed when Dinah returned with Gideon and Raisa, each of them carrying clothing and blankets.

Raisa ran up to Robert and presented the gifts she had for him. "I wore these when I was a baby. I want Lucette to have them. Tell her Auntie Raisa loves her, and I will see her soon."

Robert scooped her up and hugged her to his chest. He looked into her big brown eyes and said, "I will tell Lucette you sent all these things to her, and I will deliver your message. Thank you, my sweet Raisa."

Turning to Gideon, he clasped him in a bear hug. "Keep up your excellent work, brother. Papa needs you."

Walking to his parents, he put an arm around each of them and drew them close.

"I cannot begin to tell you how thankful I am for all you have done for me and my family. Once we have established a homestead,

John or Roger will return and let you know we are settled. And if you are ready to come, there will be help. Until then, know I love you, and we will miss you."

Releasing them, he mounted his horse, gathered the reins to the horse pulling cart and started down the road.

Turning back, he waved once more, then focused on the road ahead.

Robert felt a sense of wholeness and calm surrounding him.

All my family will be with me at last; we will be together.

eight

Ezra's Reveal

It is urgent that we prepare to leave.

As Robert approached the cottage, Nichol was alerted to his arrival by John, who was watching the road and sharpening his sword with a stone in anticipation of what might come. Robert was surprised when he saw her walking down the road with Lucette in her arms and Shadow by her side.

Increasing the pressure of his heels on the flanks, his horse picked up its gait. As Robert was close, he released the reins of his horse and dismounted quickly. Wrapping his arms around her, he stepped back to see Lucette. As Nichol passed the baby to him, a gentle cooing could be heard. Robert took in every feature of her beautiful little face.

I will do anything to protect you ….

Others were now on the road. Helene approached and he embraced her. Timo was next and started to reach for the reins of both horses. Robert stopped him and clasped his hand. Smiling, he said, "Timo, your warning to us cannot be measured. You have protected all my family." As he looked around, he could see that there had been no disruption to the family.

Timo nodded. "Of course." He and John gathered the reins and led the horse pulling the cart and Robert's horse to the cottage.

The family collected the food and other essentials that Dinah had sent and went inside. The tools were left in the cart. The small cottage was now bursting as they crowded in. Observing this, Nichol said, "When spring comes, we will be outside with plenty of room."

Everyone was eager to hear what Robert had to say as they gathered around the kitchen table.

Helene burst out, "Is there any word about Ezra? Do you know if he is safe?"

Nodding, Robert said, "Yes, Ezra is safe. I have much to tell you. Let me start at the beginning."

Unpacking the food Dinah had sent, Helene started to arrange some for eating, using the small table to unwrap the packages as the generous display unfolded.

Nichol lay Lucette down in the cradle to help, and John and Timo settled on the floor with the foodstuffs they took from the table. Robert sat on one of the four stools. They waited for his words.

And the words tumbled out—first telling them how he had gotten there and discovered an unknown man inside the home and how he saw how ransacked it was before the door was slammed on him. Then he told them about the woman across from the house who waved him over to tell him what happened. Several men took things from inside the house and loaded them in a cart. She could hear shouting and laughter after Ezra had fled. He ended by summarizing what Ezra told Achim and Dinah when he was in Antony.

Seeing Helene's concern, Robert continued, "Ezra is traveling on horseback with Roger now. I am sure he'll be here soon and he will tell you much more."

Placing a hand over her heart, Helene said, "I am relieved to hear that Ezra was not harmed, but I am also saddened that our home has been destroyed. Robert, with what you said, I now know that we can never return. Loupe misjudged what is most important to us. We will travel beyond his reach and make our new home in the land of Nichol's vision. Our family will prosper there."

Timo was disturbed by Robert's news. "What Loupe instigated and the actions he took are against everything my church teaches. It is the likes of him and other corrupt men who use the church for their own personal gain that wreaks havoc upon innocents. I pray that one day they will stop. Until it does, I no longer want to be part of it."

Nichol looked at her friend as he said his final words. "Are you sure, Timo?"

Nodding his head, he responded, "Yes, Nichol. I want to build things and encourage others to help each other. I belong here."

The following morning, Helene noticed that Nichol looked troubled as she fed Lucette at the kitchen table. "What is on your mind, Nichol?"

"The Lady has come to me for three nights now, always with the same message.

"What is she saying? Where should we go? We cannot leave before Ezra joins us."

"She is telling me that we must move for our safety. And we must do it soon. With the urgency I feel, I think we should leave no later than tomorrow."

"What if Ezra isn't here?" Helene asked, her voice cracking with emotion as the words tumbled from her lips.

"Ezra will be here, and we will all leave together. I promise," Nichol said.

Robert and Timo observed the two and overheard what was said.

Timo spoke up. "I will stay behind. When Ezra arrives, I know what direction you are heading, and we will find you."

Heads nodded in agreement.

They knew Nichol spoke from her heart. All of them trusted the Lady's guidance when Nichol revealed what she had been told.

Nichol added confidently, "The Lady has guided me from the time I was a little girl, and now she is guiding all of us. Ezra will be here. I know it."

"I'll take Shadow up to Jacob's for one more hunt in his gardens," Robert said. "I will tell him I found the farmer with the horse for sale and purchased it. I will also tell him we are leaving to return to Paris in the morning."

Late that afternoon, they heard horses approaching.

Helene was the first out of the door and was relieved to see Ezra and Roger as they dismounted in front of the cottage. The men were covered with dust and mud and looked as though they had been riding hard. The horses were sweaty.

Helene's first thought was that Ezra had bad news.

It is good that we are no longer there.

With everyone talking at once, Ezra held up his hands.

"Stop. We must gather to discuss what I have learned but first, we need food and rest. John and Timo, can you feed and water the horses?"

The Devil's Work

*If there is a devil's child, it is the priest
hiding behind the cloak of the church.*

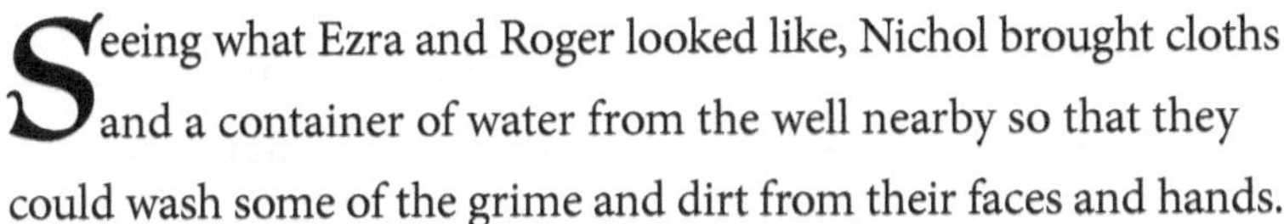

Seeing what Ezra and Roger looked like, Nichol brought cloths and a container of water from the well nearby so that they could wash some of the grime and dirt from their faces and hands.

Ezra and Roger ate the food Helene placed in front of them and then Roger joined John outside, leaning against the side of the cottage. Their heads were close together as Roger told John what he and Ezra had done after the others had set out for the cottage.

Ezra was exhausted. Moving from the table, he lay prone on the floor and was fast asleep until early evening.

When Ezra woke, he knew all were anxious to hear what he had experienced.

Roger and John came in from the cold, stationing themselves by the door. Many candles were lit to brighten the dark interior. Ezra stood while the rest sat around the only table in the cottage.

Taking a deep breath, Ezra told of the assault on their home in Paris and the thorough destruction by a priest and his henchmen. "When I opened the door, two foul-smelling men knocked me to the floor and immediately started slamming chairs on the floor to break them apart.

"When I looked at the door, a priest stood in the entrance. He demanded, 'Where is the infant that was born—the devil's child and its mother?'" Ezra paused, then continued.

"At the same time, the two men had entered the kitchen area and, with their swords, ripped everything off the walls and broke all our cooking and eating pots and anything loose. One headed up the stairs. I could hear him smashing the bed frames. Then I heard a cheer as he came to the stairs with one of the bags of coin I had purposely set out, shouting out, 'I found it!'

"The other man was ripping and destroying our paintings on the walls. At the same time, he spied the second bag of coins I had left on the floor by the chairs they had destroyed.

"The two bags of coin distracted the priest from his demand of the infant's whereabouts. When that happened, I got up and shoved past the priest, telling him, 'I must meet one of my merchants. You are mistaken … there is no infant here.'

"The room looked as though a great storm had come through. The only intact things were the roof and outer walls.

"I headed to the stables to get horses and find Roger. We gathered some coins from areas I had sequestered in safe, guarded places with some of my business partners, telling each I would someday return to collect them. I knew I had to reach Achim's home before evening."

All eyes turned to Helene as she dropped her head and slumped on her stool. Ezra immediately went and knelt by her side, embracing her. "We are all together and unharmed. I promise, you will have a new home."

Helene looked up and kissed Ezra on the cheek. "It was not the home I am upset about; it was the family inside. I wanted to show Lucette Paris and teach her to read and write. I wanted us to be a family."

Ezra took Helene's hand. "You will be by Lucette's side as she grows up in a new home. And it will be a safer place."

Nichol's words brought a smile to her face. "Helene, you are to Lucette what Margaux was to me. She needs you."

Ezra held up a hand for silence. "My story is not finished. I must continue."

What he said next put all of them on edge. Ezra's words wove an intricate tale of ruthless power and ambition.

"The priest's thirst for power has no bounds. He uses the Catholic church's wealth and power as his own, destroying whatever is in his path.

"Roger had heard of this priest when he was traveling to meet up with me. When I fled our home, I forewarned several other moneylenders that trouble was coming our way. Three of them had heard the same thing that Roger reported about a priest who was responsible for much of the mayhem other Jews encountered in Marseilles. The more I listened to this from different sources, the more I believed it was not just a rumor, but a grim warning about the priest called Loupe. Loupe wants the Jews destroyed.

"I am certain he used the rumor of the 'devil's child' as justification to invade and destroy our home. At first, I did not believe that it was because I was a Jew. Now I know this is in addition to seeking the wealth he is now after—Alexander's.

"I believe that his pursuit and assault on our home is connected to his search for Nichol and now Lucette. With what Astrid told him, he believes Nichol knows where the treasure is. If there is a 'devil's child,' it is Loupe hiding behind the cloak of the church.

"Long before the priest hammered on our door, I thought that someday this would happen, and I prepared for it. I knew our home would be the first place they would pillage. So, at that time, I began removing anything of value and hid it in a safe place.

"Alexander's goods and what I stored at the docks in Marseilles under Alexander's supervision were looted next, and I could not protect them. Loupe justified the theft by saying that Alexander owed back tithes. You are right, Nichol. Astrid did sleep with the devil, and then he stole what little was left in the villa from her and Fredric. They both got what they deserved.

"I think he knew you were living with us and used Sacha's story as an excuse to invade our home and finally capture you. Nichol, I don't think Fredric is the one we should immediately fear; the truly dangerous one is Loupe. He is a threat to all of us and anyone in his path because of his church connections. He will never stop until he finds all of Alexander's wealth and he believes Nichol is the person who knows where it is.

"After I left Achim and Dinah, I went to warn many of my associates about the peril they could face at the hands of Loupe. I told them they need to create protection for themselves and their families and find a way to conceal their wealth."

"I am glad to hear you say that. These are cruel people, and we need to have no dealings with them. Warning your partners and others like us is important, Ezra," Helene said. "Did you learn anything else about this priest? How did he become such a powerful force in Paris?"

"My sources told me that Loupe comes from a very wealthy family living near Marseilles. He had an older brother who inherited all the family's wealth. Feeling slighted and pushed aside, Loupe grew jealous and eventually murdered him. I believe he saw the church as a way of gaining personal power and used his family's name and wealth to do just that.

"His father bought his way into the church and Loupe rose to power and influence at an early age. He puts on a charming façade but is devious, just as Nichol observed in Alexander's solar. He met with the archbishop of Marseilles and convinced him he would be the ideal replacement for the bishop of Paris, who had recently died. He told the archbishop he was a fierce defender and promoter of the church.

"Not fooled by Loupe and his lust for power and greed, the archbishop of Marseilles knew he would be hard to control. He would not grant him the title of bishop, one that Loupe desired. He had other plans that would need someone with a ruthless drive for power, and Loupe had demonstrated that already. He wanted him in the position of a priest, someone he would have greater control over.

"Loupe has amassed a following of villains using church funds, and no one has the courage to challenge him. He has surrounded himself with priests who support his goals and his ways of achieving them. He gives them full authority to suppress any complaint against him or his church.

"These are the positions that Loupe supports. And there is something else of importance we must consider. The archbishop of Paris has made it known that he holds the Jewish community in the lowest regard and threatens them at every turn. That will make every Jew a target. I have a plan to protect us from them.

"People I have talked to say that Loupe has a type of power, an attraction, which convinces others to do his bidding. He doesn't have to give a direct order to the thugs that work for him; they just anticipate what Loupe wants. I fear it is going to get worse."

Reaching for Helene's hand, he said quietly, "We need to … no, we *must* … disguise who we are."

Speaking to his nephew Robert, he added, "We must protect our families and ourselves from this day forward. I will have myself baptized by a priest at one of the churches close by. I think we all should be baptized, including Lucette."

Timo took in all that Ezra had said. Leaning forward, he spoke up.

"I have heard the same thing from other priests and other monks. They tell about an outspoken Parisian priest who simply disappeared after confronting this Loupe about his abuse of church funds. His power seems to be absolute against those who challenge him. What you are saying matches the workings of this priest Loupe.

"He is developing the power of a bishop as a priest, and he has ways of persuasion, of a devious nature, beguiling his victims. What Ezra suggests is correct … you would be wise to remove the possibility of being called a heretic. Get baptized. On the outside, others will think you are a Christian. Follow your heritage privately, never demonstrating or revealing your Jewish background."

He then fell silent. Lifting his hands from his lap to the table, he spoke softly.

"I have a decision I need to make. I feel great sadness as I listen to what Ezra has discovered and experienced … what Nichol has experienced.

"After hearing all this about Loupe and his corrupt followers, I know it is time for me to step away from the church for a while and live as a common man. I will adhere to my vows; they are sacred to me. Just as you will adhere to the values of a Jew. And I can still teach others the way of planting and harvesting. If you allow me, I'd like to travel with you and help establish your new surroundings."

All of them were aware of the heightened stress in the room after hearing Timo's pointed words following Ezra's revelations.

Again, silence surrounded them.

Touching the chain that held the amulet, the feather, and the rings of Alexander around her neck, Nichol scanned the faces of her new family. With the disclosures of what Ezra said and now with Timo stating he could not be a monk under the name of the church, could another worry be added?

Nichol then turned toward Timo before anyone spoke.

"It is your choice, Timo. I think all of us support your decision, and we welcome you into our flock. But if you want to continue your work as a common man, will you do it dressed as a monk?" She gave him a rueful grin. "Sewing is not one of my talents."

It was Robert who offered help. "Timo, my mother sent me here with extra clothing. Surely some of the clothes will fit you. I will get them, and you can see what fits best."

The monk accepted the bundle Robert brought forth and went outside, beginning to shed his robes before closing the door.

Smiling at Nichol, Robert said, "I have a gift for you, Nichol. I forgot to give these things to you. Raisa sent clothing that she wore as a baby. She wants Lucette to have them. She also asked me to tell you that she misses you both and she loves you."

Taking the pile from Robert, the smile did not leave Nichol's face. "Look at all this. We will not have to make her anything new for months! I wish Raisa were here so she could see Lucette in them."

The door to the cottage opened, and Timo entered—a new Timo. Instead of his monk's robes, he was garbed in dark brown breeches and a short brown tunic.

"These fit perfectly. Do I look my new part?"

Everyone laughed, stirring Lucette as she had quietly slept in the sling draped across her mother. Smiling as she looked down at her daughter, Nichol said, "Yes, you do. Welcome to the family, farmer Timo."

As she spoke, all eyes were on her. Ezra turned to her. "I think you have something else to tell us, Nichol. You know where we are heading and when we need to leave here. Is that right? You know where we are going to stay until spring as well."

Once again, looking down at her no-longer-sleeping daughter, Nichol saw her little face as she smiled up at her mother for the first time.

A slight glow entered the room, unnoticed by all but Nichol and Lucette.

Directing a glance at Ezra while staying connected with her daughter, Nichol nodded. "We are headed to Rouen, less than a week away."

"Helene and I have friends in Rouen who will help us." *How did Nichol know about Rouen,* Ezra wondered.

"Ezra, Rouen is not our final destination. Where we are going will be safe and we will build a community for others like us. We will only stay in Rouen for two months."

Nichol told Ezra about the Lady's message and where they would live until spring allowed them to travel again. There was a combination of excitement and fear in the air as they discussed and planned their departure for early the following day.

Nichol's words energized everyone, continuing their conversation well into the night.

Ezra was still unsure what to make of Nichol's Lady and her messages, but his instincts told him it was the right thing to do. And he was relieved that everyone knew of the challenges they faced.

I wonder if the Lady will speak to me as she does to Nichol? Alexander said she spoke to him.

As night descended and quiet filled the air, Nichol reached for the quill she carried in her backpack, along with scraps of parchment.

Finding ink in the cottage and lighting a candle, she let its flame glow brightly. Then she wrote:

> Loupe, a handsome man
>
> Hair dark as night
>
> Struts with dignified might.
>
> A robe and cross projects devotion and love.
>
> Yet his eyes are of chilling ice.
>
> There is no caring.
>
> This man is no dove.
>
> His words tell one story, his deeds tell another.
>
> A man with conflicting presence.
>
> Pious outside ... devious inside.
>
> Dangerous.

ten

Not Wanted

I can feel the weight of his body suffocating me.

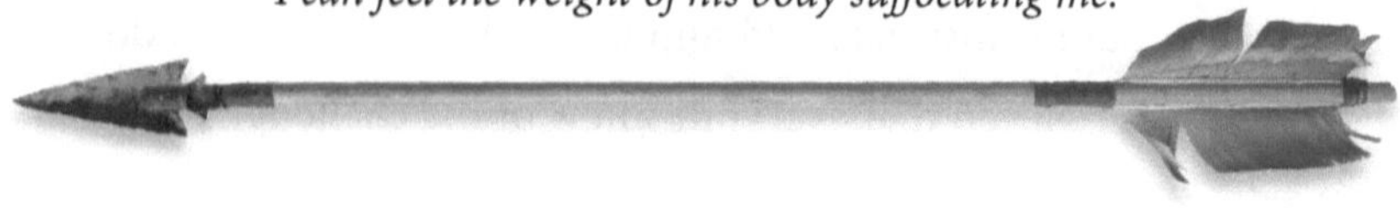

Opening the door, John and Roger felt the morning chill to their bones as they began to load items from the cottage into the cart and on the horses.

For warmth, Timo had wrapped himself in the monk's robe he had shed the night before. Moki's packs were already getting loaded. The horses' breath streamed from their nostrils, awaiting their passengers.

Inside the cottage, it was quiet as they began a day filled with anticipation of the unknown. With everyone present, Ezra was the first to speak.

"Roger and John have agreed to stay after we depart. When we leave, we will head toward Paris and then turn onto the road to Rouen. I do not think anyone should know where we are going, including Jacob. If he did, it could put him at risk. After a few days—when they are convinced that no one is looking for us— Roger and John will get on the road and join us in Rouen. Let us finish loading the cart and leave soon; we have a full day of travel."

After loading, Robert helped Helene onto one horse and Nichol with Lucette in her sling onto the other. Laughing, Timo said, "Nichol, I think if Shadow could, she would be up in the saddle with you and Lucette."

As soon as he said the baby's name, Shadow wagged her tail, and Timo reached down and patted her head. "They are fine, Shadow. Walk by me."

Suddenly Helene spoke up. "Wait … there is something we will all want to have. Timo, please go back and get the wooden sticks we use for eating."

Timo returned to the cottage and soon appeared with all the wooden rods Helene asked him to get. After adding them to one of Moki's bags, he explained, "In the monastery, we called the sticks carved into two points on one end *furcas*. The other stick is the spoon to scoop liquid as well as solids."

Nichol listened to Timo's words to Helene and then said to Robert, "I think you can create a better furca and spoon, Robert. Something that will not break, like the small sticks we have always used. We need tools stronger than the twigs we have been using to pick up meat and vegetables."

Smiling, Robert reached into one of the bags and pulled out a small silver spoon. "I made this for Lucette at the guild before I left. She can use this when she is no longer a baby. With your ideas, I will make her a furca to fit her small hand."

Handing it to Nichol, he added, "I also made these after you had showed me the sticks you were eating with, along with the drawing you made showing a different design. These can scoop and pick up food like the sticks did."

Fascinated, Nichol picked up one of the silver thick sticks, rounded into a small scoop on the end. She placed it between her fingers on one hand while she cupped her other hand, imitating the shape of a bowl. Pantomiming eating, she motioned with her hand, carrying food to her mouth.

Smiling, she said, "Everyone will want these, Robert. This is good! We can eat hot stews and broths better. When we reach our destination, would you make more of them?"

Settled on the horse with Lucette nestled into the sling across her breasts, she looked at her new family. A smile spread across her face.

Glancing back at the cottage for what she knew was the last time, she turned and said to all, "It is time. We must leave."

The narrow road only allowed a pair of side-by-side travelers.

Nichol and Helene rode in front, followed by Robert leading the horse-drawn cart, with Timo and Ezra walking behind it. Moki stayed close to Timo.

Shadow loved being on the move, traveling back and forth, then pausing to scan the countryside. She was always on the hunt; it was the wolf in her.

By late morning they found the road to Rouen. Turning on a well-traveled road, everyone knew it was the beginning of their journey to a new land.

Nichol stopped and brought everyone together.

"In the following days, we will pass merchants, peddlers, and others going in our direction or passing by. It will help our secret journey by acknowledging them with a smile and no conversation. If we separate into small groups as though we are strangers travel-ing together, especially when passing through towns or hamlets, I believe we can become ordinary travelers to those we meet. It served me well on the rode to Paris before I met Timo."

There was agreement from all as they continued toward Rouen. Each of them was deep into their own thoughts as they walked and rode silently for the first few hours.

Helene looked back and realized they had traveled more quickly than the others. They needed to let the cart catch up, along with Timo and Ezra. She looked at Nichol.

"I have seen that look on your face before—one that combines fear and confidence. We are here because of what we have no control over, not because of you. We will make a new home for all of us, a safe place to live our lives. And we would not have these gifts without you and Robert coming to Paris."

Nichol managed a slight smile. "I do not know what I would do without you, Helene. If anything were ever to happen to me, will you take care of and be a mother to …."

Robert caught up to them and Nichol stopped speaking.

Silence dropped in again as the chill in the air wrapped around her words. Helene reached for her hand and squeezed it. She knew that Nichol meant Lucette.

When the sun was overhead, Helene turned and called back, "Nichol and I will go ahead and find a spot to stop and eat."

The many trees along the road were bare except for the scattered pines. There were patches of water and heavy mud on the road, and they took care to avoid the worst areas by walking and moving the cart to the grassy shoulder of the road.

Rounding a bend in the road, they came upon a young woman sitting with her back against a tree with a trunk as wide as her body. She looked pale and sick. Her body shook with the cold, and her hand rested on a bundle in her lap.

Immediately Nichol and Helene stopped, and Nichol dismounted. Approaching the woman and crouching down, she asked, "Do you need help?"

The woman just stared blankly into the distance.

Assessing her, Nichol then asked, "What is your name?"

"Marie," the woman whispered in a weak voice as she looked at Nichol.

Just then Nichol heard the faint mewling whimper of a baby. She looked at the bundle in the woman's lap and asked, "What is your baby's name?"

"He has no name."

"How many days old is he?"

"I'm not sure," was the woman's whispered reply.

"May I see him, Marie?"

It was apparent to everyone that the woman was very weak. She could barely lift her hand. Nichol bent over, lifted the infant from her, and then passed it to Helene. Nichol's eyes traveled back and forth between Marie and Helene, who was parting the tattered rags in which the newborn was wrapped. He appeared to be no more than a day old. With his faint cry and blue-tinged skin, she knew he needed help right away and so did the mother.

"Have you nursed him?" Helene asked Marie.

Looking up at Helene, Marie replied, "No. I cannot."

Robert, Ezra, and Timo arrived, surprised to see that the women were tending to a stranger.

Relieved to see them approach, Nichol said, "Ezra, would you start a fire? Robert, please fetch some water so we can heat it. Helene will clean this baby, and I need water for its mother."

Ezra hurried to do as he was asked, and Timo brought a bowl from one of Moki's bags to hold the warmed water, along with cloths to help clean the mother and baby. Robert brought water to heat and then motioned to Nichol to give Lucette to him.

Helene tended to the new baby while Nichol cleaned and dressed Marie with warmer clothes from her own bag. Exhausted, Marie surrendered to their attentions with a confused and stoic look, almost like she was in a trance. While Nichol and Helene tended to Marie and the infant, Robert held Lucette, and Timo prepared food for everyone.

As the fire warmed her, Marie stopped shaking, though she was still weak and dazed. Nichol sat with her as Timo brought them each a bowl of dried meats and cheese.

Marie only stared at the food. She could barely lift her arm; so weak she could not move.

Touching her hand, Nichol said softly, "Marie, you must eat and drink. You have a baby who needs milk, and if you do not take care of your needs, you will not be able to take care of his." Slowly responding to Nichol's encouragement, Marie began to nibble the food and take sips of the water.

Helene handed the tiny infant to Nichol, who dropped beside Marie. "Do you know how to nurse him?" Marie gave a slight shake of her head. "All right, I will show you."

Nichol carefully brought the baby to her breast, and he suckled eagerly. When he was satisfied, he fell asleep. Smiling down at him, she said to Marie, "He is a beautiful baby. If you relax and do as I do, he will learn very quickly, and nursing him will soothe both of you. Your milk will come in soon if you let him suckle. Until that time, I will share my milk with him."

Before the afternoon had passed, Marie and the baby responded well to the nourishment and attention. Asking Helene to stay with Marie, Nichol approached the men.

"We can't just leave her here now. The baby will surely die and most likely, she will as well. She is weak, has eaten little, and is not strong enough to take care of herself or her baby. I will help feed him until she can nurse him herself. If everyone agrees, I want to take her with us until we reach the next village."

The men agreed and Nichol returned to where Helene was talking calmly to Marie and the baby. "Marie, we want you to travel with us until we can find a safe place for you. It is time to move on now."

Nodding, Marie attempted to stand up. It was soon clear to all that she was too weak to walk.

Robert came to Nichol's side. "Marie, I'll help you to the cart, where you can rest as we move ahead." Making room for her and the baby in the cart, Robert helped Marie into it and covered her with a cloak.

He then cautioned the group, "Before we depart this place, we should mask the remains of our fire by scattering the ashes and covering it with dirt so no one knows we were here. We are not yet a day's ride from Paris, and we do not know where Loupe or his men are."

Completing the task and settling the baby with Marie in the wagon, they set out and traveled the bumpy road until late afternoon. Finally, Robert found a dry area off the road where they stopped to spend the night.

A routine was begun, the animals fed, and a fire started while Nichol oversaw the feeding of the babies. Timo spread his tarp among several trees for them to sleep, nestled together for warmth. That evening after supper, the exhausted Marie fell asleep immediately.

Nichol motioned for the others to follow her to a place where they could talk out of Marie's hearing. "I do not know where Marie comes from, but I fear that she and her baby will not survive without our continued help. How do you feel about inviting her to travel with us until she is stronger and can decide where she wants to go?"

Everyone agreed that it was the right thing to do.

The next day, Marie was silent as the group headed north. When they stopped for the evening, Helene sat beside her and noticed that she was more relaxed and patient as she finally held the baby to her breast. Helene also noticed how different Marie was with her baby than how Nichol held and fed Lucette. Marie showed no affection for the little one as if she did not want him.

"Where are you from? How is it that you and your son are traveling alone?" she asked.

Marie looked nervous and did not respond.

Helene was insistent. "We just want to help you. We are traveling to a new land, and you can travel with us for as long as you like."

Helene watched as Marie gazed at the fire with a blank stare. Tears began to flow down her cheeks. Finally, she spoke.

"I do not want this baby. I hated the boy who made me pregnant," was all she said. Helene was patient, knowing there was much to her story and more to come.

Finally, Marie spoke, her words soft and hesitant. "There was a tournament of nobles and Lord Walter made several of us work there serving food, wine, and ale. The men drank too much, and Lord Walter's son dragged me into the woods and raped me.

"When it became obvious that I was pregnant, my father blamed me. I was allowed to stay in my family home only until my time came. My mother delivered the baby and immediately after, my father told me to leave. He was worried that if Lord Walter found out that I had given birth to his bastard grandson, our whole family would be punished."

She fell silent. After a moment, she added, "I have six brothers and sisters. We barely had enough to eat, and there was no room in our house for another child. I cannot take care of this baby and I do not want it. It would be best if he died."

Nichol joined the two women, hearing what Marie said. Moving slowly, she reached for Marie's hand. "Marie, do you think we should give him a name?"

Marie fired back with the first spark of energy that Nichol had seen from her. "Why? I just said I do not want him! Every time I look at him, I feel the pain of that night all over again. I can see that boy's face and feel the weight of his body smothering me with his, laughing in my face and saying awful things to me. And I can still hear my father's harsh words as he told me to leave."

Nichol's and Helene's eyes met.

"He is a handsome baby boy. You are a good person, and he has your goodness in him, a goodness that will override the meanness of his father," Helene said, her tone gentle. "I think Aiden would be a proper name for him." Turning toward Nichol, she asked, "What do you think, Nichol?"

Nichol stayed silent. She knew Helene was trying to welcome Marie into their group just as she had welcomed her. She liked the name Helene suggested and nodded her head in agreement.

"You two can call him whatever you like. I do not care," Marie said. She then fell silent once again. She finished nursing the baby, pushing him away from her body and leaning back against the tree.

For the next few days, Nichol observed Marie's lack of affection for baby Aiden. It was evident that there was no bonding happening between either. One night, Helene placed both babies on a blanket, swaddling them together, and hummed a song to lull them to sleep. The babies calmed down as they lay closely—almost as if they were connected somehow.

That gave Nichol an idea. She took the opportunity to talk to Marie alone.

Sitting beside her, she said, "Marie, what you experienced at the hands of a powerful and privileged man was horrible, and I can see the pain it still causes you. You have made it clear that you do not want to keep the baby that resulted from the attack. I have an idea that will take away part of your burden."

Marie raised her eyebrows and turned her gaze to meet Nichol's.

"Robert and I talked as we set out this morning. We could raise the children together on our own. I will pay you five silver coins if you allow me to treat Aiden as my son. But as they grow, I will not have enough milk to sustain both babies. If you stay with us until we reach our destination and continue to feed Aiden until he is off the breast, I will give you the coins, and you can go wherever you like and leave Aiden with Robert and me."

Marie's eyes widened at the suggestion. Looking at Nichol in disbelief and realizing what an opportunity had just been handed to her, she responded immediately.

"I do not understand why you want to do this, but I will do as you have suggested. Aiden is now your son, and I will feed him until he no longer needs milk."

Nichol covered Marie's hand with hers. "I am sorry this has happened to you. I promise we will care for Aiden as our own. Helene will love him as she does Lucette."

From that day forward, Marie's demeanor changed. Her strength was building. She now had a way out and began to openly converse with and give help to her traveling companions. More importantly, her treatment of Aiden changed. She became calmer and gentler with him, and he became a quieter baby.

What Marie did not know was that everyone knew of Nichol's suggestion—not just Robert, but also Helene and Ezra. Even Timo thought this was the only way to save both the baby and the mother.

Nichol had not shared with anyone that as she had nursed Lucette one night, the Lady's soft voice told her the children would grow together as brother and sister.

eleven

On the Road

I know a man who owns an inn.

For the next four days, they traveled toward Rouen.

The mornings were cold and overcast, but their spirits always improved when the sun broke through the cloud covering. Traveling together as they were, Robert and Nichol became a formidable team, working together for the benefit of all.

Along the road, there were few places where they could shelter for the night. It was a challenge to find a cluster of pines that offered protection from the winds and the weather.

Where Ezra always had others to do things for him, and Timo was connected to the monasteries and moved about with Moki as his companion, it was Nichol who became the true survivalist, adapting tree climbing and tying herself onto branches to sleep off the ground and away from anyone who might be traveling on the road.

As a monk with a donkey, Timo had some protection. However, during her earlier travels on her way to Paris, Nichol had been dressed as a boy alone. She knew she didn't have the freedom to travel in the open because others were after her. Because of that, she learned the art of being invisible and blending in. Traveling with her family was safer, even though there were still reasons to be wary of others on the road.

Moving forward, Helene became the general of the group, organizing their days and events as they unfolded and then taking both babies under her supervision so Nichol and Marie could walk independently.

As soon as a place was found where they could shelter for the evening, Nichol and Robert built a fire for warmth and the heating of food and water. Nichol had begun to add peas, beans, beets, and herbs to cook in the hot water. Bread was passed around to sop up the juices. The soothing mixture was something that everyone looked forward to as they sat around the fire at the day's end.

Nichol appreciated all that Helene was doing to tend to the children. Helene became more tired and quiet; as Nichol observed this, she became worried.

Is she ill?

On the fourth evening, with all eyes staring into the fire, Nichol sensed a feeling of gloom had come over them. She broke the silence.

"Ezra, where will we stay when we arrive in Rouen?"

"I know a man who owns an inn. We can stay there until the warm weather arrives. It has many rooms."

"I think you and Helene should take the horses, go to Rouen, and secure a place for us before we arrive. That way, you arrive ahead of us and can settle in and prepare the innkeeper for our arrival."

Nichol watched Helene's face as she suggested this and noticed a slight smile directed at her. As Helene hugged Nichol later, she whispered, "Thank you. I am weary from all this travel. I will be waiting for you and Lucette where you can rest, too."

Robert and Timo agreed. They also sensed that Helene was not well. The type of travel they were doing and the events she had gone through at the cottage affected her. Getting her to Rouen as soon as possible was a clever idea.

The next morning, Ezra gave Robert and Nichol directions to the inn. The two waved farewell to the others as they headed out. It was not long before Helene and Ezra were out of sight.

twelve

Rouen

Do you have enough rooms for all of us?

Within two days, Ezra and Helene arrived at the inn in Rouen, which now boasted many rooms for guests, plus a stable for Moki and the horses. Ezra had looked forward to seeing his old friend.

Upon entering, they were warmly greeted by Amos, the owner. He seated Ezra and Helene at a table near the fireplace and brought them food and drink. He was glad to see his old friend who helped him start the inn long ago.

"Amos, we have had a long journey from Paris, one fraught with danger. Helene and I are the first to arrive. In a day or two, there will be six more adults plus two babies. You know both John and Roger, who I usually travel with when I have business away from Paris, and I will explain about the others. Will you have enough rooms for all of us?"

"I will have your room prepared for you, and after you eat, we will talk about your needs."

Amos escorted Ezra and Helene to their room. Turning to him, Ezra said, "I will get Helene settled in bed and come talk to you later. There is much to tell."

In a short time, Ezra returned and reseated himself at the table across from Amos, who called to the server to bring them ale.

"My friends are more like family, Amos." He then told his friend the story of a priest named Loupe taking over his house in Paris and destroying it as the reason they fled. He avoided telling of the circumstances for the priest's visit or disclosing the birth of Lucette as the reason behind it.

"There are other reasons we are being pursued, but to protect you, I will not reveal them. My nephew Robert and his wife Nichol with their young baby will be here in a few days. Timo is a good friend who has helped me in the past. Marie, a young woman in distress we met on the way here who needed our help, will be with them. She also has a newborn. My two protectors could arrive at the same time or afterward."

Amos chose his words carefully. He sensed there was more to Ezra's story and why a family had fled their comfortable home and rescued a stranger in distress with an infant.

"Ezra, as you can see, your investment in the inn has brought success. I have built more rooms for visitors so I can take care of you and your friends. My friend, you look worried. What is wrong?"

"There is much to tell, Amos, and I will do so over the next few days after we are rested and Helene is stronger from our sudden departure from Paris. The church and a villainous priest are hunting down Jews and businesses. As a moneylender, I—and those I associate with—are their targets.

"We plan to leave here in the spring and travel north to find a place far away from the priest Loupe's influence. While we are here, we can help you with any needs you may have. Robert, Nichol, and Timo all have a variety of skills that will be useful to you while they are here."

Amos nodded. "Once you and Helene are rested, we will talk further about your needs. I may know of such a place for you to settle. You are welcome, my friend, as are those you bring with you. I must tell you, sadly, there has been growing hatred of Jews in Rouen. One day, we may have to follow you to where you are going," he added.

At the end of the second day, Helene was rested and feeling better but worried about her family. Just before dark, her worry was lifted, as the road-weary and hungry group arrived at the inn. Roger and John had caught up with them as they approached Rouen.

"Come in; we have been expecting you," Amos said as he greeted them. "I will have your animals and wagon tended to."

He looked down and his eyes widened as he saw Shadow leaning against Nichol. Then he smiled. "Is that the wolf that Ezra said only bites bad people?"

With a sigh of relief, Nichol smiled as she slipped her arm through Robert's. "Yes, thank you. We are glad to hear that Ezra and Helene arrived safely."

Before she could say anything else, Amos said, "Everyone, sit down; we will bring bread, hot stew, and pitchers of ale. Your travel has made you hungry and in need of nourishment. I'll let Ezra know you have arrived."

Nichol immediately scanned the room to evaluate any possible threats. She took in the many tables with chairs, illuminated with the large number of candles for the evenings. Flat stones were used for flooring. Several people were drinking ale and a hush fell over the room as the strangers and a large dog entered. All eyes in the inn were on them.

Her training from Sir Roland had proved very useful on her journey.

Motioning Shadow to stay at her side, Nichol and the others sat at the table where Amos directed them.

Amos went to Ezra's room to inform them that the rest of their group had arrived. When she heard the news, Helene almost leaped from the chair she was sitting in. She and Ezra rushed to greet them.

When they entered the inn's common room, all Ezra and Helene saw were the tops of their heads, bent down as they raised the delicious stew to their mouths with the bread that the inn provided. It did not go unnoticed by Ezra that Amos had taken care of all of them.

"Nichol, you are among friends. Let me take my Lucette," Ezra coaxed.

As Nichol handed Lucette to Ezra, she leaned forward and whispered, "Is Helene well?"

"Yes, she is better now that you have arrived."

With her voice still low, Nichol added with a smile, "Your Lucette, Ezra?"

"I think my role will be to share my wisdom with Lucette like Alexander did with you."

Her smile did not leave her face. Turning to the others, she felt joined with her friends … and new family.

Yes, I now have a family, thanks to Papa's decisions for my safety.

Helene immediately reached for Aiden, taking him from Marie. Timo and Robert pulled up stools and joined the others at the table in the corner of the room.

More bread, stew, and ale were brought, and Ezra repeated Amos' story about where they could go when spring came. Watching everyone's reaction, Ezra smiled and spoke.

"It is in Nichol's description of what she sees ahead for us, but not in her detail."

Robert put an arm around Nichol, leaned in, and kissed her on the cheek. "We believe in you, and soon, we will raise our children away from the danger of those chasing us."

The mood at the table was of relief.

Friends. Family. A destination.

thirteen

Nichol and Ezra

I see them clearly.

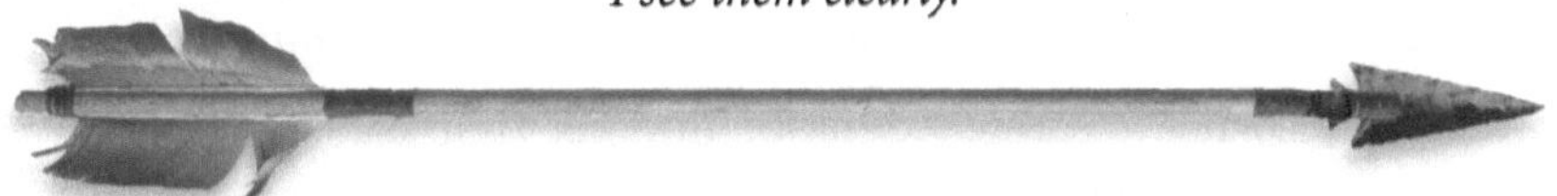

The river Seine was Rouen's southern border and primary trade access with a significant influence from Normandy. To get to Paris, the Norsemen went through Rouen on the river. The Rouen port had regular shipments unloaded from other kingdoms that surrounded France.

Nichol felt alive with the vibrations she could hear and feel when she walked outside Amos' inn. She could sense that people were making it a place to live. The similarities to Marseilles reminded her of how she used to go to the docks and watch the merchants sell their wares when she was a young girl.

The next day, it was a cold and overcast morning. Amos approached Robert and Nichol.

"As you were eating last evening, you said that you would like to experience Rouen. Would you go to the market and bring back what is fresh at the markets to feed the inn's guests?"

Almost at once, both said "Yes" to him and Nichol immediately went to Helene and Ezra's room with Lucette. She knocked at the door.

"It is Nichol. Would you watch Lucette while Robert and I go to the markets for Amos?"

Immediately, the door opened, with outstretched arms and a smile from a happy Helene. "Take your time. Ezra and I will take good care of her."

"I just fed her, and I will be back before her next feeding."

Shadow saw the two of them moving toward the inn door and quickly reached it before it could be cracked open. Laughing, Nichol reached down and scratched her behind her right ear, signaling that Shadow was included as they headed to the marketplace.

As the two stood outside the entrance to the inn, Robert was wrapped in his cloak. He pulled Nichol closer to him, helping her put on a full-length cloak with a hood. The damp, cold air blushed their cheeks as both were invigorated by the task ahead and being alone together without others' ears close by.

"Nichol, I have been thinking … when we are in Rouen, it would be safer for you if you dressed like other women so you do not attract attention. You do not have to disguise yourself as a boy any longer."

"Yes, you are right. I will do that. If Loupe is looking for me, I will be easy to recognize, dressed as I am. Have you seen how people look at Shadow? Do you think Loupe knows about Shadow? The earlier we leave Rouen, the safer we will be."

She thought for a moment. "But, Robert … the way I work and move about, the men's type of clothing is best for me. I will continue to dress that way when we are building and working in the fields where we are going.

"I am glad for the long cloak and scarf covering my tunic, breeches, and short hair and for protecting me from the cold this morning brings. If only there were someone like Margaux who could sew for me. She tried to teach me how, but I told Papa that

I was not interested because I had others to make clothing for me. We will look for a merchant when we are walking about who makes women's clothes."

They wandered up and down the row of merchants, noting which merchants were the busiest and how merchandise on their tables was displayed.

Reaching for Robert's hand, she murmured, "I think that when you have finished jewelry and items to sell, you will do well here. Another day, we will see if there are any goldsmiths selling items. You could approach to offer your items to sell with theirs."

Nichol was wearing the satchel on her back that Timo made for her. Robert carried two satchels with slings over his shoulders as they strolled from one stall to another. Walking from one place to another, they marveled at the items they saw and how some merchants displayed their goods while others just heaped them in a pile on the ground.

They purchased dried and salted fish, bread, cheese, onions, turnips, and fresh fish for Amos and a bone for Shadow.

Turning to her, Robert said, "Nichol, you seem more interested in what is happening around you than our task at hand."

"This is what I remember from Marseilles; I am drawn to the activity. I used to sit and watch people; it is how I discovered you when I was in Antony. Do you miss selling your jewelry at the markets?"

Robert paused. "Yes, I do. And one day I will sell my jewelry here in Rouen and you can watch for thieves." That brought laughter from them both and attention from those around them.

"We need to return. We have many items for Amos, and it is time to feed Lucette again. I promise we will return soon to explore all the trade shops."

Arriving back at the inn, Nichol went to nurse Lucette, found Helene alone and stayed with her. They talked about small but essential things involving the growing family and future destinations.

At the corner table that night, Nichol whispered to Ezra that they should explore Rouen.

Ezra paused. "I have merchants I would like to visit and let them know I will be in Rouen for another month. Is there anything that is of interest to you?"

"Yes, but I will tell you while we walk. Can we go tomorrow after I feed Lucette?"

"Yes, let us talk in the morning; I sense you want a private conversation."

"Yes, it must be private."

The following day, with Lucette fed, Nichol dressed as Helene usually did, donning a calf-length tunic with long sleeves, a full underskirt, a wimple around her head, and a borrowed cloak. She then entered the room where Ezra and Amos were seated.

Ezra turned and smiled. "You look different this morning." Amused, he then asked, "Are those Helene's clothes?"

"Not exactly. The tunic is Robert's and the wimple and cloak are Helene's." With hands on her hips, she continued, "I believe I am now appropriately dressed, sir. Would you like to escort me around Rouen?"

Ezra sat back and gave a hearty laugh, one that Nichol had not heard before.

"Yes, Nichol, I would like to escort you today through the streets of Rouen and even introduce you to some very influential people I know. Shall we leave now? Amos, could you inform Helene that Nichol and I are leaving?"

When they left the inn, Nichol put her arm through Ezra's and made the short walk to the markets. Once there, he introduced her as his niece to anyone he talked to.

One was Nigel, his principal agent in Rouen who created Ezra's distribution channel to Paris for merchandise he agreed to resell, along with his moneylending operations. Taller than the other men she saw talking with Ezra, he stood with confidence as she was introduced to him. After greeting him, she turned away so that Ezra could tell him his plans. Nichol acted as though she was not interested in the private conversation; although, as always, she was.

As they left Nigel, she said, "You can trust him. When you first introduced me, I saw him. He listens closely when you speak and responds with words that would affirm what you are asking for. He also thinks before he speaks, choosing his words carefully so you do not misunderstand him."

Turning his head toward her, Ezra raised his right eyebrow. Touching her arm, he guided her away from the merchant table nearby. Stopping after they had walked several paces, he asked, "What told you he could be trusted?"

"This is what I did for Papa. He and I were lonely in our own home. One day, I was in the niche, and when his guest left, he walked directly in front of the tapestry and said, 'What have you learned today?' I felt like I had been caught listening and was embarrassed. I did not speak. He repeated, 'What have you learned today?' A strong feeling came over me then, and I found my words, realizing there was no anger in his words. He was interested in what I thought and felt.

"I told him I learned that people do not trust the lords or church to keep their promises and they struggle to protect their families and keep them fed. I stepped out from behind the tapestry and Papa sat me down in front of him. With his hand under my chin, he gently lifted my head until our eyes met. At that moment we found each other; we were no longer lonely. I saw him, and he saw me.

"I then repeated to him what I heard word for word: how the man's facial expressions agreed with his words or covered up and lied. I even told him that the way his visitor sat in the chair across from his table revealed whether there was agreement or disagreement with what Papa was saying.

"Papa laughed and said, 'Lisa, you are indeed part of me. I am interested in what you have to say … about what you hear and see in the solar when you are here. I see you feel as I do about the church and the lords.'

"Almost whispering, I told Papa that I have decided I do not believe in the cruelty of this church and the men who are its messengers and will not support it.

"From that day forward, we would always leave the solar and the manor and walk in the gardens and discuss what I heard and saw, away from the eyes and ears of Astrid and Fredric. From then on, he wanted me in the solar when he had visitors, letting me know beforehand so I could be in place. When they left, he would turn to the tapestry and say, 'What did you learn today?'"

Nichol smiled at Ezra. "Papa referred to me as his secret asset."

fourteen

Gifts and Revelations

She has a power that few possess.

On their way back to the inn, Nichol noticed a shop selling herbs, spices, and potions. Stopping, she turned and entered the shop, and Ezra followed her.

As she began asking the owner questions, Ezra realized that Nichol knew more about the herbs and spices for sale than the owner. Nichol purchased some herbs and spices and they departed.

With her satchel full, they began to walk toward the inn. Before they arrived, they saw Robert carrying a wrapped bundle. Nearing them, he pulled back the edge covering their daughter's face. Lucette, upon seeing her mother, reached her arms out to her.

"She grew hungry and started crying, so I decided to take a walk to settle her down. I am glad you are back." Nichol took her satchel off and gave it to Robert while reaching for Lucette at the same time, nuzzling her daughter's neck as the baby laughed for the first time. She entered the inn and went to their room to nurse her daughter.

At the same time, Ezra headed to his room and found Helene holding Aiden, sleeping in her arms.

He gazed at his wife. "I have seen how you look when you care for these babies. I wish we could have had children."

"Ezra, we have a good marriage and now we have two children who need us. Nichol and Robert need us as well. Every morning that I wake up, the first thing I think about is them and that I am needed … that I am wanted by their mothers and the babies."

Smiling at his wife of many years, Ezra pulled over a chair in the room and leaned toward Helene. "As you know, Nichol accompanied me to the market today. I visited three merchants who have handled some of the goods I have brought into the port here to sell. I introduced her to them.

"She was cordial and then stepped back so I could privately talk with each of them. Interestingly, she turned away and pretended to ignore what was being said to me. That made the merchants say to me what would typically be said in private.

"When we left, she told me exactly what they said, and she added at times whether they were truthful or not. I asked why she thought that and what she said surprised me. She watches them out of the corner of her eye, while at the same time, she listens closely to their words and what type of voice tone they use."

Watching Helene's face as he said this, he continued speaking. "Then she added, 'After years of simply listening in Papa's solar and then watching, I see them clearly and told Papa what I saw and heard. It is what he relied on when he saw how I observed and listened behind the tapestry.'

"Helene, Nichol has remarkable gifts that I did not understand at first. I now know what she meant by seeing them clearly. What she said confirmed exactly how I felt after she explained her observations and what she said to me after we left the three merchants we visited. She was Alexander's secret asset. Now, she is our secret asset as well."

"Nichol and I have had many conversations about her gift, Ezra. When she says, 'I see him or her or them,' she has a way of seeing deeper into anyone she meets. When she speaks, I trust what she says. I am thankful that Alexander trusted you with her protection. I know what you are thinking: You want Nichol to accompany you when you meet with merchants for your business. Of course, she will have to agree."

Ezra chuckled. "She already has agreed. Alexander tried to tell me who she was; now I wish I had listened more closely to his words. She has a power that few possess. I have not experienced anyone in all my years who can so quickly assess others and do what she can do. Also, she revealed one more thing to me while we were speaking: Where she hid Alexander's fortune."

With a twinkle in his eye and a grin, Ezra continued to speak.

"The night before the funeral, she took his fortune, including some contracts, manuscripts, drawings, and poems from his solar, and buried them. Do you remember her telling us about taking his gold, silver, and gemstones and hiding them? She told us that her papa was guarding them. Well, he is! They are buried in Alexander's grave under his casket. She wants the gemstones for Robert to use while he is making jewelry for sale in Rouen and Paris."

Aiden stirred in Helene's arms as she raised her voice and straightened up in her chair.

"What? Wait … you are telling me that you want to return to Marseilles? Isn't that an unsafe place for any of us to be?"

"Yes, that's what I am saying. I can travel by boat on the rivers most of the way. At most, it will take two months down and back. I will not be of any help cutting down trees and building homes here. You know that. There are more than just gems; there is gold and silver—enough to care for all of us. Combined with what we have, we will have a great opportunity in Rouen for our growing family."

Helene heard Ezra's words. Her mind was circling, trying to fully understand what he was saying. As if the baby Aiden could sense her settling back, he sighed in his sleep, pulling his thumb to his mouth.

"Ezra, I have never seen you so excited. Of course, you should go. Have you asked Nichol?"

"It was her idea."

Helene rolled her eyes and just shook her head. "When are you planning to leave?"

"I will go with you to where you plan to build our homes, then leave from there."

"Ezra, you know that I never stopped you from anything you wanted to do. But this time, this trip will be for our family—for all of us—and for our future protection."

Weeks went by, and plans were assembled for building the homes. Detailed lists were made of what was needed once they arrived at their destination—the destination the Lady had revealed to Nichol.

Robert, Nichol, and Shadow took frequent walks through the streets of Rouen. On their walk one morning, Nichol suddenly stopped. She turned and entered a small shop, followed by Robert and Shadow.

A wizened, hunched-over old man looked up and asked Robert if he could help him.

"I think my wife would like to talk to you," Robert said.

Turning his attention to Nichol, she said, "I need a bow, short but powerful enough to bring down a deer. One that can be used to hunt in a dense forest."

Looking at Nichol, his forehead furrowed, and his eyebrows drew together as if he questioned whether this young woman would even know what to do with a bow. Getting to his feet, he used a hand to steady himself and slowly limped to the back of his shop. He returned with three bows.

Nichol quickly strung them. Pulling on all three, she decided on one, then looked at the man. "Do you have another one like this?"

Without saying a word, he again slowly moved to the back of his shop. When he returned, he had two similar bows, identical to each other but different than the one Nichol initially selected. With certainty, he said, "These are the ones you want."

Nichol strung one and evaluated the pull. "You are right. These are the ones I want. We will also need ten arrows with metal tips and two strings for each bow."

"You have not asked the cost?"

"I know what the cost should be. If we walk from here with two bows and twenty arrows, you will tell me a proper amount."

Smiling, he shook his head while they bargained, finally agreeing on the cost. Nichol paid the amount they agreed upon and complimented him on the quality of his work.

"In all my years, I have never sold a bow to a woman. I was surprised that you pulled the bowstring back with the ease of a man. Your request was not for the type of bow I usually sell. Where are you from?"

Nichol answered his question with another question. "Where did you learn to be a bowyer? You would not have learned to build this bow in Rouen."

Again, his thick eyebrows narrowed as he smiled. "It seems we both have questions but no answers. Come back, and we will talk with answers."

"I would like that," Nichol said as they turned and left.

Robert did not question Nichol about the purchase. She always had a reason for what she did, and on the way to the inn, she revealed it.

"Where we are going, there is a great forest. We can hunt for fresh meat."

Robert tilted his head. "I always wanted to shoot a bow; now I can learn. Did you ever hunt?"

"I practiced on straw targets with a man's tunic hung on them, so we will learn to hunt together. I know you will be good because of all the work you have done for your craft and working at a forge. Bows require strength, and you have plenty. Now, we must get back to the inn, as I can feel in my breasts that our daughter is hungry."

The winter was lessening. Their plans continued to evolve as they talked about preparing to leave Rouen for their next destination.

Ezra hired two skilled carpenters to help with building the homes, a father and son willing to stay with them until the houses and barn were completed.

Timo also had his plans. With the coin Helene had given him, he bought enough seed to plant summer crops for the coming season as soon as they arrived and the building began.

The infants were now cooing babies, charming all who encountered them, and their energy became a positive source for everyone.

As Timo took his turn holding and talking to them in his deep voice, Nichol marveled at their focus on his face as he spoke.

"I think these two have become an energy line for all, Timo. Each of us feels better after holding them. Sometimes in silence, and sometimes as they look at us as if they understand what we are saying."

With renewed enthusiasm, it was becoming a new world and a new family.

fifteen

Emma

*Your clothes are not of a peasant and
I know most noble families in Rouen, but not you.*

Over the next few weeks, Helene and Nichol sewed clothes that would give Nichol a look of prominence. Robert had given her a clasp he had made to fasten her new cloak. Now that her attire was complete, it was time to leave the inn as a properly dressed woman.

As she walked to the door in her new clothes, Lucette and Aiden were close by, lying prone on the blanket on the floor. Nichol bent over, kissing both and promising she would not be gone long. Eagle-eyed Helene sat and watched the two babies as they actively kicked their feet in excitement as Nichol spoke to them.

Moving toward the door, Shadow went by her and stopped to wait for Lucette and Aiden to join them.

Motioning to Shadow to come, Nichol's words stayed in her head. *It is just us today, Shadow.* Turning back to the babies, Shadow was reluctant to leave. Carefully padding toward each, then nuzzling them and licking their cheeks, Shadow finally returned to Nichol's side. As Helene closed the door, Nichol could hear their cries.

Nichol needed a quiet walk by herself, a need to reflect on the rapid changes occurring in her family's lives and to her. Suddenly, she became aware of her current location at the market. The familiar smells of fresh bread, birds squawking—the sounds and sights overwhelmed her senses.

If I closed my eyes, I could be in Marseilles.

Something woke her from her reverie.

Nichol noticed a young woman close to her age, elegantly dressed, with a head covering that matched the fabric of her dress. A beautiful piece of jewelry accented her cloak. She was more girl than woman and walked with a protector by her side.

Their eyes met and each expressed a friendly smile.

Previously, Ezra had pointed her out on one visit to the markets. Nichol remembered his words: "She is of royal blood, sister of Richard, the duke of Normandy, and William, the archbishop of Rouen. Her name is Emma. Some say that she likes to leave the castle for walks."

On this day, Nichol approached her and was stopped by Emma's protector, blocking any further view Nichol had.

Not deterred, Nichol leaned past the guard, peering around him to see Emma and spoke to her. "Your dress is of a particular color that brings out your beauty. I have not seen it except in trade from Mediterranean cities. Do you know where the dye came from?"

Surprised by Nichol's direct question and knowledge, Emma responded, "I do not know where it came from, but this color purple pleases me." She signaled her protector to step aside. Cautiously, he moved but stood beside her, hand on the hilt of his dagger and his eye on Shadow.

"Your clothes are not those of a peasant, and I know most noble families in Rouen but not you. Now that you are in front of me, I see a beautiful clasp and a silver chain around your neck. What is on the end of the chain?"

Nichol smiled. "My husband made these for me. He is a goldsmith."

"Is it carrying something special? I would like to see it."

Her protector moved slightly in Nichol's direction. It was a perceived threat, but Nichol was not intimidated. "Of course. Here, I will show you."

Nichol slowly removed the silver chain from around her neck and exposed only the feather. "At my father's funeral, a hawk appeared and swooped down and dropped this feather close to me."

Emma was not impressed and appeared bored. Her expression changed when Nichol lifted the feather, revealing the stone and rings hidden behind it.

"Oh, the stone is beautiful. Where is it from?"

"An old woman gave it to me and where she got it, I do not know. It gives me comfort. Touch this stone and tell me what you feel. What you see."

Emma was intrigued. With some hesitation, she slowly moved forward to touch it. Just when the palm of her hand was in reach, Nichol placed the stone in Emma's hand and placed her other hand under Emma's outstretched hand, cradling the union.

Still grasping the stone in her hand and Emma's hand on top of it, Nichol placed her other hand on top of Emma's. *I see you, Emma* filled Nichol's mind.

Now a willing participant, Emma's eyes closed, her head swayed, and her facial expressions began to change. She was on a journey—her own secret journey. Her protector became nervous as he observed her behavior and reached to pull Emma's hand away just as her eyes opened. A smile appeared as she raised her head.

Emma leaned closer and whispered in Nichol's ear, "I saw you; you saw me. Our meeting was not by chance. You know who I am and the castle where I live. Come within the week. We can talk and be alone in my garden."

Emma bent over and petted Shadow, sitting by Nichol's feet. As she straightened, she said, "If she has pups, I would like one."

Walking away, Emma stopped. Turning back to Nichol, she added, "When you come to see me, bring your baby daughter with you."

sixteen

Plotting

Does Amos or Ezra know anything about Emma?

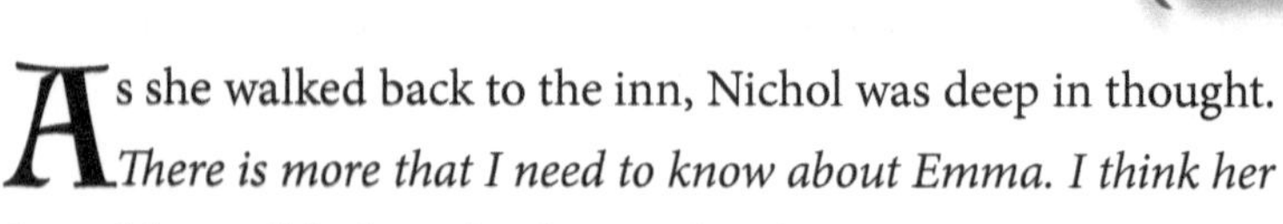

As she walked back to the inn, Nichol was deep in thought. *There is more that I need to know about Emma. I think her friendship will be beneficial to my family.*

Shadow was walking closer to her than she usually did. Reaching down to scratch her favorite spot, Nichol said to her four-legged companion, "There is much to learn, Shadow. We will return in two days to visit with her."

Walking the road, Nichol noticed that the weather was changing. There was less mud on the road and hints of greenery appeared in the bare branches of the trees. More people were traveling on the road than she had seen in the last two months.

Shadow, stay close to me.

As she noticed the changing landscape, she also paid attention to the variety of goods and trade items offered in the stores she walked by.

Ezra and I need to come back and visit them.

As she turned to walk back to the inn, her mind was filled with questions about Emma. She mused aloud to herself as she walked.

"Hmm, I wonder if Amos or Ezra know anything about Emma. When I go to her gardens in the next few days, the more information I have about her will be good for the business we want to build once we have settled further away."

As she approached the inn, she was energized and excited.

Heading to Helene's room, she found Lucette and Helene waiting for her. Marie had come by earlier for Aiden's feeding and he was fast asleep. Removing her cloak, Nichol quickly untied the extra bottom of the flap she had sewn on the fronts of all her tunics to nurse Lucette easily.

Lucette eagerly latched on and began to suckle … but not before giving her mother a gurgling smile. *Are you talking to me, little one?* Turning her attention to Helene, Nichol let the flap fall and drape around Lucette's head.

"You look well, Nichol. Being outside must have been good for you," Helene said as Nichol settled into a chair.

"Oh, Helene … I can see that spring is here. We will be moving on soon to build our own places, which excites me. I also met a woman today who is the sister of Richard, the duke of Normandy, and William, the archbishop of Rouen. Her name is Emma, and she has asked me to visit her at the duke's castle. She also asked me to bring Lucette."

Helene smiled as she spoke until Nichol said Emma wanted her to bring Lucette. "Nichol, you must be on guard. You must talk to Ezra before you go."

Nichol was puzzled by Helene's warning. *I saw her and she saw me. Would the Lady allow her to see me if it put Lucette in danger?*

That evening Ezra and Helene joined Robert and Nichol in their room, and they began quietly talking while the children were sound asleep. A few candles were lit, and the four were seated close together so their words would not be heard beyond the room's thin walls. Their secrecy was imperative as Ezra was briefed on Nichol's visit with Emma.

Ezra began by relating a story of absolute power and control from Emma's brothers, Richard and William. As a moneylender, he routinely heard the gossip and rumors about the brothers. "Once you enter their world, there is no turning back."

Much time passed as the candles burned down. It became uncomfortably quiet after Ezra gave his last thoughts—thoughts that revealed the treachery of royalty and the church toward the people. "Both hold absolute power over all, holding servants and their slaves in a type of absolute bondage.

"Nichol, be careful what you say whenever you are away from us. Emma might repeat something that should remain private. The church and royalty have eyes and ears everywhere. You don't know who might be listening."

Nichol cleared her throat. "Emma requested that I return to visit her and bring Lucette. I will do so in two days."

Robert listened closely. "Why would she want you to bring our baby? Unless it would be during Lucette's feeding time, I think she should remain here with Helene."

Helene nodded in agreement as he continued, "If you take her, Shadow must be always with you, close by. Will Emma allow that?"

Reaching for his hand, Nichol spoke. "Lucette will be safe. Emma asked if she could have one of Shadow's pups if she had any."

Then she let her stop on each face in the room—Robert's, Ezra's, Helene's—before speaking any further.

"I think Emma is lonely. The only way we can survive is by knowing who they are and what they want. I will listen and observe the family so I better understand their relationships with each other. Emma is the entrance for me. The better we understand them, the better we will be able to prevail."

Nodding at his wife's words, Robert added, "I will walk with you to the duke's castle and watch for your return."

seventeen

The Visit

I am closely watched by all the guards.

For two days, Nichol thought only about her meeting with Emma.

Will she receive me? What is it she wants from me?

She is of royal blood and I am just a goldsmith's wife.

While preparing for her trip to the duke's castle, Nichol began humming a tune she remembered Margaux singing to her when she was a child. As a gift to Emma, Nichol added a special water she had seasoned with cinnamon and honey encased in a water bag. She placed it in the side bags she had created for Shadow.

Before adding her cloak to her shoulders, she placed Lucette in her new front pack where the baby could face out in the direction her carrier was walking. Helene had created breeches for both Aiden and Lucette to keep their legs warm on the floor. As Nichol walked, Lucette's legs were in constant motion, as if she were taking steps with her mama.

The day was sunny and crisp, and she was cheered by the appearance of greenery breaking through along the roadside. Reaching her destination, she approached a tall stone wall, walking along the wall until a sentry appeared at the castle gate. Heavily armed with a pike and sword, the sentry made eye contact with Nichol as she advanced.

Noting her dress, a broad smile appeared across his heavily bearded face. "You must be the young woman that Emma is expecting?"

Nichol returned an anxious laugh as the sentry turned his eyes to Shadow. Nichol saw the look the sentry gave her dog and quickly said, "If she did not like you, she would be gnawing on your leg."

The sentry dropped to one knee and reached his open hand out to her.

Shadow cautiously approached and received a welcome pat on her back. The sentry then opened the gate and allowed both to enter.

Once inside, she slowly walked down a wide path, wanting to take in every detail of the gardens on either side. The castle had many floors and a large wooden door at the entrance, which had a knocker that Nichol lifted and released several times.

A man answered, looked them over, and shut the door, leaving her standing.

Will he open the door again?

Moments later, Emma appeared and burst out of the door. Immediately, she took Nichol's arm and blurted, "I am pleased that you came," pulling her toward a bench.

As they settled in, Shadow moved directly in front of Nichol and Lucette, watching Emma's movements.

In a low voice, Emma revealed to Nichol, "When I am outside the castle, I am closely watched by all the men-at-arms. My brothers want to know my every move and who I spend time with.

"Your and Lucette's visit allows me to have a friend they won't question. I only have older women around me in the castle or the gardens, or men-at-arms when I am out on the streets of Rouen. When you were not afraid to approach me last week about the color of my clothes, you lifted my spirits. And I have always wanted a dog like your Shadow—one that would be a companion, loyal just to me."

Of course, Emma couldn't take her eyes off Lucette. It was clear to Nichol that she wanted to hold the baby. Gently, Emma touched her daughter's cheek. As she did, Nichol said, "I think Lucette would like it if you held her." At the same time, she removed her wrapping and placed her in Emma's arms.

Taking Lucette into her arms, Emma's hand brushed against Nichol's. The gazes of the two women met, and both smiled as Emma cuddled Lucette, gazing into the baby's eyes. Emma touched Lucette's cheek and a smile emerged across both of their faces.

At the same time, Lucette laughed, creating a joyous sound with the three of them—mother, daughter, and new friend.

"Nichol, when we met in the marketplace, I noticed you had a beautiful chain around your neck with a feather. When you moved the feather and revealed the stone behind it and then pressed it to my hand, it was then that I knew you had a daughter. It is why I asked you to bring her today.

"I knew that we would become friends. I have always been alone and I believe we can help each other. Since I met you, I have had many meetings with you in my mind."

Nichol was overwhelmed with what Emma was revealing, and yet, at the same time, she was not. She felt, too, that there was a unique bond between them. The Lady had come to her in her dreams the previous night, telling her that Emma could be trusted and would become one of her advocates in the new land they were going to.

Glancing at the young woman holding her daughter, Nichol chose her words carefully.

"Emma, I felt a connection with you as well when you touched the stone. I know that my children will know and honor you. I also know that you and I will be lifelong friends and that we will support each other if the need arises."

"How do you know this?" The astonishment on Emma's face was apparent.

"I have an inner voice that has guided me all my life. You probably have one, too—one that forewarns and encourages you. My father taught me much about merchants, the trades, and how to understand those people who could be trusted and those to avoid. I became his son."

"You became a son?" Now Emma looked puzzled.

"Yes, I was his only child and he treated and taught me as if I were a son who would eventually run his business. The feather on my chain is a reminder of my father. And the chain was made by my husband Robert … a goldsmith, as I told you."

Emma held Lucette to the front of her, gently rubbing the baby's back—a gesture mirrored by mothers everywhere. At the same time her eyes found Nichol's. Nichol pulled the chain out of her tunic with the feather and the stone.

For the second time, Emma saw the rings. By looking more closely, Emma knew that Nichol came from a father of importance.

"One day, Emma, you will have special items meant only for you. And ones that you only reveal to those you trust. One day, I will tell you more about the feather I wear, the rings, and the stone."

Emma's smile had not left her face since Lucette had been in her arms. "Your daughter is special, Nichol; I can feel it in her as

I hold her. One day, I will have a daughter and I pray that she will be like yours … special as well. And I believe that you and I will become like sisters."

Nichol nodded. "I believe we are, Emma. Let us meet again at the marketplace in one week at midday where we first met. I know your protector will be with you. Now they know me and will most likely keep their distance and let us talk. I'll bring Shadow and Lucette with me."

The women stood. Emma placed Lucette in Nichol's arms. When she did, they touched their foreheads together like a secret parting. As they pulled away from each other to turn back to the castle and the entrance for Nichol to leave by, Nichol thought she heard Lucette say her first word.

Did she say Mamas?

The sentry opened the gate for Nichol, and she smiled and nodded her appreciation. The smile was not for him; it was for the Lady—her Lady.

I know now that Emma and I did not meet by chance.

Stepping away from the castle gate door, she looked up and saw Robert emerge from a shop. Her heart and step quickened; she had much to tell him.

eighteen

Friend or Foe?

Emma is naïve. She has never had to fend for herself as I have.

Offering Nichol his arm as they headed back to the inn, Robert waited for her to speak. What she said surprised him.

"I believe that Emma will become one of your patrons, Robert. She admired the chain you made for me. I feel my friendship with her will bring recognition to you and your work.

"Emma was taken with Lucette. As she held her, it was clear to me that she is fond of children, especially our daughter. She said that she hoped to have a daughter like Lucette someday."

"Let me carry Lucette," Robert said as he reached for her.

"Do you want to carry her or wear her?"

Laughing, he helped Nichol out of the front carrying pack she had created and slipped his arms through the slings, then placed Lucette in it, facing out as they walked. As soon as Lucette was positioned, her little legs were in motion, wiggling with excitement as the three of them neared the inn.

Neither were in a hurry to return to the inn. With the sky a brilliant blue with no clouds, feeling the warmth of the sun on their faces and shoulders was welcomed.

Soon, the inn came into view. Both noticed that Ezra was out front, waiting for them. So did Lucette. When she saw Ezra in front of the entrance, she directed her arms toward him, cooing as she did so.

Nichol laughed, touching the back of Lucette's head. "It looks like our daughter has a chosen person."

Greeting them, Ezra could hardly contain himself. His face softened when Lucette reached for him. Touching the baby's cheek with his large hand, he leaned in and whispered in her ear. Then he straightened to his full height and escorted them through the door. "Let's go to my room where we can talk."

Nichol spoke up. "Before I tell you of my visit, I need to feed Lucette. Let me settle her in; then, I'll join you all at the table. What I will share is for your ears only."

"Helene and I will fetch some ale and something for all of us to eat and bring it back. I will tell Roger and John that we are not to be disturbed," Ezra said.

As Ezra reached for the door pull, he added, "I want to hear of your meeting with Emma and what was said. With your memory, Nichol, I know you can give us a word-by-word account of your encounter. We need to hear everything you experienced there, if anyone else was around, and give us your impression of her."

Lucette quickly settled into her mother's breast as Nichol seated herself at the table. "Did you feel safe when you were there?" Robert asked while they were alone.

"Yes. I felt safe when just with Emma. The sentry who let me in also welcomed me because Emma had told him I was coming."

As she said that, both their eyes turned to the door as Helene and Ezra entered with two trays—one with drinks and the other with food. "Nichol, I brought bread, and some of the broth with fish, beans, and carrots you like," Helene said as she placed her tray on the table.

As the four settled in, all eyes were on Nichol.

"It was the first time we had the opportunity to speak after I approached her in the marketplace. Because of her position, she is watched closely, and she longs for a friend—a woman friend like me. What she said next surprised me. Emma said that the men-at-arms observed her and reported back to the duke and the archbishop, who she believes are both schemers despite them being her brothers. Both men want to know who she spends time with and what she does during the day. She related this to me in almost a whisper as we sat outside in her gardens."

Nichol revealed the conversation and what emotions Emma displayed when they were together. When Nichol described how Emma responded to Lucette, a smile appeared on Helene's face.

"I believe our first meeting was not by chance, and the Lady brought us together, as in providence. We are going to meet again next week in the marketplace. I will bring both Lucette and Shadow. Since her protector now knows of me, we felt they would stand back and let us be together as friends.

"As we stood to part, we leaned in and touched foreheads. I felt a connection with her when we did that. Before Papa was murdered, he and Margaux were my confidantes. Gerhardt was my friend, but not someone I could confide in like his mother and Papa. I feel that Emma will be a friend."

Ezra leaned back. "This is excellent, Nichol. It is important that we have someone that can warn us of dangers to come. You will be able to understand what her eyes and ears receive. I am pleased you have a new friend—one that you need, and one that she needs.

"Both the duke and the archbishop will want to know about someone who has captured the attention of their Emma, and is more than a peasant. It appears they both expect total obedience from family members and will be jealous of any outside influence or intrusion into the family. We need to create a safe background for Nichol."

"Emma is naïve. She has never had to fend for herself as I have. But I know she can. She did not have a papa like I did who taught me his trade."

She turned to her husband. "Robert, she admired the chain you made for me that I always wear. I would like to give Emma a small gift when we meet next—something she can tuck under her garment or sleeve. Is there something you could make for her, or that you already have, that would be small, but special? Something that she could secretly wear to remember me?"

Robert took her hand. "Of course, I have just the right gift for her. Do you remember when we first met, the bracelet I made, the one the man tried to steal?"

Nichol smiled and hugged him. She whispered, "That is the perfect gift. I want to show her a different world than the isolated one she grew up in, a world that includes all people."

The Next Meeting

Royals do not mix closely with tavern commoners.

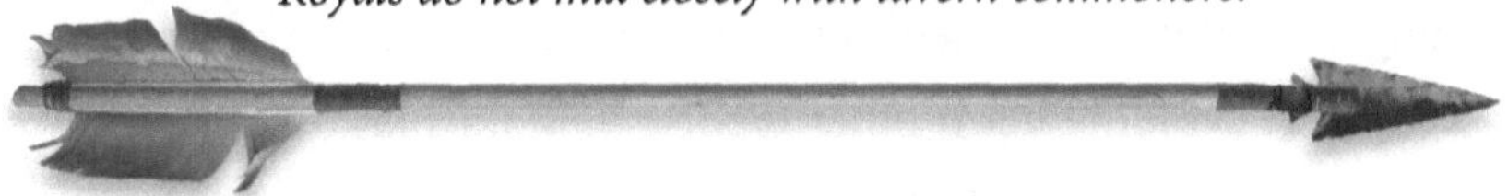

Winter was not completely gone and the air was heavy and damp. People moved quickly through the marketplace to ward off the chill. The usual marketplace chatter was muffled behind the wool wrappings surrounding villagers' faces.

A week had passed since Nichol had seen Emma.

Moving through the marketplace on her way to meet her new friend, Nichol held Lucette close to her for warmth. Settled into the unique front pack her mother had created for her, she could tell her daughter wasn't pleased.

At four months, Lucette was alert and wanted to see what was happening around her. Her little hands tried to push away the cloak her mother had wrapped around her. Suddenly, her squirming stopped. Lucette heard a voice she recognized.

And then her feet started kicking. Nichol touched the head of her daughter and leaned into her ear, whispering, "She's here …."

Emma embraced Nichol as she pulled back her cloak to see an excited Lucette. She laughed as Lucette smiled and gurgles poured forth.

Emma's protector stayed back and allowed her to approach Nichol.

"I know a tavern close by that my brothers frequent. Let's go there so we can sit and talk by a warm fire."

The protector entered first, then signaled for Emma, Nichol, and Shadow to follow. When they did, the room went silent. Everyone knew who Emma was by sight. They also knew that her sudden appearance was odd; she did not frequent taverns.

Once inside the door, Nichol scanned the space for possible danger, a habit she learned from being attacked at the Anchor Inn and while avoiding her brother Fredric in Marseilles. As she did, she immediately thought *this tavern was a better establishment than Fredric would frequent.* The walls were stone and plaster. Rough-cut oak beams supported the wood plank ceiling. Many candles were lit and those inside seemed more interested in their ale and wine until they took notice of Emma.

An attendant approached and guided them to the fireplace, the location of the room's only warmth. Those already seated there were ordered to give up their seats for the duke's sister.

Seeing this, Nichol touched Emma's arm. "Why not suggest to him that they move over and make room for us? Like us, they are only trying to stay warm." Emma nodded.

"Ask them to move over and make room for us. You have other benches," Emma demanded of the owner.

Surprised by her request, the owner shifted several benches closer to the fireplace as everyone rearranged themselves. Now, in front of the fire, Shadow settled next to Nichol. Emma was on her right and the protector stood close by. Ale, bread, and cheese were brought to them.

Nichol could feel the shared tension emanating from those around the fire.

Those of royal blood did not mix closely with tavern commoners—ever.

Nichol opened her cloak, lifted Lucette from her sling and handed her to a waiting Emma. Those around the fire stayed silent, watching intently as Nichol lifted her cup and said loudly, "Let us drink to the coming of warm spring weather."

Small talk and laughter began to resume in fits and starts. The whole establishment was now curious about their unusual visitors.

Emma, knowing little of the lives of those outside the castle, began listening intently to the conversations around the fireplace. Nichol nudged her and whispered, "They want to hear from you. Say something that pleases them."

Just then, the owner brought them more food and ale. Emma pulled off a piece of bread and told the owner to get food and ale to share with all seated around the fire with them.

Emma looked at the patrons. Seated close by was a young man clad in tattered clothes.

"What work do you do in Rouen?"

"Lady Emma, I am a baker, and I made the bread we are eating. Thank you for the ale. I must return to my duties. I have loaves to take to your castle." He stood, bowed, and left.

The conversation continued to increase among the tavern patrons as more ale was brought. Nichol noticed that, as the ale flowed freely, there were those who wanted to say more, but Emma's protector's stare made them hold back their words. The patrons all had suppressed concerns, but their uneasy movements, gestures, and facial expressions created some confusion.

Aware that there was tension in the room, the conversations she overheard confirmed to Emma that she had little in common with anyone but Nichol, her new friend. Because of the shared feelings they experienced with Nichol's stone, they both know much about each other.

Nichol knew that Emma was to leave for England and marry the king. She wanted to speak with her friend alone and understand her thoughts.

Nichol knew what it was to be alone, raised by Margaux, the housekeeper. She would have known little of the outside world if it had not been for her hiding in Alexander's solar and listening behind the tapestry. His later trust in what she learned and interpreted had taught her much. *I must share what I know with Emma. She can use my knowledge.*

For the first time, Emma was aware that there was unrest outside her gated castle.

Separately, Emma and Nichol had both walked the streets of Rouen and observed slavery, starvation, and cruelty. After the conversation around the fireplace, the opportunity to interact with these people gave Emma a closer perspective and an awareness of her own weakness. She had not been aware of the depth of misery so many were experiencing.

I have seen those in despair before. Until today, I had not seen the anger and fear of faces up close.

Lucette began to fuss. "Lucette is hungry. I must take her home. Can you walk with me for a few moments?" Nichol said in a low voice.

Emma lifted Lucette and kissed her on the cheek as she handed her to Nichol. "Our time is too short. My protector and I will escort you to where we must part ways and we can talk and plan to meet again in a quieter place."

The keeper of the tavern approached Emma. At the same time, she put silver coins in his hand. "This should cover the costs of food and ale for all those around the fireplace while I was here."

As they left the tavern, their walking pace slowed. The two women leaned their heads closer so the protector could not hear. Emma instructed him to walk ten paces behind so they could talk freely.

"You have been my sunshine on this dreary day. I am watched from the time I wake till I go to sleep. When I enter a room when one or both brothers are present and they have a guest, they stop talking and look at me as if I am an intruder," Emma whispered.

After the first conversation, Nichol realized her new friend was naïve and that she might be able to help Emma develop her own knowledge in dealing with her brothers. But she cautioned herself to be careful and not expose too much about herself and her background.

"A new priest has appeared, and I do not trust him," Emma revealed in a whisper. "I heard my brothers talking about him. They think he is a useful tool." She shuddered. "I do not like the way he looks at me."

Nichol realized that Emma knew nothing about the activities of her brothers. Observing Alexander for years with his dealings with men from all levels, Nichol learned that it was her observations that kept her safe. *She has my curiosity. I will help her, so she doesn't get entrapped by them.*

"Emma, you must position yourself where you can hear conversations. Voices echo off the stone walls, and in that way, private conversations among your brothers and guests will be yours. One day, you will depend on the knowledge you learn from these conversations, and that knowledge may save your life when you become queen."

Emma stopped. "Do you truly think so, Nichol?" Her eyes were wide as she looked at her friend.

"Yes. You will be important someday, and not just for birthing children for a royal husband. My heart tells me this is true."

Their eyes connected, and Nichol removed one of the finely crafted braided bracelets she wore on her wrist—Robert had created both. Reaching for Emma's hand, she laid the bracelet in it.

Emma's mouth opened in astonishment. "Is that for me? It is beautiful!"

"This will connect you with me. We are both different from most people here. I could sense it the day we were in your garden. I feel you are like a sister to me, Emma. Robert made this for me and I wanted you to have it. These braids of fine gold are woven together as a symbol of our friendship and unity."

Emma pulled back her cloak and extended her arm so Nichol could attach Robert's bracelet to her wrist.

Lifting her eyes again to connect with Emma's, Nichol added, "When you touch the bracelet, think of me. Soon, I must leave here, but I will return when the sun warms the ground again."

"Nichol, I will think of you often. I know my brothers will want to meet you. Nothing escapes their attention or their complete authority over me."

Nichol turned and walked away as she thought about Emma's last words. They troubled her. *They have complete authority over me.* The words vibrated through her body and kept repeating over and over in her mind. She knew they had a deeper meaning than what Emma casually said.

What are you telling me, Emma? I heard men like these in Papa's solar. When Papa argued with the evil priest Loupe, I heard, saw, and felt fear in his response. Your brothers are the duke and the archbishop and have absolute control over Rouen and the church of Rouen. They cannot tolerate doubt in their rule or wisdom. That would be their ultimate enemy.

Pulled from her thoughts, Nichol found herself in front of the inn. Her deep thoughts had taken her many steps, oblivious to her immediate surroundings. A smile spread across her face.

I see them—I know who these people are before I meet them.

Looking up, she felt warmth flow through her body. At the same time, her mind was filled with gratitude.

Thank you, Lady of the Light, for Robert, my children, and all the people you have brought into my life who support and believe in me.

twenty

Earning the Trust

I have seen this place; it is time to move on.

The end of March had arrived, and the days grew longer and warmer. The excitement and anticipation of their upcoming journey consumed their conversations. Nichol's description of their destination helped finalize the list of supplies needed and additional purchases were made.

"Good morning, sleepyhead," Robert said to Nichol as he gently moved her hair from her eyes. "Today is our day. Are you ready?"

Smiling into his face and snuggling closer, Nichol said, "I am. My hands are anxious to begin the garden Timo promised me. And I long to be in the open without eyes peering at me whenever I'm out."

The two whispered, not wanting to wake Lucette. "And I'm looking forward to creating the new land for everyone and our first home together for the three of us. I'm thankful Papa taught me about the forge before becoming a goldsmith. With his guidance, I can make the things we will need. I need to get up and head to the stables to bring the horses and cart around."

Smiling at her husband, Nichol said, "Lucette slept well last night. I'll feed her before we set out and ask Marie to take care of Aiden as well."

Before sunrise, Timo had arrived at the front of the inn with Moki loaded and ready to leave. He knew Robert would bring around the horse-drawn cart they had loaded the day before.

Joining him was Amos, carrying a cup of water. "You have a long journey ahead, Timo. It is best for you to have some water before you leave. I've got two bags full of bread, cheese, smoked fish, and vegetables for you all to share. I did not think Moki would mind being the carrier."

Thanking Amos for his hospitality, Timo asked, "Would you hold Moki's rope so I can bring around the horses?"

Nodding yes, Amos remained at the inn door.

Within a short time, everyone assembled outside the inn. The last few items were packed in the saddles on Moki and into a cart that was packed high above the side rails.

Without a spoken word, Robert, Nichol, Lucette in her front pack, and Shadow began walking. Behind the cart were Timo and Ezra, who would be on alert if anyone approached from the back. Marie now had a front pack for Aiden, like the one Nichol had made for Lucette, and walked alongside Helene.

Amos bid them a safe journey as the travelers left the inn. His sadness was evident as Helene and Ezra passed him. Ezra turned back. "No worries, my friend. I will see you again and be back with John and Roger."

The horse's hooves striking the cobblestone street, and an occasional dog barking were the only sounds to be heard at this early hour. Soon, Rouen was behind them. As they traveled on the road north that led away from their temporary home, Nichol suddenly stopped and turned to the east. The rest slowed down as she looked at her fellow travelers. With a smile she put her right hand on her heart and pointed to the horizon.

Now, everyone stopped, following her pointed arm. Smiles spread across their faces as they observed the splendor that was unfolding. The colors of the sky vibrated in front of them. A wisp of yellow clouds on the horizon blossomed into orange and red as a brilliant array of colors ascended to a light blue sky.

Nichol turned to Robert, and they embraced. She whispered in his ear, "I know this sunrise is from our Lady … a promise of good things to come."

Robert looked down at Lucette between them, her eyes moving between the two as she smiled at her parents. "When she is old enough, we will tell her of our secret journey," Robert responded in a low voice, and he put his arm around Nichol's shoulder, pulling her closer to him.

Ezra had been scanning the road ahead. Finally, he saw Roger and John waiting, still on their horses. With them were Harald and Olaf, the carpenters Ezra had hired to help build homes at their destination.

Ezra waved and shouted to the men. Hearing his voice, they all waved back. To Robert and Nichol, he said, "Roger and John are down the road waiting for us."

Slowing down as they met up with the four who had been waiting, the group was now complete. The expanded caravan moved forward, with John riding in front to spot any danger and find places to rest and stop for the night. Harald and Olaf—father and son—came next, leading the cart, followed by Marie, Nichol, Robert, and the babies. Helene stayed behind Nichol and Marie to help with the children if needed.

Everyone could sense the excitement in Ezra. He stayed busy moving up and down the caravan while engaging in lively conversation with all. Last was Roger, riding next to Timo and Moki.

Shadow was always on the move, ever watchful, stopping to look and smell the air—alert and on the hunt.

By late morning, John had found the perfect spot to stop and rest: trees for shade and a small stream to water the horses. For their first meal of the day, the food Amos had given to Timo was unpacked. As Nichol and Marie nursed Lucette and Aiden, Nichol watched Timo walk to the stream with Moki's bowl to fetch water, just as they had done many times on their journey together.

Robert surprised them with dried berries and ale to wash it all down. He sat next to Nichol and noticed her warm gaze as her eyes settled on each member of the group. "Nichol, you must eat. While you eat, tell me what you see."

"Everyone is here because the Lady brought us together." Nudging Robert, she smiled and leaned closer, softly saying, "Have you noticed Olaf and Marie? He just brought her food and then sat down next to her."

Robert took Lucette from Nichol, placed her on his shoulder, and patted her back.

Not to be outdone, he turned to Nichol, "Have you noticed Timo and Roger? They are eating together and sharing stories."

Nichol just looked at him. A few moments later, he said, with a broad grin. "Of course, you have noticed them. That is what you do so well."

Nichol leaned into him, kissed his cheek and then rested her head against his shoulder. He felt a subtle sigh flow through her body.

Shadow suddenly appeared as if she knew it was time to move on.

Without anyone speaking, the group slowly stood and made their way to the road. Everyone took the same positions, except Marie.

Nudging Robert, Nichol nodded her head toward Olaf. At his side was Marie. Roger dismounted and walked with Timo; they both strolled at Moki's speed. Nichol listened to their conversation, a Christian and a Jew talking and listening to each other.

This is what the Lady wants—common ground for all of us.

twenty-one

You Are the Reason

I see that deer and boar are in the area.

Still on the road, Nichol had lapsed into deep thought.

Robert noticed and waited for her to reveal her thoughts, no matter how long it took.

She grabbed his arm, pulled him close, and spoke softly, "When I was in the solar, I enjoyed watching and listening to Papa's guests. You and I are now doing the same thing here."

She turned toward Robert. With a slight tilt of her head, she smiled, a signal for him to respond.

"I now see why you hid there," Robert responded. "I, too, am enjoying what I am seeing and hearing. Marie and Olaf reminded me of us when we first met. This is the first time I have seen Marie at peace. Timo and Roger are of different religions, and they show respect for one another because I think they have more in common than not.

The two clasped hands as they spoke, just for their own ears. "This is the first time I have traveled without someone chasing me—and now us," Nichol said in the lowest whisper she could. "There is a reason the Lady is guiding us in this direction. Yet to what end, I do not know."

Robert took her arm and pulled her even closer. "Chasing us? We all chose to be here with you. And now the Lady is in our lives, too. Growing up in Antony, I saw Ezra and Helene one or two times a year. Papa never said much about Ezra's life as a merchant or moneylender. When you and I arrived in Paris, and I started training at the guild, I began to hear and feel others' resentments toward Jews, something that wasn't apparent to me when I lived with Papa and Mama. Now with the attack at Ezra's and the search for you and Lucette, they are chasing all of us. Until you came into our lives, I was not aware of the prejudice that surrounded Ezra and Jews and now my family. We are all Jewish. You and Marie are not, but our daughter is.

"You have opened all our eyes to the danger that comes from the duke and the archbishop. This is where I need to be—next to you, Lucette, and Aiden. My aunt and uncle. Shadow. And now our friends. I feel we have all been chosen to be together."

His last words were said as he gently moved the hair away from her face. In a quiet voice directly into her ear, he added, "You are the reason—the center of a new life and new land."

They came across small settlements, one after another. The farther they went, the settlements became fewer and the road narrowed through the forest to a path just wide enough for the cart.

Nichol felt at home in the solitude. The morning of the third day, Nichol knew she needed to reposition where she walked with the group. Moving to the front would be better and she could let John know he did not need to ride ahead for scouting.

Late that morning, she held up her hand and came to an abrupt stop.

"Nichol, why are we stopping?" Robert asked. "There is nothing here."

Everyone started looking at each other as they gathered around her.

Nichol pointed in one direction. "This is where we leave the road."

Extending her arm and pointing in a northwest direction, she firmly repeated, "This is where we leave the road." Nichol turned and noticed the bewildered stare of the group. With confidence, she said, "Look carefully. You can see an overgrown path that we will follow. That path will take us to where we will live and build our homes. Few have traveled this way. We will be more protected."

Roger and John led the way to the path and held branches back so the rest could enter while concealing the entrance.

After scrutinizing the area carefully, Timo spoke, "There are fresh animal tracks and no signs of recent human travelers. I see that deer and boar are in the area. We must walk single file and try to keep the cart from breaking branches." After all had passed and were well into the forest, Roger and John returned to the entrance with fallen branches they had picked up. Carefully, they pushed the dirt around, concealing the tracks and entrance to anyone traveling the road.

The solitude and quiet safety of the forest brought cheerful conversations. With frequent stops to rest, eat, and enjoy their personal stories, bonds were beginning to form.

Moving the cart through forest growth, as well as around an occasional downed tree slowed their progress. Working collectively to clear the cart's path united them. Timo had taken it upon himself to sweep the forest floor with dead shrubbery as they passed.

The original sense of urgency to arrive at their destination was replaced by the enjoyment of their journey. Spring was beginning to show itself with new buds on trees and wildflowers promising to show. The birds now created a symphony of sounds that several found themselves whistling to.

Nichol slipped into thoughts, moving from topic to topic. She knew she would need to return to Rouen before the growing season ended. Her friend Emma would be leaving for England and her marriage. And Ezra wanted her to meet with specific merchants to help their business thrive.

At the end of day three, with the babies fed and sound asleep, Timo brought the firewood he had gathered to Nichol. She pulled out her flint with steel and started a fire as she had done many times on their journey to Paris.

After eating, they gathered around the fire, quietly gazing at the flickering flames. When it turned to glowing embers, one by one, they began to lie down for the evening. Tired, all the travelers secretly hoped their destination was just around the next bend and were excited about what they would find.

Shadow suddenly appeared and sat next to Nichol, with blood on her mouth and rabbit fur on her coat, which let her master know that she had hunted down her meal.

In her sleep, Nichol heard from the Lady.

You are heading in the right direction. Your destination is near.

How will we know?

You will walk for several days. Then you will come upon a large hill, the hill of hope and inspiration. Cross the stream and follow the base of the hill. There will be a valley surrounded by forests. In the distance, there will be a small lake. The ocean will not be far. You will feel in your heart that it is right.

I remember you revealing that to me as we left Paris. Will we be safe?

You will create a new way for people to live and work together —a safe place.

You will create a special name for it. Do you know it?

Yes … and it will come to you when it is time.

A vision of the land, the hill, the stream, and the small lake suddenly filled Nichol's head. A smile spread across her face, knowing that this place will be ideal for all of them.

Then she heard the Lady's final words.

Remember, Nichol, always be on alert.

twenty-two

The Crossing

Finally, in a sun-drenched valley, a hamlet came into view.

Early the next afternoon, Roger, Helene, and Ezra stopped as they exited a forest and called Nichol to come forward. Pointing down the path, Helene said, "Nichol, what do you think? We just came out of a forest. Is that the hill the Lady showed you?"

In front of her was a landscape she had seen many times. The hill was greening up. She could see promises of flower buds popping up. The trees on the upper edges revealed the first offering of leaves and shading to come. She saw a few rabbits moving from budding shrub to shrub. A family of deer were clustered at the base, turning toward the new sounds that arose—their voices.

Nichol's heart began pounding with anticipation of what other proof might lay ahead. Clasping her hands to her chest, she said, "Yes, that is the hill she revealed to me. We should keep going. On the other side of it, we should arrive at a stream we can ford and a path to follow once we are across."

Excitement rippled through the travelers. As they breeched the hill, a stream came into view. Its width was the size of many men stretched across. The water was crisp and clear because of the winter flow.

With all gathered on the bank of the stream, Roger raised a concern felt by all. "It is not running fast but it is at least knee-deep, maybe more. I will try crossing first."

Roger rode his horse to the edge of the riverbank and slowly entered the water. He made his way across and then returned.

"I have crossed far worse. Let us take a rest and let the horses drink and feed on the grass on the riverbank before we all attempt to cross."

As if the horses understood what Roger said, they immediately moved to drink from the stream and turned to munch on the lush grass on its banks. The travelers filled their waterskins, then awaited Roger's guidance.

Shadow sensed what was next and approached the stream. It was her turn. The roiling water was icy cold as she eyed the other side. Immediately, she leaped in and moved swiftly across. Pulling up on the bank, she shook her body and turned to the others as if to say: *You can do this.*

Roger went first into the stream to locate the best place for the wagon to cross and determined it would also be the best place for the horses. The water was deep, above the knees. First, the cart was taken safely across, then the others crossed and dismounted. Roger returned with three horses until all had crossed except Timo and Moki.

Now, it was Moki's turn.

Roger returned with two of the horses. Timo took Moki's rope and positioned one horse next to Moki on the downstream flow of the stream. Roger and John were positioned upstream, blocking the current to lessen the force on the laden Moki.

Everyone stopped what they were doing and lined up on the riverbank, intently watching and ready to help if necessary. As the horses and men emerged from the cold water, there was a loud cheer and an immediate gathering around Moki. His ears perked up. Moki knew it was for him.

Nichol bent over and whispered in Moki's ear, while stroking it. He brayed and his head bobbed up and down. Shadow at her side got the same ear-scratch and another whisper. Leaning into Nichol, the three of them became almost one.

The group went silent about what they had just observed. They knew they were in the presence of someone who had a gift with animals. Nichol looked up and the first one she saw was John, with an ear-to-ear smile and a wink of his eye.

Robert turned to Nichol. "Let us go find the land of your dreams."

Everyone picked up their pace and spirits soared as the Lady's predictions, one after the other, proved true. They continued following the footpath's gradual rise above the stream and to the right around the base of the hill. One by one, the valley came into their view as they gathered, overlooking the sun-drenched valley and a path to a small hamlet.

Nichol took Robert's arm and exclaimed, "We are here! It is the end of our journey and the beginning of a new life for us. This is exactly what the Lady has been showing me! This is it … the dense forest to the north, and a lake gleaming on the eastern boundary. This is where we will build our homes and our future!"

Ezra motioned for Roger and John to join him. "I want both of you to stay here until I return. They may not be used to having armed men entering their hamlet. I will return after I speak with these people; I will not be long."

As they continued down the path to the center of the hamlet, Nichol counted fifteen homes clustered together. The dwellings were surrounded by fields beginning to sprout winter wheat, grazing sheep, and chicken coops. The noise from the cart and horses brought people from their homes as they passed. A constant chatter increased as they gathered and began to follow.

Nichol quickly instructed the group, "Give them smiles and friendly gestures."

Making their way close to the lake, they found a suitable place to stop for the day.

Robert, Ezra, Timo, and Nichol stepped forward to meet the villagers, now within talking distance. An elderly man broke from the group and approached Robert.

Scowling, the old man asked, "What brings you here?"

In a pleasant voice, Robert replied, "We're looking to start a new life in a peaceful land with peaceful people."

"Who are you, and who else is with you?" the old man asked with suspicion.

"I am Robert, the blacksmith. My family is traveling with me. What is your name, sir?"

"I am Garlyn." Silence fell as he looked them over. Bluntly, he asked, "Who is chasing you?"

Nichol had joined the men and stood next to Robert, who was now speechless at the man's gruff questioning. Looking confidently at the old man, she said, "No one is chasing us. We are here for the same reason you are."

"And what would that be?"

"To live in peace and to start a new life in a new land," Nichol answered him promptly.

Eyes wide, Garlyn looked at Robert. "Does this woman always speak for you?"

Smiling, Robert said, "You do not know my wife." His reply brought laughter from Garlyn as well as the other onlookers.

Finally, Ezra spoke up. "A man called Amos, who owns an inn in Rouen, told us that we would be welcomed here."

Garlyn straightened, and the look of suspicion left his face. "I know Amos from Rouen; he is a good man. We are a friendly group to those we trust, but the trust must be earned."

With that, Garlyn and the other villagers walked away, returning to their homes.

"It seems we have much to prove," Robert said to everyone.

Ezra turned to the group and spoke. "This is where I leave to head back to Paris through Rouen. John and Roger will go with me. It should take less than half the time to return. We will make sure we leave through the forest using a different route."

Taking Helene by the arm, he motioned to Nichol to join them in a private conversation. Once away from the group, he turned and faced Helene and Nichol, holding onto a hand from each woman in his.

Deep in thought, he paused for a moment, then began to speak.

"I gave this trip much thought while we were in Rouen. Then upon seeing this land, I now share Nichol's vision. I will return to Paris with John and Roger and retrieve my hidden coin. The three of us will travel by horseback and river, reaching Marseilles in a month.

"I will contact Margaux and determine when only she and Jonathan are at the villa to dig where Nichol told me to go. Once I have collected Alexander's fortune, I will purchase passage on a seaworthy boat and sail back to Rouen. It is the safest way to travel. By the time I return, the sea will be at its calmest time of the year. With fair weather and your Lady's guidance, I should return within two months."

That brought smiles from Helene and Nichol as they all embraced.

Without further words, Ezra thanked Robert for the food and water and waved farewell to the others. Mounting his horse, he rode through the hamlet and out of sight.

As he left his expanding family, he could feel that he was sitting taller on his saddle. Speaking out loud, Ezra told himself: "This is the most important trip of my life. If I fail, we all fail."

Locating a flat area near the lake, Timo unpacked a large tent he acquired in Rouen. With Robert's help, the two men put it up quickly, creating a shelter that would protect them and their belongings from the sun and any changes in the weather.

Next came unloading Moki and the cart before they could start creating a new homestead.

Harald and Olaf set out to gather wood, both for warmth and to build a small temporary shed to store what Moki had carried, along with items from the cart.

Nichol and Marie tended their babies. Feeding the infants, then placing them side-by-side within a cloak, the two women set out to sort out what Moki had carried, deciding to leave what was in the cart for Robert and Timo to organize.

Sitting on the field grass, Marie spoke up. "Nichol, you have saved the two of us. Aiden will have you as his mother. And I am feeling the same as I once felt before I was attacked.

Nichol reached out and touched her hand. "It was meant for you to be here, Marie. I can feel it."

That evening Nichol, Robert, Lucette, and Shadow took the short walk to the lake.

As the sun began its final drop before disappearing behind the horizon, the color that spread across the sky was breathtaking, rich with every hue of orange that one could imagine.

Settling in to enjoy it, they gathered close together, letting the sounds of the pending night fill the air. Lying back, Shadow nuzzled Nichol's shoulder. Surrounded by evening stars, the moon cast its glow across the travelers.

Feeling at peace, Nichol told Robert of Ezra's travel plans to Paris and then on to Marseilles. "There is more that he did not tell us. I think he did not want to disappoint us upon his return if his trip is not successful. It is a dangerous journey because of what he will be carrying."

"What is he carrying back that I do not already know?"

"The large number of beautiful gems and coins that came from my father's money chest—the same gems and coins I buried securely before I left. Of course, Ezra is after names and contracts that I also buried. It is worth a fortune; one that Fredric and Astrid want and would go to any means to acquire. And now we have priest Loupe in pursuit."

Robert said, "We need to support Helene until Ezra is back. And we will need to be strong for her if he does not return."

twenty-three

Harmonie

Our place in the sun.

The next morning, Timo saw Garlyn approaching their campsite and turned to Robert and Nichol. "We have a visitor."

When Garlyn was within speaking distance, he motioned to Robert and said loudly, "We need to talk."

Robert and Nichol stopped what they were doing and slowly walked to Garlyn. His eyes were on Robert as though Nichol was not visible to him.

Nichol noticed his bold stance and gruff demeanor, but to her, his facial expression betrayed him. Amused, smiling as she approached him, she thought, *I have seen that look before.*

Once again, Garlyn narrowed his eyes and suspiciously demanded, "Why are you here?"

"Good morning, Garlyn," Robert said. "We traveled here because we wanted a place free of oppression."

Raising his eyebrows and crossing his arms, Garlyn asked, "Whose oppression?"

"The duke and the church, their rents and tithes."

Garlyn just stared at an unflinching Robert. Without responding to what Robert said, he remarked, "For now, we welcome a blacksmith to our valley."

"Does your hamlet have a name?"

"No. As soon as we name it, the duke will try to claim it as his own. We are too far from the duke and the greedy hands of the church, and our place is too small to be bothered with. One day, that will change."

"It seems we are both here for the same reason."

"Yes, it does." Garlyn then turned and left.

Later that morning, Robert and Nichol wandered away from the group to survey the land for the site of their prospective home. Taking her hand as they walked, he leaned toward her and said, "I promise I will build a home you will be proud to live in. We will have a home big enough for us to live in comfortably, and it will be ready for us to live in before the next winter sets in."

Squeezing his arm and leaning into him, she said, "As long as I have you and our children, I will be happy."

Content in their comfort with each other, once they had completed their examination of the landscape, they turned and walked back to rejoin the rest of the family.

As everyone gathered outside the tent, each person contributed their thoughts about how they thought their new hamlet should be laid out with multiple homesites.

Nichol said, "Timo, you know how monasteries and their fields and vineyards are arranged. Tell us where we should build our homes and plant our fields. Where should a barn be? And what about creating a central longhouse like the monasteries have where we can all gather?"

Timo picked up a stick and began to explain as he drew in the dirt. "Think of where we are standing as the hub of a wheel.

The way we came in will become the road to the hub and the spokes of the wheel will lead to each of our homes."

Lifting the stick and pointing at the stream, he kept speaking. "We can direct water from the stream to provide water to some of our fields. Our cluster of homes will be surrounded by fields with a field between the homes and the northern dark forest. They should not be close to the stream. Flooding can happen. Instead, we will create a water well that serves our homesites and can be dug where we stand."

As Timo finished his drawing, Nichol asked, "What about you, Timo? Where should we build a house for you?"

"I am content to sleep in the cart until a stable is built. Then I will make the stable my home and live there with Moki and the horses."

Nichol laughed. "When winter comes, you will need more than Moki to keep you warm. You are welcome to sleep by our fire."

Helene was excited about having the garden she did not have in Paris.

Robert sensed the excitement among the others. For the first time, he expressed the desire to have a forge shop of his own.

Nichol added, "Our first home should be large enough to shelter all of us, to sleep in and take our meals. After that, we should build a place for the forge. As we begin to build, we will need to make and repair tools. Robert's skills as the only blacksmith in the hamlet has made us welcome."

Holding Aiden, Marie asked timidly, "Nichol, will there be enough room for Aiden and me to stay in your home until he no longer needs my milk?"

"Of course, there will be room for you both," Nichol reassured her.

Timo scanned the land to the south of the proposed home sites, drawing on his experience as a farmer and grower. He stood silently, contemplating the land.

Joining him, Nichol said quietly, "You seem lost in thought. Are you plotting where the orchards and vineyards will be planted?"

"You know me well. Yes, that's exactly what I am envisioning. The exposure to the sun is perfect there, and we can draw water from the stream for the fields," he said, pointing to the expanse of land to the south.

In a contented whisper, Nichol said, "I like the sound of that. The name for our new hamlet came to me in my sleep. We will call it Harmonie … our place for togetherness with our family."

Nichol told the group her idea for naming their section of land, and everyone agreed Harmonie was the ideal name.

They spent the rest of the morning making plans for what would be built first.

It was Robert who suggested they build in phases.

"We need to build a temporary large structure for all of us to live in, giving us a place to eat and sleep. It can be simple and provide shelter from the weather, more secure than the tent. When it is built, then we can use the tent as a workshop area. Later, we can convert the large structure into a barn with a stable. Timo, if the stable is to be your home, where do you want it to be?"

Nodding his head, Timo said, "I agree with your earlier suggestion. It makes sense to build it south of the forge and close to the farmlands we will plant."

Robert summed up the day's plans. "My father has provided all the tools we need to build, and we have the wood from the forest."

Nichol added, "Harmonie represents a new beginning and hope for a brighter and more peaceful future for all of us. Together, we will make it work. When Garlyn and the others see what we are doing, they may want to help us, as we can help them."

twenty-four

A New Beginning

I felt a sense of calm for the first time in many months.

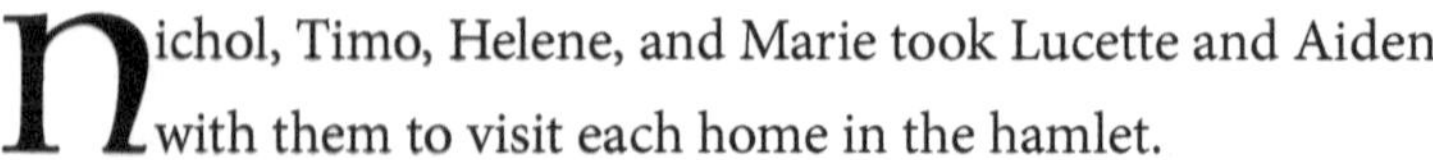

Nichol, Timo, Helene, and Marie took Lucette and Aiden with them to visit each home in the hamlet.

When Timo shared what he had learned while working at several monasteries in the past and how to grow grapes, there was excitement among the villagers that a vineyard would be possible. Timo would become the teacher once again, instructing all in planting and better ways to plow. Nichol offered coins to anyone willing to help build their homes.

For the first time, the villagers saw promise in the strangers from the south. They heard Timo would eventually raise bees after discovering a colony he could safely move. The resulting honey could be shared with all in the village.

Within days, the newcomers were working nonstop to build their new hamlet. Neighbors emerged from their homes every morning to help Harald and Olaf cut trees for their homes. Robert and Timo used the horses to drag the logs to the new home sites and begin splitting them to form the walls. Nichol, Helene, and Marie took care of the children and started planting a garden close to where the house was being built.

Robert was pleased with the quality of the construction. The walls were sturdy, made of split logs and a securely thatched roof.

Shadow staked out her territory. She would patrol the edge of the forest, then disappear into the forest on the hunt. When she was not hunting, she stayed near the children.

When they all gathered to eat, Nichol would talk to Harald and Olaf, learning their words and the customs of their native language.

Over supper, Olaf said to her one evening, "You are not from our land, but you speak our language well. Few can do this."

That evening as Robert and Nichol lay side by side, Nichol turned on her side and gazed at her husband. "I've been thinking … watching Helene with Lucette, and seeing her joy. We need to plan for her to be with us someday."

"Some day? She is here all the time."

"But she won't be. Ezra will spend much of his time in Rouen. He can always stay at Amos' inn, but I know them. Both will want their own home as well. I know that they will have a place there."

Nichol lay quietly, turned toward Robert, and added, "But I know Helene. She is like a mother to me now. She wants to be here … and she doesn't want to be away from Lucette and Aiden for long periods of time. We have become the family she always wanted. And all of us are her friends. As Harmonie adds more families, Helene will want to be part of it … part of *them*. Trust me, Robert. We need to plan for her to live with us someday. And it will be soon; I can feel it."

"We are planning on building a home for Ezra and Helene here in Harmonie."

"I know, but I want to make sure she and Ezra will always have a place in our home as well. As they get older, being in a home alone may no longer meet their needs. Promise me, as you build our home, you will make it larger than you had planned so that there is room to include them as well."

Pulling her closer, Robert murmured, "I promise."

The two hamlets—old and new—were growing and thriving, side by side.

twenty-five

Ezra Returns

I would pay one of them with the other's head.

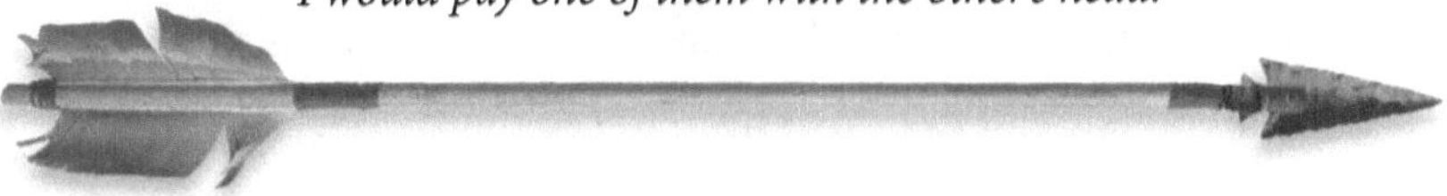

Almost three months had passed since Ezra left. The sizeable temporary shelter was like a big house that all would use, along with the barn when it was completed. By the time winter arrived, three more houses were built: one for Helene and Ezra and one for Nichol and Robert. The third one would be converted to a common longhouse, similar to those Nichol and Timo had seen in the monasteries they had visited.

Planting for summer and fall harvest was completed with help from Timo, Robert, and the neighbors. The valley was becoming a community: women from the hamlet would stop by and invite Nichol and Helene to join them at the lake to bathe, wash clothes, and enjoy the children.

Most importantly, the lake was a place for conversation among the women. They had more in common than not, talking of children, husbands, cooking, and secrets not to be repeated. Occasionally a roar of laughter was heard.

When the women were done, it was the men's turn to bathe. Their conversation was quite different, consisting of talk about building homes, farming, and plans for the valley's future.

Information about anyone's past was not asked for or freely shared. After a few months of community bathing, Nichol gathered Robert, Helene, and Timo for a private conversation. Once together, they all began to share conversations they participated in or overheard from those who lived in the hamlet.

Nichol began by describing the women and men she had talked to and then added, "I cannot see these people; they do not reveal themselves as others do. They are people of few words. They are good, though, and I feel that the Lady brought them to this location. I am sure of it. I don't need to see them; I feel that they are good people."

Robert and Timo both raised their eyebrows at her words.

Nichol smiled at their expressions. "Everyone in Garlyn's hamlet is skilled. He was a boat builder and a skilled carpenter. Do you remember when we first arrived, we all commented on how well the homes were built?"

Nichol stopped and let her words be heard. She smiled and looked at Timo. "They sorely needed your knowledge of planting and harvesting. No one in the hamlet had your knowledge or skill. Your skills are valued and needed here, Timo."

She turned to Helene, aware that Helene had become more irritable as the days went on. Her friend was worried about Ezra. She could see it on her face and even in how she moved about.

Reaching her hand toward the woman who not only was her friend but had become more of a cherished mother and grand-mama to her two babies, she said, "Helene, news of Ezra will be here soon. I know it."

The morning was overcast but with promise of the sun breaking through. On their land was the first growth of vineyards that had been planted.

Timo noticed a lone rider approaching the hamlet in a full run. Turning to the houses built and those working in the fields, he yelled, "RIDER coming!" Everyone stopped work as he approached, moving closer together.

Immediately, the rider was recognized. It was John, one of Ezra's protectors.

Nichol immediately rushed to Helene's side, fearing the news was not what she had foreseen. When she saw John approaching them riding alone, Helene turned pale.

John saw her reaction, and he dismounted and hurried to her, saying in a loud voice, "Ezra is tired and in good health in Rouen. He wants you all to join him at the inn as soon as you can. Now, I need something to eat and drink."

Speaking more softly, he continued, "I have a story to tell all of you—especially you, Nichol."

Everyone crowded into Helene's home.

Robert gestured toward a stool for John to sit on. Almost out of thin air, a cool cup of ale was placed in his hands. Gulping it down, he held it up for more, then wiped his mouth with his sleeve.

The gulp was all that everyone heard. Then silence fell. It was though all were holding their breath for what would come forth. John was aware that all eyes were on him.

Nichol's eyes fell on Olaf and Harald; she realized John didn't know them. However, he did know Marie.

"John, what you say can be trusted and heard by all in this room. Olaf and Marie are together, and Harald is Olaf's father. Harald and Olaf are skilled carpenters in our hamlet."

Relieved by her words and before taking a morsel of the food hurriedly placed in front of him, John began his promised story.

"On our way back to Rouen, Ezra told Roger and me that if we accepted his offer, it would be the most dangerous trip we have ever been on together. I laughed and asked him, 'What trouble you have gotten into now?' Then, I saw Ezra as I had never seen before. He was worried and frightened, not for himself, but all of you.

"That is when I stopped him from saying anymore. I told him, 'Yes, I will join you.' Then Roger said, 'We always work together. I am with you as well, Ezra.' It was settled.

"After Rouen, we went to Paris and got fresh horses before we left the city. Many stops were made to pick up the coin he had hidden with allies. From then on, we traveled by horseback and boat on rivers that led us to Marseilles.

"When we arrived in Marseilles, Ezra led us to a manor. He revealed that it was where Nichol had lived, and Alexander had served as the port commander. Everything and everywhere Nichol had told him to look, we did. And … we found it all." He winked at her as he said those words.

As she heard them, she felt her body relax against Robert.

"Little did Roger and I know we would become gravediggers late at night. Ezra got the caretaker's son to help us, while his father stood guard as we dug. Under Alexander's coffin a fortune was buried. We now had two fortunes: Ezra's and Alexander's.

"Ezra wanted to do something else. This time, the caretaker and his son added their shovels and efforts to ours. Ezra told us that we were to dig a new grave for Alexander and move his body away from the house. Margaux showed us the place where Nichol and Ezra would sit and talk in his garden."

When John revealed what they had done, tears glistened in Nichol's eyes. "Thank you, John."

He continued, "I then realized why Ezra was worried. If anyone became aware of what we carried when we traveled back, we would not have survived the trip. Ezra said that the Lady was smiling down upon us when we arrived at the docks."

"What Lady?" Nichol asked, puzzled.

"The Lady Ezra said was watching over us." John looked around and saw the approval of what he said. "You know about the Lady, don't you?"

Nichol laughed. *My Lady is now Ezra's Lady.*

"Yes, we all know," Helene said with a nod.

"We were blessed. A merchant came in with a cargo of silk, spices, leather, and wine. Ezra convinced him he could double his price in Rouen and Paris instead of selling in Marseilles. There is more to this story and I know Ezra wants to tell you himself. How soon can you all leave with me for Rouen? I think we should leave in the morning."

That evening, with everyone together, the discussion commenced about who was going to Rouen and the need to bring back more food, a few goats, and some chickens.

Nichol spoke first. "We have all worked for three months without stopping. I saw joy in everyone's eyes when the idea of a return trip to Rouen was mentioned. Ezra wanted to see all of us, and I believe we should all take some time and plan to restock our supplies."

Harald turned to Nichol and spoke in his native tongue. "I want to bring my wife back with our other two children."

Turning to the group, Nichol told them of Harald's wishes. Watching the group, Harald could see by everyone's reactions he had their approval.

No one wanted to be left behind, so it was agreed that they would all return to Rouen. Each wanted to reconnect with Ezra. And they all realized their supplies needed to be increased before the winter. Olaf wanted to encourage Harald to bring the rest of his family back and become part of Harmonie.

John continued to speak. "On my way here, a day's ride from Rouen, I was stopped by two men on the road. They said that for me to pass, I had to pay them. I told them that I could pay only one.

"'There are two of us,' came the quick response. The man's voice held a threat. Then I drew my sword and told them I would pay one of them with the other's head. They gave me passage as I charged by. I think there were more of them hiding off the main road, and they were armed. When we return, we must travel in a close group with weapons."

Nichol went to see Garlyn and told him of the plans and that they would soon return. She asked him, "Is there anything we can bring back for you?"

"We are in need of some cloth and leather for shoes."

"We are as well. When we return, we will have enough cloth and leather for all our needs." Nichol noticed a sudden change in Garlyn. "What worries you, Garlyn?"

"There is a man who lives in our community who has told people that you bring peril to this valley."

"Is it the man called Quinlan? He wears an angry look when he is with us."

"His wife died after he arrived here and soon after her death, he turned bitter. I fear he will turn people against one another in the valley."

"Before we leave, I will stop by and talk to him and maybe bring back something just for him."

Garlyn hesitated, taking a deep breath before he spoke again. "Nichol, make sure that you are not followed when you return from Rouen."

"We will, Garlyn. When we turned off the road halfway here, we traveled through the forest for the remainder of our journey. We were careful to leave no trace of our travel."

After leaving Garlyn, Nichol sought out Quinlan.

She found him tending to his garden, on his knees, picking weeds. He looked up to see Nichol and said with a scowl, "What do you want?"

"We are going to Rouen. Are you in need of anything?"

"Why are you going?"

Nichol's glare and brisk response startled him. "We will bring back leather and cloth for the needs of all in the valley, including you. If you desire anything, let me know."

Nichol turned and went home.

The next morning, with dawn's beginning light in the sky, they all started down the road to leave the valley.

When they were passing Quinlan's home, he was outside, anticipating their departure. He approached Nichol. "Geese—a pair of geese," he said in a humble tone.

Nichol put a hand on his arm. "Quinlan, we will bring you geese on our return."

He nodded and his facial expression softened.

Their journey to Rouen began with high spirits. Time passed unnoticed as Nichol moved from one to another as they walked, engaging in conversation and small talk.

Nichol asked each, "What do you need to bring back with you from Rouen that is important? What would you like Harmonie to become? What can you do to contribute to ensure that happens?"

Much was revealed. Each had hopes and desires that were personal. They began to openly share their thoughts, voicing them back and forth. Soon, they all began to realize they were the same.

Nichol observed Marie and Olaf walking together, and she leaned into Robert. Whispering, she said, "Olaf is taken by Marie; they have become inseparable."

Her voice was louder than she intended because the others turned to the couple and then smiled.

Marie and Olaf did not hear what Nichol had said. They were unaware of anything but themselves, with Olaf carrying Aiden as they walked.

twenty-six

Returning to Rouen

We must wait to talk until we are alone.
There are people watching us now as we eat.

When they were a day's ride from Rouen, they found themselves approaching a forest. The road narrowed, and with heavy stands of trees on both sides, it was the perfect place for the thieves to lay in wait for unwary travelers.

John turned in his saddle. Looking back, he put the group on alert.

"Everyone, be careful. This is where I encountered the outlaws. Stay close so we aren't separated if they appear. We all must be on watch. Take your weapons out and show that we are ready for battle."

When they started into the forest, Nichol commanded Shadow to lead the way. It was not long before her ears laid back, flat against her head. The dog was growling, looking side to side, and baring her teeth.

Seeing this, Nichol knew they were not alone. "Shadow, come back! The thieves have not left the forest."

She went to the cart and put Lucette in the back, along with Marie and Aiden.

Nichol commanded Shadow to get in the cart at the same time and whispered in her pet's ear as she scratched it, "Protect the children, Shadow."

Then, a loud, deep sound caught her attention overhead. Looking up, she saw a large fork-tailed hawk with red on the upper tail and belly circling the area. The majestic black tips of each wing were mesmerizing.

Papa ….

Harald and Olaf were armed with long knives and axes, and John and Robert had swords. John rode alongside Helene, telling her to drop back a bit. Robert and Timo took positions on either side of the cart as Nichol removed her bow from its cover and strung it. Sliding three arrows in her belt, she nocked one, ready for trouble.

Just as John had warned, men started to appear at the edge of the road and quickly moved in front to block their way. This time, four men appeared on the road in front of John and Helene. Behind these men stood another three.

At first glance, they were outnumbered by strength. The robbers had seven men, where their group consisted of five men, three women … two infants, and one wolf dog.

One of the four thieves spoke. "I remember you. When you passed here before, you said that you would take the head of my friend as payment." He laughed as he looked at his men on both sides of him. "Now, I think we will take your cart and your horses. Then you can pass."

"Your weapons tell me you are soldiers. Who do you fight for? You do not appear to be common thieves," John demanded.

"That is none of your concern. We need horses and you have brought them to us."

"So, you do not deny you take orders from a lord … or is it a priest?"

Becoming agitated, the man in front repeated his demand, this time louder and with a heavy threatening tone. "We will take your cart and your horses, then you can pass. Or I will put an arrow through your heart."

Talons extended, the hawk swooped down, providing the perfect distraction for Nichol's movements. Without saying a word, she suddenly appeared between John and Helene. In a motion almost too quick to be followed, she shot and released. Her arrow flew into the man's mouth, protruding from the back of his neck. He was the one who demanded their cart and horses.

Yelling at the top of his lungs, John charged ahead, waving his sword over his head. Too frightened to move, his target froze and was trampled.

The robber standing next to him raised his sword to protect himself, and John's sword descended, knocking the sword from the thief's hand and delivering a deep gash to his arm. John dismounted and, with brutal efficiency, dispatched the two battered men.

Nichol shot another arrow, impaling another robber in the chest.

Dumbfounded, the three remaining men confronting Harald and Olaf hesitated as they saw these actions. Harald raised his ax above his head and stepped forward as he released it, slamming the sharp weapon into the thief's stomach.

Olaf raised his ax and the man facing him froze.

Nichol sprinted toward the wagon to protect her children and released another arrow on the run. This one flew solidly into the shoulder of a man charging at Harald, now armed only with a knife.

The remaining two men, one with an arrow in his shoulder, immediately fled into the safety of the forest.

John shouted to Harald and Olaf, "Do not make chase! We do not know if there are more men. We must leave here at once!"

Nichol went to the cart and laid her bow down, with Robert and Timo on both sides of the cart, their weapons still in hand. Lucette and Aiden were crying, and Shadow was crouched in front of the two, ready to spring into action. Her protective instincts were raging.

Without saying a word, Nichol picked up Lucette, gave her to Robert, and handed Aiden to Marie.

Moving quickly, John stripped the fallen men of their weapons. He turned toward the wagon. "Nichol, one is still alive."

All eyes followed her as she picked up her bow and quickly went to John's side.

She knew the thief with the arrow in his chest would not live long if the arrow were in or near his heart. Even though the man was still conscious, she put her foot on his gut and pulled the arrow out of his chest. Blood flowed from the wound.

He let out a shrill scream as she demanded, "Who do you fight for?"

The man said nothing.

She pulled her dagger and knelt next to him, holding it to his throat. "I will ask one more time. What lord do you fight for?"

"It is … not … a … lord … " were his last words.

The pain disappeared from his face, followed by the blank stare of death.

Instincts on alert, Nichol quickly scanned the forest. She saw a man behind a tree, looking at her. There was something familiar about him.

The way he looks at me … does he know who I am?

He must be stopped.

Glaring back, she pointed the bloody arrow at him and mouthed the words, "I see you."

Fear shot across his face, along with surprise at being exposed. He turned to leave.

I cannot let him escape. He is greedy.

In one swift movement, she dropped the arrow she had pulled from the dead man and threw her dagger. The blade made a solid *THUNK* as it stuck in the tree he had been hiding behind.

Hearing the weapon hit the tree trunk, he turned and saw the jeweled dagger embedded in the tree. Such a fine weapon was the offering of a lifetime and his greed overcame his fear.

Prying it loose, he turned toward Nichol with a sneering smile that quickly faded.

The arrow Nichol shot pierced his chest, all the way to the fletching. He looked down with a look of disbelief and then collapsed.

Nichol walked with Shadow to the fallen man, holding a death grip around the dagger. Kneeling, she whispered to her pet as the animal aggressively sniffed the man's boots and clothing.

What does she smell that so capitates her? What is she learning about him?

After retrieving her dagger, she stood, putting her foot on the man, gripping the arrow, and pulling it out.

Stopping, she turned and stared into the forest. "Shadow … not now, but soon."

Helene was not surprised at the speed and accuracy Nichol displayed. She had seen Nichol's fighting skills before, during the incident at the cottage.

Still, this was different: No words were exchanged, but the man was dead all the same. There would be an appropriate time to talk to her but now was not the time. *We must leave right away,* Helene thought.

The others also saw the strange exchange between the man behind the tree and Nichol.

A silence fell over the group. The others had heard about Nichol's skills, but what they saw and experienced at the confrontation was something they had never encountered before.

As a soldier, John was in awe. He told the group, "With Nichol, we have a secret weapon. We must protect her and she will protect us."

He added, "I am certain there are more of them in hiding. I fear for the souls of other travelers on this road. If they do not give the outlaws what they want, these men will not leave a trace of their existence."

Traveling in haste, few words were spoken as they approached Rouen.

Finally, John said, "We must find out who attacked us. They are well-armed fighting men. They must be connected to a powerful person. And until we find out who it is, do not speak a word of what happened to anyone."

It was late afternoon when they arrived at the inn, tired and hungry.

Harald and Olaf were again cautioned not to talk about what happened on the road as they left for their home. The rest of the group entered the inn, while Timo and Robert took the horses and Moki to the stable to be fed and watered.

Seated in the inn's common room, Amos was expecting Nichol, Helene, and the group's return at any time. When the inn door opened, and they entered one by one, Amos rushed to greet each one.

Seating them at their usual table, he noticed their grim mood. Bowls of stew, bread, and ale were brought to them. Silently, they began to eat, and Nichol and Marie nursed their babies.

Nichol looked down at Lucette with a mother's loving smile.

I wonder what Lucette feels when she touches the feather and amulet while suckling. She doesn't settle down until she touches them. Does she feel what I do when I touch them; does she see Papa and Rose?

Softly, Nichol whispered to her daughter, "One day, I will see you, and you will see me."

Amos brought a stool and sat down between Nichol and John. "Ezra is meeting with merchants and will return soon. I will take you to your rooms when you are ready." His voice lowered to a whisper. "I see dried blood on your boots and clothes. Your mood and the blood suggest that you were attacked on your way here. Was anyone injured?"

Nichol turned quickly, looking at Amos. "No. If anyone asks about us, please say only that we were good guests, paid for our food and lodging, and kept to ourselves. Anything more could put you in danger."

The children were suckling as they all began eating their first good meal in over three days. With all eyes on their bowls of stew with bread and cheese, Helene's intentional cough broke the silence. Everyone looked up.

"We must wait to talk until we are alone. People are watching us now as we eat. When Ezra returns, I will tell him we all need to speak away from the ears and eyes of others."

Just as they were finishing their meals, Ezra walked in. His presence lifted everyone's spirits. Immediately, Helene and Nichol leaped from their stools and greeted Ezra with hugs. Lucette stopped nursing, turning her face up to her mother as she reached out to hug Ezra.

Seeing the joy on their faces, Ezra proclaimed, "I have good information."

Helene's eyes and head moved toward the room, and put a finger to her lips.

Observing the heads turned their way, he lowered his voice, "You are right—too many listeners."

Ezra leaned toward Nichol and murmured, "I want you, Robert, and Timo to come to our room as soon as you can."

twenty-seven

Ħarmonie

Helene felt her anxiety about
what Ezra was about to reveal increase.

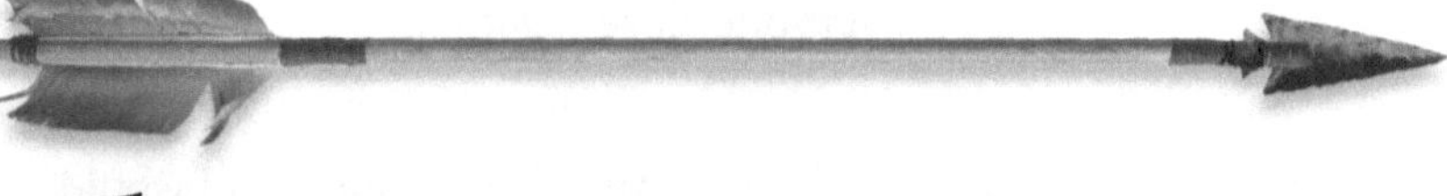

Ħelene watched as Ezra began to eat.

Looking up, he noticed his wife's attention. "What is it, Helene? You seem worried."

"Nichol has been waiting to hear what happened on your trip, especially in Marseilles." Her tone held mild reproof and a hint of impatience.

"Of course," Ezra replied, picking up bread and a slice of cheese to eat as they went to their room, the largest one in the inn. Arriving at his room, Roger, Nichol, Robert, Lucette, and Timo were already there, along with Shadow. John had stayed at the table in the inn.

Ezra knocked on the door. "Roger, it is Ezra and Helene."

Roger removed a thick wooden brace securing the door and stepped back. Nodding to Ezra, he left and joined John in the inn's tavern.

Shadow had worked her way to the front of everyone and rushed through the door as she made her entrance. Scanning the room, she then turned to the others and let out a short bark to let them know it was safe to enter.

Once inside, the group was excited to hear what Ezra would say and they all wanted to listen. It was time for some rearrangement.

Robert moved a small table and some stools to the center of the room. Timo brought more lit candles to the table. Helene sat next to Nichol and took her hand, giving it a gentle squeeze while looking into her eyes.

Nichol tried to smile but to no avail. Helene felt her anxiety about what Ezra was to reveal increase. Once seated, Ezra began in a low voice that drew everyone close together.

"John, Roger, and I traveled through Rouen, stopping to gather more food for the journey to Paris at Amos' inn. I told him I would return within two months and asked him to be on alert for anyone who showed interest in me or our group. When we got to Paris, we immediately collected the coin and contracts I had hidden there and in the surrounding villages.

"It took almost a month to reach Marseilles, traveling by boat, down rivers, and then on horseback. After arriving, the merchants I had traded with for years warned me to accept changes made for my own good and that it would be best if I left. The careful choice of words they spoke, and their lack of eye contact told me their fear was real.

"Alexander's stores—the stores I was a silent partner in—at the docks in Marseilles were pillaged by the priest Loupe. His ransacking was witnessed by many of the surrounding merchants. He justified the theft by telling them that Alexander owed back tithes. I believe only a tiny portion of the value he took went to the church.

"I also learned Astrid took up with him, sleeping with the devil. After he was done with her, he then stole from her and Fredric by raiding what was left in the warehouses where Alexander had stored merchandise to resell. What jewelry and personal items they both had were taken by his men, leaving them virtually coinless.

"From what I overheard from the merchants and those in the community, they both got what they deserved. And then I heard something interesting. Some said they heard Loupe had offered Fredric coins and supplies to hunt down Lisa if he quit the drink.

"Gossip surrounds the priest Loupe. He had stolen his brother's wealth, raped his wife in front of him, and then had his thugs slash both their throats before he became a priest. Claiming his brother's share of their father's estate, he now has the power that large amounts of money bring. It was how he got the title of priest … he bought it."

Mouths gaped open as Ezra related his story. The group around the small table leaned closer. Voices now dropped to a whisper as if anyone outside Ezra's door might overhear what he revealed.

Robert reached for Nichol's hand and squeezed it.

"And my family—all of you are my family—there's more. Now I hear he is building a small army and has become someone to fear."

Ezra took a deep breath before continuing.

"I think that we should believe what we know about the cruelty of Loupe. Just as we should believe that all the gossip is true. We must be careful and prepare for what might come."

Reaching for a piece of cheese, a cup of ale mysteriously appeared at his side. As he looked around the table, his eyes landed on Timo. Nodding his head, he was ready to speak again.

"When we arrived in Marseilles, I sent Roger ahead with word to Margaux's husband Jonathan that I needed to see her after we arrived. I asked that he meet me at Sir Roland's before I met with Margaux.

"Jonathan and his son Gerhardt met us at the end of the next day. The first thing Gerhardt asked was, 'How is Lisa?' Both were pleased when I said, 'She has become the daughter Helene and I longed for. She is now known as Nichol and is married to my nephew, Robert. And she is a mother! She has a baby girl named Lucette.'"

No one noticed the tears in Nichol's eyes when Ezra shared his heart. Where Robert was gently touching one of her hands, Helene had the other.

"A huge smile crossed Gerhardt's face when I said that. I then told them what I needed, starting with talking with Margaux at the villa when Astrid and Fredric were absent. I was surprised by his response. 'Whenever you like,' was what he said. 'No one knows where Fredric is. With what I heard about Loupe offering him coin and supplies to track Lisa and coming under Loupe's influence, I assumed that was what he was doing.'

"With Loupe gone, Astrid has been taken up as a mistress to a count, and she is staying at his home in Marseilles. This told me that the villa was almost empty except for Margaux's family, so we headed there, along with John and Roger. When we arrived, Jonathan and Gerhardt took our horses to their barn to feed and water them. They are still on the property until the duke who owns the estate names someone to take Alexander's place.

"Margaux heard our arrival and met us at her door. With a concerned look, her first word was, 'Lisa?' I told her that you are in a safe place, married, and have a daughter. She put her hand on her heart, smiled, invited us into her home, and served us bread, a warm stew, and ale. When Jonathan and Gerhardt came in, John and Roger stayed by the door to keep watch.

"I then told them why we were there. You all should have been there when I told them I was the only one Lisa had entrusted with the whereabouts of Alexander's treasures. When I got to the part where it was hidden, Margaux let out a shriek and started laughing, placing her hand over her belly as she continued laughing. 'Lisa's outsmarted them again. Astrid and Fredric are such fools.'

"Then, Margaux wanted to know more about Lucette and the rumors surrounding her birth. When I revealed why we had left Paris and that we were all getting guidance from the Lady through Nichol, Margaux took it all in and said, 'If you hear the Lady, listen to her … she is wise and has surrounded Lisa since she was a small child. Your words tell me she is now with Lucette as well.'"

As Ezra spoke, Helene watched Nichol's face. This time, she noticed her eyes brimming with tears and Helene again gave her hand a gentle squeeze. "We are all here with you, Nichol."

"Then I warned them both, 'No one is to know about Lisa's new name but you, Margaux, and Rose. She must be protected as Astrid, Fredric, and Loupe seek her capture. And I believe they will kill her after they find the secrets Alexander revealed to her. Sinister rumors are being spread about Lucette's birth by the midwife.' I did say that it was important that they always refer to Nichol as Lisa if talking about her.

"Margaux's face then changed from the softness of talking about Nichol, Lucette, and the Lady to a stern expression. In an angry voice, she revealed what happened after Lisa escaped during the funeral.

"'Astrid excused herself and went to the solar to claim her reward for murdering Alexander. The next thing I heard was a scream echoing throughout the villa. When everyone rushed to the source of Astrid's shouting, I saw her in front of Alexander's chest, kicking it. In her hand, she clutched a single coin. The box lay on the floor, empty. Immediately, she summoned Fredric and told him to find Lisa and to bring her back alive. When Fredric failed, she realized Lisa could not have carried the contents away. It's why they have pursued you.'

"Margaux continued, 'For the next few days, the two of them tore apart the inside of the manor, looking for the contents of the box. When they could not locate any, Astrid had Fredric and two of his drunken friends dig up Alexander's grave, searching through the contents of the casket. When they did not find what they were looking for, Fredric and his oafs left, leaving the casket open and the burial site in disarray.'"

Ezra broke in. "What Fredric and Loupe didn't seem to realize was that Alexander never owned the manor outright. He paid the rents he collected annually to the Duke of Provence and tithed to the church. The rest was his personal wealth. He was a Roman Catholic but kept his faith to himself. There was much happening in the church that he did not support. Astrid's frantic search was seeded by the fact she knew the manor was not hers. She had to find out where he had hidden his wealth. She failed."

Nichol was mesmerized and horrified by Ezra's words and the information he revealed. She did not know that her papa did not own the manor. *Was this why Papa made sure there was a plan for my escape to Paris and Ezra?*

The small room had gone quiet.

Finally, Nichol spoke. "Ezra was the only one that knew what I did—where Papa's treasure and contracts were hidden before he was buried. When the grave in the orchard was first dug, I had taken all his things of importance and removed them, digging a deeper hole within the gravesite. I moved all the bags of gold, silver, coins, gems, and some of his contracts, my poems, and drawings and placed them deep in the new hole. Then I covered it with dirt, smoothing it so it did not look freshly dug and climbed out of the grave.

"Early the next morning at first light, I returned to make sure that all was concealed at the bottom of the hole. When the funeral was over, Alexander's burial shroud and casket would be placed on top, protecting the treasure below.

"I remembered speaking with Margaux once, when she told me my family was complicated. I now know Fredric was not Papa's true son and, therefore, is not entitled to any inheritance because his mother, Astrid, murdered Papa. I am his sole and rightful heir, and they are trying to steal it from me."

Nichol noticed a grimace from Ezra. "Is there more, Ezra?"

twenty-eight

I Know Her

I did everything you asked me to do.

Ezra took a deep breath.

"Everything happened so fast before you left … there was more Margaux and Rose wanted to tell you."

Ezra looked down at the table, struggled with his words, then looked into Nichol's eyes. "Alexander found comfort with another woman in Marseilles, and he fathered a girl and boy with her. They are younger than you by a few years and the girl has many of your features."

Absorbing Ezra's words, a calmness began to flow through Nichol's body. "Did he love this woman?"

"Yes."

Nichol smiled. "When he was gone for a few days, he always returned in good spirits until Fredric or Astrid confronted him. Did you see the children and their mother when you were in Marseilles?"

"We stopped to see them to make sure that they had coin for their needs. I knew that Alexander had cared for them when he was alive. I know you want to return to Marseilles someday. Meeting them is now another reason for you to return. They are anxious to meet you, their older sister."

"I have a sister and brother; I may have seen them and not have known who they were." Turning to Helene, she hugged her, adding, "Yes, now I know I will return to Marseilles. Our family continues to grow. I want to meet them.

"I am pleased that you told me that Papa found the love of another; he deserved better than Astrid. What you have told me was Margaux and Rose's burden to carry. Margaux told me my family was complicated. Does the mother of my sister and brother have work that she does?"

"Yes, she is in the brewer's guild and has her own stall."

Nichol laughed. "Oh, I have met her! She knows who I am and I have talked to my sister and brother. Their names are Caterine and Piers, and Elise is their mother. We will indeed return to Marseilles."

The small group took in what Nichol had said. Even Shadow seemed to lay down, her eyes glued to her mistress. Gazes were exchanged around the circle. All were in awe of what they had just heard.

Ezra was both perplexed and amused by Nichol's reaction to the news.

Inhaling the rest of the ale in his cup, Ezra spoke once more.

"There's more to relate about the evening when we discovered Nichol's hiding place. That evening, with the aid of the moonlight and candles, Jonathan, Gerhardt, John, and Roger dug down to the now-exposed body of Alexander that had been tossed back into the open grave after Fredric had torn it apart. We carefully lifted the casket, placed it on the upper ground and continued to dig to the bottom of the hole.

"Margaux and I were the watchers, looking for anyone who might come by. They had to dig another foot deeper from where Alexander had lain. Then, we found what we were looking for.

Cloth bags of silver and gold coins, and handfuls of the gems that I knew he had. We also found contracts, poems, and drawings. It was all there—everything that Nichol told me she had hidden. All were intact and undisturbed.

"Nichol … I decided to do one more thing: properly bury your papa. You have talked about the walks you and he took after your meetings in the solar. Margaux showed us the area of the garden you used and we selected a new place. We started digging by the bench that was off the path and under the flowering tree, and that is where we chose to bury Alexander. The old gravesite was filled in. We left the grave marker, knowing that your bench and tree were more appropriate to celebrate who your papa was."

Ezra then spoke directly to Nichol, handing the poems and drawings she had created to her at the same time.

"I did everything you asked me to do. It was the exact number of items you said you left; all were retrieved. The contracts you buried have value and we can discuss them later. I gave Margaux, Jonathan, and Gerhardt the amount of coin you told me to give them. They were grateful. Because of this, they do not have to rely on the duke, who now gives them coins to manage the fields. They are maintaining the condition of the villa and fields as best they can. Margaux misses you dearly. The last thing she said was, 'The Lady willing … one day Lisa will come home to me.'"

Holding the poems and drawings to her breast, Nichol began to cry. "I miss her; she was always my true mother," she said softly.

Ezra's story stopped as each said words of kindness to her. "Thank you, you are all so kind." Then, leaning forward, Nichol asked in a hushed voice, "Ezra, is there more?"

Ezra took another deep breath. "With the good fortune from your Lady in her guidance for you, we came across a merchant that I only know by the name of Diego, and he knew the same of me—only as Ezra, the merchant. We talked about ships, sailing, and fair weather. As our conversation continued, it was easy to see that we both wanted something.

"Diego revealed that the merchant he always sold his cargo to had died. He was now searching for a new merchant to sponsor his voyages and another port where he could unload and continue to earn money. I asked who the merchant was. He said, 'Alexander.'

"When he said that, I told him Alexander was also my merchant. I asked him what his cargo was. When he responded, I knew we could work together. Feeling that I had found the connection that had been missing, I told him about Rouen and then added that his cargo would sell for top price in Rouen and Paris.

"He knew of Rouen. Then his face brightened. 'Paris,' he said, 'That is where I have heard of you. If you worked with Alexander, I can work with you.'

"It turns out I was the merchant in Paris that Alexander had told him about. We immediately decided that we would work together. I sold our horses and loaded our supplies, and the three of us, with his crew, set sail on his ship. We stayed in sight of land the whole way … except when pirates approached us. They kept gaining because we were heavy with cargo. At one point, we could plainly see their faces.

"I looked at Diego and to my surprise, he was not concerned. Neither was his crew. Diego then turned our ship out to sea; he said that pirates always stay in sight of land. As we sailed further out, we saw the pirates turn around. We sailed the rest of the way in good weather. Once we arrived at the inlet leading to Rouen, the word spread quickly when people heard of the cargo being carried. Our cargo was rich; we had sweet salt, pepper, cotton, and silk.

"Diego made double the coin he would have made if he had sold his goods in Marseilles. He paid me to find the buyers, and I paid John and Roger. We have agreed to partner going forward, including what cargo to carry. We also discussed trading with England. He plans to return in about a year. With his profits, he will buy a bigger and faster ship."

Nichol looked at her drawings of family and friends. When she looked at the drawing of her papa, she softly touched it. She showed one drawing to Robert. "Papa," came from her lips in a faint, broken voice. Robert put his arm around her, pulling her closer.

Moments later, she looked at another drawing she had created from the perch in the tree overlooking the villa.

Her active mind took over when she saw a chimney—a new idea. Proudly she displayed the drawing to all.

"If we build a chimney in our longhouse, in the winter we can have a bread oven like we had in our villa, an oven to warm our houses while baking bread."

Timo let out a hearty laugh that changed the mood in the room. "You always bring a smile to my face. One minute, you are pondering our fate, and the next minute, you create something new. I am so glad you found Moki and me on the road that day. I cannot imagine my life without your presence in it."

What Timo shared was agreed in unison by all.

twenty-nine

Ezra and Helene

I believe we are in the company of someone who has great powers.

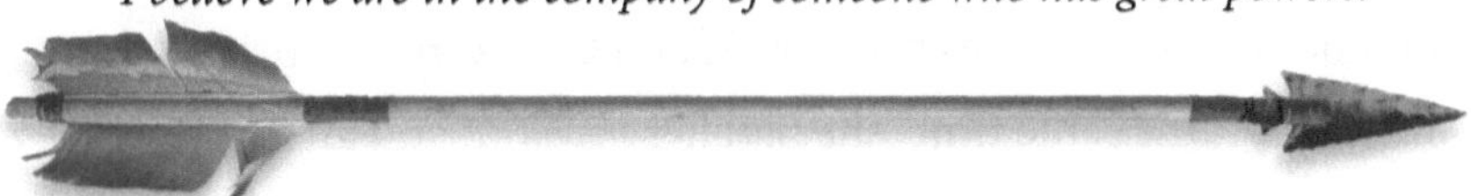

That evening, after all had left, Helene and Ezra huddled in their room, lit by a lone candle, sitting at a small table across from each other. Their acquired wealth was carefully stored in a series of small chests disguised as food storage, in the room and covered with cloth. John and Roger took turns guarding their door.

Ezra could sense that there was something big Helene needed to tell him; maybe more significant than his news about what happened in Marseilles.

Helene beckoned him to lean in closer and lowered her voice to a whisper.

"We were attacked as we traveled. I do not think we would have survived if Nichol had not been there. John and I were riding just ahead of the rest of our group, and Robert and Timo were walking with Nichol and Marie next to the wagon. Harald and Olaf were last, behind everyone. As we approached the forest, John warned us again to stay close together and have our weapons ready, reminding us that thieves could be lurking in the forests. Each of us needed to be on the lookout; he had encountered them before.

"With his warning, Nichol sent Shadow ahead to warn us of any danger. Shadow immediately smelled the air and bared her teeth, warning us that we were not alone. Nichol became the Nichol I witnessed at the cottage when the two men burst through the door to attack her.

"Immediately, she moved Marie into the cart with Aiden and Lucette and called Shadow back to protect the babies. Nichol repositioned herself between John and me, with Robert and Timo behind her, next to the cart. Harald and Olaf were last, behind the cart. At the same time, she had her bow out and an arrow ready to aim.

"Suddenly, men appeared from the forest. Four big men were in front and three more behind them, all with swords. We knew they were not peasants; they were dressed in more presentable clothing. Peasants would not have swords. Later, John said he thought they were soldiers. The leader of the group also had a bow.

"John remembered him from the last time he came through this pass. Each of us sensed the danger. Then the man said, 'Give us your cart and horses. We will let you pass.'

"Suddenly, a hawk swooped in, making sounds like I had never heard before, as if it were attempting to warn him off. The man who demanded our horses and supplies looked up and saw the bird's talons within a few feet of his face. He swung wildly with his bow and the hawk flew to a nearby tree.

"Ezra, I've never seen a hawk like this one before. Its tail was massive, and its belly feathers almost glowed a reddish-brown color, like a warning.

"The distraction was just enough for Nichol. She stepped out between the two horses John and I were on. Her bow was already strung and she instantly let an arrow go, piercing the leader through his mouth and killing him. John already had his sword out and charged two of the men, attacking and killing both.

"Everyone froze—except Nichol. She had already nocked another arrow and she released it quickly. Her target was the fourth man's chest. He then dropped to the ground, still alive. Harald threw his ax and hit one of the three in the stomach. That left two of the men.

"I turned to see Nichol run back toward the wagon. As she was running, she let another arrow go that hit a man who was behind the wagon in the shoulder. The last two men fled, one with an arrow through his shoulder, leaving their dead behind. John chased down the wounded man, killed him not far off the road, and retrieved Nichol's arrow.

"Then Nichol went to the children. After she knew they were safe, she returned to the man she shot in the chest. John told her that one of the downed men was moving and still alive. Pulling her arrow out, she knelt by the fallen man and spoke to him. He whispered something, and then he died. We watched her scan the tree line once again. Then she pointed the bloody arrow at another man, another man who wasn't in the original attack. He was peering from behind a tree.

"My eyes followed where she was pointing and immediately saw what she saw … an eighth man. His face turned crimson, as if he was filled with fear, and he started to move. He almost disappeared when Nichol swiftly threw her dagger, embedding it in the tree the man was standing behind. He must have heard the dagger hit the tree because he turned and came back to the tree. Pulling the dagger out, he smiled, holding it up. His smile was short-lived. Nichol had already nocked another arrow and made another perfect shot. He fell to the ground, still clasping the dagger.

"Ezra, when she turned toward us to walk back to our wagon, our eyes met. I saw that same look she had at the cottage when she saved us both. She is a warrior, a mother, a wife, and a protector —truly someone to behold—and I think her Lucette might have more gifts than her mother. After the birth and the Lady's visit, the attacks at the cottage, and on the road, I believe we are in the company of someone with great powers that none of us have seen or experienced. Nichol is someone who will protect us all."

Nodding, Ezra reached for Helene's hand. Matching her whispered voice, their eyes never broke contact.

"I have thought the same thing. On the voyage home with many days to think, I journeyed back to the day I opened the door to Robert and Nichol. I believe Alexander honored me with the protection of his daughter who, in turn, will shield us and lead us to a new life.

"The comfortable life we led before had no meaning, and it became clear that change was coming, with or without Nichol. I have loaned coins or sold items to powerful people; I knew each one I dealt with carried a threat with them. Our wealth would become too great an attraction that others would want. It is why I had John and Roger to help protect us and our coin. The church wants its tithes, and the nobles want their rents. They will take the wealth of those who have it and use it to further dominate their subjects like us.

"When we escaped from Paris, I know that the priest Loupe was behind the theft and destruction of our home. His actions showed us he has no fear of retribution for his actions or what he deems to be righteous justice.

"I fear there is no place—no matter how remote—where we can escape being discovered. The only way to compete with the lords and the church is to create something more powerful. Something that they will envy and be afraid of."

"Ezra, you are talking in riddles. What are the answers?"

Ezra looked up at Helene and let out a deep sigh. "It is a riddle … that is why I am worried. I do not have the full answer to it yet. With Nichol and the Lady, I think it will come."

Helene reached across the table and put her hands on his hands. "Maybe there needs to be a true sovereign, a righteous power that doesn't need to take food and coin from the poor and then send away their young men to fight their wars.

Ezra jumped up, leaned over the table, and kissed Helene on her forehead. Then, he began his usual pacing.

"That is what is happening right before our eyes. That is why the Lady and her apprentice, Nichol, are in our lives. As a merchant, I have access to powerful people. I will take Nichol with me to meet them, and she can see who they are. Nichol will be a direct challenge to their power, but they will not be aware of it. I want us to have a home here in Rouen and one in Harmonie."

Helene sat, her face expressing amusement at what Ezra had said. *Two homes? I will be able to be with my babies often.*

"When are you going to tell Nichol of your plans for her? When you do, you must include Robert. Timo knows about the Lady as well. Let us get some rest. Tomorrow will be a long day. I know you and Nichol had planned to visit merchants in town. Being alone with her, you will have the opportunity to share your thoughts."

Before Helene could say goodnight to John or Roger outside their room, Ezra had laid down on their bed and closed his eyes. Joining him, she let out a sigh and then sat up.

"Ezra, there is one more thing I need to ask Nichol about. Why was the man behind the tree so important that she risked losing her dagger? How did she know he could not resist the lure of it? Did she know he would try to retrieve it?"

Ezra mumbled, "There is a curse. You asked the right question and…." He had fallen fast asleep.

"What curse?" she said loudly to the motionless man beside her.

Now, how am I going to sleep ….

thirty

Creation of the Dagger

The dagger's true owner would eventually be found.

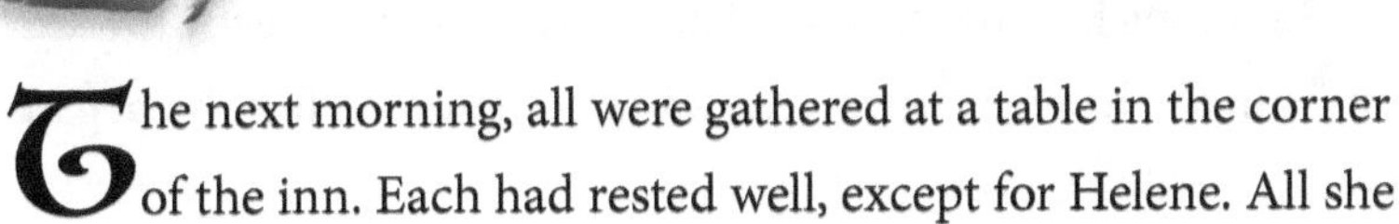

The next morning, all were gathered at a table in the corner of the inn. Each had rested well, except for Helene. All she could think about was the curse, whatever that meant.

"Ezra, you said something about a curse when I asked about Nichol's willingness to risk losing her dagger when she threw it. Then you fell fast asleep. What curse?"

"Curse?" Nichol said. "My dagger has a curse?"

"Nichol, did you ever see your papa take the dagger off the wall in his solar or use it?" Ezra asked her.

Thinking, she replied, "Once, when he had to rid Marseilles of some pirates stealing from all the merchants on the docks. I was behind the tapestry in the solar listening to one of them talking to Papa and asking for help. Papa planned to meet at the tavern the pirates favored with several of his men-at-arms. He removed the dagger from the wall and laid it on his desk. I decided to follow him when he left, and I saw Papa and the men kill the pirates. The next morning the dagger was back in its place on the wall and wasn't taken down until I took it when I escaped."

Ezra was surprised at her words. *So, perhaps she is the rightful owner … ?*

What followed from Ezra shocked everyone present. He wove an incredible story—or perhaps a fable—leaving what to believe to their imagination. In a low voice—just enough for all to hear at the table—Ezra began to speak.

"Many years ago, a weary nomad slept on the vast desert floor in the cold of the night. Suddenly, he awoke when a bright light in the dark sky created a vibrating array of light on his face. The nomad raised his hand to shield his eyes and wondered, *what was the source of this light?*

"Squinting his eyes, he saw a ball of fire heading directly toward him from the heavens. Paralyzed and terrified with fear, he began to pray, begging God to let him live.

"Immediately, he saw a slight shift in the trajectory of the fireball, just before it struck the desert floor with a huge booming noise. Clasping his hands, he thanked God for sparing his life and promised to help others, and veer away from false promises.

"Approaching where the fireball fell from the heavens, he saw what landed. It was a fiery ball with its heat vibrating toward him. Reaching down to pick it up, he quickly yanked his hand away. It was hot as any fire he had been around.

"A shudder flowed through his body. He sunk to his knees in the sand, heated from the ball's presence, and dropped into a deep sleep. When daylight broke, he lifted what looked like a very large rock from the sand and noticed how heavy it was for its size.

"The nomad set out for the last town he passed through. His new quest was now to find a buyer and secure wealth from the sale of this rock. *Surely, this rock from the heavens must be valuable and sacred,* he thought. *It must be worth great sums. Maybe the prince who lives there will want it.*

"Quickly, his promises to God of the previous night joined the string of his forgotten promises of the past. Helping others and veering away from false promises had become a passing thought.

"Through his messengers, the prince had heard the story of the fiery rock that had dropped from the heavens. 'Find this man with the heavy rock and bring him to me,' the prince commanded of his protectors.

"Before the day had passed, the rock came into the prince's possession along with the nomad who found it. Realizing that it was too heavy to be a rock, he demanded of his metal workers, 'Take this and tell me what it is made of.'

"The next day the prince had his answer. 'We have never seen something such as this, your Highness. It is not a rock. We believe it is stronger than any metal we have ever seen or worked with. It is different. A sheen protects it as if it is a shell. It is a new metal.'

"The prince turned to the nomad. 'I will offer you your weight in silver for the truth.'

"The nomad's eyes widened. 'The truth?'

"Repeatedly, the nomad never wavered from his story. As he weakened under the prince's whips and torture, each time retelling the event of the night in the desert, the prince realized the nomad was speaking the truth. But it was too late, for he died early the next morning.

"*'This man told the truth. This is important and a gift from God. I know it was destined for me. There is no need for me to honor my promise of silver. God wants me to have it,'* the prince thought.

"The metal workers were summoned before the prince once again. The prince ordered, 'You will make a dagger, one that will be the envy of all those who view it. The handle will be gilded in gold and embedded with my most precious gems. The metal is a gift to me from God .... You will not fail. My protectors will be by your side and reporting to me of your progress.'

"Many months later, the dagger was finished and presented to the prince. It was magnificently crafted with a long, thin, double-edged blade. It had a delicately scrolled, gold-inlaid hilt with intense blue sapphires embedded along its length. The double-edged blade reflected a color never seen before. The dagger's sheath was of equal beauty, supported by a gold chain attached to his waist for all to see. The prince now had a dagger fit for a king. It was destined for a god and as beautiful as any dagger ever crafted.

"Word of the dagger's magnificence spread. Knowing its extreme value, the prince kept it by his side day and night—even as he slept.

"And then he began to change. His wife noticed it first. He no longer had any desire for her as his obsession now focused on what he believed the dagger would bring him—immense power.

"Whatever power it would bring would not be bestowed upon the prince. He became bedridden and out of his mind. No one could understand the words he uttered and seizures possessed his body. His death came quickly.

"He was buried with the dagger. His wife thought it was the cause of his death and wanted it buried with him and away from her.

"Within two days, grave robbers removed the dagger and other valuables from his tomb.

"The story and mystery of the dagger quickly spread throughout Persia. Those who were beguiled as the prince once was and consumed by its beauty fell under the dagger's spell. Its captivating beauty shrouded its hidden danger for anyone who was power-hungry.

"Gossip spread. When the death of the prince and his claims that the dagger was a gift from God were spoken, no one believed it. Instead, it was said the dagger was cursed. The new gossip pro-claimed that the curse could only be lifted when the true owner was found.

"The tragic story that came with it was deleted as it passed ownership … and the eventual death of the new owner. Greed was at its center. As it passed from man to man, the beauty and luster of the dagger became the magnet, dangling a promise of power. No one understood that the power would come to some-one who did not crave power.

"Death followed from one owner to the another until its misfortune was realized. The dagger was bad. Dangerous. And whoever owned it would die. One day, a Persian merchant entered the port of Marseilles, carrying with him a locked box."

Everyone around the table was barely breathing as Ezra spoke. The tale that was being woven in front of them was exciting … and promised more danger and death to come.

No one spoke. The silence begged him to continue. He did.

"Word came to Astrid that a Persian merchant had just arrived and was unloading his ship. She had Jonathan bring a horse-drawn cart around, prepare it for her, and take her to the port. Being kind to others was not something Astrid did. As they set off, she demanded that he whip the horse to increase their speed. Silk was on her mind; she wanted the cargo … all of it.

"Upon arrival, she noticed a group gathered on the street as cargo was being unloaded from a ship. Dismounting, she rushed to the group and pushed her way through the crowd until she came face-to-face with the Persian merchant. There were no bolts of silk as she desired. What she saw was a locked box in front of him.

"Disappointed, she listened to the merchant as he began to weave a tale about the contents of the box. As the story of the dagger unfolded, she became captivated with each word of the merchant's tale. While he was telling his story, his eyes scanned the crowd. One by one, people lost interest and left. Eventually only Astrid and the merchant remained.

"Focusing on her, the merchant knew his story captivated her. Her eyes betrayed the depth of her intense interest. The merchant's slave opened the box that shielded the dagger's curse and stepped away. Astrid silently stood and stared into it.

"What she said next surprised even the merchant. Raising her head and looking at him, her eyes were glazed over. A wicked smile spread across her face. 'This is beautiful. I know my husband would cherish it.'

"Relieved, the merchant knew he had found the buyer he sought. Silently, Astrid moved her hands to the box and removed the jeweled dagger. The wicked smile grew larger. She had found her perfect gift for Alexander."

A gasp could be heard around the table.

Helene was the first to speak. "What do you mean, Ezra … a perfect gift for Alexander?"

Reaching for another drink, Ezra stopped. His small audience was spellbound. His eyes turned to Nichol. *She knows.*

Ezra once again began to speak. "In Marseilles, not much went on that Alexander did not hear about. He was aware of the story of the dagger and Astrid being the only one interested in purchasing it. When she gave it to him as a gift that evening, he was immediately suspicious of her motive. Knowing its story connected to it, he chose to hang it on a wall in his solar as a reminder: greed never wins. And he vowed never to touch or handle it again unless it was necessary to remove evil.

"Years passed and the dagger's curse did not affect Alexander. He lacked the greed, lust, and drive for ultimate power that destroyed the other men who possessed the dagger. Only once did he use it to deal with the pirates who threatened the ships in the Marseilles port."

Ezra had stopped to take another drink from his goblet. He continued, "From what I have heard and seen with my own eyes, I believe the dagger was meant to be in a woman's possession. The curse only pertained to men who were evil in nature."

Everyone was captivated by his every word as the mystery behind the dagger was revealed, along with Astrid's involvement in bringing it to the manor.

Nichol reached across the table and clasped his hand as he spoke.

Pausing, Ezra turned to Nichol. "And now, it belongs to its rightful owner … Nichol."

All eyes turned toward Nichol.

Silence filled the room. Locking eyes with Ezra, she spoke, "The night before Papa's funeral, I entered the solar and removed the contents from the chest. As I was leaving, candlelight reflected off the jeweled handle of the dagger, as if it was calling to me. Then, another light entered the room, landing on the dagger and guiding my eyes to it.

"Moving toward the wall, I removed it from its perch and tucked the dagger and sheath into my tunic. I remember taking a deep breath as I looked around the solar and saying a silent goodbye to all my fondest memories with Papa. Then I prepared to leave with the dagger hidden in my clothes. I blew out the candle and left.

"The letter I placed in the niche behind the tapestry and one coin I left in Papa's box was meant to send Astrid a strong message. I wanted to hurt her as much as she hurt me. I knew when she found the coin, she would go into a rage. I did not expect that, in her anger, she would pull down the tapestry and discover the letter as soon as she did … before I was well on the road to Paris.

"Thank you for telling the story of the dagger, Ezra. You are right … it was meant for me. I can feel that it is so."

thirty-one

Another New Beginning

We have become the family I always wanted.

Late that evening, there was a knock on Ezra and Helene's door.

"It is me, Nichol. I'm with Robert and Lucette."

Holding a candle, Ezra slowly opened the door. "Come in. What brings you to our room at this late hour?"

Helene was behind him, already moving from her bed with the first knock. As Ezra opened the door to allow them to enter, she quickly scooped Lucette into her arms.

Ezra motioned them all to sit around their table. As usual, Shadow settled by Nichol's side. Before Ezra closed the door, he noticed that John had positioned himself in front of it.

In a soft voice, Nichol began. "I could not sleep until I talked to you and Helene privately. When I told Robert what I was thinking, he agreed. Neither of you are peasants."

As she said this, she reached for Ezra's hand, placed hers over his, and rested it there. "Your hands are not those of a peasant farmer. They are the hands to care for others ... not wto work in fields.

"With the fortune we both have now, Robert and I think you should do what is best for you both. We would like you to be with us. But we know that Ezra needs to be in Rouen most of the time. And we know that Helene wants to be with the babies.

"We will build and add to our existing home so Helene can be with us in Harmonie and when you are there. It will be your second home away from Rouen. We could also build another home, maybe like the cottage Helene loved so she could have her own if she would like that."

Nichol could sense relief from Helene when she made the offer.

Looking at Ezra, Helene added, "You are a merchant, and with both your old and new connections, why not set up your new business in Rouen now? Why wait any longer? I like what Nichol suggests."

Ezra sat back in thought, looking at Nichol affectionately as a father to a daughter while finding his words. "I know a young woman who has often said these words, 'I see you.' I now see that you are your father's daughter and much more. Yes, I can start a merchant business in Rouen. But it is not just me … it is you and me, Nichol."

For a moment all sat in silence, waiting for Nichol to respond.

She released his hand and sat back, first looking at Robert, who nodded his approval. Then she turned to Helene holding Lucette, then back to Ezra and spoke.

"Papa welcomed me into his solar and his world. Now, you ask me to continue the journey he started, inviting me into a world ruled by men. It will be dangerous for all of us," she said. Then she paused. A broad smile appeared as she leaned forward, looking confidently into Ezra's eyes. "But it is a world I understand and embrace."

Ezra stood, placing both hands on her cheeks, and kissed her forehead.

"Tomorrow, we will look for a new home in Rouen that will hold all of us when you and Robert and the babies are in Rouen." Turning his head to Helene, he continued, "What do you think? Would you like two homes—one here and one in Harmonie? And when Nichol is here, you will have the babies as well?"

Hugging the sleeping Lucette, Helene looked around the table and blinked away tears. "Oh, yes." Then sitting a little taller in the chair, she continued, "We have become the family I always wanted. I never had a brother, sister, or children, but now I have much more. I will be in Harmonie most of the time and Rouen will become my home away from home."

The next morning, Robert and Nichol joined Ezra and Helene in the inn's main room.

After meeting with Robert and Nichol, a transformation had taken place. Faces that normally would show weariness and fatigue from their travels instead reflected wonderment and excitement. The late-night conversation in Ezra and Helene's room created a new energy within everyone. Ezra had asked John and Roger to join them, so they were also included in the new plans.

As the group settled at a large table in the corner of the main room, Ezra was pleased they were the only ones in the room. *This is now my family*, he thought. Having food brought for all, he began to explain what would be happening.

"Helene and I will make Rouen home from now on. I like the idea of being attached to Nichol and Robert's home. Helene will be happier.

"Immediately, I will buy a home here that will provide a place for anyone who needs to be in Rouen. When any of you come to Rouen, you will stay with us. Nichol and I together will look for a site to create our merchant business here in Rouen tomorrow as well.

"Many of the merchants who live here are Jews. I have heard gossip of persecution of those of our faith—their families and their businesses. I think we need to now think of how to protect ourselves—including Lucette."

Hearing Ezra speak the name of their daughter, Robert could sense his wife's body stiffening at his side.

Ezra continued, "We have talked about being baptized as Christians to protect our Jewish heritage from the persecution and power of the church. I need to talk with my brother. Because of me, he and his family are being watched as well. And I want to encourage him to bring Dinah, Gideon, and Raisa to join all of us in Harmonie."

Little did Ezra know that Achim was already planning to move his family to Harmonie.

Surprisingly, Roger spoke up. "Ezra, if you are going to encourage others to come here, you should talk to Joshua. We have always trusted him and he is a Jew. If we are all to be baptized, then we need to do it quickly. We should include him as well."

Nodding his head, Ezra added, "There is much planning we all must do, starting now. As soon as Helene and I get our home here, Nichol and I will plan what we need to set up as merchants. Then Helene and I will return to Paris with Roger to get baptized.

"I can talk with Achim and Dinah. Nichol's guidance is needed in most of what we do. I think it is important that our women are included in our plans. When in Rouen, we need to be seen at the church."

thirty-two

Nichol the Merchant

You will become a welcome asset for women in our community.

Within the day, Ezra had found a suitable home in Rouen. Once the official sale document was signed, Nichol, Robert, Ezra, and Helene gathered in his new solar. Centered in the room were only three items: a table and two chairs. The walls were bare, and the window shutters were open, overlooking the street next to the river. All the markets were within walking distance and the port was visible from one of the windows. The home also had two extra rooms, where Nichol and others could stay when they were in Rouen.

Looking the room over, Helene said, "I will seek out more chairs and another table, Ezra. Also, we will need a pallet for sleeping and some other items. Robert, Nichol, and I will gather supplies so that you will be as comfortable here as you were in our previous home."

"This reminds me of Papa's room without his wall hangings. All it needs is a niche and tapestry for Lucette to hide behind," Nichol said as she took in the room.

As she looked out one of the windows, she saw the hawk with the red markings and split tail circling above.

I see and feel you ....

Ezra sensed that Nichol was thinking of her papa. "I always liked Alexander's solar and felt that, with us working together, we can bring his memory here. You carry many of his business ideas and practices with you.

"Being a merchant will not be easy for you, Nichol. It is not that I do not think you will be a good one. It is because there are no women in this trade and I think you will get much resistance. You have more skills and determination than the men you will encounter. You know more and you are smarter than most. You must be patient; one day, you will be accepted. I am confident you will learn to bring people to your side."

The compliment brought a smile across Nichol's face. Changing the subject, she said, "I know the perfect addition to this room. You brought the tapestry I hid behind in Papa's solar when you returned from Marseilles."

Gesturing toward one of the bare walls, she asked, "Why not hang it on that wall for now?"

As she spoke, Ezra nodded his head. "Just like with Helene, I will leave the rooms for you to adorn."

What Nichol said next surprised him.

"I know inns and taverns have names, but the other merchants do not. Why not us? I cannot reveal my connection to Alexander. Why not refer to ourselves as E & N Merchants?"

Now Ezra's smile matched Nichol's earlier one. Turning to Robert and Helene, he stated, "Nichol and I will call our business E & N Merchants. What do you think?"

"I like the idea," Helene said. "And I like Nichol's idea of hanging Alexander's tapestry in your solar. There are things I can also bring in when you and the children are not here."

As Robert and Ezra talked, Nichol turned to Helene. Touching her arm, the two women moved out of the solar to the front door.

Lowering her voice, she said, "Helene, if you decide that you would prefer to live in Harmonie most of the time, you can make that choice at any time."

Tears welled in Helene's eyes. Nichol reached up and gently dabbed them away.

"Thank you, Nichol. There is no other place I would rather be than with you and our children. I have already decided."

Nichol smiled. "We will share our desires with Robert and ask for the building to start right away."

Ezra's mood shifted as his business mind took over. "Nichol, the next thing we need to do is find warehouse space to bring merchandise into Rouen for distribution and to store imported goods. My old connections will be helpful to us.

"We are heading out to talk to the local merchants about their needs and let them know what we have coming into the port. We are also looking for merchandise we can resell to other cities."

Helene took Aiden from Robert to hold him. Robert then reached for Lucette from Nichol. As they opened the door, Robert said over his shoulder, "We will see you back at the inn."

As they set off, Ezra headed toward the main marketing area of Rouen.

"Nichol, will you listen with your eyes and ears? What is in the shops you enter? Does it appear that there is much of one kind of item, is it very limited, and is there a variety of items for sale? Talk to the merchants and ask them what their needs are.

Do the customers ask for items that they do not carry? I also think that, when you are working in Rouen or other cities, it is important for you to dress as a successful merchant, which would be different from what the women wear in Harmonie."

Upon entering the first store, Ezra was greeted by a welcoming voice.

"Ezra, my old friend, I heard you were now living in Rouen. What brings you to my humble store?"

"Joseph, I could not live in Rouen without visiting you, and I see that you have prospered. Your shelves are full of cloth and I hear you provide silk, linen, and cotton to the royals. I, too, have a source for those items that you may want to use as well. Before we talk of your success, I would like you to meet my niece, Nichol. She is married to Achim's son, Robert."

Joseph's hair and beard were dark and streaked with gray on the sides. Thin and short in stature, he walked with a slight limp and was garbed in dark clothing. His store had a few shelves of colored cloth displayed behind the counter. Most of his goods were displayed on small tables, in direct view for his customers as they entered his store.

He emerged from behind his counter and approached Nichol. Reaching out, he took her hand. "What a lovely young woman you are, Nichol. I believe I know why you are here. You look like you need new clothes. I have several bundles of cloth that may interest you. And I have someone who can make them for you."

Turning his head over his shoulder, he shouted, "Rose, come here; Ezra is here with his niece, Nichol."

Nichol looked toward the back of the store. Her heart began pounding as a petite older woman, also garbed in dark clothing, came through the door behind the counter.

After hugging her, Rose took Nichol's hand. "Come with me while the men talk. I have beautiful cloth that is perfect for a beautiful young woman like you."

A watery smile and a tear appeared on Nichol's face, and Rose noticed.

Moving to the rear of the shop, Rose placed her at a table. Pulling a few bolts of fabric from a nearby table, she laid them in front of Nichol.

Quietly, Nichol reached for the fabric closest to her. The fabric was beautiful, tightly woven, and of high quality. Turning to Rose, she asked, "Where did these come from? The colors are vibrant and different from most fabrics I've seen or touched."

The old women studied Nichol's face and hands. Lifting one of the bolts, she unwrapped some of the cloth and held it against Nichol, close to her face. "This would be beautiful on you. It brings out the unusual color of your eyes."

Hesitating, Nichol looked at her. "You remind me of a wise woman who shares your name. Rose taught me about herbs and healing, and she helped me to travel to Paris. I'm glad to be here with you."

Letting Rose hear her words, she continued, "I would like to buy cloth from each of the bolts you have on the table. There should be sufficient cloth to make my outer tunic more substantial than the women wear here in Rouen. I do not want long tunics that reach the ground—they will soil quickly and show the dirt on them—so the new tunics should fall only to my ankles, and have two layers of cloth. Wearing a long tunic gets in my way when working in the fields and at home. I would like several pairs of braies made from sturdy cloth as well."

Rose was surprised at Nichol's request. "Do you have someone that can make your new garments?"

"Helene is skilled in stitching and will be able to make them once I explain how I want them made. She will create the new street tunics for me to wear when I work with Ezra and the other merchants. I will add the final stitchery to them when completed. Would you like to make some, too?"

"Other merchants …?" Rose looked even more surprised.

"Yes, Ezra and I will work together. Our business is called E & N Merchants, and it is based here in Rouen."

Rose's mouth dropped open when she heard Nichol's explanation.

"A woman merchant … I know of no other such thing! You have the best instructor and guide in Ezra. No one knows how to buy the exact merchandise that others desire. And he has always paid a fair price when he buys. You will become a welcome asset for our community, and all the women in it."

Rose smiled as Nichol spoke. "Where I live in the north, I will create a common house for those in the village to gather for the purpose of creating goods for sale and to be a place for tending the children as we women work. Before I return there with Ezra, I'll come back to buy much of your cloth for the women in my village and take it back to them. They will be happy to work with such beautiful fabrics."

The two women shared a knowing silence, each understanding that they would support the other.

"I am pleased to work with you. I have other women who stitch well. By tomorrow, I will have braies made for you from the new material. Nichol, you may want several in the dark cloth on this table. Perhaps then you could create new shorter tunics to wear with them."

As she got up, Nichol said, "I like your idea. I will come by the store tomorrow to get the cloth. I look forward to working with you and to welcome you as a friend. Thank you."

Ezra finished the business he needed to transact with Joseph.

Seeing Nichol returning from the backroom with Rose, he stood from his chair. "Joseph, I look forward to working with you again. Nichol and I will walk around the area soon. We are hoping to find a suitable site for a warehouse. I want her to meet many of my old business associates and the merchants and store owners of Rouen."

"I know of no available warehouses here, Ezra. You best look down by the river. There may be some there."

Bidding Rose and Joseph goodbye, they returned to the inn.

In the following days, the duo traveled about town, searching for a suitable warehouse.

Nichol became more confident in revealing her observations to Ezra. With each one, he was pleased to hear what she had to say—and often surprised.

On their way home at the end of one day, he stopped and turned to her. "I thought I could easily see a person's intentions in contract negotiations. I was wrong. Your judgment of conversations and interpretation reveals much to me. One day, all that we create here in Rouen will be yours and the rest of the merchants will fail in comparison to you. I now see the potential that you have and I know why your papa was so proud of you."

Nichol put her arms around Ezra and they embraced in the middle of the street as people passed by. As their embrace ended, the sound of a hawk overhead caught Nichol's attention.

Looking up, she thought, *I see you, and I will follow.* Pointing up, she said, "The hawk is circling overhead, Ezra. He is telling us to follow him, to see what he sees."

They followed the hawk, noting that it would circle back and look down at them as they traveled. The two kept their eyes on the sky, Nichol leading the way as they briskly walked down streets, turning corners, and always looking skyward to catch the hawk's direction. Nichol glanced from the hawk and saw people in the street looking up to see what they were watching. Children began laughing as they followed them. Ezra's excitement in the chase and anticipation of what lay ahead kept him close behind Nichol.

Finally, they arrived at the edge of the river. Ezra bent over, trying to breathe, and Nichol went to him, put her hand on his back, and said, "When you have your breath back, look to the right—you will be pleased."

Ezra straightened up immediately and turned to his right to see what she saw—the reason for the chase. In front of them was a large building.

"Our warehouse," they said in unison.

On the highest peak of the roof, the hawk perched. When it saw them looking at the warehouse, it fluttered its wings and took flight, circling upward into the sky.

"Thank you, Papa."

"Papa?" Ezra was puzzled.

Reaching for Ezra's arm, Nichol lowered her voice. "That hawk has been with me since Papa's funeral. He swooped down, tipping his wing at me, and flew out to sea. I next saw him when I slept in the trees hiding from travelers and Fredric as I traveled to Paris. I've seen him in Harmonie and now here. I know Papa has sent the hawk. His spirit is with us."

Tapping her arm, Ezra smiled at her story. "I am glad to have Alexander with us, too."

thirty-three

Nichol and Loupe

Something was different here.
Shadow can sense it, too.

Nichol knew she could not return to Harmonie without seeing Emma first.

Ezra encouraged her to go, intrigued by what she might hear. Even the slightest information might prove beneficial.

Everyone was busy preparing to leave when Nichol announced her plans to visit Emma.

Robert, with a concerned look, turned to her. "I will go with you."

Nichol shook her head. "Not this time. Stay and prepare for our return trip to Harmonie. I will go alone with Shadow and I will not be long. Marie and Helene will watch the children."

On her way, she stopped by a goldsmith's shop and bought a necklace that appeared much like hers. Once at the castle's gate, the sentry acknowledged her with a smile. "Nichol, I was concerned you would not visit us again. Where is your baby?"

"I left her asleep in her papa's care."

Opening the gate, he added, "Emma will be pleased to see you."

Nichol slowly walked to the door and stopped. The thought *something is different* raced through her mind. With apprehension, she lifted the heavy door knocker and let it fall against the wooden door several times.

A servant slowly opened the door with a stern look on his face. Eyeing Nichol up and down, he then stepped back and shut the door.

Moments later, Emma opened the door and stepped out. She took Nichol by the arm and without a word, led her to a secluded part of the garden. Shadow moved closer to Nichol, matching every step she took.

Something was different here. Shadow can sense it, too. What has changed?

"Emma, what is wrong? You are acting strangely."

Emma bit her lip. "There is a priest named Loupe in my brother's home who met with him in Richard's solar. I overheard him saying terrible things about you to my brothers. Nichol, tell me … who are you, really?" Her eyes were wide with concern.

Nichol gave her friend a level look. "Am I in danger if I stay and talk to you?"

With a frightened look and quivering voice, Emma replied, "Yes, you should leave at once."

"I can tell you this, Emma. Do not trust Loupe. He is an evil person."

Emma's eyes narrowed. "How do you know this?"

"A man that I trust with my life told me that Loupe coveted the wealth of his own family—wealth and power that his older brother controlled as the firstborn. He captured and raped his brother's wife in front of him and then had all the family members killed to inherit the family's fortune. Loupe thinks I hid my papa's gold and silver and he wants that, too. I know that he bedded my mother, seized the contents of Papa's warehouse, and sold everything. He has also sent men to kill me; it is why he has been after me. And he knows that I know what he has done. Did he tell your brothers of these deeds?"

Looking at her, all Emma could say was, "No … none of it."

Nichol then stood, took out the silver chain, and placed it in Emma's hand. "You will find a stone meant only for you to put on this chain. You will know it when you see it."

They both embraced, and then Emma bent down and rubbed Shadow's head. "I still want one of her pups. You must go now. I will walk you to the gate."

"We will meet again; I will find a way to let you know the time and place."

Just before the gate, Nichol turned, stopped, and looked up at a window. One of Emma's brothers stood motionless, watching them.

As Nichol met his eyes, she mouthed the words, "I see you."

His direct glare at her showed no emotion, an act of control and intimidation used by powerful people she had seen before in her papa's solar.

The man looking at her must be Richard. *Emma is a slave in her own home.*

Emma opened the gate, and Nichol and Shadow exited the castle grounds.

Nichol ran through it and moved down the road to the inn. Slowing to a walk, she decided to take a different route back to avoid being followed.

Turning a corner, she abruptly came face-to-face with Loupe and his protector. He was not surprised, a slimy grin on his face. *He was waiting for me.*

"What good fortune we have come upon this morning."

Turning to his protector, he said, "This woman's name is Nichol." Turning back, staring, his eyes slowly narrowed. "Or is it Lisa?"

His chilling voice dropped to a snarl. "How fortunate it is we meet when you are alone."

Shadow immediately went to the protector and smelled his feet and legs as she did the man trying to steal the dagger. *I think he was there in the forest; he was the one who escaped unharmed when I threw my dagger.* The protector kicked at Shadow.

"Come," Nichol commanded. Shadow backed away with her teeth bared.

That gave Nichol a moment to gather strength and confidence for what was to come. In a calm voice, she said loudly, "Are you stealing coin purses from ladies on this fine day?"

Angered, Loupe glared at her as his eyes narrowed. "You have something of mine."

"I have nothing of yours. You are a murderer and thief."

Loupe was surprised by her strong words.

"Oh, are you referring to the fortune my whore mother promised you that does not exist? What pleasures did you have to perform on her for that information? I was told by villagers in Marseilles that she enjoyed a certain priest's face between her legs. Was that you?"

Loupe's cheeks turned red with anger. He was unaccustomed to his authority as priest being challenged—or being humiliated by a commoner in front of another person.

"Now, I know why I was not welcomed at Emma's. As I was leaving, I turned to see her brother glaring at me from a window." Nichol's eyes narrowed and a knowing grin appeared. "You told him that I murdered my papa, even though you know that I did not. One day everyone will know the truth."

The protector stepped toward her as Loupe became even more furious. Nichol showed him no fear or the respect that he was accustomed to—that he *demanded*.

Backing a step away, she pulled out her dagger. Pointing it at him, she said, "You have seen this dagger before. My papa gave it to me."

A strange look appeared on Loupe's and the protector's faces.

Again, Loupe demanded, "I want what is mine." Pointing to the protector, he added, "You will tell me where it is, or he will cut you down."

Loupe's threat didn't stop Nichol. She kept speaking.

"Astrid had no idea what Alexander did. He gave everything to the people he loved and he was a good Christian, unlike you, who worship only power and coin. How can you be a priest? You are a murderer of your own brother; you raped his wife, and then you killed her. You have followed me from Marseilles to here. How could I have carried a fortune all that way without anyone seeing me do it?"

Anger vibrated through Loupe's body and mind. He wanted to destroy her with his hands. Moving closer, he sneered, fogging her senses with his foul breath. "Your days are numbered. Duke Richard is going to drive you and your Jewish family from Rouen and we will take what is ours. That includes the merchant business and your family's wealth."

Extending his hand, he said, "Right now, I will take that dagger, peasant. Give it over."

Nichol pushed the dagger, blade first, at Loupe's outstretched hand, drawing blood—a warning.

Loupe grimaced in pain. He grabbed the blade, turned it around, and pointed it at Nichol, blood dripping from the blade.

In one swift motion, she pushed Loupe's dagger arm away, hooked one leg behind his, and with all her force, struck his chin with the palm of her hand. He fell back, hitting his head on the cobblestone road, breathing but lying motionless on his back with his elbow on the ground, his forearm and the dagger pointing straight up.

Shadow lunged at the protector's throat and sunk her teeth in, violently shaking her head and body. Her teeth penetrated deep into his neck before he collapsed to the ground, eyes bulging, as Shadow continued her suffocating grip on his neck.

A wolf's kill.

Nichol knelt by Loupe's side, snatched the dagger from his hand, and wiped the blade on his vestment.

Bending low, she murmured to his expressionless face: "I see you … and you are mine."

Loupe did not move.

Nichol stood and began to run, calling Shadow to her side. She stopped, looking back at Loupe, who still was lying motionless on his back.

His protector was glaring at her, gasping for his last breath.

With Shadow at her side, she knelt and wrapped her arm around Shadow's neck and pulled her close, nuzzling her neck. Triumph flowed through their bodies.

thirty-four

Leaving Rouen

You must leave at once ....

Clear skies on a warm summer day greeted the eager travelers, preparing for their departure. This time, they knew their destination and their spirits were high for their return to Harmonie.

Outside the inn, the group waited for Nichol's return. The horse-drawn cart and Moki were heavily packed and in the cart were two very active seven-month-old babies, who were the delight of everyone. Harald and his wife Freyja waited next to their mule, packed with their possessions.

Their daughters—Gunvor, fourteen years old, and Tova, who was twelve—stayed close to Lucette and Aiden, like bees to a hive. Their task was to keep the two active young ones from falling out of the cart. Olaf and Marie watched the children play as they enjoyed being together again.

Nichol and Shadow walked at a rapid pace as they turned a corner with the inn now in sight. As it came into view, Nichol felt a sigh of relief when she saw everyone ready to leave.

Robert and Timo were standing next to the cart when Robert looked up and saw Nichol and Shadow approaching. Seeing her face and noticing her fast pace, he knew something was wrong. Alerting Timo, they both moved to greet her, with Robert arriving first.

"What happened? Are you hurt?"

A defiant Nichol stood straight with shoulders back. "I am fine, but Loupe and his protector are not."

Looking down, she gestured at Shadow, who had blood on her face. "She enjoyed a taste of the protector's neck. We must leave at once. I will explain when we are on the road and can talk freely.

"Timo, can you take Shadow and wash the blood off her face? Shadow, go with Timo," Nichol commanded.

Robert knew there was urgency in her words and continued preparing the group to leave, even though he wanted to know more about what happened.

In front of the inn, Ezra and Helene were waiting to see them off on their return trip.

Seeing them, Nichol knew they were both happy and sad: happy that they were together and in a community that Ezra knew and could begin to do again what he did for his business; and sad to see their extended family depart for an unknown amount of time.

Nichol moved toward them and took Helene's hand. In a low voice, she revealed what had happened as she left Emma's.

Ezra spoke first. "I am not surprised. It was only a matter of time, Nichol. What I have been hearing is that the archbishop and the duke have already begun to persecute Jews. I planned to return to Paris within days to see a priest I know and I hope would be sympathetic to our concerns. I will ask him to baptize Helene and me.

"I suspect, with a substantial donation of coin, he will not refuse. Next, I will contact Achim and tell him of our plans. He may want to be baptized with us. And I will encourage him to bring his family and move them to Harmonie. With Robert and the growing hamlet, I think he and Dinah will welcome it.

"After our anticipated baptism, Helene and I will return to Rouen and the merchant business, but not without asking the Christian community for their consent and blessings. Your papa and I have dealt with people like Emma's brothers. You have witnessed this in the solar. They appear pious, but under their fine clothes, there is a relentless drive for power and wealth.

"Nichol, I want John to stay with you. Helene, Roger, and I will leave now. You must leave at once, especially with what you have just told us. I will inform Amos that we are leaving but not tell him of our plans so if asked, he will not have to lie."

As Ezra spoke, the two women never released their grasp. With his final words, both squeezed each other's hands as a silent message of love and support.

Nichol released her grip and took Helene into her arms, whispering, "You came into my life, filling the hole that Margaux left. I will miss you and keep you in my thoughts until we are together again."

Saddened, Helene began to cry at the thought of Nichol and her family leaving.

In his heart, Ezra knew it was selfish to expect Helene to lose her family. She had been devoted to him through their years together, never wanting anything for herself until now.

Ezra stepped in and said to Helene, "Go with them; they need you, and you need them. I will be busy with the merchant business. I know where you are, and one day, Roger and I will suddenly appear."

Helene turned and hugged him, whispering, "I married you because I know the man you are. You have always thought of me."

Helene and Nichol grabbed her clothes and returned to the cart. Hastily, they set her clothes on top and around the children. As they set out, all were silent at first.

Once Rouen was out of sight, the chatter among them began.

Harald and Freyja led the cart with the babies safely riding inside. Gunvor and Tova walked close by and kept their eyes on the two little ones, entertaining them and at times, carrying them as well. Timo and Moki moved at Moki's pace and the other six adults mingled with the walkers, ensuring there was always someone behind the cart as well as in front.

John, on horseback riding ahead and leading the pack horse, became a watchman. His eyes and experiences of travel with Ezra made him careful.

Because they were passing travelers bringing their goods to the markets in Rouen, Nichol warned everyone not to make conversation.

"A smile and head nod, a simple greeting; we do not want to be their gossip to others when they reach Rouen. We should separate so we are seen as individuals, not as a group."

Nichol, as always, was on alert, and the group was thankful for her protection. They had seen her in action at a moment's notice. Separating slightly but always keeping within earshot and sight of each other, Robert turned to Nichol and noticed she had a concerned look.

"I think the Lady brought all of us together for a purpose. What do you think?"

Before answering, she turned to look back down the road. When she saw no one approaching, just Timo and Moki behind them, a small smile appeared on her face.

Taking his arm, she spoke softly, "She chose you for me at the fair. I believe that one day she will talk to you. You will suddenly hear a woman's soft voice in your ear and turn and see no one there. You will become another of her chosen ones she communicates with directly, just as our children will. Rose, Margaux, and Papa heard her as well.

"Look around at our group; we were all chosen. When I first heard her voice, I was not sure what to believe. I was a young girl. Margaux later told me that she was communicating with both her and Rose. And I know that she communicated with Papa. Margaux and Rose understood it. Papa did not at first.

"On my journey to Paris, I would not have survived without her guidance. She would come to me at night, often in my sleep, after I had climbed a tall pine to settle in. When I woke, her words were with me. The wisdom of her words will always be with me. She gave me hope and strength to continue the journey to Paris. I know she will talk to you and guide you. I am sure of it."

Robert turned to Nichol. With concern in his voice, he asked, "What happened at Emma's?" Then he looked up to see Helene approaching.

Seeing Helene walking toward them, Nichol said quietly, "I will tell you after Helene joins us." She stepped away from Robert and took Helene by the arm, leaning in to walk with her. "We are pleased that Ezra understood your desire and your wish to be with the children, so he allowed you to freely join us in Harmonie."

Timo was not far behind, looking down as he walked, still a humble man of the cloth.

As they approached, looking up, his first words were, "I brought new seeds for different plantings. I think we can grow everything our hamlet needs. And I found two goats, many chickens, and a pair of geese."

Silence followed, then he stopped and turned to Nichol. "I think you are here to tell me what happened at Emma's this morning."

With Timo on one side and Robert, Helene, and Shadow on the other, they slowly continued. Nichol began a detailed account of what had happened, including Loupe's confrontation. "I had some thoughts on the way back to the inn. I know we will be safe once we get to Harmonie, but we must prepare. No matter what we do or how far we go, someone will come and attempt to take everything from us.

"None of us knows what drives the archbishop and the duke. And we are both aware of the evil within Loupe. Emma now knows of Loupe and his evil deeds as well. They do not know us. To them, we are just the food that feeds their power. But we know them and what drives their greed. We cannot become idle. Their fear will become our power. I know them; I see them. The arrogant fools will not know what is happening to them."

Robert stopped, turned to Nichol, and gently touched her cheek. "My love, I see that we have no choice. Harmonie will be good for us all."

"We will plant the seeds of change while doing God's work—and the Lady's. And we will support the others who live close to us. I know Garlyn did not want a name for his hamlet, for fear others would find them. But when I think of them as we travel between here and Rouen, I call his small hamlet No Name," Timo added.

Nichol smiled when he said No Name. "Why not, Timo? I think Garlyn would even be amused when he hears us refer to them as No Name."

As she walked, a sense of well-being flowed through her body. Hooking an arm through both Robert's and Timo's, they continued down the road.

A smile spread across her face and her thoughts reached out to the Lady.

This is what you planned …?

Nichol saw a slight glow emerge when she took her next step.

thirty-five

The Truth

This is my family now.

The warm summer day wore on. Nichol was keeping her eye out for any trees that would offer shade. Hearing a horse approach, she was relieved to see John riding toward them.

"There is a shaded place just ahead where we can stay the night, with water for us and the animals," were his first words when he approached her.

"How far off?"

"It's around the next bend on the road," he replied as he turned his horse to ride alongside where she and Robert walked. With John's words, the pace picked up along with the chatter, bringing an end to the first day of travel to Harmonie.

As they rounded the bend, Nichol's eyes took in the site. It was ideal. John had picked a grove of trees with a small stream close by. The entire group of travelers was pleased to stop, rest, eat, and just be together.

Timo unpacked Moki while Robert, Harald, and Olaf unhitched the horse from the wagon and unloaded the packhorse. The men led the animals to the water, with Shadow enthusiastically running ahead. Marie and Nichol took their babies from the cart to nurse, encouraging Gunvor and Tova to go with the men to the stream.

Once the horses were taken care of and before the food was brought out, they sat in the shade to rest as they talked of the day's travel.

Nichol was leaning against a tree with her head back and eyes closed, loving the closeness of her daughter while she nursed, gently cupping her head. She heard Shadow's paw steps approaching. Without opening her eyes, she knew Shadow was moving her eyes back and forth between mother and daughter.

Then, Shadow put her nose to Lucette's cheek.

What is she doing? Nichol thought as she took in the two of them. And then Nichol knew something important was going to happen.

Lucette rolled out of Nichol's arms, grabbed Shadow's fur, and began pulling herself up. Standing and holding on with one hand and patting Shadow's head with the other, a joyful scream from Lucette brought everyone's attention and laughter. Lucette fell back into her mother's lap.

Shadow lay down next to them with her head on her paws.

"Marie, bring Aiden and sit next to me," Nichol requested. Gunvor and Tova jumped up and joined them, all eyes now on the babies.

Nichol put Lucette and Aiden on the ground, sitting up. What happened next even surprised Nichol. Shadow jumped up and hopped around, then got down and crawled on her belly to the babies, tail wagging. Sniffing both, she jumped up and pranced around just like when she was a pup.

Nichol glaced at Timo with a surprised look, then back to Shadow. Shadow's actions brought laughter, and Lucette and Aiden squealed with delight.

As quick as it started, Shadow stopped, lay down and rolled on the ground, looking at Nichol for approval. Patting her thigh to summon her pet, Shadow quickly went to her. Nichol whispered in her ear and the animal remained with her and the babies.

Freyja and her daughters were delighted to witness what Harald and Olaf told them about Nichol and Shadow. It was obvious how special their relationship was.

Timo looked at Nichol, Shadow, and the babies, bringing him memories of his journey to Paris with Nichol. *There is something about looking into a fire, to relax and let good memories enter. I will undertake this task for these people—my family.*

He stepped away to begin gathering fuel.

After Timo returned with an armful of firewood, Nichol asked Gunvor and Tova to find tinder to start the fire. When they returned, Nichol gave them her flint and steel. With Harald's help, a fire was started.

Nichol looked toward Freyja, who was guiding her daughters to set up their sleeping arrangements. Watching the girls' interaction with their mother and how active and eager they were to be involved in all the activities around them, Nichol felt happy. *She is a good mother; I can learn from her.*

Just then, Freyja turned toward Nichol. As their eyes met, Nichol looked at the girls and smiled. She then looked back at Freyja and put her hand on her heart. Freyja smiled in return with her hand on her heart, a silent compliment from one mother to another.

The night sky arrived and the fire did what Timo thought it would. He watched the light and shadows flicker off the faces of those in the fire's embrace. Smiling faces glowed back, basking in the warmth. Timo felt happy; a quiet joy that resonated within his spirit.

Robert leaned toward Nichol and spoke softly. "I see you are doing what you do best. What do you see?"

"I see them as you do; they are good people. They want what we want, a safe place to live with their family. The children are asleep. Neither of us is. Let us go for a walk so we can talk and not disturb the others."

Robert noticed a rapid change come over her. "What is it? Is something wrong?"

Nichol smiled at him. "No, I just want to be alone with you."

Robert stood and offered her his hand. Nichol rose, and they quietly left. Shadow raised her head toward both and then moved toward the sleeping babies, taking her watchful position.

Walking far away from the fire's light and the others, Nichol turned to Robert. "Hold me," she whispered.

Robert wrapped her in his arms and pulled her in forcefully, her arms by her side. He felt her quivering body as he silently embraced her. Robert wanted her to speak first but knew she was struggling with her thoughts. He whispered, "I loved you from the first time I laid eyes on you, and that will never change."

Nichol quietly sobbed. The events of the last year finally came raining down on her, and her emotions flooded out with her tears.

At that moment, Robert heard a woman's soft voice in his head: *She needs you; stay strong for her.*

Stroking her head, he shared with Nichol, "I just heard from your Lady. I know that she is now with me, too."

The two stayed entwined as they continued to move deeper into the darkness.

"She has always been with you; she brought us together. The children are sleeping and taken care of. We are alone … remember our trip to Paris?" The moonlight picked up the whites of Nichol's eyes.

Smiling, Robert pulled her even closer, bestowing a tender kiss on his wife, followed by another and still another, as each one intensified the hunger that grew between them. Caressing hands moved up and down their bodies, touching and stroking. Each was a vulnerable and willing captive to the other.

Gently, Robert slowly moved his hands to lift her tunic as his kisses continued. Lifting it over her head, Nichol reached for his breeches; she could feel her legs trembling. Pulling back, she teased softly, "What is good for you is good for me."

Her body went limp, and Robert gently guided her to the ground, settling on their dropped clothes. At the same time, they slipped off their remaining clothing.

Robert knew what she liked. He began kissing her, starting at the nape of her neck. A soft moan emerged that increased in volume as he moved down to her breasts. His hands and kisses lovingly followed the curves of her body until he felt the warmth of her mound and the wetness at its center. Nuzzling to absorb her smell, Robert inhaled deeply as his lower body erupted in its response. How he wanted her.

Nichol nibbled on his lower side, slowly moving her nose and taking in his essence. At the same time, she pressed his face closer to her body. Her own desire wanted him within her.

She reached for his shoulder, to pull him more fully into her embrace, higher on her body. Their gazes met, eye to eye, noses touching. As she stroked his forehead, she whispered, "You are everything to me."

As Nichol spoke, he moved his body over hers to become one, their union surrounded by a soft light. Their movements became magical, paralleling the music of the night sounds.

Robert filled her as her eyes slowly closed, both desiring this moment and time to last forever. He felt himself higher in her body as he had never experienced before.

Within moments, the two shivered in unison.

Something special had happened.

They both knew it.

The Secret Way

*Shadow appeared to nod her head
as she heard the words in her ear.*

With the first hint of light, Nichol opened her eyes.

Robert was facing her, lying close, with Lucette and Aiden snuggled between them. With a smile, Robert blew her a kiss as their hands reached for each other.

Their shifting was just enough movement for Aiden to wake from his sleep, crying to be fed. That woke Lucette and she joined him in demanding to be fed.

Gunvor came and quickly carried Aiden to Marie. Nichol sat up and began to nurse Lucette when she saw Shadow strolling into the camp. The dog curled next to Nichol.

She felt Shadow's belly and patted it, knowing her pet had success while hunting during the night. "Curl up and sleep. We will leave soon."

The morning overcast sky was a relief for the travelers. Quietly, everyone went about preparing for the day's travel: Helene and Freyja served pottage and bread. The animals were packed and the horse was hitched to the cart. They set off at a brisk pace.

By midday, Nichol told the group she would lead them on a different path to Harmonie. "It is to protect us and the other hamlet. We do not want to overly beat down a path easily viewed by anyone on this road. We should take care to conceal where we are building."

John noticed Helene was tired from the day before and offered his horse for her to ride. For some time, Helene rode with John walking by her side, ahead of the rest.

Later that morning, John offered Nichol his horse to search for their new path—a secret path—to Harmonie. Nichol looked for the path the Lady showed her in her dreams during the night.

With a clear image in her head, she found the path that she saw in her vision. She was not far ahead of the rest, and when they came to her, she pointed and said so all could hear: "This is where we leave the road."

Turning to John, she added, "Would you cover our tracks leading into the forest until we are out of sight?"

Nichol stepped down from John's horse and handed him the rope attached to the horse's bridle. Moving toward Robert, she took his hand, and the two led their group off the main road, traveling into the forest far away from the road and the possibility of outlaws.

Guiding the cart through the thickets between trees took extra time. Nichol realized that the new path could add another day to their travels before their arrival at Harmonie.

She smiled to herself. *Nine adults, two children, and two infants are now part of my family, plus a wolf dog and a donkey. And now goats, chickens, and geese.* Nichol thought about the time over a year ago when she escaped from the wrath of Fredric and the evil Astrid, mourning that her beloved papa was not with her and wishing for him to be able to see her baby daughter.

Now, she was cared for, having a husband, his family that had become hers, new friendships that had grown along the way, and even a new Shadow who watched out for her.

The group moved forward. Nichol carried Lucette in her sling, close to her breasts. Glancing at her daughter throughout the day, she felt her heart warm each time Lucette looked up at her or reached up to touch her face, always with an instant smile. Sometimes she felt that her daughter was talking to her with her eyes.

In the early afternoon, she glanced back at Marie and Olaf as they walked together. Smiling, she nudged Robert, who was carrying Aiden and nodded her head toward the two.

Robert leaned in and whispered, "They are just like us," as he took Nichol's hand and continued to walk. Shadow looked up at the two of them and nuzzled Nichol's leg as if she approved. Nichol sensed that her family was strengthening and that she and Robert had created a new bond between them the previous night.

John had caught up with them. Seeing him approaching, she suggested that they take a short rest. As they settled in and the quiet of the forest surrounded them, small amounts of food were passed around and the two women nursed the babies.

Seeing that all had eaten something and Lucette was done feeding, Nichol pulled Shadow close to her, her ears erect to receive a message from her owner. Nichol whispered, "Guide us home to Harmonie, Shadow. Walk ahead of John to lead the way."

Turning her face to Nichol, Shadow appeared to nod her head as she heard the words in her ear. She then moved toward John and pawed his leg. When she did, he looked back at Nichol, who smiled and mouthed *follow her*. He winked at her, and then moved to his horse and mounted it.

At the same time, Robert stood and told everyone to get ready, as they were traveling forward again. *He knows what I am thinking and what Shadow is doing!* Smiling at her husband, Nichol added, "John and Shadow will be ahead of us, making sure that it is safe as we walk. They will circle back if our direction needs to change."

As they walked, she noticed that Timo and Moki were in their travel mode. They were longtime friends, content with each other's company. Both seemed to thrive on whatever the new day sent their way.

Gunvor and Tova—Harald's and Freyja's daughters—could hardly wait to play with Lucette and Aiden. When they were not with their mother, they had become like older sisters. Whenever they stopped for rest and food, they would quickly go to Nichol and Marie's side and asked to play with the babies.

At one of their stops, Nichol turned to Robert as they watched the girls play with Lucette and Aiden. "Have you noticed how different Lucette and Aiden are? Aiden is always cheerful. He kicks his feet, moves his arms out to be held and plays with anyone who is close by. I think he will charm his way through life.

"Lucette looks frustrated sometimes. Even though she is too young to have words, I think she has them in her head. I think she wants to talk. I sense that when she looks up at me as we walk and she is in the sling."

With a smile, Robert leaned into her and quietly said, "I, too, have noticed that, and I see you in her. One day soon, you will see her, and she will see you. You are one."

Nichol turned to watch Lucette with the girls. *Soon, Lucette, soon, all will discover who you are.*

The third evening was enjoyed as they camped in an open meadow.

Timo and Harald had gathered wood for a fire. As the skies darkened, they all enjoyed the magic of the glowing flies that rose above them, dancing overhead and around them, as they settled down after a long day of walking. All of them knew that they were getting closer to Harmonie.

Nichol leaned into Robert and softly spoke as they lay side by side.

"Ezra and Helene had their house stolen and their lives threatened. Everyone here has given up so much to be here—not all of us by choice. Harald and his family are with us because he wants to live in Harmonie. Timo walked away from his monastery life to be with us. Every time I think about you and our children, I know we created something special, and I feel that Harmonie will be the only safe place for all of us. There will be no tithes to pay to the church, no rents to pay a lord, or a ring to kiss. No knee to bend. Only our journey with the Lady who comes to me as a guide. Sometimes, I feel the light surrounding me when I hear her voice. It was what I heard two nights ago when we lay together."

Turning to her, Robert reached for her hand, pulling it across his chest as he slowly turned toward her and whispered back, "We are all in the place we are supposed to be. Without you finding me, no one here would have the promise of what is beginning to unfold. I am thankful to your Lady, and for you, our daughter, and now Aiden who has become our son."

Snuggling, each lapsed into their thoughts.

Words did not need to be spoken.

The following morning, Nichol walked with Harald and Freyja, hungry to learn their language so she could continue to improve her ability to speak with them and their daughters.

Knowing little about where they came from, she wanted to hear about their land and culture. She learned more of their history and that they were not in Rouen by choice. They had been driven from their homes by rival tribal leaders who were constantly at war with each other.

Harald admitted, "When Ezra hired Olaf and me to help build the first home, I knew it was where I wanted to bring Freyja and our daughters."

Freyja listened to Nichol and her husband speaking. "When Harald told me about this Harmonie, it gave me hope. I wanted a home where we could have a small farm like my family had back in my homeland, Norway."

It was to become a new land and beginning for all of them. Nichol sensed the need for her to increase her walking pace. *We all need to get there soon.*

Late the next morning, they arrived at the stream they had crossed before. It was not as deep as before and they all crossed with ease. New energy increased with each person as they stepped from the water. They felt… they knew … their new homeland was close.

As they circled the hill and came into view of the valley, Harmonie came into view. Nichol watched Freyja as she first viewed the valley; her face reflected her immediate approval.

Garlyn was working in the field beside his home and heard them coming. He began waving as he shouted, "Welcome back!" Hearing Garlyn's voice, more shouts could be heard as excitement grew to see their return.

Stopping in the middle of the hamlet, the party became surrounded by everyone talking at once. Robert and Timo unpacked the requested cloth and leather, and Nichol had brought cups and bowls for each family.

Garlyn motioned to Nichol for a private talk, and they moved away from the group. Nichol saw the smile on his face change to a worried look.

"Nichol, were you careful not to be followed on your return?"

Nichol looked directly at Garlyn. "We were not followed, and when we left the road, John covered our tracks into the forest."

Nichol paused in thought. *Garlyn will not like what I have to say.*

"Garlyn, the valley will be discovered. When, I do not know. A new church is being built, and more people are moving to another village as well, no more than a day's ride south of here. We must prepare for that day.

"For now, Ezra sent a small cask of wine with us. Let us gather to celebrate our return and talk of preparation tomorrow."

Without a response, Garlyn put his hand on her forearm and gently squeezed as he nodded in agreement.

The women and children went to the lake to bathe. Later, it would be the men's turn.

As they all gathered for the evening meal, the new energy increased. It—along with excitement—was felt everywhere. Plans were made on where to start the next day for the barn and additional homes.

Timo was glad that the barn would be built next. It was summertime and he wanted to concentrate on laying out his plantings and the future farming for their community. He was already thinking of ways to create a type of plant wall to keep animals away from a growing garden and the foods it produced.

The group agreed that there was a sense of urgency to complete all the buildings before the next winter set in again.

Timo shared what summer crops he would plant and when the winter wheat would be added. He had planted apple trees, grapevines, and spring wheat when they first discovered where Harmonie would be. Future harvesting would be from early spring to late fall.

He quickly became a welcome addition to the valley, sharing his farming skills to enrich their harvest. The No Name hamlet and Harmonie had become a secret village in a secret valley.

The stage was set for Harmonie to become the ideal place for families to grow and help others.

Reflections

I'd like to bless this house before we celebrate.

One afternoon in October, Robert summoned Nichol and the rest of the group—including Harald's family—to the front of their finished home. The warm days of summer had passed, and the current month delivered sunlight that allowed them to work long days plowing and planting the fields for the spring and summer harvests.

Turning to Nichol, he said, "You were the inspiration behind all of this."

He turned to the others. "I was not sure we could achieve all that we have by this time, but due to the efforts of many good and determined people, we did it."

As usual, Timo topped off the conversation. "It was Nichol's dream; we simply followed her. Now let us go make supper in your new home!"

Nichol brought out the new cups and wine Ezra had purchased in Rouen and filled them for everyone to drink.

Timo said, "There's something I must do first. I'd like to bless this house before we celebrate." Heads nodded and everyone encouraged him to continue.

"Thank you, God. We were guided here by the Lady. We thank her for choosing Nichol to be her instrument of communication, and we thank Nichol for having the courage to heed her message and for sharing it with us. We ask the Lady to bless this house and protect everyone in it."

Nichol had been unusually quiet for the last few days and Timo finally asked her about it. "Nichol, you have been so quiet lately. Is something bothering you?"

"Timo, I am just savoring all the beauty around me. We all have new homes, a stable for our animals, a forge shop for Robert, future fields of grain, fruits, and vegetables, and the start of our very own vineyard. Most of all, I appreciate all the talented and loving people I call my family.

"I am thankful every day for all of you who have made my life complete and that's something I thought I'd never get to say.

"I know the Lady brought us all together for a purpose. Just what that purpose might be is not yet clear to me, but I believe somehow that Lucette and Aiden are the keys to finding out.

"When I woke this morning, I felt a sense of calm for the first time in many months. No one is chasing us to cause us harm, and no lord or priest is hammering at our door, demanding a share of what we have worked so hard for. For now, we are not in danger, and I value that. We will build a different future for our children … a life free of hate and fear and one of promise and respect. Harmonites is the perfect name for us and for all to be in Harmonie."

Timo absorbed her words. "I, too, woke this morning with a sense of well-being. I will continue God's work here in Harmonie, to sow and reap our plentiful harvest and teach the villagers how to do the same."

Nichol and Robert looked at each other and Nichol smiled.

Robert said, "After many conversations, my Uncle Ezra saw what was coming long before Nichol came into our lives. Because my family were Jews, we knew that we had always been considered outcasts by powerful lords and church leaders. They only tolerated us because of Ezra's wealth, and they could demand coin from him. Now, here we all sit as one. We're like a pot of stew, full of various kinds of meats and vegetables, and we all work together to make one delicious meal. This is how a family and how villages should blend. We love one another despite our differences and we're better because of it."

Finally, Marie quietly said, "I owe everyone here more than I can ever repay. You saved Aiden's and my life. I am forever grateful. You have shown me more kindness and generosity than I have ever known. I know Aiden will become a good man because he has all of you to love and guide him. Thank you for including us, saving our lives, and for making him one of your own."

Silence followed Marie's statement. Nichol wiped tears from her eyes and nodded her understanding to Marie.

They ate and celebrated together, blending their joy.

As the evening ended, Marie gathered Aiden and Lucette, and moved toward the bedroom she shared with the two children. Shadow, who insisted on staying close to Lucette and Aiden, slept on the floor next to their bed.

Timo and Moki headed for the stables.

Harald and the family went to their home.

All was right with the world—their world. The hamlet of Harmonie.

Nichol stood and wrapped her cloak around her shoulders. Stretching her hand to the sitting Robert, she said, "The night is cooling. Let us take a short walk before we sleep. I have something to tell you."

Moving to open the door, they quietly left. Nichol tucked her arm through Robert's and pulled him close. Now, within a short distance, they were surrounded by the stars that filled the night sky.

Nichol looked up. "I have not seen the night stars so clear since I was nestled in the treetops while running to Paris."

Robert squeezed her hand gently. "The stars are for us. I have always believed that messages are within them."

As the words left his mouth, a brilliant light moved high in the sky, landing as if it was on top of the hill that oversaw their new home.

Nichol knew.

She felt it—the message.

Nichol turned to Robert and smiled as she lifted her eyes to meet his. "A new life is within me once again, another child for us."

The Harmonie House

You have a bigger role to play in our village.

One frosty winter morning, Nichol and Robert sat by the fire, the only light in the room, as they played with Lucette and Aiden on the floor. Now both walking, they had to be watched, especially with the fire burning for warmth. They were into everything now.

An unexpected knock sounded at the door.

As Robert opened it, he was surprised to see Timo, Harald, and his family on the other side. As they entered, Gunvor's and Tova's eyes sought their targets. Immediately, they moved toward Lucette and Aiden, reaching them with arms stretched and huge smiles as Lucette and Aiden both were on their feet and toddled to the welcoming hands.

"Come join us," Robert offered. "Where are Olaf and Marie?"

"They wanted to be alone," Harald replied. His response brought smiles from everyone.

As Nichol listened to the conversation, she sensed how natural it was for people to seek companionship. Conversations usually begin with trivial things, eventually leading to more critical issues in each person's life.

Another knock sounded on the door. This time Robert opened the door to Garlyn, wearing a cloak for warmth. "Come in and join us by the fire."

Garlyn enters and gathers around the now-crowded hearth.

"Garlyn, what is on your mind?" Robert asked. "You look troubled."

The man shrugged. "I just wanted to be with all of you."

"You are always welcome in our home," Nichol said.

Nichol listened quietly, and then her face lit up as an idea started to evolve: the vision she had earlier of the common house. "I have noticed how people tend to congregate around a fire when the weather cools, and I have seen how people like to gather in one place just for conversation. I have fond memories of going to the market in Marseilles with Margaux and Gerhardt and visiting Rose, listening to the peddlers selling their wares and sharing their ideas as people milled about talking with each other. The same thing happened at the fairs I visited while making my way to Paris. People came together in one place. We could build a place for people to gather and share ideas."

Garlyn asked, "What do you have in mind, Nichol?" She had shared her initial vision a long time ago but now she would reveal the vision in more detail.

"I see a longhouse, something like the monasteries have, where the monks feed and house many travelers. We could gather there year-round, but mainly in the winter after the harvest is done and hands are idle. It could be a place where everyone in Harmonie could share their skills and knowledge.

"It can be an indoor gathering place where we would bake bread, make clothing, shoes, and other crafts. We can make goods that could be sold in Rouen. We could also make a space for children to play and a place for them to learn. I was taught how to read and write as a child. I know many don't know how. We can teach those in our community to do both. I'm grateful that I learned. Timo has always kept written records to share with the monasteries he visited so they could follow his advice.

"I know that he will gladly share his written work with you. It could create a plan to have our ideas, and what we do so it is accessible to all. I believe our children should learn what and how we do things."

What Nichol had said was met with silence at first.

Then she continued, "What do you think?"

Harald was the first to speak. It was slow and halted, not fluent in the language the others spoke. "We have places in homeland."

Nichol then spoke to him in his native language, asking several questions and then turned back to the others. "Harald told me he knows how to build what I described. They have them where he came from. What shall we call this place to represent what it will be used for?"

Timo added, "There's more to think about and what we could do. Nichol, you envision a place for everyone here to gather as one. What about others? Why not open it to other families here and even merchants who have things they would like to sell or trade?"

Nichol and Garlyn's eyes met. As she spoke, Garlyn nodded his head. "Timo, that could be later. Right now, we are all not seen by the outer world. It is why we are careful with our tracks when we travel from here to Rouen and back. When it is time to welcome others, we will know … and we can be prepared if trouble arises.

"Ezra can find markets outside our village where we could sell our goods, and he could import the supplies and materials the villagers need to make their crafts. We could even bring in supplies that those here desire—supplies that they will need to pay coin for. New items can be made and sold amongst ourselves or when we take them to Rouen for Ezra to place."

Excitedly, Helene added, "I could teach people how to sew and cook. Timo could share his knowledge about the proper methods for sowing and reaping, as well as reading and writing. And he knows how to work with leather for footwear, pouches, and front packs like Nichol uses to carry Lucette. Robert could teach smithing and goldsmithing. Nichol, you could also teach reading and writing, and methods for using herbs and spices for healing.

"And Nichol, I believe you have a bigger role to play in our village. People are drawn to you, your energy, and your approach to solving problems. Maybe you could be the leader of the gathering place and host community meetings to discuss issues important to them."

Nichol was surprised by the unexpected and optimistic response from her family. "I am encouraged by your thoughts and ideas. What should we call a place where so many people could gather and create their crafts?"

Timo offered his thoughts. "Since you are fashioning the structure after the longhouse the monks use, what if we called it the Harmonie House? A place where everyone can gather for conversation, companionship, and solutions for us and No Name."

Nichol added eagerly, "Great idea, Timo. I like the name. What does everyone else think?" Everyone nodded in agreement at the same time.

"The Harmonie House it is!" Nichol exclaimed.

"No Name … what is No Name?" Garlyn asked, puzzled.

"Garlyn, remember when we first came here, and you told us that your hamlet didn't want a name because people would attempt to seek its whereabouts? We honored that so we always refer to it as No Name," Nichol responded.

Silence hung in the air. Then Garlyn did the unexpected. His head went slightly back and a big belly laugh flowed through his mouth. A smile spread across his face. "No Name … I like it! No Name!"

More conversation ensued about how and when to build the Harmonie House and how they would all be involved in the decision making.

"How can we convince people that this is a promising idea for all of us and that we should start building the Harmonie House before spring planting?" Robert asked.

Nichol looked at Garlyn. "Garlyn, you are deep in thought. What is on your mind?"

"Robert asked the right question." Looking at Nichol, then Helene, he asked, "How do we convince people that your Harmonie House will benefit everyone in No Name?"

As Nichol turned her head toward Helene, she thought about how grateful she was that she was here. *Helene would be perfect to act as the overseer of the Harmonie House.* Nichol gestured to Helene for the answer they both knew.

"We convince the women that it is a place for them to gather, especially in the winter. They will make sure that it will be built," Helene responded enthusiastically.

"Of course," Robert responded with a cheerful laugh.

But there was more on his mind, more to be said, as well as more on Nichol's mind.

Nichol added, "Now that our homes are built, and the Harmonie House will be built by next year, I have been thinking about we Harmonites. We must prepare for our trips to Rouen when I work with Ezra. I'll stay at Ezra's Rouen home and use the warehouse to store goods from Harmonie and merchants in Paris and Rouen. And the jewelry that Robert makes, along with whatever anyone else in Harmonie creates that can be sold.

"Robert and I have much to consider before Ezra and I establish a merchant business in Rouen. The most important things are our families, the children, and how we best share the responsibilities between the two homes."

As all left through the door, the sense of shared excitement could be felt.

Closing it, Robert turned to Nichol. "Did you notice how Garlyn relaxed and enjoyed himself? No longer is he grumpy and defensive around any of us. He wants us here. And I believe he wants to belong, just as he wants the two hamlets—his and ours—to live in harmony with each other."

The next day, Gunvor and Tova stayed with Lucette and Aiden while Nichol, Robert, Helene, Timo, and Garlyn visited every home in No Name to discuss their thoughts on the Harmonie House. The idea was well received, and many offered to help build it.

The group was encouraged by the reaction of those in the valley, and they returned home feeling that the Harmonie House would indeed be built long before spring came. With all the men and the women helping from both hamlets, it would be possible.

Because of his knowledge, Harald became the leader of the workforce to build the Harmonie House. He paced off the length and width of the land to be cleared. Every morning, men and women arrived to help. Harald and Olaf then took a group of men to the forest and chose trees to be felled to the length and size required.

Nichol had one more request for the Harmonie homes. To Harald, she had asked the day before, "All our homes were originally planned to have packed soil and straw as flooring. This is not good for us, with the mice and rats that will come. I would like all homes to have smooth wood floors, like those the Norse ships are made of. Can you do that, Harald?"

Harald agreed. "Yes. It will be best for all and free from dirt. I saw much oak in the forest that will be strong. We can make the wood floors. When winter comes first, we must have a roof over us."

The next day, the women began to level the floor areas and stack the sod that was removed. Each was excited about having a home with a floor above the land where each home was built. The Harmonie House would have a floor built around the firepit space.

Timo worked with Harald and Olaf to identify which trees would be felled and split.

As they did, Timo planted a few tree seeds for every tree chopped down. Every able person in the hamlet contributed and there was a feeling of goodwill and happiness with the new floors and the other improvements that would come.

thirty-nine

The Tell

I will always be with you for this.

Nichol had slept little during the night; it was becoming a habit that Robert noticed. One candle was always lit, if needed, to tend to the children; when he turned to Nichol, he could clearly see her face. Her eyes were wide open, and he gently touched her cheek, whispering, "What is keeping you awake?"

"I do not want to burden you with my thoughts."

Robert paused, trying to find his words. "We are husband and wife. It is best that we do not have secrets … and that we share our concerns with one another."

Nichol was silent, then turned on her side, finding his eyes. "I need to meet with Emma again. She will soon be the queen of England and whatever the king demands of her will take preference … I fear I may already be too late. When I am in Rouen, I need to meet with her before she travels across the sea. I will ask her to properly introduce me to her brothers, the archbishop and the duke. Both are important to our merchant business."

She took a deep breath. "Robert, you should know they are also a danger to it … to me … to all of us in Harmonie if they have the ear of and are working with the evil priest Loupe. You know that if I am introduced, I will hear them. And I will see them. Then, I will know who they truly are."

Robert was silent for a moment. "When you are ready, leave the next morning. The children will be cared for and I will ask John to ride with you. Now, my wife, go to sleep."

Sleep was still elusive. Nichol's mind raced. Now, she had plans for travel to make, her departure, and what supplies to bring back. Finally, she drifted off.

A few hours later, Nichol woke with a fright, sitting up and scanning the room for threats. There were none.

She heard Robert's voice speaking and the children and Helene laughing. The aroma that had drifted to the bedchamber promised a hearty, warm meal. She smelled food being cooked. Suddenly, nausea overwhelmed her.

I know ... you are beginning to let me know you will come this summer.

Rising, she dressed and went to greet them.

"I tried to keep them quiet and did not succeed. But I did keep them from jumping on you."

Hugging both children and then Robert, she sat next to him, gently touching his hand. "Thank you for listening to me in the night and letting me sleep."

Shadow was at her feet, wanting attention.

Nichol gave her a hug and whispered, "Are you ready for a trip?" Shadow's tail went into a circling gyration. She went to the door and lay down.

Nichol turned to Robert, "I will prepare for the trip today and leave at first light in the morning. I will make a list of everyone's needs and bring back what we can."

Helene observed her, noticing that her color was pale and how she persisted with the gentle touching of her belly. Their eyes met.

She knows.

Helene's eyebrows rose and a smile crossed her face. "Would you like the special warm drink I used to make for you, Nichol?"

Yes, she knows.

Nichol spoke to Helene as if no one else was in the room. "Our next adventure has begun. The light is with me. I am grateful that you are with me again for it."

The two women maintained eye contact. Helene nodded. "I will always be with you for this." Then, Helene took a few steps to embrace her.

As Robert watched them, all he could think was, *what just happened?*

Nichol and Helene worked closely all day, not speaking much but in total harmony and sync, each sensing what the other needed.

As the daughter she never had, Helene wanted to protect her. She knew that Nichol could defend herself and the Lady would also be at her side. She also would care for her children while their mother was away.

Nichol knew that, just as she knew Robert and Timo would be there for her always and the children when she was away. Those in her life have been chosen to be there and they cherish her for who she is.

"Helene," she spoke aloud, "I will see Ezra soon. Is there something I should carry to him or a special message to share?"

Looking at Lucette and Aiden, Helene responded, "I have all I need in this home. Ezra knows that I am safe and cared for. Tell him what is happening with you and that I will come to Rouen the next time you go down.

"I will have food for you to carry. Mix the ginger you like with hot water when you stop for a fire in the evening at the end of your day. Shadow will not have to hunt; I have included food for her as well."

With Shadow by her side, Nichol walked over to Robert's forge. Finding him, she asked, "Have you spoken to John about leaving with me in the morning?"

"I have. He is looking forward to it. John will have two horses ready to ride by first light and a pack horse for the return trip. And please talk to Timo. He is making a list of the items you will need to bring back with you upon your return to Harmonie.

"I will have some jewelry and other things for you to take for Ezra and to place with merchants. I know he will be pleased to see you and hear of our progress here."

With excitement in her step, she was anxious to see Ezra and the warehouse. She knew it was time for her to become a merchant and follow the path of what her papa had done.

She had not fully realized that she had sown the same seeds of success and prosperity in Harmonie as well.

It was part of her destiny.

Many Eyes and Ears

She will protect me if needed … don't worry.

An overcast morning greeted the residents of Harmonie the next day. Nichol and John were in front of her home, surrounded by loved ones. Helene was holding Lucette and Nichol took Aiden from Marie. Helene brought Lucette to Nichol as Lucette reached for her.

Taking both infants in her arms, the two giggled and squirmed. Kissing both, she passed them back to Helene and Marie. One by one, she hugged them all, as everyone wished her well on the journey back to Rouen.

John was already on his horse with the pack horse lead in his hand. Mounting her horse, John said in a commanding voice, "Nichol …." She turned to him and was greeted with his customary tribute, a wink of his eye. "Are you not forgetting something?"

Nichol looked down and came up with a smile. "Yes, John, how could I forget?" Turning to Robert, she asked, "Could you get my bow and the quiver of arrows?"

Robert returned with her request, and as he handed them to her, he held her hand and said in a soft voice, just for her ears, "I love you." He then released her hand.

John had started and she gave her horse's flanks a quick kick with her heels. Their journey had begun. Nichol could hear the children's cries fade as they went down the road, but the memory of their little voices would last until she returned, and they were back in her arms once again.

As they passed No Name, they were greeted by waving hands and shouts of goodwill. Riding side by side as they arrived at the base of the hill, they both stopped and turned to view the valley. John spoke first. "We have a lot of hard riding ahead of us." She nodded.

Pausing for a few moments, they turned at the same time and continued with Shadow by their side.

The evening darkness began to take over the skies when they stopped. John took the horses to water, then hobbled them and dropped hay the pack horse was carrying. While he tended the horses, Nichol started a fire to help ward off the night chill. Thoughts of sleeping next to Moki on her cold winter nights of the past brought a smile.

Bread, cheese, and dried fish from the lake were enjoyed as the night closed in on them. Nichol sat down next to John for shared warmth. "John, when Timo, Moki, and I were traveling to Paris the nights were cold, just like tonight. I slept up against Moki for warmth."

John's laugh bellowed from deep inside his chest. "So, you are comparing me to Moki?"

"Well, you are not as big as Moki, and you smell better, and you are certainly better looking."

John's laughter boomed once more, and then he fell silent. Nichol turned to see sorrow on his face as she had never seen from him. "Did I offend you?"

"I was married once. When a lord decided to fight a war with a neighboring lord, I was required to fight for him. The battles lasted months and when I returned, I found that both my wife and child had died in childbirth. I should have been there."

He turned to Nichol with tears in his eyes. "You brought back feelings and memories that I had given up on—fond memories— and I thank you and Robert for that. We should never forget the ones we love. When you compared me to Moki, in my mind I saw her saying those words. Yes, we can sleep side by side and I am glad I do not smell like Moki."

Nichol put an arm on John's back and smiled at him. "When we first met, I saw you."

"What did you see?"

"The gentle man and husband I see sitting next to me now. Let us get some sleep and start at first light."

Lying on the ground, with John on one side and Shadow on the other, covered in their cloaks, John's soft snore and the chatter of the forest were the only sounds to be heard in the cold night air. The fire slowly changed to glowing embers, revealing a full moon.

Sleep would not come easily for Nichol—not until all her thoughts were resolved. Her concern about Emma was the key to her wakefulness and the most troubling to her mind.

The next day when the path was wide enough, they rode side by side, continuing their conversation from the previous day and night. Each spoke frankly and revealed their journey from begin- ning to their current circumstances.

John was interested in the Lady; he had witnessed events that could not be explained. Nichol revealed her childhood, and how the Lady had influenced and guided her, and occasionally warned and protected her.

"John, both my mother and brother are bad people and want to destroy me. My mother sent Fredric to capture me, but I escaped each time. Fredric is evil and believes that I took Papa's coins. I must be alert because he could still be looking for me. They knew me by my birth name, Lisa."

"When Ezra took Roger and me with him, he shared with us much of what you are saying. He left out the part that Fredric may still be looking for you. I will be on alert in everything we do from here forward."

John pointed in the air. "I see the hawk … your papa has been with us the whole way. It is time to ride with care and stay quiet, as we are close to where we join the road."

The morning of the third day, tired and hungry, they arrived at Ezra's home in Rouen. John pounded on Ezra's door and, in his deep voice, demanded that the door be opened. Moments later, they heard the solid brace lift that secured the door.

Ezra's face showed concern. His first words were, "Is all well?"

Nichol embraced him. "All is well and Helene sends her love," she whispered.

Ezra stepped back and waved them inside, then stepped outside and looked up and down the street. His actions did not go unnoticed.

"I will bring in our satchels and tend to the horses, and then I will go to the inn and meet up with Roger. I know you and Nichol have much to talk about."

As Ezra looked at Nichol's bow and quiver, he asked, "Was your trip without danger?"

Nichol nodded. "It was. John is a good companion—formidable foe on the outside and a caring soul on the inside. At night, we talked about our pasts, and what brought us to you."

"Come sit at the table. I will bring food and ale so you may eat while you tell me about Harmonie. Tell me everything, no matter how small it seems."

As they sat down, Shadow approached Ezra, wagging her tail. He broke off a large piece of bread and set out a bowl of water for her on the floor.

Looking up from petting Shadow, Nichol began, "Ezra, everyone is in good health and spirits. Helene sends her love; I know she misses you. The two children are walking and keeping her busy, and she likes being needed."

Ezra was pleased with the progress being made in Harmonie that Nichol revealed. He was attentive at first as Nichol continued her story, and then she could see his attention drift away. She reached across the table, placed her hands on his, and smiled. She saw loneliness in his eyes, the longing for all to be together again.

His shoulders dropped as he let out a sigh. "What brings only you and John to Rouen?"

"I came to see Emma before she leaves to marry. I want to find out what danger I am in and if Loupe is spreading more lies. If I am in danger, to protect you, we must not be seen together. I will go to the market today at the time of our past visits, with hopes of seeing her."

"I have heard she will leave soon for England when the tides and winds are favorable. Several merchants by the docks have told me. I suspect that is not your only reason. I think you should have John follow you."

Nichol shook her head. "I have Shadow with me. She will protect me if needed; don't worry."

She straightened and leaned forward in her chair. "Harmonie House is now built and I want to discuss what types of goods we should make to market here. I will return to Harmonie with the supplies needed to create them. Robert and Timo have already given me a list of things to get. Robert sent some of his jewelry that he thought your merchants might be interested in selling."

Pulling several pieces from the bag at her side, she placed them on the table. Picking them up one by one, Ezra carefully looked at them. "These are all desirable pieces and would sell quickly. I know the ideal merchant to carry Robert's work."

Smiling, she relaxed. "Now, tell me about the merchant business and what you have done for E & N since we left."

Ezra tilted his head. "Ahh, you miss the markets; they call to you to fill your hunger. I also have a passion for business, which is why I know. Someone I know who is very wise would say *I see you*."

Nichol stood and placed her hands on Ezra's cheeks as she kissed his balding head. "Let's talk over supper. Can we meet later with John and Roger at the inn?"

Before she turned toward the door, Nichol reached for his hand. "Ezra, after John and I knocked and you opened the door, you stepped out and looked around. Are you all right? Should I be concerned?"

"There are many ears and eyes around here and too many gossips. I have learned that, with my work, I can never be too careful. There is a strong Jewish quarter here in Rouen and I know that eventually, the church will seek them out to destroy their homes and businesses as they did in Paris with mine. When I was in Paris, I was baptized for the protection of all of us—my family."

Nichol thought about what he said. *We must all be on alert and ready to protect ourselves.*

Opening the door for her to leave, Ezra added, "I am going to the inn now to talk to John and Roger. Amos, the innkeeper, said he likes having Roger around to deal with unwanted customers."

forty-one

The Reunion

Who will be left standing?

Nichol strolled through the marketplace. As she walked, her thoughts flowed to Emma.

Is she still here?

People gave her ample room to walk once they saw Shadow by her side. Finally, she arrived at the place where the two first met.

Her mind was still filled with Emma. *I wonder if Emma will be here today? Will she be able to talk with me if she is? Does she know I am here?*

Standing close to a building so she could observe happenings and passersby, self-doubt crept in. Nichol began to question herself, wondering if her marketplace visit was a good idea.

As she stepped away from the building she was leaning against and turned to leave, Shadow left her side. As Nichol watched her pet move away, a smiling Emma appeared and walked in her direction. A guard trailed several steps behind her.

The two women met and embraced. Emma took Nichol by the arm. "Shall we go to the inn where we warmed up by the fire before? I have much to tell you."

Once inside the dimly lit inn, their presence, as before, drew much attention. The owner quickly came to them.

Emma said, "We want a table to have a private conversation. Bring us wine."

They were quickly escorted to a corner table and the proprietor placed two cups of wine on their table. Emma handed him some silver coins in payment as her guard moved to stand by the door.

When he left, Emma lowered her voice and leaned close. "Do you remember when you told me how to hear conversations of my brothers, counselors, and their visitors?"

Nichol nodded.

With a grin, Emma leaned in further and softly added, "I found out that my brother, Duke Richard, owns this inn. There are many ears in it." Her expression and tone then changed to one of longing. "I thought I would never see you again and I miss seeing Lucette."

"I've missed you, too, Emma. Lucette is in a safe place. I had a strong feeling that I had to come back to see you before you left for England."

Nichol took a deep breath and lowered her volume to match Emma's. "Emma, have you heard anything about me? When I return to Rouen to stay for a longer time and you are no longer here, will my family or me be in danger?"

"I do not know, but you were right about the priest Loupe. I think he is a bad person. I overheard my brothers talking about him, and their conversation confirmed the story you told me. My view of my brothers and my position has changed. I realized that I am only used for their convenience.

"Nichol, I fear for both of us and your Lucette. If you return, do not trust them—any of them. You are older than I am and have experienced much. I sensed it when we used the stone between us. You are stronger than me, and what you and Shadow did to the priest and his protector gave me the courage to speak out to you.

"Loupe is a coward. My brothers are the ones to be feared, for there is no power greater than what they have here in Normandy. They know who you are, and they also know the merchant, Ezra. I overheard his name when the two were talking. Nothing happens in Rouen without their knowledge. If you are generous with them, they may leave you alone. Work with them, but do not fully trust them or their words.

"My brother Richard used to protect me from William when I was little. William would hit me if Richard were not nearby. I am always hopeful that now that Richard is the duke of Normandy, he will still watch over his little sister, who will soon be the queen of another country. I heard Richard say England needed his support to hold back the raids from the north. The marriage they planned for me was to create an alliance.

"When I become queen, I believe he will need my support, possibly more than what my brothers were talking about, and maybe your help as well."

Nichol reached beneath her tunic and removed the amulet. Emma extended her hand, waiting to receive it. As she did before, Nichol pressed the amulet into Emma's hand and then placed her hand on top of her friend's.

Thoughts, not words, were exchanged between the two friends … friends who had become allies.

Nichol lifted her hand and Emma murmured, "You are with child. Lucette is to have a sister. When your daughter Athena is born and you can travel, you must come to England. Who is the young boy?"

"I would like that. Aiden is their brother. Robert and I raised him as our own son since his birth when his mother could not.

He is of the same age as Lucette. With what you have told me of Richard protecting you from William, I believe Aiden will do the same for his sisters."

Over their wine, they talked and laughed as only true friends can.

Suddenly, Emma stiffened and motioned with her head, saying, "My protector is getting restless. He keeps looking my way as if to say *it is time to go*."

Emma rose from her seat and Nichol quickly followed. As the two moved toward the door, Emma said over her shoulder, "The merchants have displays. Let us walk and enjoy them so we can continue our conversation."

Reaching the entrance, the guard opened the door. As Emma passed by him, she said, "We will walk in the streets to look at the shops and stalls."

As Emma and Nichol spoke, Emma's brother William came into view—the archbishop of Rouen. He was dressed in his regalia; long, flowing white robes informing all who saw him of his wealth and high ranking. An ornate cross hung mid-level on his chest from a thick gold chain. His fingers bore several rings, some with glistening gems.

Nichol thought, *what a fool he was to appear in public like this*. His rich garb was in sharp contrast to the rags worn by the men and women in the marketplace. She could see by his gaze that he dismissed the peasants and merchants as unworthy of his notice.

First, Emma showed the respect required in public as she curtsied.

Saying "Your Excellency," Nichol then bent down and kissed the ring on his index finger, which she identified quickly as his signet ring, used when he sealed documents in wax. After kissing the ring, she studied its design more carefully.

Upon examining the ring, Nichol thought, *Robert could make this.*

She lingered a little too long for the archbishop's liking. Frowning, he pulled his hand back, away from her.

Nichol glanced up with a flirtatious smile. "The ring's beauty enhances your masculine hands, Your Excellency."

Quickly, his frown disappeared as the archbishop looked at her. "Do I know you?" he asked.

"We have never met, Your Excellency."

"Very well. I will see you at mass this Sunday." With a swish of his robes, he turned and left.

The two women watched his back as the distance between them lengthened.

Nichol turned to Emma, who began to laugh. "You played him well, my friend."

Slowly, they strolled and chatted as they passed the stalls of the merchants. While not in a hurry, they both knew that it might be a long time before they could be together again.

Eventually, their conversation ceased and their pace slowed. Nichol looked at Emma, who appeared to be in deep thought, staring into the distance. "What are you thinking?" she asked.

Emma revealed, "Now that I have met you, the thought of marriage brings me sadness. I have you as a friend, and now I must travel across the sea to marry a man not of my choosing— a man I don't know. To a place where I know of no one."

Staring into the distance, she continued, "I wish we had grown up together. I feel so alone. I was always close to my brother Richard, but now I know that he and William see me as an object; someone to maintain their power and bred like cattle to provide male heirs that they will have a strong influence over.

"I have accepted my role, but now, not so willingly as I did. Not one time have they asked me what I want; they only tell me what I must do."

As Nichol took her hand, they stopped and turned toward each other.

"I will come to England and bring Robert and our children, I promise. You will see then how he treats me and them. Perhaps your king will be inspired."

Eventually, it was time for them to separate. They embraced, and tears flowed. Each had found a close sisterly bond they had never experienced and their parting was fraught with pain.

Emma looked around. "Richard has many of his men-in-arms positioned on the streets today. I do not know why. We must always be careful."

Those were her last words as the two turned and traveled in opposite directions.

forty-two

Shadow and the Hawk

We are protected.

Nichol and Shadow slowly walked toward Ezra's house, preoccupied with her fond thoughts of Emma, and saddened by their short time together. Shadow, always alert when on the streets of Rouen, sensed her calm and walked easily at her side.

Without notice, Nichol was suddenly surrounded by guards wearing the gold lion emblem of the duke of Normandy.

One guard spoke, his tone harsh. "The duke wishes to speak with you. Control your wolf, or we will slit its throat."

Alarmed, Nichol gave Shadow a command to obey and not to attack.

The guard who spoke grasped Nichol by her arm as the others tightened their presence, forming a circle around her. Others in the streets moved away, giving the group room as they moved toward the duke's castle.

Suddenly, a hawk swooped down, shrieking while sinking its talons into the guard's shoulder close to his neck. Instantly, the man released his grasp of Nichol's arm, screaming in pain. Startled, the other guards stopped moving, stepping away from her.

Maintaining her calm demeanor, Nichol tapped the top of Shadow's ear. Softly, she whispered, "We are protected."

The hawk soared to the rooftop close by. Upon landing, it shrieked once more. Nichol glanced up. A soft light surrounded Nichol at the same time—a light no one else saw.

Thank you, Papa.

The guard cupped his hand on his shoulder. Blood was running down his upper arm and back, staining his clothing. In obvious pain, he motioned the others to resume their escort around Nichol and her wolf dog.

"Move to the hall. The duke awaits us."

Emma's brother.

Led directly into the great hall, Nichol and one of the guards awaited the duke's arrival. As she waited, Nichol scanned the hall, looking for an escape route. Unfortunately, the only door was guarded and the windows were too high to reach.

Suddenly, the door opened, and an entourage began to arrive. The first to appear was the duke's marshal, followed by an adviser carrying a staff. Both took positions on opposite sides of the duke's throne. They were followed by a priest and a monk.

What could they want? Is it about my visits with Emma? Could it be about Loupe and the attack?

The duke finally entered the room. Moving briskly, the duke did not acknowledge her as he moved past Nichol and the two guards by her side. Ascending the five stairs up the dais to his throne, the duke seated himself. Placing his arms on the armrests, he glared intensely at Nichol and snapped, "Bring in her accuser!"

From behind her, Nichol heard the footsteps of two more people as they entered the hall. The steps drew closer and finally ceased.

Nichol stiffened, showing no expression as she struggled to maintain her outward show of courage. Dread filled her heart. *You must maintain control, Nichol. Be on alert.*

Standing ten paces away was Loupe.

Beside him was the half-brother she despised—Fredric.

Their grins of triumph were too much.

Her body felt numb. *I fought my way to Paris, then to Rouen, and now I am cornered. I am four long steps from thrusting my dagger into the duke's heart if I must, to protect myself.*

Duke Richard turned to his marshal and commanded him to state Nichol's charges: assault on a priest and the killing of his protector. As the marshal began, the duke closely watched Nichol's response as she turned to face Loupe and Fredric, standing closely together. Her defiance was evident.

When the marshal finished reading the charges, the duke looked down at Nichol and Shadow.

He then turned to Loupe and without a word, glared at him.

The grin on Loupe's face vanished, replaced by confusion and then outright fear. Leaning forward, the duke commanded the priest, "Tell me the reason you confronted this woman."

Loupe tried to find words, but he had none.

Silence filled the room.

A spark grew in Nichol. *Loupe is acting like a coward.*

Leaning back in the throne, the duke turned to Nichol. "I will fine you one hundred silver coins for the attack on the priest. Your dog must be put to death for killing the priest's protector."

"Your Grace, my dog acted to protect me. He does not randomly attack unless I am threatened, and I can prove it. Order Loupe to stand in front of me."

Loupe did not move until the duke ordered him.

"My dog Shadow can sense the priest's anger and hatred of me. But as you can see, she is calm. Now, have one of your guards give the priest a knife."

"She carries a hidden dagger … I have seen it!" Loupe shouted.

The duke's thick eyebrows furrowed, his patience waning. "Give the priest your dagger."

Nichol removed her golden, bejeweled dagger from its sheath under her tunic.

"I gave it to him before the attack. He demanded it," Nichol added.

"Guard, bring the dagger to me and give him your knife." The duke's eyes never left the dagger as it was brought to him.

Complete silence again filled the hall; not a soul moved. All eyes were on Nichol and Loupe as a guard gave Loupe his knife. Beads of sweat could be seen on the priest's forehead.

Still Shadow did nothing, alert and waiting by Nichol's side.

Nichol said, "Point the knife at me" in a strong voice to Loupe as she moved toward him.

Loupe did nothing. The coward feared what would happen next … afraid of what Shadow would do to him.

Nichol could sense anger filling the air. Not directed at her, it was focused on the weakling Loupe, and it was emanating from the duke, who then shouted, "Point the knife at her, priest!"

Nichol looked into Loupe's eyes, knowing he wanted to bury the knife deep into her gut.

Finally, Loupe grabbed her cloak and stabbed the knife toward her with an evil smile.

With all her fury, Shadow lunged and latched on to Loupe's knife-wielding wrist. The dog began to shake her head, tearing flesh from the priest's wrist down to the bone.

"You are a stupid fool," Nichol whispered to him. She had outsmarted and humiliated him once again.

Loupe cried out in anger and pain, attempting to shake Shadow off his wrist, hitting her head repeatedly with his other fist. Shadow didn't let go. The dog's growls and utter determination told Nichol she was ready to take Loupe to the ground and destroy him.

"Stop, Shadow."

Obeying her mistress, Shadow immediately let go of Loupe's wrist and sat by her side quietly. Stunned silence filled the hall, broken by the pain-filled whimpering of Loupe.

The soft light suddenly appeared again, settling over the duke's throne.

The Lady, my Lady, is with us. Quickly glancing around the hall, it appeared to Nichol that she was the only one to see it.

Richard stood and stepped away from his chair. "Out of the hall! Everyone leaves, NOW!" he barked and then pointed at her. "Nichol, you will stay."

She could feel a power surging within herself that she had never felt before, almost as if the Lady's light was weaving throughout her body. Tapping Shadow's ear, she crouched down and whispered, "We are one. I will tap your ear again if I need you to protect me."

Confusion from his advisers and guards, and fear from Loupe and Fredric were apparent. The marshal muttered, "What has come over him ..." as he stomped toward the door.

When the last person left, the guard turned and closed the door, leaving Nichol with just the duke.

The duke turned to the wall on his left. "You can come in now."

Nichol was stunned.

What was happening?

forty-three

I Saw You ... I See You

You will then know who not to trust.

A secret panel opened close to the duke's throne. Emma walked in, with an ear-to-ear smile, moving toward Nichol. Nichol was surprised to see her friend, and both embraced.

"Remember when you told me to listen to conversations? I found a way to listen and see into the hall. I overheard private conversations that were important to my brothers and told them," Emma explained.

With an extended hand, Duke Richard gestured toward a small table at the side of the hall. "Sit down. We three need to talk," he said as he placed the dagger on the table in front of Nichol.

Nichol sat with Shadow between the Duke and her. "Do not worry, Your Grace. Shadow only bites bad people." As she spoke, Nichol once again saw the light over his head.

Shaking his head, Richard laughed and reached down and scratched behind Shadow's ear. "Your humiliation of Loupe was only exceeded by your wolf dog. Shadow is an appropriate name for a loyal protector.

"Nichol, you have shamed Loupe in front of the guards and my advisers. He will not soon forget. Because of that, he is a significant danger to you. I will talk to the archbishop about his bringing false charges to me. He knows of Loupe's reputation and lies. I do not expect he will receive more than a reprimand." The duke sighed. "Apparently, the archbishop finds him useful, along with Fredric.

"Emma and I have spoken about you. She explained what had happened and why Shadow had attacked Loupe. To bring you before me to resolve this, I could not appear biased, and I enjoyed watching you and Shadow expose Loupe's villainy." He waved his hand dismissively.

"Do not pay the one hundred silver coins. Before Emma leaves, we must have another conversation. I believe you could be an emissary between Emma and me once she is in England."

Nichol's eyes went from the duke to Emma. *She is in disbelief at what he is saying. I will ask her in private what her true thoughts are.*

Duke Richard continued, "I also wish to know what you said when you and I looked at each other when you left after visiting Emma. Your lips were moving, but I could not hear the words."

Nichol calmly said, "The first time I saw you, you were in the window of this castle. I said *I see you.*"

"What does that mean … I see you?"

"I saw you as a just man, and when I say *I see you* to someone, I know if they are good, bad, trustworthy, or an outlaw. Loupe and Fredric are bad, untrustworthy outlaws and murderers."

"What did you see in the people today in this room? I am interested in how you see others." The duke was intrigued by Nichol's words.

Taking a deep breath, Nichol said, "Loupe revealed himself to all today. My brother Fredric sold me to two friends to be raped for a cup of ale. My father, Alexander, stopped them from hurting me and they paid the ultimate price."

Nichol dropped her head and then resumed gazing at the duke. "Your adviser, the one with the staff, is not trustworthy. He is a good person, but someone in his position should not gossip and tell tales that are incomplete."

Richard leaned back in his chair, a slight look of relief on his face. "I have been concerned that my private conversations were being revealed, and now you have told me who it is."

"I have a suggestion for you that can protect you and you can use to your advantage. When it will benefit you, tell someone, including an enemy, what you want them to think and he will pass on that information. Do this by giving them wrong or misleading words. See what comes back to you. If it is wrong or misleading, you will then know who not to trust."

Nodding his head, he smiled and turned to Emma. "You two will stay connected. I will make sure that will happen."

The duke slapped his hands on the table and abruptly got to his feet. "We will talk later."

He walked to the end of the hall and turned back to Nichol. "I am now aware of Fredric and Loupe's intent to cause you harm and how my brother uses them. I will tell William that it must stop.

"I must know where your dagger came from and how you came into its possession. There must be a story with it. Am I to learn if it is good or bad?"

He then spun around and walked out the door.

forty-four

The Turnabout

*They had created a code between the two ...
code that could be communicated silently as well as with words.*

Once the duke had left, Nichol turned to Emma. "Your brother, Emma, did you expect him to act and speak as he did? To let me go and not punish me?"

"Not at first. But I saw a soft light around you, and I knew that you were safe. Then, when you were taken to the great hall, I slipped behind a long tapestry where I had created an opening, like what you told me you did in your papa's solar. Once there, I could hear and see. And I saw a soft light around Richard, similar to yours. I knew you would come to no harm."

"Do you know why the duke would focus on the priest and not so much on me?"

Speaking more softly, Emma took her friend's arm and leaned into her.

Shadow immediately sensed Nichol's shift and felt the gentle tap on her ear. She heard Nichol say, "All is well." Shadow relaxed by her side but continued to monitor those in the street.

"Richard is aware that the priest is not a good man. I overheard a conversation between my brothers, listening in secret as you advised me. When I was peering through the cut I made in the tapestry, Richard and William were talking about Loupe. Richard told him that the priest had murdered his brother for his wealth, and that he was torturing villagers and stealing what he could. Then he said, 'If it were up to me, I would have dealt with him, destroying his power.

"'You are the archbishop, William. It is your responsibility to deal with those who violate and break their vows—those who cause harm. Stop him before he does great harm to the church … and to you.' That's when I knew that the duke was the brother who would help protect me … and now you."

Emma swallowed. "Nichol … I will leave for England in less than a week. Could you stay in Rouen for a few more days?"

Nodding her head, all Nichol could say was, "I will be here."

The two women gazed at each other fondly. Emma and Nichol knew they would be allies for the rest of their lives. They were released from female bondage restrictions normal for other women. They felt the soft light flow through their veins.

Nichol and Emma parted in good spirits, promising to meet the next day. Both realized they had to choose their words wisely, just as women have learned to temper their actions. but their thoughts were nonstop.

They could now talk in ways they could not just the day before. They had created a code between the two … code that could be communicated silently as well as with words using their eyes, facial expressions, and hands. As time evolved, they would be able to sense each other's thoughts.

On her way back to Ezra's, Nichol's thoughts ranged from Harmonie to the merchant business and having the children and Robert with her as she headed to the inn.

She woke from her thoughts only to find she was standing in front of the inn door, not Ezra's home.

Kneeling, she whispered in Shadow's ear, "You are my protector," and then looked up, "Thank you, my Lady." Seeing the hawk perched at the top of the roofline, she added a final *thank you* to her papa.

Nichol entered the inn and saw Ezra, John, and Roger sitting at a table. She approached the table and in the dim candlelight, they all saw her broad smile. "I have much to tell you, but first, I need to eat."

John stood and brought her a stool as Ezra made a wry comment. "Your joy tells me we will not have to run for our lives tonight."

Roger shared the bread and poured her ale.

"This is the first food I have had all day," were Nichol's muffled words coming from a mouth full of bread. Washing it down with ale, she placed her cup on the table and motioned for them to lean into each other.

"Earlier today I was brought before the duke and charged with attacking the priest and killing his protector. Fredric was there," she revealed with pleasure.

Alarmed with her words, Ezra said, "You are pleased about him being there?"

"Yes, now I know that he is in Rouen. Where Loupe is, so will be Fredric. They are bonded together by their evil ways. We must all go to your home for a private conversation. I have much to tell you."

"Let us stop talking here. This conversation needs to be out of the ears of others." With that, the four rose and moved out of the inn and swiftly to Ezra's home, with Nichol's words, *I have much to tell you,* racing through their minds.

Ezra unlocked the door and went to the kitchen. "Roger, secure the door. John, we will need more wine and food for Nichol's story. I will light more candles."

The kitchen was cold as the fire went out a long time ago. The anticipation of Nichol's story was their only thought as they huddled around the table and chairs Helene had added.

Nichol did not disappoint them.

"I went to the market and waited, hoping Emma would arrive. I was about to leave when Shadow felt her presence. We went to the inn and had a lovely conversation. I told her she was the sister I never had and now that she is leaving, I will miss her terribly.

"When the time had come for us to part, she walked me to a point where we went in opposite directions. Shadow and I were slowly walking when suddenly, we were surrounded by the duke's guards. They took Shadow and me to the castle's great hall. Within moments of my arrival, I am told that I am to be charged for the attack on Loupe and his protector. And that Shadow was to be killed for defending me."

The men were silently listening, spellbound by her tale. Nichol's eyes darted back and forth in the candlelight as if spirits were dancing, holding the small group together. Each was captivated by the power in her words and actions.

When she finished relating the private conversation with the duke and Emma after Loupe and Fredric were dismissed, only then did the three men at the table take a deep breath. John's and Nichol's eyes met and his wink was given, his silent salute from one warrior to another.

Ezra looked at Nichol with the pride of a father to his daughter. "You and the Lady have captivated and charmed the duke. We will not fail you and this gift to our families. But make no mistake, old loyalties do not turn overnight. Nichol, you must build his trust and confidence. Be patient. At first, he will question your judgment, but as time goes by, he will learn to respect your advice. You will bring out the best in him. Remember not to lecture him; you are only his adviser. Talk *to* him, not *at* him."

"Within a week, Emma will sail to England with favorable wind and tide. I will see Emma at the castle tomorrow. I am sure that when the duke learns of my presence, he will ask to see me. At the end of the five days, I will know if we can live here or only in Harmonie.

"Emma and I have a special code of communication. We will be using it for us ... and for you."

forty-five

The Table Between Us

You will leave only when I tell you to leave.

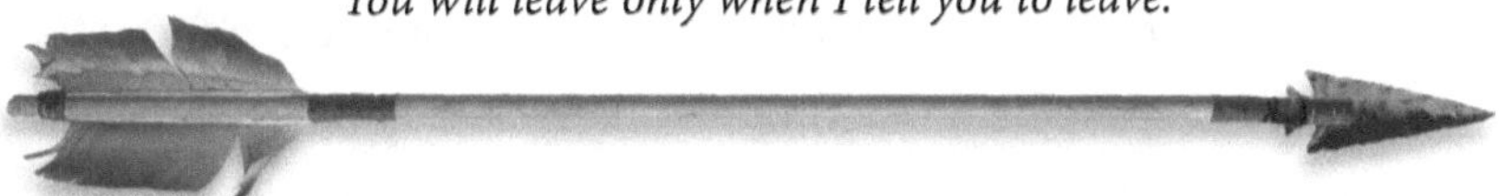

Nichol woke in a cold, dark room. Shivering and unaware of the time, she moved closer to Shadow, pulling her cloak over her head for added warmth. With just a hole to breathe through, she closed her eyes with thoughts cascading through her now-awake and active mind.

My once-private conversations with Emma may have been shared with her brother. How much of my past does he know and how much should I reveal? I must remember … Papa never gave his private information to those in the solar, only confiding his private life to his most trusted friends and allies. Ezra was the one that he trusted the most. I now have many chosen friends and a family I must protect. Ughh … what is that odor?

Throwing the cloak off, she realized the odor was herself.

I must bathe and put on clean clothes.

Ezra was in the kitchen starting a fire as Nichol descended the stairs. "Did you sleep well?" he asked.

"I had strange dreams."

"Either we had guests I did not know of last night, or you were talking loudly in your sleep. What troubles you?"

"The Lady has given me the means to make good decisions, but the choices I must make are troubling. Should I stay here and work hard to be a successful merchant as you and Papa did while trying to avoid the intrigues of the church, or go back to Harmonie and be part of helping build the village while establishing our home?" Both stopped and looked at each other while pondering her words.

Ezra broke the silence. "Nichol, I do not believe you are meant to be here all the time. We will work together. Your dream for Harmonie needs to be fulfilled when others hear about a better way of living together. It will soon be discovered and the Lady did not choose you to be hidden. Have faith in her. You are meant to be a leader and adviser to many."

Nichol approached Ezra, put both hands on his face, and kissed his bald spot, an affection he always welcomed.

Ezra sniffed and wrinkled his nose. "I will heat last night's meal if you fetch water from the well for a bath and put on clean clothes."

Nichol laughed. "I will fetch water for both of us." She had picked up two buckets just as they heard a pounding on the door. "It is Roger and John." Removing the bar from the door, they greeted their friends as they entered.

John took the buckets from her, making multiple trips as he brought enough for Nichol's bath.

After a bath and morning meal, Nichol and Shadow left for the castle after receiving fatherly advice from all three—Ezra, John, and Roger.

At the castle gate, the sentry said that Emma was expecting her. Once at the door, she knocked. This time, she and Shadow had a warm welcome. A servant was sent for Emma and soon she appeared.

Observing her friend as she approached, Nichol slightly tilted her head and saw a look on Emma's face she had not seen before. *I see her*, appearing with a glow of true pleasure and excitement.

After they embraced, Emma dismissed her maid. "We must go to the garden for our conversation." Before they sat at a bench in the middle of the garden, Emma bent down and gave Shadow a welcoming rub. With a heavy sigh, she said, "I may never see this garden in bloom again."

Nichol felt the melancholy in Emma's words. She, too, had those feelings when she left Marseilles and her loved ones. She reminded herself she was there to support her friend, not to think of sad memories.

"Emma, look at me!" she insisted. Their eyes met. "In a few short weeks, you will become queen of England, and that is your destiny. You must learn their ways and demand respect for the position given to you. Become visible to your subjects and learn the intrigues of those around you. You must see them."

Emma looked bewildered by Nichol's words. She then asked, "Where is Lucette? I hoped you would bring her."

"Without knowing where Loupe and Fredric are, the children must stay safe where they are. I cannot expose them to the danger that follows me or my family. Please ask the duke, 'Is it safe for Nichol and her family to walk the streets of Rouen?' You must listen to how he responds with both your eyes and ears."

As the two talked, their heads bent closely together, Nichol sensed a new presence in the garden. The duke had been informed of Nichol's arrival and soon arrived in the garden where the two were seated.

Nodding to Emma, he then spoke directly to Nichol. "You must come in and sit by the fire."

Emma displayed anger at her brother's intrusion. "We are having a private conversation away from my nosy servants and their constant chatter. They bore me, Richard. Why have you come for Nichol?"

Richard spoke to Nichol only. "Yes, when you are done, Nichol, come and see me. My steward will direct you." Smiling at Emma, Richard turned and walked away.

Nichol put her hand on Emma's. "Your response was strong. As a monarch, you will soon learn to make your place. Do not appear weak or without power, but always be compassionate and understanding to those you serve. If you do this, you will be respected by those in the king's court and loved by your subjects."

Nichol paused and looked into Emma's eyes, anxiously waiting for her friend's response until the silence was too long.

She continued, "You will be queen, a stranger from another land, and some will be jealous of your immediate rise to power. The ones to watch are the king's council and those who have his ear. Use your wit, Emma, for they will eventually reveal themselves. The ones who are driven by greed and a lust for power will betray themselves. They always do."

Nichol removed the stone from around her neck and placed it into Emma's waiting hand. She cupped her hand holding the stone under Emma's, and covered it with her other hand. She covered their hands with part of her cloak. They both closed their eyes.

When they opened them, Nichol saw movement from the corner of her eye.

We are being observed.

Leaning in, Nichol lowered her voice. "Emma, always be present for the council meetings and engage in the game of power. I think you will like the intrigue. And above all, always remember that you are the queen of England. When I see you again, you will be in England, and with me will be my children. You and I will remain as sisters for the rest of our lives." She smiled. "Now I think I have kept Richard waiting long enough."

With that said, they both stood and embraced. "I will return tomorrow."

After Nichol entered the castle to meet with the duke, Emma stayed in the garden, turning her face to the warm sun, relaxing in thought while avoiding her return to the smells and dampness of the castle. A smile spread on her face. *I have a sister.*

Nichol and Shadow entered the castle and were escorted to a floor above the main entrance. The male servant announced her arrival and then left.

Nichol stepped into the room and observed Richard sitting in a high-backed chair behind a thick oak table with piles of parchments covering the desk. In one corner were papers that had been bound on one side. He placed his quill on the table and looked up. "Come in and sit down."

Nichol went to the stool in front of the desk and pulled it forward with thoughts of seeing or reading the contents of the parchments on his desk. Shadow sat by her side and she commanded him with a hand motion to lie down.

The duke's chair was high with a stool for his feet. Meanwhile, Nichol's stool was low, allowing the duke to look down on her. She could not read the documents as she had hoped to.

Her gaze continued sweeping the solar. She noticed that he had no male protectors with him in the room, yet a sentry was stationed outside it. Now, she and the duke were alone in the solar, along with Shadow, her protector.

Richard sat back in his chair and observed Nichol. Internally, he marveled at her skill in controlling the wolf. He then asked, "What do you see?"

"Your Grace, I see a solar not unlike my papa's in Marseilles. Another tapestry would make the room warmer and complement your good choice of placing the table for the best use of light from the window."

Richard frowned as he leaned forward and placed both arms on the table, eyebrows narrowed—a pause and stare to intimidate. *I think he does this to most of his subjects who sit on this stool.*

Nichol did not flinch; she faced many men who tried to threaten her.

Finally, she saw a softening of his expression. With a slight grin, he asked. "Who are you?"

"I am what you see. Emma and I found each other at the market one day and she is the sister I never had—the one I always wanted. I have a family that needs me, and when Emma leaves, I will leave to return to them. I see you are busy with important work and if this conversation is over, I will leave you to it."

"You will leave only when I tell you to leave," Richard responded harshly.

Again, she was steadfast and expressionless, showing no reaction to his intimidation.

Richard, though, was speechless and deep in thought as he studied her, unaccustomed to this direct response, especially from a young woman. "Your direct responses to my questions are not what I expected. Did your papa approve of this?"

"He expected it. I did not tell him what he wanted to hear. I told him exactly what I saw and heard. Trust was important and I became his trusted eyes and ears with the many people he had to deal with as a merchant and port commander. Emma has not told me of your conversations with her. They are your words together and private, not for my ears, just as our conversations between Emma and me are—private. It is a bond between sisters."

The room went silent, mental combat with no quarter given.

Richard became agitated as he fell back into his chair, glaring at her. His face tightened and his lips pursed. "After your visit with Emma tomorrow, I want you to come here. I have need of your skills, and I expect you to answer my questions. Leave now," he snapped.

"I will promise to be here tomorrow." As Nichol stood, she added, "And Your Grace, I want to sit in a chair, not on a stool. It is important that I see the faces and expressions of others when I am speaking."

She again motioned to Shadow with her hand. The two turned together and walked toward the door that led to the castle gate.

I know he is at the window watching me. He is sending his sister to England to be married and fears that he is losing control over her. Now he needs me.

forty-six

Common Ground

Have your pride but know when to bite your tongue.

Thoughts, conversations, and plans raced through her mind. The excitement of another meeting with the duke flowed through her veins.

Tomorrow I will heed Ezra's advice and choose my words wisely. I have emerged from hiding in a niche in Papa's solar and risen to a seat in the Duke of Normandy's solar. Everything I have learned from Papa and the Lady will be useful.

With those thoughts, she and Shadow found themselves at Ezra's door. Nichol pounded on the massive oak door and announced her arrival. John lifted a small flap of leather covering a peephole in the door and winked.

Seeing him peek at her, Nichol laughed out loud.

As he opened the door, Shadow rushed past him. Nichol entered and hugged John, who was smiling from ear to ear. Ezra and Roger rose from their seats at the table, and she gave them the same welcome as she had John.

Roger poured a cup of ale as Ezra brought cheese, salted fish, and bread. Not a word was said as they watched her eat a piece of bread followed by a long drink of ale.

Ezra's impatience surfaced. "They did not offer you something to drink or eat? Your mood suggests that all went well."

"I must gain his confidence before I am invited to his table. I know I left him wondering, who is this young woman who does not show the kind of respect I am accustomed to? Tomorrow I will go to see Emma and Richard again.

"He told me he needs my skills. I know that to be successful in Rouen and Harmonie, we will need his support. I felt after our short meeting, he demands respect and, above all, loyalty.

"I suggest that when Diego's ship arrives in port, Richard and the archbishop should have the first choice of his cargo as a sign of respect.

"I will give him loyalty, and in time, I will know of his to me. Today, I did not show weakness; tomorrow, I will bow to his Grace and show my respect." A glowing smile erupted. "After he told me to return tomorrow and dismissed me, I told him I wanted a chair to sit on, not the short stool he provided me today. If he has a chair for me tomorrow, I will know he has respect for me.

"And there's more. Twice, I have seen a light appear around him when he is speaking and I am in the same space. Since then, I have felt his attitude change toward me. It was apparent after Loupe and Fredric were dismissed, and Emma joined us."

Ezra's eyes opened wide as he shook his head. "You must temper your reactions with the duke. You are a master at seeing someone's true self, so do not display yours to him. Learn his desires before you commit yours to him. Take your time and do not rush into a place of no return."

"Tomorrow will be different than today; I will do what you say, Ezra. Your words have always been true. Remember, you are not alone."

Nichol stood. "Tomorrow is a long and important day for all of us. I need a long night's sleep and will say good night to you all."

Where is Shadow?

Quickly going downstairs, Nichol discovers John is not at the door, and the wood beam is missing. She opens the door and steps outside. Looking down the street, a figure is standing in the shadows, watching her.

Pulling her dagger, she approaches the dark figure. Drawing closer in the gloomy darkness, she realized the shape had disappeared.

Where did he go?

Turning back to the open door she had left, she sees the mysterious image enter the house and close the door. *Lucette!* Running back to the now closed door, she hears the wood beam being slammed into its brackets just as she arrives.

Turning back to where the dark shape was, she sees another man in a hood, a man she knows well.

Loupe.

He brandishes a sword held high above his head, within striking distance.

Nichol freezes, unable to move, barely able to breathe.

Something was wet on her face. *Was it blood?*

Jerking awake, eyes wide open, startled by her vivid dream, she immediately sat up and looked around her room. Shadow was licking the sweat off her face.

Nichol put her arm around her pet. "I must put an end to them, Shadow … and soon."

Carrying a lit candle, she went downstairs, stepping over John and Roger sleeping on the floor. She found a pitcher and filled a pan with water.

Returning to her room, she bathed and dressed. Her dress today was befitting for what she believed an adviser to the duke would wear: an ankle-length dress of deep blue. A blue wimple head covering was added.

She returned to the kitchen. All three men had watched her descend the stairs. Their stares and broad smiles signified their approval. John approached, bowed, and put his hand out for hers. Nichol extended hers and John received it with a gentle kiss. "You will have their complete attention. May Roger and I escort you to the castle?"

"Yes, you may, for a lady should not travel without protectors. I will take my dagger. It has served me well and I do not want to be without it. I feel it was destined to be mine and one day Lucette's."

Ezra enjoyed the lighthearted start to the day. He nodded his approval at John and Roger's devotion to Nichol.

Ezra gestured with an open hand. "Nichol, come sit down and eat. We must talk before you visit Emma and Duke Richard."

Roger and John began preparing a meal as they listened to his thoughts for her. After years of lending and trading with powerful people, Ezra was familiar with the customs of the upper classes.

He added, "Do not counsel without a request for it first. Be humble in their presence. It is wise to never reveal too much at once. Hold back so that you have something to add when the timing is right and to your advantage. Have your pride but know when to bite your tongue."

Nichol clung to every word Ezra spoke, knowing his words came from a lifetime of knowledge and were more valuable than gold. They were priceless.

When advice was given to her, Nichol always judged its merit by whomever delivered it. Ezra was now the voice of her papa.

"You have given me your years of wisdom on these matters, and you know me well. I will do as you say and I will make you proud, just as I did for Papa."

The candlelight revealed a shine from his moist eyes.

Nichol put a hand on his and one over her heart. The room was silent with reverence.

forty-seven

The Acceptance

He wants more of me ... a me that he cannot and will not have.

Nichol and Shadow entered the castle courtyard and slowly made their way to the heavy wood plank door. Before knocking on the door, she took a deep breath as she lifted and dropped the metal ring, striking the metal door plate three times. Then she stood back.

A male servant answered and said, "The duke is expecting you and should not be kept waiting." As she was climbing the stairs to his solar, her heart started pounding. Arriving at an opened door, the servant announced her and stepped aside.

Nichol immediately noticed a chair opposite Richard's desk. Inwardly, she smiled. She bowed and said, "Your Grace," and straightened up.

Looking at her directly, Richard asked sarcastically, "Does this meet with your approval?"

"Yes, Your Grace."

As she moved toward the desk, he added, "Take the parchment from my table and sit down. Then read the passage on it." Shadow sat beside her.

Richard keenly watched her as she sat down, lifted the parchment, and began to read.

"1 Timothy 2:11-12 …, *Let the woman learn in silence with all subjection. But I suffer not a woman to teach, nor to usurp authority over the man, but to be in silence.*

"Your Grace, you know I can read and write. Why this passage from a letter?"

Richard's standard stoic look changed with a slight smile. "Does this letter from Paul offend you?"

"No, men think women are not their equal. Their unawareness makes it easy to listen and not be suspected of understanding men's conversations. Notice that I am wearing a pale blue tunic, a color that does not attract attention. To most men, I would be invisible in their midst. When I was running from Fredric, I dressed as a boy, chopped my hair short, and wore peasant clothes."

"How do you know these things and where did you learn to read and write?"

"I have learned to observe since I was a young girl. My papa encouraged it and instructed our steward and my tutor, Margaux, to teach me how to read and write. She had been trained in a convent. My mother wanted nothing to do with me and deemed me worthless. Papa and Margaux did not. The only thing that mattered to my mother was her son Fredric, my half-brother. You have already met him."

Silence filled the room. Richard then stood and pushed his chair back. "We have much to discuss, but now I am thirsty. We will go to my inn. I will have Emma join us. I hear you both have been seen meeting there."

As they left, a guard led in front, another at his side, and one trailed behind. Emma and Nichol were on the duke's right side, with Emma close to him. All wore cloaks and walked briskly to ward off the late morning chill in the damp air.

Upon arrival, the lead man entered the inn as the three waited at the door. He returned with a nod, signifying it was safe for the duke to enter.

Emma and Nichol stepped forward to enter the inn when a man on the street rapidly approached the duke. A guard stepped forward to protect Richard.

Richard noted the man's identity as he drew near, and he gestured to the guard to let him pass.

"Willem, what troubles you today?"

Bowing, Willem said, "Your Grace, there is trouble at the wharf. A group threatens the peace of the marketplace and the merchants. I need your advice. Can we talk in private?"

Speaking to the guard, Richard said, "Have wine ready and a place for me at the fire." Turning to Emma, he said, "Go with him. Nichol and Shadow can stay with me while my protector is with you."

Richard returned a knowing half-smile as Nichol knelt, tapped Shadow's ear, and petted her. Looking up at Willem's expressions, she focused on his face and how he used his hands.

At first, Willem appeared hesitant to say anything with her there. Richard became impatient and his displeasure was evident. "Out with your story, Willem! She is a woman and does not understand or care about these matters."

Willem began a story of bribery, theft, and violence at the wharf, leaving out the names of the perpetrators. He paused several times to see the duke's reaction. When he was done relating his tale of activities, Richard quickly waved him away.

"Your information is most important and I will find these men and punish them. Now I am wanted inside."

Willem's shoulders slumped. Nodding, with a look of defeat, he turned and walked away.

Richard and Nichol entered the inn and were given wine and a bench by the fire. With Emma at Nichol's side, Richard sat down beside Nichol, surprised that Shadow sat next to him. Nichol signaled to her to lie down.

Richard ordered the innkeeper to bring food and a bone for Shadow.

Looking at Nichol, he asked, "Now, who do you see Willem as?"

After a moment of thought, Nichol spoke. "He became troubled when you were annoyed by his presence and said, 'Out with your story.' He did not want to be seen at your castle and followed you here. Willem is a weak man and I believe him to be part of the gang, but not by choice. Now he is afraid of them and their growing power. He is desperate for himself and because of that, he turned to you. You can use him to confirm your other sources' stories. If he is found out to have spoken to you, he will end up floating in the river."

Richard's eyes narrowed. "You are right. I have subjects near the harbor that have come to me with the same story. Some theft and violence are tolerated, but it has increased lately. The thieves are growing too powerful. You know this just by listening to him? By observing him?"

"Ezra and I have been to the harbor and know Willem's words are true. He confirmed what we had observed. He came to you for help and protection, but you gave him nothing in return for his information."

Richard paused in thought, then took a long drink of his wine.

Nichol looked affectionately at Emma as she reached out under the table and squeezed Emma's hand. She squeezed back.

Richard put his cup down. "For now, let us enjoy our wine and food and we will talk later in private. There are too many ears and eyes about."

Nichol stared at the fire as they all ate. Now, her thoughts were with Robert, Helene, and the children. *How can I be in Harmonie and serve the demands of the duke? But I am intrigued about what comes next ….*

Leaving the inn, they walked until they had to part ways.

Nichol promised Emma that she would return in the morning and then turned to Richard to bid him farewell. She noticed he had a different look on his face, one that she had seen before on other men.

The Opening

There is much to tell of my meetings with Richard.

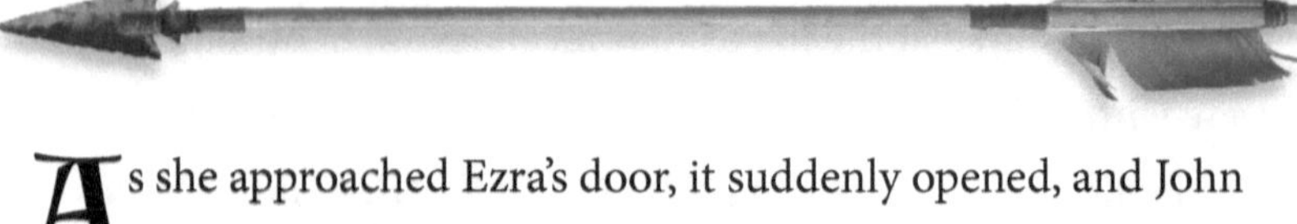

As she approached Ezra's door, it suddenly opened, and John almost pulled her in. He shut it after Shadow followed Nichol through the doorway. Ezra sat at the table with his ale. Cheeses and fresh bread from the bakery were arrayed on a plate, ready to eat.

Nichol removed her cloak and hung it on the empty peg on the wall next to the door.

Her eyes took in the room filled with men. The table had become the focal point. They ate there. They planned there. All decisions were made there.

As she moved toward it, John pulled a chair away from it for her to sit.

"Sit, Nichol. We are all anxious to hear what happened at your meeting with the duke." As Ezra spoke, Roger joined them.

Surprisingly, John went to a pot that held hot water. A goblet containing Helene's herbs was filled with water and placed in front of Nichol.

Looking at the goblet, and then at the faces around the table, she saw grins appearing.

"I know … we know … you are with child again, Nichol." They all spoke at once.

"How did you know?" She was astonished.

"I remember that glow you had with Lucette. And now I know why Helene gave you the special herbs for your tea when you were tired. John has made a tea for you with them."

Nichol smiled. "Ezra … did you know when Lucette sees Helene, her word for her is *Mamatoo*. And then she laughs. She says *Papa* when Robert is with her, and she can say *Timo* as well. I think you might be her *Papatoo*. What do you think?"

Ezra was delighted with his new name. "When will the new baby come?"

"It will be many months … in the late summer. Her name will be Athena and she will be born at the small lake within Harmonie."

The three men were surprised and yet not surprised with her response.

How did she know this? Did the Lady tell her she would have a daughter … or is Nichol revealing new gifts she has?

Becoming serious, Nichol said, "There is much to tell of my meetings with Richard. I believe that he can be valuable to E & N and all of us. Today, he asked me to read a letter from Paul, 1 Timothy 2:11–12. He was surprised that I could read. He is also aware that I read people as I observe them. Then he asked Emma and I to go with him to the inn for food and drink.

"As we approached the entry, one of the workers at the wharf asked to speak to him. He told him a tale of recurring bribery, theft, and violence and was seeking help to stop it. Richard said he would handle it. After the man left, Richard asked me, 'Now, who do you see Willem as?' And I told him. His response to me was, 'You know this just by listening to him? By observing him?'"

Ezra, John, and Roger nodded their heads as she spoke.

"Nichol, you are gaining his confidence. The duke could be helpful to our business and our safety in Rouen," Ezra said with conviction. "What about Loupe and your brother? Are they a danger to you and us?"

John and Roger listened intently to this conversation, knowing their paths would be set by the outcome of what happened around this table.

Nichol groaned. "Emma also told me that she overheard the archbishop tell the duke that he would not discipline Loupe. He has become the perfect messenger; his reputation precedes him. When he hands letters to other members of the clergy, they understand the letters' importance before opening, as the recipients know the letters are from the archbishop. I wish they would send him to another diocese, one located far from Rouen. I am tired of looking over my shoulder."

Nichol looked at John. His bushy eyebrows dropped, and his teeth clenched at the mere mention of Fredric and Loupe. He said, "If the duke and archbishop will not deal with them, there are other way for us to deal with them. The pleasure will be mine."

Roger was the quiet one and listened with a sly smile of pleasure. His words were usually few, but when spoken, they carried meaning. "When you and John return to Harmonie, I will find Fredric and Loupe and send them to hell, where they belong."

Heads nodded in agreement as they watched and listened to Roger.

The four were quiet for a few minutes, hands holding their goblets, mulling over the words that had now been spoken, each deep in their own thoughts.

Nichol straightened in her chair. Leaning forward, she said, "I have been thinking we need our own system of messengers … for here and for Harmonie."

Ezra sensed her concern and meaning. "I will send for Joshua. He has always done this service for me. He will stay with me here in Rouen and move about when needed."

And then Nichol spoke again. "I know the perfect person in Harmonie," Nichol quickly added. "One who knows all of France. This person is smart, invisible to most others, and is loyal to us."

"Who?" the men asked in unison.

"Timo."

forty-nine

Coming Out in Rouen

I must help her. I must help others like her.

The evening's conversations had calmed her fears. Exhausted by the mental maneuverings with Richard, Nichol retired for the evening.

As she lay on her bed, the wharf, Emma, and the stirring of the little one within her beginning to make her presence known wove in and out of her thoughts.

The Lady came to her as she slept.

It is time, Nichol. Your journey is continuing, and it is time to begin to let others know of your presence and strength. You are no less than any man and your skills will grow. You will see others beyond what you now see. You are everything I saw you as a child to be. People need you to bring a new understanding of what a community is and can do together.

As the promise of morning light approached, her eyes opened. Her mind picked up where it had left off when she had closed her eyes. The Lady's visit swirled within her. Caressing her belly and the slight swell growing within her, she spoke softly to her child.

Little one … you and your sister will make the difference for many. Your brother will be a protector of you both.

I like the idea of Timo working with us as a messenger. Using his outerwear habit will create trust around him as he listens and observes as he did in Paris to warn us. His eyes and ears will help protect Harmonie. Our vines and plantings are completed. He is training those in Harmonie and No Name like he did at the monasteries. I think he would welcome other tasks.

A thin beam of light pierced the shutters with just enough light to see Shadow staring at her. Nichol jumped up and slipped an old tunic over her head to attend to her own needs.

Shadow was at the front door before she made the last step at the bottom of the stairs. Roger opened it and Shadow bolted out to relieve herself. Nichol went to the back of the house to the closet, returned to her room, and poured water into a wash basin, freshening and cleaning herself.

Choosing her blue gown that hung loosely from her shoulders, she slipped her dagger and sheath into the hidden deep pockets Helene had created for her. Her belly was beginning to swell and was hidden, along with her dagger, by the long pleats sewn into the front of the gown.

As she stepped toward the short stairway, she was pleased that she had decided to shorten all her garments to allow them to stop at her ankles. Each step made it easier to move without the hindrance of a garment touching the ground. *This is ideal as we walk in Rouen and the fields of Harmonie.*

Descending the stairs once again, John and Roger watched as she stood still at the bottom and spun around. John winked and said, "You will be unseen next to us."

Nichol looked at Roger, who was motionless in thought; his face revealed a yearning for a time and a woman that once was his.

"I see you," she said softly to her friend. Nichol approached and embraced him. "One day you will tell me about her."

Ezra was next down the stairs. His first words were, "We must be on our way. There are many people I wish Nichol to meet."

Ezra and John put on their cloaks. Both had hoods; Ezra's was fur-lined. Nichol had a cloak and a head covering that matched her gown. Shadow returned, and Nichol knelt by her side and whispered in her ear, "Protect and stay with Roger today."

She stood and pointed to Roger. Shadow slowly went to him with her head down and looked back to her mistress. Nichol went back to Shadow and hugged her, then stood. The three left for the wharf, with Nichol carrying six arrows that needed new fletching.

On their way, Nichol walked between Ezra and John. She chose to walk with the men and not behind them, which was more typical for the times.

Their destination was the wharf. Along the way, they planned to stop at merchants Ezra needed to meet with. The streets were crowded as people were going about their daily activities. Chatter could be heard from those who had gathered together.

Their first stop was Joseph's cloth shop. Nichol and Rose selected cloth to take back to Harmonie for the women to stitch new clothes. Ezra had thoughts of trade on his mind and enjoyed speaking with Joseph.

Part of Diego's cargo would be silk and linen from Italy. Nichol talked of the fashion from Marseilles with colored cloth and described silk with raised patterns of silver and gold. When they left, they shared the excitement of new markets.

The second stop was with George at the bowyer's shop. Nichol entered first.

He immediately noticed her, and raised his aging body from the stool he sat on. "Ahh, you are the woman who bought two bows and twenty arrows." And with a grin, he continued, "I see you brought arrows in need of new fletching. I hope the bows served you well?" He peered over the counter, looking at the floor. "Where is your dog or should I say wolf?"

A young man came in from the back of the store. George beckoned him over. "Nichol, this is my apprentice. He will put new fletching on your arrows."

Nichol was surprised. "I never told you my name but you remember me and my dog?"

"Only fighting men and nobles have enough coin to buy what I make and you are well-known to those people in Rouen. More than once, people have seen you with a bow I made. Now, others want that same bow; your patronage of my shop has created demand."

The apprentice looked over the arrows George had handed to him. He noticed that one arrow metal tip was loose and the tips were stained dark red. George noticed this as well.

"Nichol, I see you have had success with these arrows."

Pleased with his statement and with a half-smile, she nodded. "I have achieved great success. In a week, Ezra or his man Roger will be here for the arrows. I need more of them as well. Could I pick up more at the end of the day so I don't have to carry them with me now?"

"I will have ten arrows available for you at the end of the day. We will need several days to add the new fletchings to the ones you leave with me today."

Turning toward the door, Ezra and Nichol said at the same time, "Thank you, George," and left. The wharf was their next stop.

A breeze from the river past the fish market told Nichol they were close. When they arrived, Ezra moved immediately to each moored ship and inspected what goods were being loaded or unloaded. Nichol walked close to him and John dropped back on the lookout for possible danger.

From the corner of his eye, Ezra saw a man approach. As he turned, he recognized the man. It was Gerard, the owner of several ships and a trusted business associate. Warm greetings were exchanged between the two men as John moved away to allow for a private conversation. Nichol stood close by as they spoke. She listened as she continued to watch him and the other people at the wharf.

In the distance, she recognized Willem, talking with a group of men.

Hmm, that is a conversation I would like to hear.

A few steps away, Ezra laughed heartily. Leaning into his friend, he said, "I know. It's time for you to meet my niece, the daughter of my business partner who was murdered in Marseilles. He has taught her much about business and she is helping me. I want you to meet her and know that you can trust her just as I do if we continue working together or if anything happens to me."

Gerard raised his brow as Ezra said those words. "Anything happens to you, my friend? What harm would come to you?"

"You and I both know there is danger in what we do—dealing with pirates, and those who want what we have. We both take risks every day. Nichol has become my ears and eyes in ways that Roger and John cannot. I trust her. You should, too."

Nodding, Gerard smiled. "We all need trusted ears and eyes. I knew Alexander. If this is the daughter he trained, I trust her." He turned to greet Nichol, and they spoke for a few minutes, discussing topics of mutual interest.

Bidding goodbye to Gerard, Ezra offered Nichol his arm. "Nichol, there is much more to show you and we will have years to build our trade. In the merchant business, as you know, you are a woman in a man's world. You understand the merchant business better than most men, and it is your ability to see people that gives us an advantage over others. If your trade with men fills their purses with coin, they will accept you with open arms."

Nichol acknowledged his words by pulling their arms tightly together.

"Lately at times, you have seemed quiet and distant in your thoughts. Is it Robert and children you have been thinking of?" Nichol bowed her head and nodded.

Ezra continued, "John told me he saw a change in you and is concerned. You must return to Harmonie for the present. Come back after you have Athena and bring Helene. I miss her and will be waiting for you all."

Nichol, stunned by his words, looked into his eyes.

Suddenly, she heard a scream emanating from farther down on the wharf.

Turning, she saw a woman bound in leather straps and heavy shackles lying on the pier, holding her face. A tall, brawny man stood over her. His light-colored hair and bushy beard told her he was a Norseman.

Breaking away from Ezra, she ran toward where the woman lay and knelt by her.

She is a slave and others like her have been around me all my life, from Marseilles to Paris, and I chose not to see them. It is my shame and now I feel her pain. I must help her. I must help others like her.

Angered, the Norseman grabbed Nichol by the arm and pulled her away, tossing her down on the wooden planks of the wharf.

Showing no fear, Nichol jumped up, a hand in her pocket grasping the concealed dagger. "How much do you want for her?" she asked.

He glared at her. "She is not for sale."

Quickly, John was on him with sword out, held high. "Answer her or die."

"Twenty silver," was the grunted response.

Ezra took a quick count from his purse and threw the coins on the ground. As he did, Nichol said, "Remove her shackles and we will be on our way."

The Norseman glared at her, as if he was daring her. Slowly, he began to remove the key tied to a leather strap around his neck.

It was too slow for Nichol.

She had already pulled the dagger and the light reflected on the blade. It caught his eye as she instantly cut the leather strap and released the slave, grabbing the key at the same time. Dropping down to the woman, Nichol unlocked her shackles. "You are safe with us. I will protect you."

Men on the wharf were slowly moving toward them, but John's size and sword kept them from being overwhelmed. Slowly they backed away.

Nichol saw clearly on the men's faces that the slave was not worth dying for.

When the wharf was out of sight, they turned and picked up their pace. The slave began to stumble, so John picked her up and carried her the rest of the way to Ezra's home.

When they arrived at Ezra's home, a hawk appeared overhead. With one screech, it made its presence known and then landed on the rooftop of the closest house. As it landed, it spread its golden tail as if to announce, *I am watching.*

As they entered, Shadow rushed to see and smell the woman. "Come," Nichol said. Shadow went to her side as John placed the young woman on a chair.

Nichol removed her cloak and wrapped it around the woman's shaking body. "I will need water from the well heated and placed in the wood tub in my room. Someone, bring bread and ale."

Nichol knelt before the young woman, her head down, staring at the floor. Long hair matted with dirt was covering her face. Nichol put her hand under her chin and began to lift her head gently, but she pulled away.

Nichol could see her clenched fists on her lap. Placing her hands on the woman's, she began to hum as she did to calm Lucette and Aiden.

The house was busy with activity, fetching food, heating water, and preparing a bath.

Ezra brought a cup of ale. Nichol took the cup and encouraged the woman to open her hands and accept it. With the ale in her hands, Nichol again began to carefully remove the matted hair from her face and encouraged her to take a drink. As she lifted the cup, their eyes met.

Nichol's warm smile hid the rage building inside. The woman's face was swollen and bruised from many beatings. Nichol turned and looked at Ezra. "She has been beaten, and needs broth to soften the bread."

As she began to eat, Nichol asked her questions to see where she was from.

"She is frightened and does not want to talk. All she said was the name *Cara*. I believe that is her name. I will take her to my room and bathe her."

Roger overheard Nichol and hurried to caution her, "The water is not warm."

"I will bathe her as best as I can and put her in my bed."

Once Cara was asleep, Nichol descended the stairs and went to the table where the three were now gathered.

Roger had put bowls of stew with fish, turnips, carrots, onions, and bread to sop up the juice. Tension was in the air. There was an uneasy silence as they ate.

Roger did his best to lighten the dour mood of the foursome. "Shadow and I went to the market and stopped by the fishmonger. I bought three fish, two to make this stew. Shadow could not wait, so I gave her a fish. She carried it in her mouth with pride and tail wagging until we arrived at the door."

He added, "I left the door open, and before long, Shadow was looking for more. I gave her a fish head and she took it outside. Later, when I looked where she was lying by the door, nothing was left."

Roger's words put a smile on Nichol's face.

Then, remembering the stranger in her bed, she stopped eating. Everyone knew she was distraught over Cara and the activities at the wharf.

Putting her spoon down, she said, "At the wharf, Cara looked at me with the same blank stare that Marie had when we found her with a newborn baby. At that time, Marie could barely say a word;

all I knew was that she needed care. It was some time before we knew the rest of what happened to her.

"I fear that it is even worse for Cara. We don't know how long she has been a captive or how many beatings or rapes she's endured as a slave. She probably feels she has nothing to live for, no family, and no more tears to give. It will take a long time for her to heal, longer than Marie needed. We can help her in many ways and others like her."

Turning to Ezra, Nichol said, "When you pass by Joseph's and Rose's shop, tell them I will visit and select more cloth the next time I am in Rouen."

To all, she said, "I plan for Cara to leave with John and me after I say goodbye to Emma and have a final meeting with the duke tomorrow."

fifty

Goodbye to Emma

Be yourself and walk with your people.

As Nichol arrived at the castle's walled entry, the sentry told her, "It is good to see you and Shadow this morning. Emma and the duke are expecting you."

Nichol reached out, put her hand on the sentry's arm, and smiled as he opened the gate. Once inside, she was met at the door by Thomas, the duke's steward.

"Emma will see you in the garden; I will announce your arrival to the duke."

Nichol strolled slowly along a different path toward the garden bench. Flower and leaf buds were beginning to appear. Touching flower buds, she closed her eyes and envisioned the gardens in Marseilles in full spring and summer bloom with butterflies and bees going from flower to flower. Now, she tilted her head back, breathing the hint of a sweet-smelling fragrance from garden flowers.

A noise brought her from her enchantment.

Opening her eyes, she saw Emma emerge at the end of the path where she stood.

Emma's pace was quick and she began talking as soon as she was within four arm-lengths of Nichol. Her words flowed, tumbling over each other as she blurted them out, and Nichol heard fear in her voice.

"I am to leave in two days, and all I will have with me is my staff and I will be surrounded by strangers in a strange land. I don't want to go. I want you to be with me …."

She put her arms around Emma as her friend began to sob. Nichol had experienced this, and she knew the depth of her feelings, the fear and the stressful feeling of being alone in unknown places.

Time ceased to exist. The women were alone in their thoughts as the world around them disappeared. Nichol then slowly lifted the stone lying on her breast and the two clutched it in their hands.

Nichol whispered, "Fear not; she is with you." As their eyes met, Nichol could see Emma relax. "You are young, Emma, and you are wise. I sense that your reign and rule will be much bigger than you or your brothers ever foresaw."

"Do you think I'll find joy being queen, Nichol?"

Before she could answer, Thomas interrupted them to announce that the duke was waiting to see Nichol. Both rose to follow Thomas.

Entering the castle, Nichol turned to Emma. "It will be a long time before we see each other again. Tomorrow I will leave Rouen. My children and Robert need me, and I miss them. I promise you that I will come to England as soon as I can. With me will be Robert, Lucette, Aiden, and Athena." Hugging her friend tightly, she whispered, "We will always be sisters no matter how far apart we are."

Suddenly, a man with a disgruntled scowl on his face came storming out of the castle door, pushing Nichol and Emma aside. As he moved away, Emma revealed in a soft voice that was almost a whisper, "That is Hugh, a baron who manages one of Richard's estates and is always late with his rent. It must not have been a good meeting."

Nodding at Emma, Thomas led Nichol up the stairs to Richard's solar, stopping to announce Nichol.

The duke waved her in. Taking his appearance in and the motion of his arm, she knew that anger still filled him from the last visitor. As she entered, Nichol bowed, saying, "Your Grace."

Nothing more. Silence filled the air.

The duke's face was stern, unforgiving. "I wish you would have been here to see what you see and advise me about the baron who just left." He shook his head.

Then, the duke smiled at her. Nichol sensed that he was forcing himself to relax a bit and let his exterior guard down. "I have been so taken with estate matters that I have forgotten that Emma's time to leave for England is near. How was your time with her?"

Almost as an afterthought, he said to Shadow, "You sit, too, Shadow."

Nichol gazed at him calmly. "You heard the baron speak. What did you see?"

"See … what do you think I saw? A lying man who does not want to pay his rent." The duke's ill temper returned in a flash.

Silence.

Then Nichol asked, "What else did you see? What could be behind his nonpayment? Is he sick? Is he loose with his coin? He smelled strongly of drink.

"How was the coloring of his face when you asked for money? Did he appear calm as he responded to your questions? Did he look at the ground or at you when he spoke? Or when you spoke? What did he look at when you spoke to him? Did he meet your eyes or stare at the floor? How do you know that he was lying?"

Silence.

Richard exhaled harshly and then spoke in a softer tone, almost coaxing. "If I could see—or had someone who could guide me in how to see—I would know the answers to your questions."

"Yes. Learning how to see them, even before they speak, will reveal much about their character. It will help you to know who to trust and who to avoid. And what kind of words to use with them."

Richard's expression changed from anger to one of apprehension. He said, "You must know there is very little that happens in Rouen that I do not hear about. Yesterday, you had an altercation at the wharf. Tell me what happened there."

"Ezra, John, and I were at the wharf when I heard a woman scream. She was lying on the wharf, her hands covering her face. I ran to her. When I reached her side, her hands were shackled. By this, I knew she was a slave. I knelt next to her to see if I could help her and the man grabbed me and pulled me away from her, shoving me to the ground.

"I asked him how much he wanted for her and he said she was not for sale. John, Ezra's protector, moved to my side and pulled his sword to defend me. The Norseman saw John's sword and said, 'Twenty silver.' Ezra paid him the coins, and we left."

Nichol held her anger inside, then calmly spoke. "I know that Norsemen bring many of their captives and plunder from raids to sell here in Rouen. I do not agree with slavery, but it is accepted here, and if there is a profit to be made, it will always exist. She is a slave but did not deserve to be beaten to death on the wharf of Rouen."

"I received word this morning that the slaver is coming here to the castle. He wants his slave back and said that she is worth more than the twenty silver coins you paid him."

"I paid him the amount he asked for."

Richard was stunned by her response.

Nichol stood to face him. "Your Grace, I paid him what he asked for her, and she is my slave now. I will wait for him, and I will explain this to him."

Why is the duke involved with a Norseman slaver and hearing his grievance?

"Your Grace, I am with child, and I desire to be with my husband when our daughter arrives. With your blessing, I will return to Rouen with Robert and my children to stay with Ezra after the birth. I also told Emma that I would visit her with my family in England.

"When I return with my family to Rouen, I would like them all to be baptized. Would you arrange this with the archbishop?"

Richard nodded his head affirmatively.

Nichol continued, "Emma is anxious and feeling alone because she will be moving to a land of strangers. With your consent, after I leave you today, I would like to see her once more before I return to Ezra's home."

Surprising her, he stood as she did and came around the table. "Nichol … you have a gift. I have never experienced anyone with your understanding of how others behave. Your ability to interpret their lack of words or the true words behind what is said is beyond what I have seen. You will continue to be a guide and adviser for me. I look forward to meeting your daughters and husband, Nichol. If I need to get a message to you, I will do it through Ezra."

Emma was waiting for her outside Richard's door.

As they walked back toward the garden, Nichol said, "Emma, do you remember the first time we met in the street? After you settle in England, do the same. Be yourself and walk with your people. Once they know you, they will love you."

Nichol heard a clatter at the gate. As she looked up, she saw the man from the wharf and another well-armed man enter the compound gate and move toward the castle door. They did not see Nichol and Emma.

Nichol asked Emma to help lift her ankle-length tunic to her waist and tie it up with her rope belt.

Emma looked confused. "Why, Nichol?"

"This is a bad man, Emma. I saved a woman from certain death at the wharf yesterday, a woman he was beating. I paid him twenty silver pieces—the price he asked for—and I took her away from him. Now she belongs to me. Richard knows about it and told me he would be here today. Now, wait … soon we will know why he came."

Nichol knelt and whispered in Shadow's ear. Walking side by side, Shadow was now poised for a battle. The hair on her back bristled as they approached her adversary.

Out in the courtyard appeared the slaver and his man-in-arms. Duke Richard and his armed marshal appeared with him, but not close to him and waved to the gate guard to approach.

"The duke's concern over this was evident. When this is done, I wonder what side he will choose?" Nichol mumbled to herself.

The duke turned to where Nichol and Emma were standing. The slaver's eyes followed and turned toward Nichol. A broad smile and gleaming eyes were all that could be seen through his face covered with hair.

Nichol shouted in a thunderous voice as she walked toward him, "I see a man who beats shackled women!" Holding her hands high, she continued, "I am not shackled—try to beat me."

Laughter could be heard from those standing in the open castle doorway and windows, observing the activities in the courtyard.

His smile disappeared. The Norseman demanded in a voice all could hear, "I will take my slave back," and tossed the twenty silver coins on the ground. "There is your silver. Count it."

Now standing in front of him, still smiling, Nichol turned to those watching. "Should I give her back to be beaten and raped?"

A woman's voice shouted in response, "Never!" Nichol turned to see whose voice it was and saw Judith, the duke's wife.

Glaring at Nichol, his eyes full of rage, the Norseman said, "Then I will take you instead. One bitch is the same as another."

Nichol's smile disappeared. Her eyes narrowed and she growled as she pulled out her dagger. "You heard the woman shout *never*. I agree! I paid what you asked and she is mine!"

Shadow started a guttural growl and barred her teeth, poised to attack.

As a man, being humiliated by a lone young woman was unacceptable. He had to act.

He chose unwisely as Nichol stood defiant. With his left hand, he grabbed her by the hair and pulled her close.

Boldly, she shouted, "You stink like rotten fish," and then kneed him in his groin when the last word came out of her mouth.

Roaring with pain, he pulled out his knife. "I am going to hurt you just like I did the slave bitch," and raised his knife to her face.

Shadow latched onto his leg, ripping his flesh open to the bone. The snarls issuing from her throat were truly terrifying.

Moving swiftly, Nichol dodged his knife and drove her dagger to its hilt, under his chin, and through the back of his neck. The Norseman's eyes rolled back as he collapsed. Shadow released her grip on the slaver's leg.

Stunned by what he had just witnessed and the speed with which Nichol dispatched the slaver, his accomplice pulled out his sword and knife. He moved toward Nichol, ready to avenge his companion.

Shadow again crouched, ready to attack, and Nichol stood poised to engage, seemingly unaffected by her previous actions.

Seeing this, the accomplice hesitated.

At the same time, the gate sentry approached from behind him. With the flat of his sword, he slammed it against the accomplice's head, rendering him unconscious.

Shadow moved to her side as Nichol bent, pulling her knife from the Norseman's neck and cleaning off the blade's gore on his tunic. Blood was splattered on her face and clothes, but she made no move to wipe it away.

Anger making her voice harsh, she addressed the duke and those watching from the castle. "I am a woman. Men see women as weak. That is a mistake." With her dagger pointing to the man dead on the ground, she finished, "A deadly mistake."

Nichol's gaze sought out Emma. She knew her friend had seen, had heard. The two sets of eyes found each other.

With a slight nod, she turned toward Duke Richard and bowed her head.

Her eyes met the gate sentry's gaze and she tipped her head to her right, acknowledging him as well. As she moved to the gate, she slowed and as she passed him, she said, "Thank you."

Walking away from the castle, Shadow at her side, she veered right toward Ezra's home, walking speedily.

On her way as she often did, she was lost in deep thought.

I have been invited to dine with the royals and all the dangers associated with them. When the day comes, will the Lady save us from them?

fifty-one

The Unknown

Tomorrow, you and Cara must be ready by first light.

When she reached Ezra's house, Nichol knocked on the door and announced herself. John opened the door and Shadow rushed in as she always did.

John took one look at Nichol with blood on her face and the tunic still tied at her waist. "What happened? Are you hurt?"

"Do I look that bad? No, I am not hurt." With a smirk, she added, "I just killed that bastard."

"What bastard?"

Nichol looked at Cara and smiled. "The slaver that beat Cara and imprisoned her."

John's silence filled the small room. "Tell me what happened."

"Where are Ezra and Roger?"

"They went to the markets."

"Find them and bring them back. I will tell everything when we are all together."

"I do not want to leave you and Cara alone."

"There is no one coming for me, I promise you, not after what I just did in front of the duke and his servants and guards. Go find Ezra and Roger and bring them home. I will tell all of you together."

John buckled his sword on and left. Nichol barred the door after his departure.

Nichol went to the table and sat across from Cara, while finishing John's stew and bread. She broke off a large piece of bread that she sopped in the stew and gave it to Shadow.

Once the two women were alone, Nichol told Cara the man who hurt her was dead.

The former slave began to cry.

Nichol and Shadow huddled around her. "We will not let others harm you, Cara. You will be under our protection. I promise you." Nichol embraced her gently and Shadow nestled her head on Cara's lap.

Cara was still weak. With Nichol's help, they went upstairs to Nichol's bed and she lay down. Slowly, her eyes closed as she drifted into an exhausted sleep.

Nichol covered her and returned to the kitchen table to wait for Ezra, Roger, and John. She did not have to wait long.

After Nichol unbarred the door at their knock, Ezra was first in. Nichol put a finger to her lips and pointed her hand up. "She is asleep."

They sat around the table and the men waited with intense concern.

Ezra knew Nichol's skills enabled her to remember their conversations and their meaning. Every detail would be accounted for, especially facial expressions and gestures. Nichol did not disappoint the men at the table.

Nichol began describing her visit from the time the guard greeted her to the time she left.

When she finished her tale, all men at the table breathed a sigh of relief. Roger and John showed their joy when she described the final placement of her dagger.

All eyes fell on Ezra. With his merchant's stoic non-expression, he said, "Duke Richard could have interfered when you confronted the Norseman. And he allowed you to leave without any recourse for your action because you just defended yourself. There is an uneasy peace between the Norse raids and the slave trade and with many in Rouen. They are given safe harbor in Rouen and then sail to English waters, plundering and taking slaves, killing anyone who gets in the way.

"How they treat the slaves is none of Richard's concern because the slaves are just a different type of merchandise, like goats or sheep or wine. The same thing happens in Marseilles. Alexander didn't like it, but it was too difficult to counter the accepted norms of the trade."

As Nichol heard Ezra's words, she asked, "Do you think that's why he watched after so many of the orphaned children near the harbor? He always made sure that Rose had coin to help them."

"Knowing your papa as I did, I think so. You remember Marseilles. There was a slave trade there as well and it is no different here. I see you disapprove of what I say, but there are things that simply need to be left alone. You know that is why Emma is going to England to marry King Ethelred, to make peace and stop the raids."

"Ezra, her marriage to the King of England will not stop the raiders. There is too much profit and these men are not farmers. Why would they stop?"

Ezra sighed. "Nichol, it is not our problem. As long as there are riches to be made, there will be slavery."

"One day, when Richard and the archbishop are together, I will ask them if their merciful God condones slavery, torture, and murder. I will ask the archbishop if God has asked him to repent his sins for the slaves he owns. I have murdered only to defend myself and others, so I guess God will forgive me. He will tell me, yes, if I confess my sins. I will tell him that we can confess our sins together."

With a sly look on her face, Nichol smiled. "Of course, I will not ask them that. It would be dangerous and foolish of me. I would like to ask them if they think that God will accept them into the kingdom of heaven—and why?"

"Nichol, I share your anger but do not let it destroy you. Religion is used to control people and the only Christian I know that will be invited into heaven without confession is Timo."

"When the Lady comes to me, she does not make demands; she gives a vision. Her words support it. She brings knowledge and guidance, not hate and fear. That man's God demands you must kneel and fight with those who speak for him or against those who do not." Nichol's anger was palpable.

Ezra spoke up. "Nichol, your Lady is why we are here. You have no argument from us. We support and stand by you. Tomorrow you and Cara must be ready by first light. Roger and John will bring the horses to the warehouse and load the pack horse. You both will leave from there and go to Harmonie. I will visit the duke and see if he is concerned about what happened today. If we are in danger, John and I will follow you within the hour of my meeting with him. If not, John will catch up to you where you leave the road and enter the forest. Wait for him there."

Ezra put his hand on Nichol's. "Tell Helene that I love her and hug your family for me. You must take care of your family first. And now you will add Cara to our growing family in Harmonie.

"I have been a moneylender and merchant most of my life. If we are able to stay here, we will do well in Rouen."

Cara

That is what I must do, create a hamlet that needs no walls.

Nichol and Cara rode out of the city of Rouen through the wall's west gate. The sun was just over the horizon, promising a full day's light ahead. Shadow stayed close, even though there were few travelers on the road at this time of day.

Nichol glanced at Cara. The woman had healed from her beating, and some of her most prominent bruises had faded. She seemed to be a capable rider, telling Nichol that she was not a simple peasant. Nichol hoped to learn more about her in the next three days.

There was a slight incline ahead and before they came to the road's crest overlooking Rouen, Nichol stopped and turned to view the city.

Cara did the same, squinting with the morning light in her eyes.

Nichol saw something different about Rouen in the distance, seated at the higher advantage point. Pausing in thought, it finally came to her.

Nichol looked at Cara and pointed to Rouen. Speaking out loud, she said, "I see a river that brings life to a city with walls for protection. What do you see, Cara?"

A slight smile appeared on her still-swollen face. No words came from her mouth.

Nichol's gaze turned back to Rouen. "I see a moat rising to a rampart and parapets built to protect a city from men. Women do not lead armies against towns and cities; only men do. Cara, what happened to you demonstrates that those same walls are used to keep others enslaved."

Pausing and placing her hand above her eyes to shade from the sun, she continued, "I think our hamlet of Harmonie will not have a wall. There will be no castle or church on the hill of hope and inspiration. We will not waste time building monuments to men. Harmonie will be for everyone. That is what I must do, create a hamlet that needs no walls."

Nichol turned to Cara who seemed to understand what Nichol was saying.

"We have a long day ahead. Let's go." They turned their horses and continued as Rouen disappeared from their sight. Nichol rode in front and Cara followed.

Late in the morning, Nichol turned to see her struggling to stay on her horse. She dismounted next to her side and took her reins. They moved off the road to a shaded spot where they could not be seen from the road.

Before the horse came to a complete stop, Cara fell off.

Nichol caught her in her arms and carried her to the shade. Bringing water and food, Nichol sat beside her and lifted her into a sitting position. Lifting the waterskin to her lips, she urged the woman to drink.

"You must eat," Nichol told her as she gave her bread. Slowly, she did. Shadow lay down next to her and put her head on Cara's lap, looking up at her in sympathy. Unafraid of the wolf, she put a hand on Shadow's back and fell asleep in Nichol's arms.

She is too weak to go on. We will stay here until she is ready to travel. We both need to rest.

When Cara woke, still in Nichol's arms, she sat up and turned to Nichol. To Nichol's surprise, she spoke and thanked her.

Nichol laughed. "You know how we speak?"

Cara looked down and paused. Nichol knew that her swollen face came with a story.

Eventually, she spoke. "The village where I lived had people who spoke the north tongue and English. They came at night, and we ran from our village. Most did not escape."

Looking up at Nichol, she continued, "They took me as their slave, which was the last time I saw my family. It was this season, last year. I was taken to a land where they speak your language, where I was sold. I spent a season with a family that treated me poorly but did not beat me. The man you bought me from bought me from them. He did horrible things to me."

Nichol reached out and grasped Cara's hand.

"We did not buy you; we *freed* you. You are free to go wherever you want, when you want. I will never ask what he did to you but if someday you want to tell me, I will listen."

Cara's eyes widened in surprise. "I want to go with you."

"You will like where we are going because no one there is a slave. I must tend to the horses. If you are strong enough, we will continue to travel in the morning."

Nichol looked to Shadow staring at her. "Go hunt."

Shadow trotted off.

fifty-three

Ezra and the Duke

Destiny ... it is our destiny to be here at this moment.

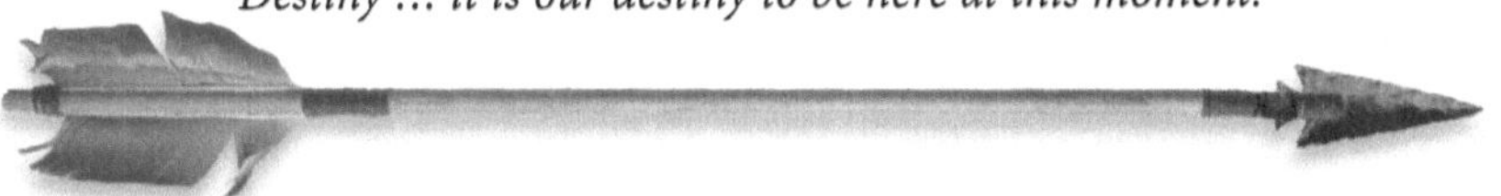

Ezra, John, and Roger watched Nichol and Cara ride away.

Ezra turned to John and Roger. "We have much to discuss when we return home from the duke's castle. Today we will find out if we have a place in Rouen or only in Harmonie. Whatever the outcome, we will take action. Either we all pick up and leave —or John immediately sets out to join Nichol and continue onto Harmonie, and I go forward to expand our merchant business."

The table was the center of many important conversations, but today, it was not for conversations. It was the unknown that weighed heavily on their minds. They were all aware that one man held their fate.

John broke the silence. Looking at Ezra, he asked, "What shall we do? What will you say to the duke?"

Ezra slapped both hands on the table and stood, pushing his chair away from the table. He walked to a shelf and brought three cups to the table. Then he slowly walked to another shelf and retrieved the wine he kept for a special occasion. He poured a full cup for each, the whole time under the bewildered and watchful eyes of John and Roger.

Roger then asked, with a sarcastic grin, "What is the special occasion ... our demise?"

Ezra answered. "Destiny … it is our destiny to be here at this moment, from Marseilles to Paris and now here. I do not want to continue without you being part of the journey—wherever it takes me. Whatever our fate, at the end of this day, we are in the Lady's hands. She brought Nichol into our lives and now we must believe there is purpose.

"Roger, you escort me to the castle gate and only I will enter. I will plead for a meeting with the duke. If I do not come out, go back, get John and leave for Harmonie. I will do my best to convince him that Nichol means no harm to him and can greatly help him."

Silently they raised their cups and finished their wine.

Ezra and Roger began their walk to the castle, with Ezra in deep thought.

I knew this day would come. I have been preparing for this my whole life. If I fail, we all fail. My biggest fear is that she will be accused of being a witch. How will I defend her from the church? Our only hope is that Richard will see her virtue.

Ezra and Roger approached the sentry at the outer wall gate. "I am Ezra, Nichol's uncle, and I would like to speak to the duke. With me is Roger, my protector. He will stay here until I come out."

The gate sentry escorted Ezra to the castle and knocked on the door. Thomas, the duke's steward, answered, and Ezra explained his reason for the visit. He was told to wait and the door was closed.

Moments later, the door opened and Ezra was escorted to the duke's solar.

Ezra bowed and said, "Your Grace," with a composure he did not feel.

Smiling, the duke surprised him with his words. "Sit in Nichol's chair and tell me about your niece. She freely talks to Emma, but

I know little of her past. In her few visits here, she has helped me on several matters."

His fears disappeared, and Ezra relaxed as he sat down. Taking in the room he was sitting in, he remembered Nichol telling him of the light that had shown above the duke in her trial with the priest. *The Lady has been here.*

Ezra began relating Nichol's story.

The duke learned of her early years in Marseilles and the love Nichol had for her papa and his love for her. Nothing was omitted: the defensive training she received at the behest of her father, Alexander, and why she had received it; the dangers she endured from her mother and half-brother; and how she became a trusted ally to him and her understanding of his merchant business.

The duke was utterly immersed in Ezra's storytelling as he told of Nichol removing the dagger from the wall before her escape to Paris because it called to her. Traveling, disguised as a boy, she defended herself with the dagger and climbed trees at night, tying herself to upper branches to be protected from men, other travelers, and, of course, from Fredric.

Ezra noticed how the duke's eyes grew bigger when the dagger was mentioned.

He needs to know the story.

Ezra explained the history of the dagger and finished with why Nichol was the rightful owner of it. If another person attempted to use the dagger, it created a bad power and would heap harm on the user. Ezra explained the dagger was not to be gifted; it sought its own rightful owner and belonged to Nichol at this time. The value was not the gold, the gems, or the perfect blade; it was the weapon's virtue in the hands of the rightful owner.

He told of Loupe and the nonexistent fortune he sought to obtain first from Astrid and later from Nichol. Ezra spoke fondly about Nichol's daughter Lucette whom Emma was so fond of. He was quick to praise Nichol's perfect memory for detail and her gift for "seeing" people that helped her papa and him.

"Nichol and I were at the wharf yesterday. Her papa was once my partner, and she is now my partner in a merchant business. When we heard the woman's cries and saw her in chains while being beaten, Nichol went to help her when no man dared to do so. She knew that you could not become involved. It became her dispute and as you saw, she completed the challenge."

Ezra ended with the most important part of Nichol. "She is pure of heart, and what you have seen is who she is. She does not live in Rouen, and this is because she does not know where Loupe and Fredric are. Both mean to do her harm, possibly to kill her if they can. She knows too much of the evil both have done to others. As you have seen, she does not fear either one but fears what they might do to her family."

The duke finally sat back in his chair, stroking his chin in reflection.

"Her valor is without question and she is more righteous than most men of the cloth. Tell Nichol that she is welcome here and I look forward to her advising me as she does you when she returns. Emma has told me she is with child again. As Nichol's uncle, you are also welcome here. Now, you and I will talk about the merchant business."

Ezra had been very open with the duke, but he left out many details in Nichol's life.

He felt it best not to say anything about the Lady and the fortune that was hers from Alexander. When that day came, that tale would be hers to tell.

fifty-four

John's Reveal

*There would be grave consequences
for a certain priest or anyone else.*

Nichol and Cara slept close together for warmth throughout the night.

Shadow returned from her hunt and lay next to Nichol. The movement brought her out of a strange dream, one that she could no longer remember.

Looking up at the stars glittering through the sparse tree canopy, she saw a shooting star as it left a streak of light across the sky. Tears filled her eyes.

I need my family. I want to lie with Robert and feel the weight of his body as he fills me with pleasure. I want to hug and kiss Lucette and Aiden, and not let them out of my sight. I want Helene and Timo back in my life. I will not be denied—not now.

Nichol woke again as the stars began to disappear, with pain shooting through her body. A soft bed was her first thought.

Cara whimpered as she woke. Nichol slowly stood and stretched, took a drink from her waterskin, and handed it to her. Then she took food from a satchel and unwrapped bread, cheese, and dried fish and they ate silently.

When finished, Nichol stood and offered her hand to Cara. The girl struggled to stand. While helping her up, Nichol noticed how weak and light she was.

"Cara … how many years are you?"

"I do not know."

"I think you may be close to my years. I will be nineteen years when my new baby is born. How many years ago did you start your courses?"

Cara looked down and, on her fingers, began to count. "I was in the field working when it started and a small church was just finished. I count this many Christmases until I was taken."

Holding up six fingers, she stopped and then continued in a halting voice. "I had a very heavy bleed two months ago after a beating that made me ill."

"Heavy bleed? I think you were with a child and lost it from the beating."

"Before that, I had a man and we were married. I remember." Then she started choking on her last words and stopped talking.

Nichol looked at Cara and spoke slowly. "I want you to tell me about all the Christmases and your husband, but now we have a full day's ride ahead. If you need to stop, let me know." Cara acknowledged Nichol's words with a nod of her head.

Nichol saddled the horses, helped her mount her horse and the two left.

I will not fail her!

By late morning, she heard horses coming up behind her. She was relieved to see John with a big smile. "Good morning, ladies," he said as he greeted them cheerfully.

"John, is it good fortune that Ezra and Roger are not with you?"

"Yes, I have much to tell you if I can remember it all."

"Begin while you have memory." Nichol smiled at her joke.

Nichol rode next to John; Cara rode behind them.

John started with, "Ezra and Roger went to the castle, and Roger stayed outside the wall as Ezra entered. He was given an audience with the duke in his solar. I do not know what it means, but he told Ezra to sit in Nichol's chair."

Nichol let out a loud laugh. "The meeting went well then."

John looked slightly confused. "The meeting went very well. What did the chair have to do with the meeting?"

"I will tell you later. Continue, John."

"When the meeting began, the duke was only interested in hearing about you. Ezra began with the story of you as a child in Marseilles and how you survived the long journey to Rouen. He did not mention what was found with your father or about the Lady. The duke was impressed with your prowess and wanted you and Ezra to visit often.

"Then they began to talk about trade, lending, and the markets in Rouen. The duke was particularly interested in Ezra's Far East trade. Then he and Ezra discussed Emma and his desire for you to visit her in England. He offered to pay for your expenses when you did visit her.

"Ezra said he believed that the duke wanted you to do for him what you did for your papa. Before Ezra left, the duke said that he would inform the archbishop that if anything happened to you or if any harm befell you, the duke would take it as a direct assault on him. There would be grave consequences for a certain priest— or anyone else. Emma had told him that you were with child. He told Ezra he looked forward to seeing you after the birth."

Patting his horse's neck, John added, "These horses need water. If I remember, there is a stream not far ahead."

Looking behind Nichol, John quickly handed the pack horse's tether to Nichol and dropped back beside Cara. He lifted her off her horse as she began to fall. He placed her in front of him with her legs on one side, his arms wrapped around her, with her head resting on his chest. Nichol and John's eyes met.

I see him. He has heartfelt sorrow for this young woman.

After a few short bends in the road, Nichol saw Shadow had stopped and looked back. Shadow then disappeared into the brush thickets. When they arrived where Shadow had left the road, they turned to follow her.

Nichol then heard the trickle of water while continuing through the tall brush. Coming to a stream, they crossed it to a place where there were plenty of trees for protection. Shadow led the way.

Nichol made a bed for Cara as John dismounted and gently lay her down. Covering her with his cloak, he said, "I will unpack and care for the horses. We may be here for a while. This girl is too weak to ride anymore today and maybe tomorrow as well."

Silently, each went about making a place to stay for as long as Cara needed rest. "Did you pack more food when you left Ezra's?" Nichol asked John softly.

"I did. Ezra sent along your favorites and made me promise not to eat them until we met up."

"My favorites? Roasted rabbit? And the cheese that Rose makes at Joseph's store?"

Grinning, all John could say was, "Yes."

The sun and clouds took their turns passing overhead. Nichol hummed a song that suddenly came to her, one that Margaux would hum while she worked in the kitchen at the villa.

She began preparing their meal with her favorites, sneaking tasting bites as she cut pieces of the rabbit with her dagger. From the corner of her eye, she saw Cara raise her head to see what she was doing.

At the same time, John saw her head move. He walked to where she lay on the ground and encouraged her to drink. "We will have food to eat soon. I want you to eat to start gaining strength."

Their eyes met. She lifted her hand to touch his, nodding her head slightly at the same time.

When night fell, they huddled by the small fire. As if in a trance, the three silently watched the flames flicker. John rose and stirred the fire with a stick, adding dried branches to keep it going.

John broke the silence. "I remember more of what Ezra told me. The duke told him that his wife Judith yelled 'Never' when you asked a question about Cara to the watchers at the castle. You asked if she should be given back to the slaver.

"Nichol, you then repeated 'Never' after the voice in the crowd said it. I would have liked to have been there. The slaver must have thought that you were just another woman he could abuse. The fool did not realize that he had already lost and would soon lose his life. Oh, to be there and see the faces of the duke, the duke's wife, and those around him as you and Shadow defeated the slaver and his protector.

"When the duke described the fight to Ezra, there was excitement in his words—both for your actions and what you did. I think he is in awe of you."

Nichol absorbed his words.

Before she said anything, John smiled. "When Shadow has pups, I would like to have one."

Cara heard them talking but couldn't comprehend all the references to the duke. She just knew that Nichol had saved her. Again, struggling to keep her eyes open, she could do so no longer. She lay down and fell into a deep sleep.

John was staring into the fire. "Who are you?" he asked as he turned to Nichol, and their eyes met.

Nichol had a puzzled look on her face and shrugged her shoulders. He pointed to his heart and asked, "Inside, who are you? We all know about the brave young woman who talks to a spirit. We know that you think of others before you think of yourself. We all have seen the outside of Nichol. But tell me who is on the inside. Will you?"

Nichol looked back into the fire.

"I have not given it much thought, John. You are the first to ask me.

"Most times, I want to go to Harmonie and never leave. I want to be a wife and a mother, but I know that I cannot be just that for me … for Robert … for my daughters and son.

"I learned that my papa had another family in Marseilles. I would like to meet with my other brother and sister and their mother. He loved them and I know I will, too. Sometimes, I want to be with Emma, destined to be the queen of England. She has become like a sister to me.

"And Timo—I taught him how to protect himself by observing how I fought to protect the two of us and Moki. Timo walked with me to Paris and he became the brother that my evil half-brother had never been.

"John, I know I have the weight of many people on my shoulders, and it is a heavy load to carry. I accept that burden. I know that there is much to come; it just has not been revealed."

John's head was nodding as she spoke, affirming her words.

Moving his eyes from the serenity of the evening and fire, he stretched his hand out to her. She took it as he said, "You forget all those who have joined you on your journey—all of us. As you give them what is expected of you, they will respond in kind. When you do this, you will become a better leader.

"You and Cara must recover from your experience. Stay in Harmonie until your daughter is born and then decide what you want to do. Your family needs you."

fifty-five

Return to Harmonie

"Come with me," she said as she took his hand
and moved toward the water.

On the afternoon of the fifth day, the trio rode into Harmonie. Nichol was excited when she first glimpsed the barn from a distance, surrounded by a field of winter wheat. Both she and John were exhausted but in good spirits. Cara sensed that they were close to their destination.

Helene was the first to see her and went to the Harmonie House to ring the bell. Three rings and a pause, then three more rings told everyone of three riders approaching.

Lucette and Aiden were at Helene's feet when Nichol spotted them. Nichol broke away from John and Cara and galloped to them, with Shadow running alongside. Pulling her horse up just short of them, she jumped off and fell to her knees.

Lucette and Aiden moved to her as fast as their little legs could carry them. Both had their arms in the air and were gleefully crying, "Mama! Mama!"

Hearing the bell, Robert came out of his shop, ran to her, and knelt as he wrapped his arms around all three of them. "I have missed you; we all have missed you!"

Shadow was not to be denied and gave a seldom heard bark for attention. Lucette and Aiden turned their attention to Shadow and reached out to her.

Robert released them and turned his attention to Nichol. They stood and kissed in a tender embrace. His lips moved to her ear and he whispered, "I was worried that something had happened to you. What would we do without you?"

That brought Nichol to tears. As he held her, he nuzzled her neck. Whispering, he said, "I feel our daughter is healthy within you."

Their eyes met, speaking a language only the two of them knew.

Standing with Timo, Helene noticed there was someone else riding with them. Catching her eye, John grinned with heartfelt joy as Helene and Timo approached him.

"I would like you two to meet Cara." Gently lifting the woman off the horse and into his arms, he held her as he spoke, not putting her down.

Helene and Timo immediately knew that she needed care.

Helene put her hand over Cara's. "Take her to my home, John. She needs food and drink and rest." John turned and started toward Helene's home. As he did, Helene turned to Timo and quietly said, "Pray for her."

Helene moved quickly to catch up with John's stride. "She can sleep in my bedchamber," Helene said as she opened the door. John entered and gently lay Cara down on Helene's bed. "Help me support her as I feed her."

She left and returned shortly with and returned with warmed stew, bread, and ale. Slowly she began to feed her, whispering, "You are safe here with us."

Nichol was now surrounded by the people of Harmonie—her people. Others from the hamlet were now walking down the road to welcome her back.

She called out to Harald and Olaf, "Would you unload the pack horse into the Harmonie House and feed and water the horses before settling them in the barn? The satchels on our horses contain the tools you requested, and some new seeds for Timo."

Looking at Tova and Gunvor, she said, "I have brought cloth, and tonight we must gather and talk of clothes to be made. Would you watch over Lucette and Aiden while I wash up?"

Lucette and Aiden were running around with Shadow.

Robert just watched all the activity and marveled at how it was normal again now that Nichol was back. The cloud that had begun to gather with concern of her delay had broken. Everyone had expected Nichol back sooner, and it was a relief to all that she was now home.

Marie was standing by herself, and Nichol went and embraced her. "What is wrong? Is it Olaf?"

"No, Olaf is good to me. What happened to that woman?" Marie looked at Nichol.

"She was hurt by a man that owned her. He will no longer harm her. I took care of that."

Marie knew what that meant. Nichol had stepped in and removed the problem forever.

"I know of her pain and I will help her." Marie stood straight, proud that she could help someone else.

Nichol embraced her. "You are brave, Marie, and you never deserved what happened to you. No woman does."

Loosening their embrace, Marie turned and went to Helene's and entered the open door.

With Robert at her side, Nichol took in the changing landscape that was revealing itself over the few weeks she had been away. *This valley will be rich with food for all of us. I have missed the river that runs through our lands.*

"Come with me," she said as she took his hand and moved toward the water. "I need to wash the smell of horses and the ride from me." She carried one of the new pieces of cloth Rose had given her days earlier.

In her hidden pocket, she removed a small package. It was a soap Emma had given to her in Rouen, one that had a pleasant odor and had been made with olive oil and herbs.

"I could join you," Robert said with a smile in his voice.

"Let's do that later when the little ones are sleeping," she murmured, kissing him softly. "Now, I just want to wash quickly and have you here with me when I do."

As they neared the water, she was already removing her outer tunic that covered her dagger. She stripped her leg wrappings off and stepped into the water with her new soap, creating lather.

Robert sucked in his breath as he watched her move quickly. He caught a glimpse of a light moving around her at the same time. *Is the Lady here, too?*

Nichol rubbed her arms and her gently swelling body with her new soap. Looking at Robert, she said with a smile, "You will love this scent when we bathe together."

As she stepped out of the stream, Robert rose and wrapped her in the new cloth she had carried. Draping her in it, he murmured, "I know I will. Would you like me to carry you back to our home?"

Laughing, she responded, "No. Let's slowly walk together, just us alone. I'll fully dress when I get to our house and then spend the afternoon with Lucette and Aiden."

That night as the sun was going down, Nichol met the women and men of the valley in Harmonie House as promised. Candles were lit, and the women gathered around the table covered by the new cloth Nichol had brought back from Rouen. Each piece of fabric was inspected and plans were made for new clothing and coverings.

Timo was delighted with the parchment that Nichol had brought back. Now he could begin to write the story of Nichol and the founding of Harmonie. The skins and leather would cover and protect many feet once shoes were fabricated.

Robert had a surprise gift for Olaf. Handing him a bow, he said, "This is now yours. You, Nichol, and Shadow can hunt and put meat in our pots."

The common house door opened and John walked in, holding Cara's hand. A stool was brought for her and placed close to the fire. By now everyone in the valley knew of her, but not all the brutality generated by her captivity. John settled her on the stool and was pleased to see others coming forward and welcoming her to the hamlet. Then he sat with her.

Those two will become one, thought Nichol.

Aiden and Lucette were running around until exhaustion took them over. As usual, all Aiden needed was to lie down to go to sleep. Nichol picked up Lucette, who snuggled in her arms. She then covered herself with a wrap and went outside. Robert followed with Aiden cuddled against his chest. Nichol heard him say "Papa," as Robert scooped him up and pulled his head to his shoulder.

A full moon shrouded the valley with the hill in plain view, beckoning them forward. Nichol hummed softly as she swayed back and forth, holding Lucette. Before falling asleep, her daughter peeked out from her covering, pointed to the hill, saying, "Mama go," and closed her eyes.

"Yes, I know, little one," Nichol said quietly as she kissed her daughter's head.

As Robert and Nichol approached their home, she noticed the extra-wide and oversized chair in front of the door. It wasn't there earlier when they went for a walk.

"Robert, where did this come from? Did Timo build this?" she asked. "It looks comfortable and different from any bench I have seen before, especially one that would be for outdoor use."

"No, I did. I'm working on some ideas that would be more comfortable for us. I asked Timo to place it here as a surprise before we headed to the Harmony House this evening. Come sit with me and tell me what you think."

Each one holding a child, they settled into Robert's extra-wide big chair.

Nichol immediately noticed that her arm felt more comfortable with the side support Robert had added. She liked that she could lean her head back and have something to rest it against.

Closing her eyes, she said softly, "Robert, I like this. I like the size. More than two of us can sit together and not feel squashed. I like that I can rest my head and my arm as well. Even Papa didn't have a big chair like this in our manor."

Then she noticed the carving on the back—two sprigs of flowers that looked like violets. "This is beautiful, Robert," as her hand glided over each sprig. "And it will be ideal when I have a baby at my breast again. Can we have chairs like this inside our home as well? Helene and I could sew fabric around cushions for extra comfort."

"I will do all that for you," Robert whispered, brushing a strand of hair behind her ear. "Let's put the little ones in their bed. I want to hold you."

Nichol smiled, grateful for his support and love. Moving inside, both Aiden and Lucette were lying on their bed already, sound asleep in the room next to theirs. Their parents' hands touched and then their eyes met. At the same time, their heads turned toward their children sleeping peacefully, their tiny chests moving in a gentle rhythm.

Returning to their own bedchamber, Robert extinguished the candle, enveloping the room in a soothing darkness.

Nichol sighed contently as she settled into bed, feeling the exhaustion from her day finally melting away. Her body was growing heavier; she could feel it daily. With the weight of this second baby and the trip and horse ride, she desperately missed the warmth and comfort of Robert's touch and his kind words—sometimes spoken, sometimes felt.

She could hear him removing his clothing—everything. Lifting the bed covers, he lay down. As he moved closer to her, their bodies gravitated toward one another as they intertwined their fingers.

Without a word, Robert glided his hand over the roundness of Nichol's growing belly, feeling the life growing inside her. The baby kicked lightly in response as if acknowledging his presence. Lifting the cover, his lips easily found the mound that hid its treasure within.

Following the curve of her belly, he kissed the skin protecting it. When a gentle kick reminded him of what was within, his lips found the source and kissed it.

As he moved his head up to taste her lips, his hand still gently cupped and massaged her belly. Robert pulled her closer; his touch remained soft yet possessive. He marveled at the miracle of their unborn child, his fingertips tracing the contours of the precious life they had created together.

Whispering in the darkness, his voice was filled with awe and tenderness as he asked, "Will our new daughter be like Lucette? Will she have your radiant smile, your captivating eyes … perhaps your active mind?"

Nichol's heart fluttered at his words, her love for him deepening every time she was around him. She turned to face him, her hand reaching up to caress his cheek in the dim moonlight that peeked through the window.

"She will carry all the love and kindness we share," she replied, her voice filled with affection. "May she have your strength and your gentle spirit. In her, as I did with Lucette, I see our future, our influence of who we are with and where we live."

Robert moved his arm under her, raising her to a sitting position. At the same time, he lifted her bedclothes over her head and then lay her back. As he did, his lips caressed her breasts.

In the silence of the night, Robert had carefully rolled on his back. His mouth found spots he hadn't touched before. As he explored her, he slowly moved her body to lay on top of him, settling on him as he did within her.

Looking into his eyes, she felt a smile spread across her face. "I am complete when you are in me, and we are joined." Time stood still as their bodies gently rocked, almost as if they were on a gentle sea. As the rocking increased in intensity, each rode the wave to the crest until the peacefully rolling sea returned.

As they lay together basking in the quiet intimacy of the moment, their bodies molded together. They were surrounded by a cocoon of warmth and affection that sheltered them and their growing family.

Time stood still in that embrace, surrounded by love and anticipation, as each experienced solace and a renewed sense of purpose.

Nichol spoke with a soft giggle, "Can we do this again?"

They were one.

fifty-six

Lucette and Aiden

I will meet you before the summer passes.

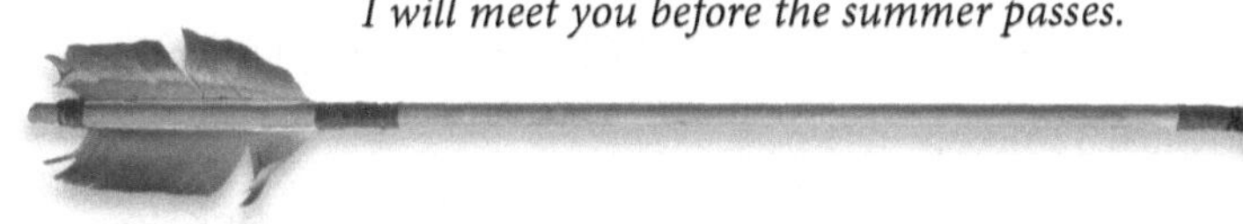

The morning arrived. Random thoughts flowed through Nichol's mind as she emerged slowly from sleep.

Lucette and Aiden are giggling.

Attention is needed.

Shadow wants in.

The children will be in my bed soon.

My eyes do not want to open.

Just one more moment of rest.

Not to be given.

Robert laughs.

I am loved.

I am home.

At last.

Seeing no help for it, she surrendered to the day and rose from her bed.

Noise from squealing Lucette and Aiden resounded throughout the house.

Nichol picked them up, tucked one under each arm, and carried them to the kitchen table. Setting each on it, hugging and kissing them at the same time, it only heightened their laughter.

"Robert, what should I do with them?" she asked.

Just then there was a knock on the door. Amused by his wife's actions, Robert moved to open the door.

"The answer to your question has arrived. Timo and Moki are here."

Both children were now standing on the table with their arms stretched out. Lucette and Aiden cried, "Down, Mama! Down!" and ran toward Timo.

Nichol eyed Moki. "I see a basket on Moki. What is Moki to carry now?"

Timo replied, laughing, "Children to the hill."

Tears filled Nichol's eyes as she embraced Timo, whispering, "God sent you to us; what would we do without you?"

"And God sent you to me that day at the fair. Now, I am here to take these spirited children to the hill. I have their ride, food, and drink for the day."

Once Lucette and Aiden heard the word *hill*, they knew the basket was for them. "Up … up, Papa. Up …."

Stretching their arms upward, Robert and Nichol lifted them into the cloth-and-cloak-lined basket. Nichol kissed them both and lowered her face to her two excited children.

Lucette's hair had darkened over the past year. Her curls bounced around her face as if they were doing a dance, highlighting her green eyes. Nichol fitted the hats that Helene had made for each child on top of their heads. As she did it, more giggles were produced from the two.

She could tell Aiden would stand taller than Lucette when they became older. His brown eyes had a hint of gold in them, like the straw of a summer harvest.

I wonder if Athena will be a version of Lucette?

"You do what Uncle Timo and Papa tell you to." Both children nodded their heads, smiling and giggling at the same time.

"I will join you later, Timo, after I spend time with Helene and Cara."

Timo, Robert, Moki, and Shadow started up the road toward No Name. As they passed through the hamlet, Lucette and Aiden waved to those they saw. Their words of greeting echoed around them.

Gradually, they worked their way up from the base of the valley, following a path they had made for Moki when they came upon a flat area that faced the south. To the north, the hill continued to rise to a rounded grassy knoll.

Moki knew where to stop. So did Aiden and Lucette. There was no time to take in the serenity around them. Aiden was already climbing outside of the basket, hanging on the edge.

Robert lifted him and Lucette to the ground.

Shadow took her position and began patrolling the edge of the flat area as it was part of her new domain. She found the best vantage point that stood apart from the hill and surveyed her hunting grounds, moving her eyes back to follow what Lucette and Aiden were doing.

As they left, Nichol settled into the big chair Robert had surprised her with by their front door. Wrapping a soft cloak around her shoulders, her hands enjoyed the warmth of the cup of hot spiced water. Resting her head against its back, she was filled with contentment. Her hand rounded her expanding belly as Athena moved within her.

I will meet you before the summer passes.

Her eyes followed the breadth of the open area in front of her chair. Speaking aloud, she murmured, "I will ask Helene to help me make cushions to sit on." Finishing her herbal drink, she got up and walked to Helene's.

As she opened the door, the aromas of drying herbs were in the air. These were the same herbs Helene had mixed with hot water when she had been pregnant with Lucette.

I need to ask her for more of her herbs.

Calling out, "Hello," she took in Helene's home. *This reminds me of the comfort of her Paris home.* Immediately, Helene appeared, moving toward Nichol, and hugging her.

"I am happy you are here. I want to hear everything … about Ezra and what is planned. You are glowing and I see our baby is growing. And—"

Nichol stopped her. "First, tell me about Cara. Then I will take a turn."

Smiling, Helene reached for her hand as they sat down. "Cara understands our language and knows that we—you—will protect her. She is safe.

"She is weak and is regaining her strength a little as each day passes. Let her stay here until we find where she will live. I think John will become part of her life. He has been here since she arrived."

Helene got up to refill Nichol's cup and get one for herself.

Sitting down again, she said, "I have missed Ezra, but know this is where I want to be—with my babies and my family. I know that Ezra has reached out to Achim to join him in Rouen and be part of E & N. That means that Dinah and their children will move from Antony. I believe she and the children will eventually be here with us and the men will travel two or three times a year."

Helene settled in. "Nichol, I would not be surprised if Dinah chooses to stay here with the children. Gideon has apprenticed with his father to become quite good on the forge, and I see him continuing to learn, working under Robert's guidance. Maybe Achim will spend most of his time in Rouen with Ezra."

fifty-seven

The Hill

I know that one day No Name
and Harmonie will be discovered.

Robert and Timo followed Lucette and Aiden running and playing until they began to tire.

A large flat stone rested by itself as though it was placed on purpose to sit or stand on to view the valley, the lake, and the vast forests beyond. Timo unpacked the food and drink while Robert placed the children on the stone.

A large red-tailed hawk had been circling overhead.

Nichol had arrived at the top of the hill just in time to see the hawk swoop down and drop a squirrel in front of Shadow. The winged predator then landed on the stone and screeched, to the amusement of Lucette and Aiden.

Slowly the hawk walked between Lucette and Aiden.

Robert thought that he heard Aiden say, "Papa."

"Timo," Nichol said softly, "give them each a piece of the dried fish you packed to feed the hawk. It is my papa."

Absorbing her words, Timo took small pieces of fish and gave Aiden and Lucette pieces for their offering. The three adults watched silently as the two talked gibberish and giggled as they fed "Papa."

Shadow devoured the squirrel as she looked toward the hawk between bites as if to thank him. Watching the display between the hawk and Shadow, Timo and Robert were both amazed.

"It's as if the two are friends," Robert said with wonder.

"They are … and more," Timo responded. "They are allies, protecting the ones they care for."

This is our hill of hope, Nichol thought. *This is just the beginning.*

Once Papa the hawk had enough, he flew to a nearby tree.

Timo unpacked the remaining dried fish and cheese and passed small pieces to Nichol.

Lucette and Aiden were like little birds. Their mouths opened for food when they saw Timo breaking up pieces from the food he was holding. At the same time, Nichol encouraged them to drink from the special cups that Timo had made. Soon, the children could not keep their eyes open.

Robert had made a bed of soft cloaks nearby. Nichol and Timo gently lay them down with Shadow beside them and Papa watching from above.

Nichol took Robert and Timo by the hand and led them to the edge of the hill.

"Look at this valley. What do you see?" As she spoke, clouds began to part with a contrast of bright light and soft shade moving throughout the valley below.

Gazing down into the valley, Timo and Robert were drawn into the depth of the question and were enchanted with the view.

Timo murmured with a faint, trembling voice, "I see paradise."

Robert agreed. "The Lady brought us here. The sight of such beauty humbles me. When we arrived, it was hard to explain but I felt a sense of calm and well-being like never before."

Nichol squeezed their hands. "We all did. This hill is special. And for the children, it is their hill of hope and inspiration, where they will be embraced and prepared for their future. No church or castle will be built on this hill. I have seen what evil men can do and I will not accept it in our valley. My burden is this: I know the past, and I know what is to come."

Nichol turned and walked to the sleeping children, followed by Robert and Timo.

"Look at Lucette and Aiden; and soon there will be one more. We must teach them the skills to succeed in our world, while the Lady will teach them what is needed for her world."

Timo spoke warmly, "I promise I will teach them to read and write and how to plant and harvest. I will also show them how to make their shoes and the special satchel you carry on your back."

Robert smiled as he spoke, "As their papa, I will teach them metalworking and I will always be there when they need someone to talk to. They will need our love even if, at times, we do not understand them and they will always have a home to come back to. And I will always be here to support you, Nichol."

Their words warmed Nichol's heart. She added, "When Athena is old enough to travel, I will return to Rouen. It appears we have a future there as well."

She frowned a bit. "I know that one day No Name and Harmonie will be discovered. If I gain the duke's trust, I will ask to be given this land and in return, I will pledge my loyalty to him. We will have to pay rents, and the men may have to fight for the duke, but he must protect us from others."

When Lucette and Aiden woke, everything was gathered up and repacked to return to their homesteads. As they were lifted into the basket on Moki, their giggles returned.

Before descending, they paused at the ridge for one last look into the valley before they descended. Timo took Moki's bridle in his hand and started down on the same path they came up. Nichol and Robert followed close by, fearing Aiden would not stay in the basket for long. Shadow disappeared to her new hunting grounds.

When they were at the bottom of the hill, Nichol abruptly stopped and turned, looking up at the summit where they had spent the day.

Softly, she said, "One day, all three of our children will run straight up this hill. When they arrive at the top, the Lady will greet them. They will become the first of their kind."

Robert and Timo remained silent as their eyes met. There was no denying or doubting her prophecy, just as there was no escape from her words.

Thoughtfully, Timo added, "I will write their story."

fifty-eight

Timo

"What if we .... What if we ...."
Then he smiled as his head bobbed up and down.

Timo slept little that night. He heard the wind howling and felt the cold air, but that was not what kept him awake. His passion, a lifelong dream, was about to unfold … he could feel it.

In the morning as dawn was breaking, he packed Moki for a day trip to the top of the hill of hope. When they arrived at the base of the hill, Timo guided Moki to the same trail up the hill they made the day before. As they reached the top, a cool breeze greeted them; a breeze that unconsciously caused Timo to pull his cloak closer to his body. He climbed onto the large flat stone and studied the valley below.

No Name, Harmonie, and the lake were in full grandeur, just as they had been the previous day. What held his interest today was the stream that flowed from the lake. Providing water from the stream to the fields would greatly increase their harvests.

Timo retrieved a satchel from Moki and spread straw on the ground for his trusted companion. Sitting on the flat stone, he removed from the satchel a piece of parchment, a quill pen, a knife, and a pot of ink he had made from oak galls.

With the sun casting a perfect light on the valley below, highlighting the landscape in crisp detail, the target of his interest was highlighted. He pulled his cloak hood over his head, cupped his hands, and blew into them to warm his fingers, a minor discomfort.

Timo turned and spoke to Moki. "Yesterday, my friend, when we were on this hill, I felt God's presence. I felt that all I have done in my life has led me to this valley and these people. I will not fail God or the people of this valley."

With an unobstructed view of the valley, Timo studied every feature and the position of every house in relationship to the forest, the road, and the slope of the land. The valley was blessed with full sunshine and rich pasture for grazing.

Using his quill and ink, he drew the valley and all the structures on his parchment. Then, he drew in the orchard and vineyard and planted fields. Smiling, he thought, *what would bread be without honey?* Then, he drew a place for a new bee colony and hives.

That day, he focused on the life-giving water flowing through the valley.

Knowing the contour of the land and now observing from the hill's elevated vantage point, he drew a series of ditches that would flow from the stream to irrigate crops.

One day, we will have a fishpond.

Once the plan was finished, he climbed to the top of the grass and rocky summit and turned around for a panoramic view.

Nichol is right. This hill belongs to everyone. It is the Hill of Hope and Inspiration and will be known by that name to all.

As his plans expanded, new ideas entered.

What if we had a way to capture the rain as it fell, close to the barn, Harmonie House, and each home?

Thinking that, he started a new series of drawings, saying aloud, "What if we …. What if we …. " Then smiling as his head bobbed up and down, looking from the parchment in his hands to the valley before him.

As the spring unfolded, using his plan, Timo taught the villagers in No Name and Harmonie the proper way to plant the fields and what crops they should grow. He showed them how to protect the small gardens of herbs each had close to their houses. Harvesting the winter wheat and planting for summer and fall crops was ready to commence.

Timo decided it was time. He gathered all able workers in the valley to the Harmonie House. With everyone's attention, Timo organized everyone's work to get the best results.

He was distracted from his instructions when Garlyn squinted and pointed to a lone rider approaching in the distance. "Someone is coming, riding a horse with three horses behind!"

The mysterious traveler wore a cloak and hood covering his head to protect him from the elements. No one could identify him.

John stepped forward as the traveler rode closer. "I will greet him. Come, Shadow, he does not look to be armed with a sword."

The rider and three horses came closer to the villagers. John dropped his head as he leaned forward to see the face under the hood. Suddenly, he shouted, laughing, "Did they throw you out of Paris?"

The rider pushed his hood back and Nichol exclaimed, "It's Joshua!"

When he slowed his horse down to a walk near the group, she spoke directly to him. "Welcome to Harmonie, my friend. You arrived just in time to help with spring planting."

Halting in front of Nichol, he dismounted and embraced her. Shadow demanded to be greeted. Joshua knelt and rubbed her neck with both hands. "She didn't bite me; she still thinks I am not a bad man," he exclaimed.

Aiden had been taken with Joshua as soon as he was off his horse, like metal attracted to a magnet. As if sensing the pull, Joshua went right to Aiden and picked him up.

"Hello," Joshua murmured, then studied Aiden's facial features closely. "You look like an old friend I delivered messages to."

His statement did not go unnoticed by Nichol. *A family resemblance—I will ask later who the old friend was who received these messages.*

Standing, he announced, "I am here to deliver a message, along with these plow horses and harnesses. Then I will return. But for you, Nichol, I will help as long as I have drink and food." Then, with a devilish look and an ear-to-ear grin, he added, "And a promise to hear the tale of the battle at the duke's castle—a battle that would make a fighting man envious."

Murmurs surfaced. "Battle at the duke's castle? What is he talking about?"

Sensing the residents' curiosity, Nichol turned to all and held her hand up to quiet the murmuring. "Yes, I promise to tell the story. It is a story that you will enjoy." She then took his hand and introduced him to the gathering.

Timo was excited to have a team of horses for the new plow he and Robert had designed and built. His plans for the valley were coming together. Connecting eye to eye with Joshua, he nodded his head toward him.

Usually, Timo was the quiet, thoughtful one. When he spoke, they all listened.

"I'm going to divide us into work groups. With what Joshua has brought us, there is much we can do over the summer months to prepare us for our food and shelter needs in the next winter."

After forming work groups, Timo set them to their tasks planned days earlier in the Harmonie House.

fifty-nine

The Gathering

The silence in the room was loud.

armonie House was growing with inhabitants. The tables were pulled together that evening in the corner and the Harmonie family welcomed Joshua, the newest member. Lucette and Aiden were fast asleep close by, with Shadow next to them.

It was late when Garlyn closed the door to Harmonie House. People still lingered around the fire, as they all knew a much-anticipated story awaited those still present.

Joshua had everyone's attention. His news lifted Helene's spirits higher than they had been in a long time as he brought news of Ezra and her family.

"Robert, Ezra wants Achim to help him with E & N Merchants. Your family is soon to arrive in Rouen. Achim's days of blacksmithing are over and Gideon's skills can help you here. Dinah has her own plans. She wants to be with Lucette, Aiden, and Helene. And, of course, Raisa wants to be here, too. Ezra is pleased that you are with your husband and children again and eagerly awaits news of the arrival of your new daughter, Athena."

Joshua took a long drink and then continued. First turning toward Nichol, he asked in curiosity as he raised his right eyebrow, "How does Ezra know you will have a girl child?"

Her response was a smile.

Joshua continued to speak. "Ezra has been lending and trading with dukes and counts for years and knows they have all the power. He reminded me of his knowledge when he said, 'You have to understand their wants and needs, Joshua. Then you let them think they are in control and make them understand that you must succeed for them to succeed. That's the secret of working with them.'

"When Ezra was telling me this, he stopped in thought, then spoke again. 'It has occurred to me that the duke is using me to keep in contact with Nichol—it is she he wants.'

"Ezra then had a look on his face that I had never seen before, and a clever, knowing grin appeared. I cannot forget his next words: 'The game has begun.'"

Joshua then spoke directly to Helene. "When Ezra said, 'The game has begun,' he told me you would know what he meant."

Helene looked down and placed a hand to her lips. When she looked up, everyone's attention was on her. She took a deep breath as a knowing grin appeared on her face.

She spoke, "I have often wondered if it was the chase in a hunt or the victory at the end that pleasured him. Now, I believe it is his love of the chase because there can be no true victory without knowing the game, and Ezra is the best at playing it … whatever it is."

She tilted her head ruefully. "I wish Ezra and I could be together but I am needed here. Joshua, what are you doing for Ezra?"

"He needs my eyes and ears at the wharf and markets. And, of course, I will be the Rouen-to-Harmonie messenger," Joshua replied.

Turning to Nichol, the glint in Joshua's eyes had returned. "It is your turn, Nichol. All of us want to know: What was the story of the battle at the duke's castle? I am a fighting man and I want to hear if it would make me envious."

The silence in the room was loud. It seemed as if everyone was holding their breath, including Shadow and the sleeping babies.

"I went to the duke's manor to see Emma; she would depart in a few days to become the queen of England. I knew that the duke also wanted to see me. When I got to the gate, the sentry greeted me and said that the duke and Emma wanted to see me. I first saw the duke and when he dismissed me, I met Emma in the garden.

"I was with her when the slaver and a man-in-arms entered the gate. He bellowed 'The duke is expecting me,' and brushed by the guard, marching to the castle entrance. I knew there was going to be trouble. Quickly, I lifted my tunic, tied it up at my waist with my rope belt, and waited.

"The slaver appeared in the courtyard with his man-in-arms and the duke followed with his armed marshal. People from the castle gathered at the opened castle door and windows. The Norseman slaver did not see me until the duke looked my way. He turned toward me and smiled as I walked toward him.

"I saw Richard look directly at Emma, holding his hand up, warning her not to intercede. Emma stopped.

"I was standing in front of the slaver when he threw the silver coins I had given him for Cara down on the ground, demanding her return.

"I turned to the crowd and shouted out, 'Should I give her back to be beaten and raped?' I heard a woman's voice respond loudly, 'Never!'"

Those listening around the table murmured, enthralled with her tale.

Nichol could hear the word *never* said in a whisper. Feeling energized as she retold the story, she continued.

"I dropped my palm down to Shadow, signaling her to stay by my side and not move. The slaver grabbed me by my hair and pulled me close. When he did, I yelled in his face, 'You smell like rotten fish!' Quickly I raised my knee and rammed him in his groin when the last word came out of my mouth."

As Nichol said this, a slight smile spread across her face. At the same time, she brushed the hair on her right side that had fallen forward and rose from where she was sitting.

As Robert watched his wife, his mouth had fallen open with the words he had just heard.

John laughed out loud and slammed his hand on the table. "Yes!" he shouted out.

Standing, Nichol continued, her facial expressions changing as she relived the moment.

"In pain, he pulled out his knife and yelled at me, 'I am going to hurt you just like the slave bitch.' He then put his knife to my face, like this. Shadow lunged and sunk her teeth into his leg, distracting him."

All eyes were wide in the room as she picked up a knife from the table she was standing by. The women gasped as she did it. Robert's face went white and the other men leaned in to hear her next words.

"Swiftly, I pulled my dagger and jammed it under his chin toward the back of his mouth. His eyes rolled back as he collapsed."

"Of course you did. Any man is a fool to confront you and Shadow," Helene said with some authority. She added, "I was there when Nichol was attacked before …." Then her voice trailed off as she reached her hand across to Nichol's.

Nichol stopped and took a deep breath before she continued. "It was over. The slaver's accomplice pulled his sword and with his other hand, pulled out a knife. He then started toward me. Shadow growled, ready to attack. From behind the accomplice, the gate sentry approached him. I knew him, as he was the one who routinely welcomed me when I visited Emma and the duke. With the flat of his sword, he slammed it against the accomplice's head, rendering him senseless.

"With both men down, I put my foot on the slain slaver's chest, pulled my dagger from his neck, wiping it on his tunic. Shadow was now at my side. As I scanned the crowd, I said, 'I am a woman. Men see women as weak. That is a mistake. A deadly mistake.'

"As I looked around the courtyard, I saw Emma. She had seen and heard what happened. With a slight nod and smile toward her, I turned toward Duke Richard and bowed my head. I knew that the gate sentry was watching. I tipped my head his way, acknowledging him as well.

"Slowly, I moved toward the gate. I could feel eyes at my back; everyone was looking at me. As I passed the sentry, I said, 'Thank you,' nodding to him again, and walked through the gate quickly with Shadow at my side. As soon as I heard the gate close, we headed to Ezra's as fast as my feet would carry me without running."

Everyone listened intently and when she finished, John nodded his head, obviously approving of all she said and did.

With a stunned look, Joshua said, "Nichol, you have done more in your short life than most do in two lifetimes. Now I know who you are; you are what others are not. You are what God aspires us to be."

No one stirred or spoke as an uneasy quiet came over the group, but heads nodded, and smiles on their faces spread, agreeing with his words.

Joshua had said what others thought but would not say.

Nichol was embarrassed and could not speak any longer. She had just revealed in detail a selfless and heroic happening.

Helene tilted her head and nodded toward her—this fearless woman warrior who had become her daughter. Robert, who was next to her, just took her hand and gave it a gentle squeeze. Looking around the table, she stopped at John, who smiled and winked.

Then John's eyebrows narrowed and in a deep voice he said, "Our past is not to be shared with others outside of Harmonie. There are things that only a few of us will know or need to know. One day I fear others will know too much. What has been said at this table stays at this table; it stays within this room."

Everyone knew the meaning of his words.

Nichol added, "We need to go to our beds; we have many days of hard work ahead."

Robert picked up Aiden and Nichol picked up Lucette and took them home.

When they reached their bed, Nichol was on her back. Robert moved close and put his arm around her, urging her to curl against his side. Tears welled in her eyes and Robert could feel them as they dropped on his shoulder. He said nothing, allowing her to release the burden placed upon her by the Lady, a burden she freely accepted.

Finally, the tears stopped.

Quietly, she snuggled closer. "I am not crying for myself. I am crying because of the danger that has been around me. It is now around you, Lucette, Aiden, and Athena if Loupe and Fredric succeed in their quest to harm me. I can't forget that Loupe used Lucette as an excuse to get to me when he came to Ezra's in Paris. What if they hire and send others to find me … or her? What have I done?" Turning to meet his eyes, she asked again, "What have I done, Robert?"

"You have always done what you most need to do for yourself and others. My love, you must take care of yourself. After what we saw on the Hill of Hope and Inspiration, I am confident that both of us and our children are protected by the Lady. Neither Loupe nor Fredric will bring us harm."

Holding her even closer, he kissed her swollen eyelids. "Tomorrow, we will enjoy a beautiful day in Harmonie with our friends and family. Now sleep."

As she closed her eyes, she felt his gentle lips once more.

sixty

The Community Quilt

It was odd … it came to me in a dream.

By the time spring arrived, those who lived in the two hamlets were adopting the common name "Harmonie" for themselves.

With the coming of warmer weather, it seemed as if a renewed energy filled the valley. Everyone in the settlement had participated in some way to complete the Harmonie House. It was a remarkable sight … an imposing wood building with a high-peaked thatched roof.

The building could easily host all the individuals who lived in their valley at one time and had room to accommodate the tradecrafts that would be housed there. Windows lined the perimeter of the structure, providing daytime lighting. Shutters were installed to protect the occupants from the rain and cold when necessary.

Several stone hearth ovens for baking warmed the members as they created their crafts. Space was allocated for weavers, wool spinners, and cloth makers. The thought of creating separate guilds for crafts, leather, tannery, ale brewing, baking, weaving, goldsmithing, and silverworking became part of the community chatter. They liked working with each other.

In the beginning, Harmonie House was intended for those living in Harmonie. Eventually, finished products would be transported to Rouen and beyond. Merchants would buy them for their stores and reselling at fairs.

As Nichol looked around the vibrant room, she wondered, *What is needed in Rouen that Harmonie could supply? I will need to ask Ezra for suggestions.*

Robert had set up an area for finishing his goldsmithing. The bigger work was initially done in his forge area.

Not to be outdone, Helene had a spot close to one of the ovens, where she demonstrated how to cook with the herbs and spices Ezra had imported to Rouen and sent to Harmonie with Joshua and John. Nichol taught people how to make and use lotions and potions in the art of healing.

Timo became the most popular person in the Harmonie House. He had enclosed a large room where the children could play and created an inviting space for them to learn how to read and write.

Shadow immediately went to the children's room when she was in the Harmonie House. She helped keep the children calm and quiet during study times when Nichol taught.

Celeste, a young widow who lived at the north end of the valley, worked at a large table in the center of the room, sewing quilts.

One day, as Helene walked by her table, she stopped to admire Celeste's stitchery and to ask what she had been working on. When Celeste spread her work out, Helene was stunned. She beckoned Nichol over to see it.

When Nichol saw the fruits of Celeste's labors, she gasped as she saw the scene depicted in embroidery stitches. It displayed a woman dressed in flowing white robes walking behind two young girls and a boy as they crossed a wooden bridge. Rays of white light emanated from her hands as she guided the children across the rickety bridge.

The image struck a chord with Nichol, and she asked Celeste what inspired her to create the scene.

Looking at Nichol, she said, "It was odd; it came to me in a dream. It was so real and vivid, and the image stayed with me for days. After dreaming about it again, I knew I had to stitch it into a quilt I planned to sew."

Exhaling, Nichol said, "This design came to you in a dream? Tell me about it."

"It was more than a dream. A woman with a soothing voice talked to me and showed me the scene with the children. We talked about it, and after the second dream I knew what I had to do. That is how the idea for the quilt came to me."

Helene lifted her eyes. "What do you think of it, Nichol?"

Could my Lady also be guiding others … right here?

"It is beautiful! You have captured the essence of what I call the Lady. She is someone who has been in my dreams since I was a young girl. Now, I believe she is guiding my children, and she protects them without them knowing it.

"What do you plan on doing with it when it is complete, Celeste?"

"I don't know. I have not given it any thought except planning to include it in my next quilt. Do you have something in mind?"

"Yes. Would you accept coin for it? I think it would be perfect for the main wall by the children's area. If we hang it there, every-one can see it and enjoy your work."

Celeste was stunned. "I am happy to do that, Nichol, but you do not have to pay me for it."

Nichol was adamant. "You deserve to be paid for your work and creativity. I can hardly wait to see what else you do."

Helene was holding a portion of the cloth that Celeste had worked on. "I think there is something else to be done, something that would involve all of us."

All eyes turned toward her. Nichol asked, "What?"

As Nichol watched Helene reach for some of Celeste's thread, she asked, "How many of you have threads of different colors in your homes that you have not used?"

Quickly, the women spoke up. They all did.

Helene continued, "What if we created a quilt together, all of us working on different parts? It would be about us: our lives and what brought us to Harmonie and No Name. It would tell the story so that our children and others will know who we are … who each of us is."

Nichol could feel excitement and skepticism in the room at the same time.

"Look at all of us. We are the same and we are different. We can celebrate our memories and our hopes. And we will do it together, each contributing a part of the whole. With Celeste's sewing skills, I would like to see her take all our pieces and create one quilt. The quilt will be us—all of us. And we can hang it on the wall so all can see when they enter the Harmonie House."

Celeste stood. "I know it will be beautiful. I will be glad to bring all our work together and unite it into one piece." Her smile was radiant.

The women exchanged glances and stirred on their benches. One by one, each of the women stood and hugged each other. They had become one.

The weeks passed and activity in the Harmonie House never seemed to stop.

Some came up to the Harmonie House to work on the sewing, others to cook, and still others brought their children to be with other children.

One night after supper, Helene suggested to Robert and Nichol, "Now that the Harmonie House has been accepted and utilized by many in the valley, why not hold a community supper there to celebrate our success? We could ask the others if they would like to come."

The idea was circulated throughout, and plans were made to hold the celebration at the end of the month.

Before the month ended, Celeste came to Nichol. "The women have all given me their stitchery pieces. Helene brought me yours as well, including sewing you did for Lucette before she was born. I will have it assembled and ready in a few days. Can I ask Timo to help hang it on the big wall when it is done?"

"Of course. I will tell him you need his help before the community supper."

It was an amazing and glorious event, bringing all together with joy. Everyone participated in cooking, baking, and decorating the Harmonie House for the event. It was noisy. Everyone was talking and laughing, and the children flocked around Shadow. The wolf dog had become a friend and protector to all of them.

No one there had ever experienced a gathering such as this.

The wall hanging that had been finished the previous day hung perfectly on the large rod Robert had forged for that purpose after Timo had revealed to him what the women in the two villages were doing.

When the food had been consumed and the crowd had quieted, the women gathered under the quilt. Celeste said, "Nichol, none of this would have happened if it were not for you."

During the building of the Harmonie House, the women in the valley witnessed what a natural and charismatic leader Nichol was. Nichol got things done. She was kind to the other women and looked out for them. She even was able to take some of the gruffness out of Garlyn. There was something good and different about her. They looked up to her and they were drawn to her. She had not revealed the details of her life to anyone, and no one cared. They respected her and wanted to be like her.

Nichol was reluctant to speak, but finally dropped her eyes from the hanging.

"Celeste, we all made it a reality, something to belong to all of us. It is a safe place where we can work on our crafts and come together to share ideas, support each other, and if necessary, solve grievances. Those in Harmonie from the beginning are like a large family, and we can prosper as a family, using all of our talents. That, of course, will add to everyone's fortunes."

The men were laughing in the background as the ale flowed. Timo moved over to join the women by the quilt. Robert joined him as the two of them admired the hanging handiwork. Soon, the other men joined them.

Pointing up to the quilt Celeste had finished, Nichol continued speaking and turned to include the men in her response.

"So that all of you know, the idea for building the Harmonie House came to me the same way the idea for Celeste's quilt with the image of the Lady came to her ... in a dream.

"The message I received was clear: We should build a safe place for all of us to gather. I have been thinking about an official name for the place we live. When we first arrived, we called where you lived the *hamlet*, and then *No Name*. We called our community Harmonie.

"Over time, many of you started calling us that as well. Now that we're all together, why not combine both hamlets into one village? Let us call the combined village Harmonie; that means all of us. It is our place together for peace, caring, and the acceptance of differences."

Nichol's suggestion was met with approval. Comments were shared all at once.

"Yes!"

"We like the name."

"It is perfect!"

"Of course!"

All agreed, except for Garlyn.

Nichol turned to him. "Garlyn, you do not want us to be known as Harmonie?"

"It could create problems, Nichol. Once Harmonie is spoken of in Rouen, people will come here. It will be those same people that we have tried to avoid. Do we want that? Do you?"

Nichol paused in thought.

Garlyn waited for her answer.

"We cannot hide forever. It would be wise for us to prepare for eventual discovery. I know the duke who controls this area, and I can communicate with him. Perhaps that will help us possibly gain some protection."

Bowing his head, Garland conceded to the inevitable. "Yes, we must prepare. And we should start now."

sixty-one

Starting Now

Do we really know why others have joined us?

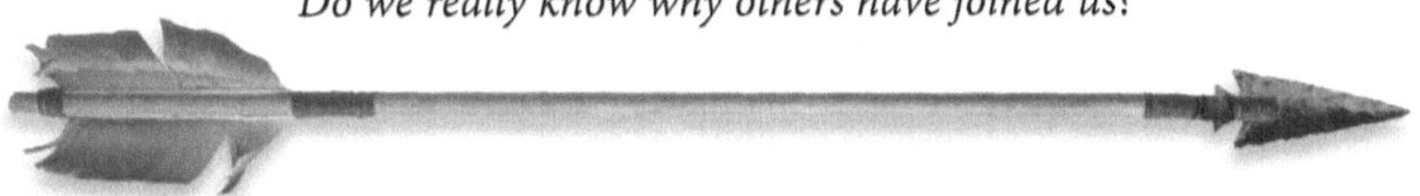

Several days had passed since Garlyn's words were first said: "And we should start now." They vibrated in Nichol's head.

He is right. We must start now. We must be prepared for being discovered by others.

Nichol saw John working with Robert. Approaching the two, she joined them.

"I have been thinking about what Garlyn said. Both hamlets need to start preparing for our discovery. It will happen. When or by whom, I am not sure, but we must be ready!"

With her words, both men stopped working. Robert leaned against his anvil as he directed his attention to Nichol.

Knowing she had their full attention, she continued, "Do we really know why others have joined us? And does Garlyn know why those who lived in No Name came there? I feel it is important to know the thoughts and motives of anyone who lives here and how dedicated they are to protecting our mutual way of life in the valley.

"None of us own this land. We are squatters on the duke's land. And we are vulnerable if he chooses to remove us. We are less than a week's journey from Rouen. Travelers could show up unexpectantly from many other places. Even Norsemen could arrive."

She turned to John. "Do you think those living here will stay or run at the first sign of someone unknown arriving?"

"Nichol, you know the unknown or danger doesn't scare me. I don't run. What you are saying is important and we all need to be prepared when it comes. I can help here." John's voice was firm.

"To get some of our questions about what goods would be desired from Ezra, Joshua can travel to Rouen. And after I give birth, it will be important for me to return to Rouen to talk to the duke. We need his protection here from others swooping in to claim what we are building. I have a few thoughts and before I start out, I will share them with you."

As Robert listened to what Nichol had proposed, he added, "It is time that all in the community reveal their commitment to it."

Turning to her, he continued, "You were taught as a young girl how to defend yourself—things that most men and women never learn. Is it time to share and teach those in Harmonie how to do the same? I know I could learn much."

"I will go to Garlyn's home and tell him that we agree with what he said about being discovered. I will ask him to meet us at the Harmonie House tomorrow after supper, to start plans for preparing for our eventual discovery. I will tell him who I am, starting with being Lisa before I became Nichol, why we are here, and the dangers following us. And I will tell him of my meetings with the duke and how I plan to make him an ally for us.

"It is crucial that he understands our commitment to this valley, which includes him and those with him. And, that *I see him* as he reveals himself to me. He needs to be aware of things that I have done," she took a deep breath, "and reminded of what I can do."

Nichol thought a moment. "After the children are asleep tonight, we will talk with Helene, Timo, and Joshua. Marie and

Olaf can watch over them. Then when we gather again at the Harmonie House tomorrow, we will ask Garlyn to join us there."

Nichol went back to Helene's to let her know that she was going to see Garlyn and ask him to come up for a meeting with everyone the next night in the Harmonie House.

As she headed toward No Name, she was struck by the beauty of the valley and the serenity. It was something she experienced when she walked with Papa in the seclusion of the villa's inner gardens.

Hearing a screech above her, she looked up and saw the red-tailed hawk. A smile crossed her face. *I knew you would be with me today.*

Seeing Garlyn in front of his house, she drew near and greeted him. The hawk landed on his rooftop and watched the two of them.

"Hail, neighbor," were Nichol's first words.

"What brings you, Nichol?"

"Your words have been in my head since we last met. You said that we must prepare, and we should start now. We all agree with you. We would like to gather tomorrow after the evening meal in the Harmonie House. Will you come?"

Listening to her, Garlyn was not entirely sure. *Can I trust these people? I don't truly know them.*

Nichol knew what he was thinking. "You can trust us. I came to ask you to come ... and to tell you why and how I had to flee from Marseilles. May I?"

Garlyn invited her into his house, motioning her to sit at the table.

Once seated, Nichol began her story.

"My name at birth was Lisa, the only daughter of Alexander, the port commander of Marseilles. My father was a skilled and successful merchant and protector of the port. We lived in a villa and Papa had instructed his steward to teach me how to read and write. When I was a small girl, I discovered that I could hide behind a large tapestry in my papa's solar. I learned about business from listening to the many meetings that Papa had with others.

"One day, I made a small hole in the tapestry so I could see what the men Papa met with looked like. Soon, I could tell if they were truthful or liars. One day, after a meeting was over, Papa stood up and turned toward the tapestry and said, 'What did you learn today?' From then on, he relied on me to tell what I saw and heard."

Nichol paused as Garlyn asked, his tone skeptical. "Your papa trusted the opinion of a girl?"

"He did. And there is more. I also had a brutal older brother, Fredric. When I hid behind the tapestry, I was safe from Fredric. When my brother attacked me and set me up to be raped by his friends, Papa rescued me and then had a knight named Sir Roland train me to think and act like a soldier. From then on, I became Papa's aide. He didn't believe that Fredric was his true son and I found out later he was correct.

"Papa revealed his secrets and showed me where his coin and treasures were. He created a map and a plan for me to follow if something bad ever happened to him. I knew where to go and who to connect with.

"I began to follow the plan when my mother poisoned Papa and sent Fredric and the priest Loupe to find me, learn Papa's secrets, and then kill me. That didn't happen. When Papa was murdered, my life changed and the plan became real.

"I walked from Marseilles to Paris and Papa's partner Ezra took me in. Along my walk, Timo and Moki became my trusted allies. Timo was a monk who sheltered me in monasteries he was visiting to train other monks about their vineyards. A pup found us in the woods and became Shadow. And I met Robert and married him before getting to Paris. Robert is Ezra's nephew.

"That's much of my personal story, Garlyn. I have had a woman's voice guide me since I was a little girl. It's her voice that led us to this valley."

Nichol stopped, waiting to hear what Garlyn's reaction would be.

Leaning forward, Garlyn reached out and took her hand. "I have never heard of anyone experience what you have told me. If I had not witnessed some of the things you have said and done here, I would not have believed it." He heaved a deep sigh. "But I believe you."

"Garlyn, you are now part of our journey. Come to the Harmonie House just before the sun sets tomorrow. The others will tell you their stories. You said that we must be prepared for being discovered by others. This will be the beginning of our preparation."

sixty-two

Garlyn and John Speak

Keep your eyes open, your mouth shut,
and always do as I say.

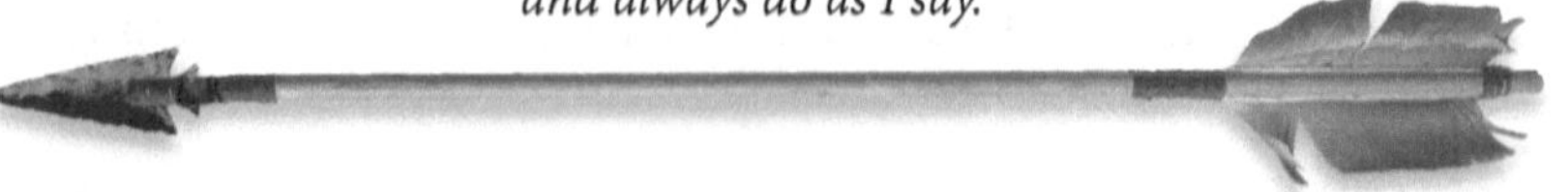

The next evening, after many others had left, Nichol, Robert, Helene, Timo, John, and Joshua gathered in the Harmonie House, along with Garlyn. As before, Lucette and Aiden were sound asleep, protected by Shadow.

When Nichol had approached Garlyn the day before and revealed her past, she felt he was initially shocked and saw her in a much different light than the one he thought of when he first encountered her—as a pushy woman who didn't know her place.

Nichol sensed Garlyn was hesitant to speak about his past to others. Was he too embarrassed to tell his secrets that had been locked away for years … ones he never revealed to another living soul?

The group gathered around and pulled tables together. Nichol lit eight candles and purposefully placed them in front of each person to see the expressions of those who spoke or the reactions of those who listened.

Nichol began to speak. "I was born in Marseilles, and my baptized name was Lisa. My papa was a merchant …."

All there already knew this part of her story; most did not know the rest.

As she disclosed the details she revealed to Garlyn the day before, she scanned the faces in the candlelight. Everyone was caught up in her story. She knew it was her thoughts she added to the events that captured everyone's attention. And sometimes their mouths dropped open when they heard her words.

As she spoke, the crowded table was silent. No one wanted to miss a word or overlook Nichol's expressions. Even those who had heard her stories before were spellbound, but this time, it was different. Her pain and raw emotions spilled out with every word.

Time passed unnoticed as the candles burned down, and new ones were lit.

When she finished, silence blanketed the table until Robert spoke. "You must write your story as you told it tonight. It is a courageous path for those who choose to follow in your footsteps."

Those at the table understood her papa's guidance in dealing with others; how she acquired her physical and mental skills with Sir Roland; and how women could be partners, not servants. They understood Timo's caring for animals and people, and where he learned about vineyards and other planting skills.

Even though some were hearing it for the first time, they also understood her experiences with the Lady, and how the guidance from the Lady had shaped her life. When she mentioned the Lady, several murmured, "Yes, the Lady …."

Nichol could see that Garlyn was stunned by everything she had just disclosed. It was certainly much more than what she had told him the previous afternoon.

When Nichol asked, "Garlyn, what of your past? What brought you to this valley?" all eyes pivoted to him. Unfolding his arms that lay on the table, Garlyn sat back.

Now, it was his turn.

He hesitated for a moment, then began to speak.

"I was the oldest, and we had little to eat. At eight, I was sold to the butcher. He was a cruel man, having his way with me in ways that I cannot speak about. I ran away from him, stealing food to survive. After being caught several times and suspected of many more thefts, I was run out of Rouen. The words shouted at me when I left still echo in my ears: 'If you are ever seen in Rouen again, we will cut your hands off!' I made sure to escape, telling myself never to go near Rouen again.

"I was a young boy when I left. No one would recognize me now but I stayed away. Even though it has been many years, I still miss my brothers and sisters. I doubt that Mama and Papa are yet alive."

Garlyn looked down and stopped. Everyone waited patiently for him to continue. When he looked back up, his eyes were wet and glazed over, staring blankly ahead.

In a gentle voice, Nichol said, "Take your time, Garlyn. We are here for you."

"I traveled from village to village, working sunrise to sunset just for a place to sleep on a dirty floor or in a barn. I never had enough to eat; sometimes I did not eat for several days. I thought that the further away I was from Rouen, the better I would become. Instead, I just got more angry and bitter as the years passed. I was able to save silver coins when I learned that I had a way with large animals. I could tell when they were ill and created remedies with herbs along with pastes for their open wounds so they could heal.

"Finally with coins in my purse, I set out and many days passed before I came out of a forest into this valley. I knew that I had found my home. The peace I felt when I discovered this valley was what I sought. I survived alone in this valley for several years. At times, I would go to other cities, sometimes even Paris, bringing back supplies on my donkey. When I passed farms with large animals, I always stopped and asked if their stock was ill. If so, I would see if I could help them. The owners were grateful and paid me coin. Over time, I came across people with stories like mine and brought them here."

Slowly, looking into the eyes of those seated around the table one by one, he added, "Whatever happens from here on, I am pleased that all of you came into this valley. You are truly one of us."

Looking at Garlyn, Nichol saw him as someone who had also endured. He was now a willing participant, an ally in and to Harmonie.

Sitting next to Garlyn, John began to speak in his deep voice.

"I was always big for my age. When I was twelve years, I was taller and bigger than my papa. One summer day, I was in the fields loading grain into our wagon after it had been threshed.

"On that day, a count rode through our village but I was unaware of his presence. He was leading a procession and everyone bowed or lowered their heads as he approached them … everyone except me.

"I became aware of his presence when I was kicked in the back by one of his men-at-arms. His blow knocked me to the ground.

"Angry, I jumped up, threw down my shovel, and ran at the soldier. Leaping up on his horse, I pulled him to the ground. The count turned around after hearing the commotion and rode back to where we were fighting. I saw him hold his hand up toward the other men who were already dismounting to stop me.

"The count watched and would not let his other men-at-arms interfere in the fight until I had his man on the ground and had beaten him senseless.

"I looked up, and that is when I became scared; a count on horseback looking down on me. I knew I was dead. To this day, I don't know why I did what I did. I picked up the sword from the man I had just beaten and asked the count, 'Is that the best you have?'

"He laughed and then got off his horse and came face to face with me. Clear as sunlight, I remember exactly what happened next. I heard a man say loudly, 'Bow in the presence of Count Walter.' I knew he had the fate of me and my family in his hands. He then asked for the sword I had used to defend myself. I surrendered it, hilt first, as I bowed and knelt respectfully, a mere peasant kneeling in front of a count.

"He asked my name. I struggled to find my voice; I could barely speak. Still looking to the ground, I quietly said, 'John.'

"He then told me to stand and pressed the length of the sword against my chest. 'The horse and sword are yours now, boy. I want you to come with us.'

"Then he looked at the man that I had defeated. His next words were as clear as the cloudless sky. He said to him, 'Get up and finish loading the wagon.'

"I mounted the horse. It was the first time I had ever been on a horse. It did not like my weight and began to jump and spin to get rid of me. The count turned his horse and said, 'Let us go. The sooner we leave, the sooner the horse will settle down.'

"He was right. The horse calmed down and adjusted to my weight. I stayed in formation all the way to the count's walled castle. When we dismounted, I was approached by the count's marshal. I was greater in height than he was. As he looked up at me, his face became angry. Then his eyes narrowed and in a threatening voice, he shouted, 'Keep your eyes open, your mouth shut, and always do as I say.' The next day I began to train as a man-at-arms."

Nichol took in what John had told the others. "You and I have much in common, John. My papa sent me for daily training with his close friend who trained soldiers. It was for my protection from my mother and brother."

John met her eyes, nodding as he did.

"I learned much from the count. When he died, he had two sons. The cruel one became the new count, his every action fueled with hate and a need to brutalize those who were beneath him. It was known that he would rape young girls. One day, I walked out of the castle compound and never returned. I had been to Paris before and decided to return there, knowing my size alone would find me work at the port.

"My size did bring me work. Unloading a ship one morning, a man smaller in stature approached me. I knew he had been watching me for several days and had asked others on the dock about me. I could tell he was a man of importance because of his dress and his command of the port area. 'I have not seen you here before. What other work can you do?' were his words.

"'I was a man-at-arms for Count Walter. When he died, his title passed to his oldest son, a ruthless man. If you know of the new count, you will know why I no longer work for him.'

"He told me, 'My name is Ezra. I know of Count Walter and of his son. I am not like him, and I treat those who work for me with coin and fairness. I want you to be my protector—for my trade and my family. I am a moneylender and merchant. I have a wife, Helene. And I will pay you for your services in coin. Would that be agreeable?'

"And that is how I came into Ezra and Helene's lives. I have now been with Ezra for many years."

His tale now complete, John paused to drink from his ale.

Nichol's mind was filled with John's words. She remembered the story that Marie had told her over a year ago of her rape by the son of a powerful man. *We must always be watchful for our daughters.*

sixty-three

Joshua and the Others Speak

The Lady you told me about, she has brought us all together.

Joshua spoke next.

"I, too, was taken from my family when I was young. I wasn't trained to be a fighter like John was. I became a carrier of messages. I could always remember the details of things I heard and saw. The secrets of my surroundings—I knew them all.

"When a baron discovered that I had this skill, he sent someone to bring me to him. He needed someone who could ride fast and deliver messages correctly. I became that someone.

"One day, I was delivering a message to a priest in Paris. I had noticed a short, balding man observing me as I dismounted my horse to seek out the priest. When I reappeared an hour later, he was still there, as if he was waiting for me.

"'You are a messenger, are you not?' he asked.

"Surprised by his boldness, I was intrigued by his question. Shrugging in response, I mounted my horse to return to the baron, but he did not move.

"'My name is Ezra. I need a messenger for my merchant business. I pay well,' was his response. I dismounted and we went into the inn for ale.

"As a keeper of secrets, I worked for both the baron and Ezra. My loyalties to Ezra deepened, shadowing anything I did or wanted to do for the baron. I became Ezra's eyes and ears around Paris, eventually only working for him."

One by one, each at the table told his story.

And then Helene added hers—a story that most knew but never tired of hearing.

"One night, there was a pounding on our front door in Paris. When Ezra opened it, he was delighted to see his nephew on the outside. Calling to me that Robert was here, I quickly got up from the table to greet him and then I noticed there was someone else standing behind him. It was Nichol, but not the Nichol you all see in front of you tonight.

"I had no idea of the power she carried behind her tattered clothes and disheveled appearance. Within days, we learned why she was in hiding, that her father had been Ezra's partner, and why he had sent her to him for protection … to us. With the information she shared, Ezra, John, and Roger traveled back to Marseilles to collect what Nichol could not escape with when she fled Marseilles after her mother murdered her father.

"While they were away, Robert was in Paris studying at the goldsmith guild. I told him that Nichol and I were going to be at our cottage outside of Paris for a few weeks. During that time, I saw all that she could do—things that few men could.

"One night, while we settled into our supper, Shadow's hair on her back raised, followed by an increasingly loud growl. Suddenly, the door burst open, and a huge man with a dagger in his hand appeared.

"And—to my surprise—so did a different Nichol. Not the kind, intelligent young woman I had come to love. This one was a warrior and she became one with Shadow as the attack began.

"I have never seen anyone move so fast. The man met her dagger and was down. Shadow still had the attacker's hand in her mouth. A second man appeared right behind the downed man. Nichol pulled out the dagger from the dead one, and took the other one down with one slash of her weapon.

"She was covered with blood. Shadow stayed close to her. I was frozen by what happened. And then Nichol said, 'I must move the bodies and bury them.'"

As Helene spoke, everyone's eyes were huge around the table, moving back and forth between Helene and Nichol. Nichol reached her hand to Helene's, gently covering it … as if to say *it is all right to tell all.*

Helene continued. "I came out of the trance I had been in, watching all this unfold. I said to her, 'There are two shovels by the garden. We will bury them there.' And we did."

Taking a deep breath and receiving a squeeze from Nichol, Helene paused, then added, "Nichol has become the daughter Ezra and I longed for. She's kind and cares for her family and us all. And when needed, she has insight and skills that will help us survive."

As she said that, she leaned over and hugged Nichol.

Timo was visibly nervous, being the next in the circle of participants around the table to share his story. But first Nichol spoke to him, saying, "Timo, you are with friends."

Then she told the group, "Timo is a monk and hesitant to talk about himself. He is our spiritual leader and strength. Please, Timo, do tell us your story."

"We are all God's children. My father is a tanner and so was his father before him. At an early age I knew that tannery work was not for me, as I enjoyed working with my mother in her garden.

"One day passing a monastery near our home, I saw fields of plants we had grown in our garden. There were orchards and a vineyard. I walked into the monastery and an abbot approached me. I asked how I could work in their fields. And a week later, I was training to become a monk.

"For many years, I traveled from monastery to monastery, teaching monks how to nurture their orchards and grow them better. I would work with them in the fields and carry seeds and clippings to other monasteries throughout France.

"My only companion was Moki. You all know him. He was good at carrying my supplies and easing my burden as I traveled by foot. When I met a lost boy at one of the fairs the monks sponsored at one of the monasteries, I knew he was special when he purchased food with silver coins and thanked me using words not often spoken by a peasant. When we met again on the road, Moki perked up.

"I soon realized that he was not a boy and that there was a secret. Until Nichol revealed who she was and what had happened to her, I didn't say anything. What I did know was that she could communicate with Moki when she scratched his ear and that there was some reason we were brought together.

"I have witnessed the cruelty heaped on innocents and the theft from too many honest men that greedy men in the church have been behind. Some of both have been directed at Nichol and her family. After much thinking, I decided I could not be part of it and removed my robe.

"I never regretted my decision to become a monk and vow one day to return. God wants me to be here, for some reason I do not know. When it is time for me to return to the brotherhood, I will know through prayer.

"What I learned working with the brotherhood is now being used in the fields of Harmonie. I will also teach the children to read and write. And I will continue to teach the skill of tanning to all who want to learn."

Garlyn's eyes got big. As he looked around the table, he pointed to each, saying, "A soldier; a woman who has visions and can communicate with animals; a blacksmith; a messenger and keeper of secrets; a merchant's wife; and a monk. But each of you has more than one identity. You are many things like those who live in our part of the valley are many things. Some have had guild training in their skills; many of the women sew and bake; and some have had children. One woman brewed ale before coming to the valley with her husband."

He shook his head in disbelief, and as a slight smile appeared on his face, he added, "The Lady you told me about, she has brought us all together."

Hearing him, Nichol responded, for herself and the others around the table, saying, "Garlyn, everyone has a story. It's how a community gets built."

Everyone took a breath. As the second set of candles burned down, Robert added good news that not everyone knew. He could see Helene's eyes glisten as he began.

"You will soon meet Achim and Dinah, along with Gideon and Raisa—my papa, mama, brother, and sister. They are on their way here. My papa is Achim, and will be working with Ezra in Rouen and traveling sometimes to be here. Dinah is my mama and will live here. Gideon will become my apprentice at the forge, and my sister Raisa is very eager to be with Lucette … and the new baby girl who will arrive soon."

One by one, the stories had one common element.

Nichol knew what it was. Garlyn had said it: *The Lady brought all of us together.*

Nichol reached one hand to Helen and the other to Robert.

One by one, each person around the table took the hand being offered by his neighbor. Garlyn stretched his hand across the table to connect with Joshua's.

As the group united, Nichol spoke.

"I believe that the Lady has brought us together as one. We have endured hardships and have strength through determination, with a perspective and insight that will benefit others. Both are needed when discovery happens. The bond we share must not be broken by jealousy, envy, fear, or hate. Our success and the success of Harmonie will depend on those of us sitting at this table."

A burst of energy was immediately felt and seen on the faces of those present. The candles began to burn brighter as each looked into the eyes of those present.

Nichol knew what was happening.

SHE IS HERE!

Marie

Your past is safe with us.

A week passed since the meeting with Garlyn.

One morning, Marie slowly approached Nichol's home. In her head, she was rehearsing what she would say to her, someone who saved her life and showed her love, caring, and kindness she had never experienced before.

Stopping at the open door, she hesitated for a moment, looking down at the ground. Nichol saw her approach and waited.

Finally, Marie quietly asked, "Nichol, can we talk?"

"Of course. Come in and sit at the table with me."

Lucette and Aiden were on the floor playing with wooden animal figures Robert had carved for them. They would giggle together when one would hold a toy and move it around. It was a joy to watch them.

Faltering at first, Marie finally found her words.

"I am grateful for all you have given me. I appreciate all you have taught me, Nichol. I wouldn't have survived if you and Robert had not found me and I know that Aiden would not have either. Now that he is over a year old, I think it is time for me to be on my own and with Olaf.

"I have made arrangements with a woman in the other hamlet to help care for and nurse him twice a day if you approve."

Nichol smiled as she heard Marie's words. Stretching her hand across to Marie's, she said, "I've been waiting for you to come and tell of your news. You and Olaf have been one since you met. You both will always be part of our family, just as Aiden became my son when he was two days old. How he came to us through you, Robert and I are grateful.

"You and Robert and I made a deal. It is time to complete it. We can take care of Aiden's feedings now."

Marie was taken aback by Nichol's words. "Nichol, he is a baby, and he still needs milk. How will he survive if he can no longer nurse and you don't have a woman to take care of him?"

Nichol smiled. "Marie, I have a surprise I was waiting to tell you. I've started to wean Lucette from my milk, and she no longer needs it. I have been giving her drinks of goat's milk in a special cup Robert made for her. He made one for Aiden, too. Timo stretched thin lambskin over the opening of the cup. He punched several holes close together on one side and added a thin cord holding the lambskin in place that I could remove to fill the cup and secure it again. Lucette holds it and happily drinks from it, like a wineskin."

"Are you sure this is safe for her? I have never seen such a thing as you describe, Nichol."

"Nor have I … but it frees me to do things I need to do here. And I will be in Rouen for many days at a time. Helene and Robert are pleased with how well Lucette does. When Aiden saw her drinking from her cup, he wanted one, too. The last time we put the two in a basket on Moki, both had cups they could drink from without me being there to nurse. When you leave, Aiden can use his cup all the time."

Marie was relieved to hear Nichol's words and relaxed in the chair. She was amazed at what Nichol described. *What made her think of creating such a cup?*

Marie continued to speak.

"Now that Harmonie House is built and the other homes will be ready before the winter, Olaf wants to return to Rouen, and he wants me to go with him. He is good to me. I am happy when I am around him and I cannot bear the thought of never seeing him again. And we could someday have our own child.

"Olaf knows what I have been through, and he knows I have given Aiden to you to raise as your son. He knows of our agreement." Marie hesitated, then added, "Do I have your blessing to leave?"

"Oh, Marie, of course, you have my blessing! You have more than fulfilled your part of our agreement. I will miss you, though. Olaf is a good man, and he shows you kindness. You will always be a part of our family. I want you to come back to visit; you are always welcome here. Please watch the children for a moment. I will be right back."

Nichol returned from her sleeping room with a leather purse and handed it to Marie. "I know you and Olaf will put this coin to good use."

Marie could tell from the bag's weight that it contained more than the five silver coins Nichol had promised her if she stayed to nurse Aiden.

Tears filled her eyes, and she stammered, "Nichol, this is more than you promised. My own papa treated me like I was a whore when he found out I was pregnant, and you did the opposite. You picked me up off the road and showed me that I am worth so much more. I will always remember that.

"I will miss you and Robert and all your family. I will miss Aiden, too, but I know you will be a better mother to him than I could ever be. Thank you for being so kind to me and thank you for giving me your blessing to leave with Olaf."

As she stood to leave, Nichol put her arms around her. As they separated, she took Marie's hand and said, "I ask that you do not use the name *Harmonie* or tell anyone what you have learned about me or my family since you have been with us. We could all be in peril if word gets out of our existence. I know that you would not want harm to come to any of us. Will you promise me?"

"Yes, I do and I understand. I promise, and I will also tell Olaf. He must promise, too."

Nichol released Marie from her grasp. "The day you leave I will give you a letter. When you arrive in Rouen, I want you to give the letter only to Ezra. He will help you both."

The fields were plowed and planted.

It was time for Marie, Olaf, and Joshua to leave Harmonie for Rouen. The night before they were to depart, family and friends gathered at the Harmonie House to wish them well on their journey.

Tears were abundant from Freyja, Gunvor, Tova, and Harald as they embraced Olaf. Harald told him, "You must send word back with Joshua. It will please your mother and me to know you and Marie are well."

With Robert at her side, Nichol motioned to Joshua to join them for a private conversation. Gathering at a candlelit table out of hearing distance of others, they sat down, and Joshua took a drink of ale while Robert, with both hands surrounding his mug, waited patiently for Nichol to speak. She was swirling the herbed water in her cup, somewhat hesitant to begin. Finally, she looked up at them.

"I must return to Rouen as well. With Athena due soon, I cannot leave until she is ready to travel. Ezra needs my support so our business can continue to grow. I also need to meet with the duke. Our paths are connected, and I believe he can be helpful to us."

John and Cara entered and moved to the table to join Nichol, Robert, and Joshua.

Nichol continued, "Joshua has been here longer than he intended. Ezra must be concerned by now."

Turning to John, she spoke.

"Tomorrow, I would like you to return with Olaf and Marie. I need to know more about what is happening in Rouen, and the only way is to have you as another messenger that both Ezra and I can trust. Will you become a messenger for us as well?"

As he heard her words, a smile appeared on John's face. Before her words were out, he nodded. Then John looked at Cara. "Yes, I will. And now I have more than one reason to return."

Joshua raised his mug. "Here is a toast to the new Harmonie messenger."

All at the table raised their mugs to Joshua's words. Then he added, "The new keeper of secrets."

Joshua, John, Marie, and Olaf left Harmonie the next morning with a parting word from Nichol to the couple: "Just remember, if you choose to return, you will always be welcomed back." Marie and Olaf started to walk down the road while Joshua and John rode their horses.

Robert turned to Nichol. "I can tell you are continuing to worry. What is wrong?"

"When you have a stream or river, you build a bridge to cross over. I feel like I am a bridge from Rouen to Harmonie, but I cannot let people cross yet. I must continue to build the bridge to benefit all, not just the powerful."

Robert took her in his arms. "You will not fail and it is not only your bridge to build. I know you worry about losing the trust that you have earned with the duke. What you have told me, I know he will wait for your return. He knows your value, just as I do, my wife."

With those words, he pulled her closer, leaving a kiss on her neck.

sixty-five

A Day at the Lake

She stepped into the water and marveled at its warmth.

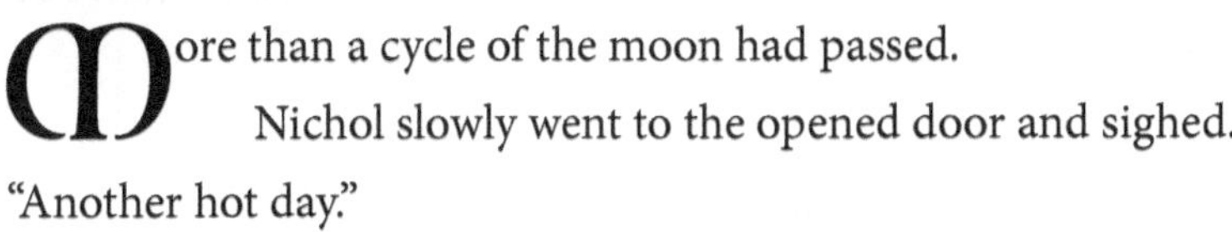

More than a cycle of the moon had passed.

Nichol slowly went to the opened door and sighed. "Another hot day."

She placed both hands on her back, leaned back, and grimaced in pain while Lucette and Aiden were at her feet, begging for attention.

Helene took their hands, diverting their attention from Nichol.

Robert was returning with water from the communal well and noticed Nichol's movements.

"Robert, we have been working so hard lately that I'd like to take time out to rest. My back hurts and I feel that our daughter will come soon. Can we not work and spend the day with the children?"

Robert set the bucket of water down. Without saying a word, he lifted Aiden to sit on his shoulders. Lucette reached her hands up. "My turn, Papa."

He scooped her up and then reached out to Nichol.

"Where would you like me to carry you?" he said with a huge grin.

"You have another arm. Would you like me to climb on it, too?"

They all laughed as she moved closer, making a jest that she was going to climb on him without any help.

Robert continued laughing. "Better yet, I just want to put my arm around you. And let's all go to the lake. The children can play at the lake's edge and we can take a relaxing soak in the cool water. I think it will help your back and body."

That was all Nichol needed to hear.

"Helene and I will pack food for the day. She will join us."

Robert packed clothes, soap to bathe with, and a cloak to lay on. He put the backpack on, picked up the children, and went out the door, with Nichol following.

He saw Tova and shouted, "We are going to the lake for the day. Would you and Gunvor like to go?"

"I will go ask Mama." Tova disappeared into her home. A moment later, both Tova and Gunvor came running. Soon, they were all on their way.

The children were laughing and playing together. It was the first time they would all enjoy a rest day together. As they walked, they spied a grassy area under a large shade tree. The space was ideal for spreading a large cloth where they could later eat and rest.

Lucette and Aiden were less than two years old and full of energy. They saw the lake and could hardly wait to get in the water.

Robert removed their clothes. Tova and Gunvor lifted their tunics, tucked them in their belts, and grasped Lucette and Aiden's hands. Slowly, they waded in the clear cool water.

Nichol removed all her clothes and waded in with a lightweight cloth draped around her bulging body.

Shadow took a running leap and landed in the middle of the frolicking children. Helene spread a cloth, leaned against a tree, and watched with pleasure, reminding herself why she chose to leave Rouen. *If only Ezra could be here …*

The sun was warm, the water was cool but not cold, and they laughed and chased Shadow until Aiden announced that he was hungry.

He was always hungry, Nichol thought.

While the children were playing and splashing each other, Robert laid another cloth to sit on under the shade tree and called everyone to come and eat.

Helene had laid out food for all. She and Aiden had become inseparable when it came to eating. When she heard his food request, bread, cheese, dried fish, and berries appeared like magic. She had the special cups ready that Robert had made for both Lucette and Aiden.

Filling each cup from the waterskin, she offered food to everyone except Nichol.

Shadow shook the excess water off her body, causing Lucette to laugh.

Nichol had not followed the children out.

As Robert looked back at the lake, he saw Nichol's body almost floating on top of the water, her belly protruding like a mound. Both her hands were moving around its contour.

"Nichol, come out of the water and eat. You must be cold."

She did not respond.

Robert ran to the lake and waded out to her. "What is wrong? Are you all right?"

Nichol smiled through a painful cramp and turned her head toward him. "She is on her way."

He reached for her hands as she started to turn her body, landing on her knees in the shallow water.

"I will carry you to the shore. The water is too …" and then he paused in mid-sentence. "No … the water where we are is now much warmer."

She removed her hands from his and moved them to his cheeks, looking directly into his eyes. "I will remain here. This is where Athena will be born. The Lady has warmed the water and made it safe for me and our daughter."

"But should I not carry you home?"

"No, this lake is where she will be born." Nichol leaned past Robert where she could see the girls. "Tova, run home; I need your mama to come right away. My baby will arrive soon. Gunvor, watch the children. When they are asleep, then you can help. Helene, it is time—stay with me."

Tova was up and running with great purpose. Her only thought was of being back in time to witness the birth.

Robert was already in the water. He pressed his chest against her back and wrapped his arms around her.

Nichol laid her head back on his shoulder, closed her eyes, and smiled. *This is where I belong with all whom I love.*

The large hawk with the red tail landed on the lowest tree branch, just above the now-napping Lucette and Aiden. A low screech emerged from its beak.

A familiar voice filled her head: *I will be here to help you, Nichol.*

With both babies asleep, Gunvor slowly moved toward the lake, thrilled at the coming birth.

Seeing that Aiden and Lucette were now sleeping, Helene moved toward Nichol, entering the water and marveling at its warmth. Gently moving to Nichol, she knelt in front of her and took her hands.

Gunvor had followed Helene, connecting her eyes with Nichol's.

"You are meant to be here with me, Gunvor."

Nichol then turned her face to Helene and then to Robert. "This birth will be different from Lucette's. It will be fast, not as many hours as before. It will be just us here."

As she rested with her back wedged against Robert and Gunvor at her lower side, Nichol felt a massive inner force move from under her breasts toward her lower belly. She knew her time had come.

She squeezed Gunvor's hand, and took Helene's, saying, "Be ready for my daughter."

And then her legs opened and the water seemed to get warmer than it already was—not hot, just pleasant.

Nichol looked up at Robert. "It … is … now …."

With a low humming coming from Nichol, her body started to vibrate.

All heard a *whoosh* and then the baby left her body.

Robert's and Gunvor's mouths dropped open at the same time.

Calmly, as she panted in relief, Nichol said, "Lift my baby and place her in my arms, Gunvor."

As she did, Nichol said, "Welcome, Athena."

As the birth occurred, Freyja arrived at the lake. She rushed to the edge where the water lapped and observed what was happening. At her side were Timo and Tova.

All were speechless.

With the baby now in her arms, Nichol knew what to do. So did Helene.

A soft light had emerged as she was born, a light she was aware of and surrounded all in the water, wavering in its movement.

Helene watched its movement and Nichol's as she lifted her new daughter to see her eyes. Helene reached up, helping to turn the newborn so Nichol could raise her even further.

Once again, a newborn was shared with the Lady. The light danced around her and a humming sound was heard from the baby girl as her legs and arms moved about.

Suddenly Robert reached up and placed his hands over Nichol's as they held their new daughter to the light together.

Now the light moved around all and into the water.

Bouncing out of it, moving toward the sleeping Lucette and Aiden and circling them, back toward the edge of the water and weaving in and around Timo, Tova, Freyja, and finally Gunvor, Helene, Robert, Nichol … and returning to Athena.

Finally, the light faded and disappeared.

sixty-six

The Day after the Lake

She is the one who will light the way.

Several days were spent at the lake. Food was brought and shared, this time with Moki.

It had become a Harmonie celebration … a quiet but joyous event among those who had witnessed the miraculous water birth. Each had experienced an inner epiphany of spiritual significance.

The hawk never left Lucette while they were at the lake. She started talking to it. Her new word usage was leaping forward each day. Her words to the hawk were clear responses to a question that could have been *what have you learned today*?

Nichol watched them interact and placed her hand on the feather and stone on the beautiful silver chain around her neck.

Alexander. My papa. He is here.

Aiden formed a fist with his tiny hand as he moved toward the branch the hawk rested on, offering the contents of his hand to it. Shadow was lying down, simply watching.

Slowly, the hawk dropped down and landed on the ground. Aiden knelt and extended his hand that contained an offering. The hawk now in front of him, Aiden slowly opened his hand and revealed a cricket.

The hawk snatched it from his hand and flew back to its perch in the tree.

Robert was amazed—both at the actions of the hawk and Aiden's connection with it. Turning to Nichol, he said, "I think a bond has been made between the hawk and Aiden. I guess only time will tell."

Nichol smiled. She already knew.

A while later, Robert was lying on his back with his eyes closed and Nichol lay beside him.

Quietly she said, "I remember Lisa—the old me—and my former life. I miss Margaux, Rose, and Gerhardt. I miss the excitement of the docks and markets in Marseilles. But I do not miss Astrid or Fredric and their cruelty.

"The person I miss the most is Papa. He taught me how to survive in this life if I was alone. He was just here. The red-tailed hawk has visited me many times. It appeared first at his funeral, circling all of us, squawking at me, then heading out to sea. Papa taught me that I could do what any man could do."

As she spoke, Robert's eyes were closed. He opened them and turned his face to hers.

She continued, "There was something about his words and how he used them that told me what he said was important—to listen carefully.

"I have become a believer. Many times, I would hear the Lady's words. Words that said I could be what I wanted to be and I had different abilities than others. I remember hearing her say that as a woman, I was not subject to the wishes of men. I did not have to act like most women were expected to act and to be.

"Now I know how important Papa's teachings were to my survival. He encouraged me to be curious and ask questions. I dream of my childhood, yet when I wake from my dream and see you and our children, I know Lisa is from a time long ago … a lifetime ago. Now I am Nichol and my life has meaning and purpose with you."

With a smile, Robert gently ran his fingers through her hair. "Alexander taught you to become a warrior, and you have survived a lifetime of peril and distress in just a few years. I wish I had met him. From all you have told me, I know he was a kind and caring man, a successful merchant, and he passed all his strengths to you."

Rolling on her side to face him fully, Nichol put her hand on his cheek. "I am so fortunate to have found you. I am sorry I took you away from school and caused Helene and Ezra to leave their home in Paris."

Robert laughed and put his hand on hers. "None of us are sorry you took us away. I am fortunate that you stopped that day at the fair in Antony. I was yours from the first time I saw you. The only reason I chose to go to school to become a goldsmith was because I did not want to be a blacksmith. Now, I am here in Harmonie working as a blacksmith and I do gold and silver-smithing. I regret none of my choices, and I know Helene, Ezra, and even Timo share my views.

"I want to be by your side; there is no place I'd rather be. With your father's fortune and the Harmonie House, I can begin goldsmithing again, teaching another to be a blacksmith."

As he sat up, Robert's voice had a different tone to it, a more serious tone. "There is one question I have. You have never described the Lady. What does she look like? I have seen a different look in your eyes and face when she is present. And now, I have seen a light. Is that her?"

Nichol paused in thought. "She is not the same each time she comes to me. Sometimes she has dark or black hair, and sometimes white. Sometimes she has light-colored skin and sometimes dark. Sometimes she looks and sounds young, other times, she is older. I see her as the spirit of all women.

"I feel like I have been guided my whole life. I am convinced that the Lady's voice has not only occupied my dreams but she has also directed my actions and decisions. She led me to you and to safety. We are together because of her."

Now, lying on his back, Robert revealed, "I had some doubts until your description of Harmonie became real. You could not know what to look for unless someone told you. You saved Helene and yourself at the cottage. On the road to Rouen, you saved all of us that day when we were attacked. And the day you purchased the bow, you said it was for hunting deer. Now that I know you, I do not think so. Did you get it to protect us?"

Nichol just smiled as she lay back, enjoying the warmth of the sun on her face.

"Robert, none of what we have experienced is a coincidence. I am not sure what the Lady has in mind for us, but I know Lucette is important.

"I believe that Lucette is the one she seeks, not me. And Athena has importance as well. When I gave birth to both, the Lady visited them and me. You saw and experienced it as Helene did when Lucette was born. Both will take her vision and guidance further than what I can do.

"Our children have special gifts … and that includes Aiden."

Silence fell between them. Nichol knew that she needed to reveal more to Robert.

How much should I tell him?

She took a deep breath. "Robert, I hear many messages. I know that there is a greater purpose for our children. Only the Lady knows that purpose and she has not revealed it yet. It is Lucette who will eventually lead this journey we started on. I know our lives—including yours—will contain the light."

Moments later, Robert looked at Nichol, thinking she had fallen asleep. He noticed how relaxed and serene she looked.

She is in a trance.

Robert had witnessed this several times before and knew what was happening.

The Lady is here with her.

Lying quiet and still, Nichol invited the Lady to come to her. She saw her, reminding her of Rose and she saw the light that glowed around her and heard her gentle voice.

I have chosen Lucette and Athena to carry my message of love and equality. They are the ones who will lead, teach, and light the way. You and Robert will protect them, with Aiden at their side.

sixty-seven

Our Lady

Yes, Lucette, I see her.

Something shook Nichol from her dream.

Opening her eyes, she found Lucette sitting next to her, Lucette began patting her face, trying to get her attention.

"Mama .... Mama ...."

A glowing bright light lit her tiny frame. Pointing upward at the source of the light, she said, "See, Mama, see! Lady! My Lady!"

Hugging her daughter to her breast and holding her tightly, a tear rolled down Nichol's cheek. "Yes, Lucette, I see her. It is our Lady."

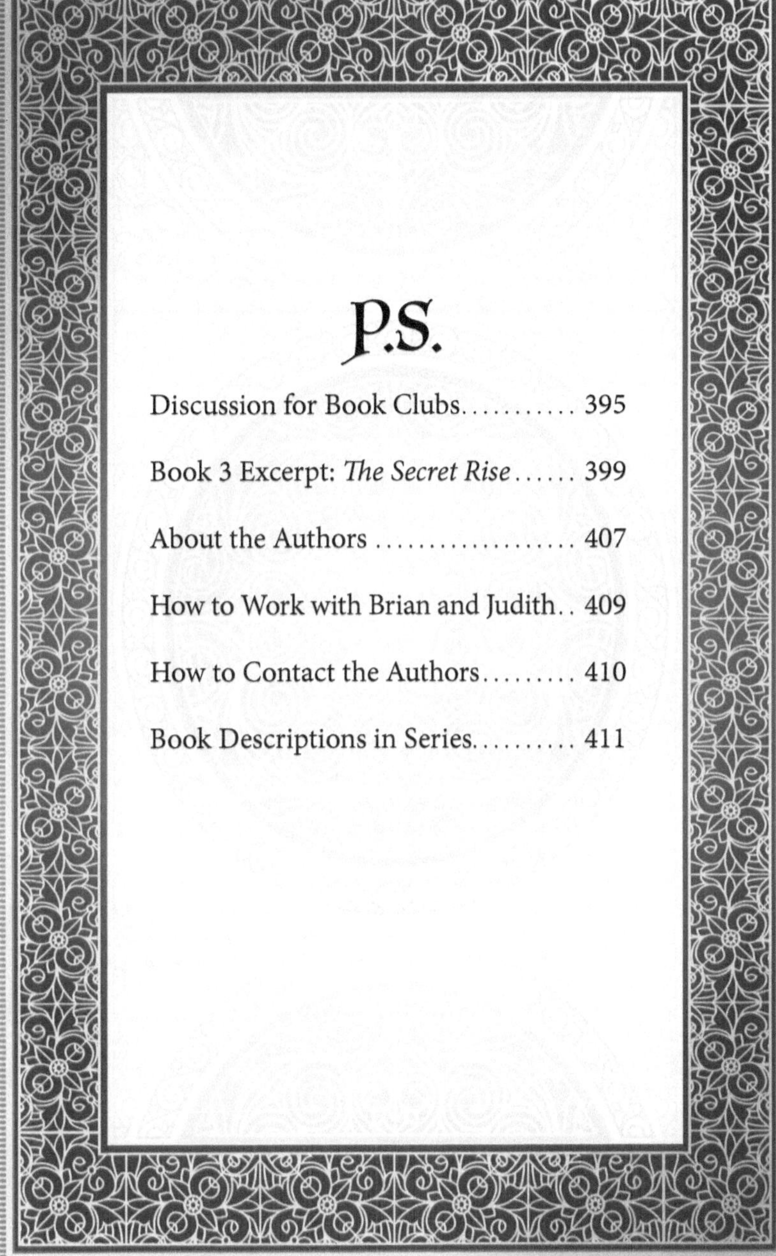

P.S.

Discussion for Book Clubs

The Secret Hamlet

Book Club Leaders … contact Brian and/or Judith to participate in a special meeting to discuss the book; the concepts; and the evolution of the series. We always encourage readers to post individual reviews on *Amazon.com* and we thank you.

In-person author visits are possible if you are in Colorado. Otherwise, Zoom is always an option.

Did *The Secret Hamlet* pull you in? Did you want more?

- Were you satisfied or disappointed with how it ended?

- How do you picture the characters' lives going forward?

- If you were to identify the most important theme within *The Secret Hamlet,* what would it be?

Do you have a favorite part(s)?

- What was it?

- Were you surprised with its reveal?

- Would you like to see more reveals in the next book, *The Secret Rise?*

Do you have a favorite character?

- Who?

- Why?

- Is there anything you particularly liked or disliked about him or her?

What do you think of Nichol's ability to defend herself and others?

- Do you know anyone like her?

- Do you think that there are women like her today?

- Do you think it's important for a woman to be able to physically defend herself?

Was it right for Nichol to listen to the duke's meetings without the other's knowledge?

- Why do you think she didn't tell him what she was doing?

- If he had known earlier, would he have forbidden her to do so?

- Once the duke invited Nichol to listen and watch, do you think he will place too much responsibility on her?

What risks did Nichol undertake as she fled from Paris with Timo's warning?

- Should she have left Ezra and Helene's home as suddenly as she did?

- Should she and the others have disguised themselves?

- Was she right to think the priest was behind it?

Could a young woman in the year 1000 be a merchant, mother, and confident of a future queen?

- How can the two women stay in contact when a country will separate them?

- What could Queen Emma do for Nichol?

- Will men seek to destroy Nichol's presence?

Duke Richard wants Nichol's guidance. Should she give it?

- Should Nichol trust the duke?

- How could Nichol and the hamlet create an alliance with the duke?

- What danger could Nichol bring to the hamlet and to her family?

Would you offer unconditional help to another as Nichol did to Marie and Cara? Have you ever had to ask a stranger for help?

- What fears could asking for help generate?

- What is the likelihood that adequate help would appear?

- What risks did Nichol and Robert take when they agreed to raise and support another infant?

When Nichol slayed the men in the forest, was it the Lady guiding her actions?

- Did her actions and skills surprise you?

- Should she have let the men take the lead in protecting the travelers?

- Should she have risked throwing the dagger?

If Nichol didn't have the voice of the Lady as a support, comfort, and guide, would she have succeeded in her quest?

- Was the Lady real or part of Nichol's imagination?

- What would she have done if the Lady wasn't real?

- Did the Lady always have good intentions for Nichol? Could she turn against her?

When Nichol first met Garlyn, he was caustic. Should she have been cautious?

- When did Garlyn accept her as a spokesperson for Harmonie?

- Could Nichol have garnered his support sooner?

- Will Garlyn be able to get those in No Name to support the Harmonites?

What themes surfaced in the story?

- Have you ever been in a situation where you needed someone to save you?

- Have you ever been in a situation where you did not want someone to save you?

- Have you ever had to step in and help someone out of a dire situation?

- Have you ever had to overlook or accept something so that you could have a relationship with someone?

- Have you ever had to trust someone you barely knew?

- Have you ever offered to help another you barely knew?

- Have you ever allowed yourself to cut off others you knew well because you felt they had become bad?

- Have you ever had inner voices and feelings that guide you?

www.HarmonieBooks.com

www.JudithBrilesBooks.com

Enjoy Book 3 Excerpt of …

the
Secret
Rise

available 2025

Prologue

In the year 1004, Nichol and Robert and a small group of other travelers have founded Harmonie, a new, hidden hamlet in Normandy, less than sixty miles from Paris, France.

Since childhood, Nichol has been gifted with her ability to see and hear others. Her papa valued her advice and sought it in his role as port commander and merchant in Marseilles, France. She was trained to protect herself with a bow and arrow, and a unique jeweled dagger.

She escaped to Paris when he was poisoned by her mother, carrying the map he created that would lead her to Ezra, his partner. Her guide on this dangerous journey was the Lady, a voice and protector, who directed her actions and protected her from harm.

Now, the mother of three and the leader of the hamlet of Harmonie, she has befriended Emma, the young queen of England. Nichol has also intrigued Emma's brother, Duke Richard, owner of the land that Harmonie resides within, unbeknownst to him.

Will Duke Richard provide his protection to Nichol and the hamlet of Harmonie?

Will the alliance and sisterhood of Queen Emma and Nichol continue?

Will the merchants of Rouen, Paris, and the Kingdom of England accept a woman merchant?

Will the red-tailed hawk continue to look over Nichol and the children?

Will the endearing monk Timo become even more valuable as messenger Timo?

Will Ezra's merchant and moneylender business thrive?

Will the evil priest Loupe track Nichol down?

When will the secret hamlet be discovered?

Nichol and Robert are now the parents of three children, Lucette, Aiden, and Athena.

The founders of Harmonie created a unique gathering place called the Harmonie House where hamlet residents gathered to work, cook, and learn together.

The Lady's role has grown, setting the stage for a vibrant community within and external surprises with the adjacent hamlet and the overseer of Normandy.

Each of their children has a special destiny that is revealed in *The Secret Rise,* Book 3, ten years later.

one

The Reunion

He does not look well. Could it be the candlelight?

The trip to Rouen was uneventful but longer than usual. There were no threats from thieves as they walked the entire way, a distance of three days. When they stopped for the evening, the children were delighted with the sleeping cloths Timo laid out for them and the warm cloaks Robert added.

The large cloth that Timo and Robert stretched and tied to three trees created a rough roof over them all. Before everyone settled down to sleep, more wood had been added to the cooking fire.

Timo spread feed for Moki and then lay down for the night. Shadow stayed close to the children as they settled in, between Timo and where Robert and Nichol slept.

In the mornings, the embers from the fire heated any leftovers from supper. Bread and cheese were added and Nichol filled Lucette and Aiden's special lidded cups with fresh water from the nearby stream.

At the end of the third day, they arrived in Rouen as the sun hung low in the sky. Lucette and Aiden were tired and hungry and let everyone know it.

A sudden chill came over everyone.

Winding through the narrow streets, they soon were at Ezra's door. Ezra and Roger were at the kitchen table when Robert rapped at the door. Roger went to the door and asked who was there.

"It is Robert and Nichol."

Ezra leaped to his feet when he heard the names, as Roger unlocked and lifted the wooden beam from the brackets and pulled the door open.

Shadow rushed past Ezra, turned, and wagged her tail, declaring it safe. Nichol entered with Athena snuggled to her breast in her sling and covered by her cloak. Helene followed and flew into Ezra's arms. Her first words were, "Lucette and Aiden must be cared for."

Ezra released his grasp and, as he gazed into her eyes, put both hands on her cheeks and with an enduring look, bent down and kissed her. "Of course, my wife, it will be so. And how I have missed you!"

Roger took a sleeping Aiden into his arms from Robert. Lucette woke up and looked around. It was apparent that she was not going to leave Timo's arms until she knew more of what was happening around her.

Later in the evening, after everyone had eaten and the children were asleep, a gathering around the table took place. Nichol noticed all eyes were on her. Ezra said, "Tell Roger and me about what you have done in Harmonie."

Nichol paused. *He does not look well. Could it be the candlelight?*

She then shared some of the accomplishments: the building and planting successes in Harmonie. When she told him of the trip to the Hill of Hope and Inspiration, he sat straight up. She knew by his look he was intrigued by the children's behavior; he would ask for more details later.

"When we left Harmonie, I told John that we would not return until spring. Robert and I would remain in Rouen for many months." That brought a smile to Ezra as he looked at Helene sitting next to him.

Now, it was Ezra's turn to tell them all of what was happening in Rouen. He began with the business of E & N Merchants.

"Joshua came to my door one afternoon with Diego, who had just sailed in with our cargo. I paid him for his cargo and underwrote his next trip. I took silk, pepper, and sweet salt to the duke, and he was pleased with the gifts."

Turning to Nichol, he added, "His thoughts quickly turned to you. His mannerisms told me that he was impatient for your return and he wishes to see you soon. I heard him say the word *wishes*, but his tone was more of a demand. I think you should see him soon. I can have Roger send word to him that you are back in Rouen."

Nodding her head, Nichol turned to Roger. "Take a message to the duke and tell him that I am here and will see him at his convenience."

They were exhausted from the lengthy walk from Harmonie.

Timo asked Roger if there were rooms at Amos' inn. When Ezra heard the question, he immediately said that he would take care of a room for Timo, and Moki could stay in the stable nearby. Nichol, Robert, and the children would stay in Ezra's home while they were in Rouen.

Ezra wanted to hear more. But he knew that with winter close, they would be together and have much time for more serious conversations.

Of course, he knew that when the new spring approached, they again be returning to Harmonie.

The next morning, the conversation picked up where the tired travelers had stopped sharing the prior evening.

It was mostly about family, children, and successes in Harmonie and Rouen. Plans were made for a supper gathering that included Olaf and Marie, as well as Timo and Roger.

As Nichol looked at Ezra, she thought, *he is livelier this morning. He needed Helene. And he needed to see our children.*

Picking up a piece of bread to sop up the warm broth Helene had placed in front of her, Nichol laughed as Lucette reached her arms up to Ezra and said, "Up, GranPaPa." And Ezra happily added Lucette to his lap.

Brian Barnes

Barnes spent decades in construction. While he built and could fix anything that required a hammer, screwdriver, saw, or drill, his mind filled with stories that only retirement gave him the time to write.

An avid reader of history, historical fiction and a follower of politics and world events, he is appalled when injustice and stupidity are prevalent in the behaviors of those who are in leadership roles. Much of the underlying theme within *The Secret Journey* was ignited by such events and the ignorance of what women are capable of accomplishing and achieving.

The Secret Journey is Brian's debut novel in the Harmonie Books series followed by *The Secret Hamlet*. He is currently creating *The Secret Rise* due out next spring.

Calling Colorado home, he's known as the "fixit guy" to family and friends. Summers pull him and wife Julie into gardening and maintenance within their community of townhomes.

Judith Briles

Briles is the author of 45 books and known as The Book Shepherd to thousands of authors she's worked with. Her construction tools are her words and imagination.

She is a book publishing expert and coach. Often, she must roll up her writing sleeves and become a "book doctor," juicing up storylines and author words. Judith empowers authors and works directly with those who want to be seriously successful. Her recent books include *The Author's Walk, How to Avoid Book Publishing Blunders.* Her books have all been #1 bestsellers on Amazon. Collectively, her books have earned over 50 book awards.

Throughout the year, she holds *Judith Briles Book Unplugged* in-person and online experiences: Publishing, Speaking, Marketing, and Social Media. All are intensives limited to small groups.

Join Judith for the "AuthorU: Your Guide to Book Publishing" podcast she hosts on the Toginet Radio Network.

Calling Colorado home, when not writing, she is most likely in the garden; the kitchen; or planning author events.

Brian and Judith

Book Clubs

Both Brian and Judith are available to book clubs to talk about *The Secret Journey* and forthcoming books in the series in-person in Colorado or on Zoom.

Judith is sole author of dozens of books. Her memoir, *When Gods Says NO: Revealing the YES When Adversity and Loss Are Present*, is about survival and resiliency. Her many books on writing and publishing are ideal to create a discussion for club members who aspire to write and publish.

Bookstore Signings

Veterans at multiple book signings throughout the year, either or both would be delighted to come to your store, creating an event that customers will enjoy. They also will create a press release to support their appearance and push out social media as well.

Speaking

Both Brian and Judith would be delighted to speak about the process of writing; creating a series; and creating voices, attitudes, and behaviors for characters in fiction.

Judith has extensive expertise in publishing: how to get published; how to market books; how to use social media; how to create a successful crowdfunding program; how to avoid publishing mistakes; and how to find the author's voice.

How to Contact the Authors

For Brian

Brian@AuthorBrianBarnes.com

 @HarmonieBooks

 HarmonieBooksSeries

 Harmonie Books

 @HarmonieBooks

For Judith

Judith@Briles.com

303-885-2207

 @MyBookShepherd

 JudithBriles/

 JudithBriles

 BookPublishingHelp/

 Judith.TheBookShepherd

 http://bit.ly/BookPublishingPodcast

 https://bit.ly/Author-PublishingTips

TheBookShepherd.com

JudithBrilesBooks.com

Book 1

The Secret Journey

At 16, Lisa's world unravels. Forced to run to Paris for her survival when her papa is murdered. Will she get there? Will Alexander's partner welcome and help her? Will she discover who killed her papa? Will the Voice that invades her sleep continue to guide her? Will she ever feel safe and loved again? The year is 1000 AD.

Book 2

The Secret Hamlet

With a priest coming for Nichol and her growing family, the *Lady* forewarns her that she must leave Paris at once and seek a new and distant land ... one that will bring peace and prosperity. Nichol's skills and movements are called upon repeatedly to protect them from thieves and the priest as they move toward their destination, the new hamlet of Harmonie. Available 2024.

Book 3

The Secret Rise

Harmonie has prospered under Nichol's leadership and vision. With Ezra's partnership, their commercial ventures have grown greater than her papa's were. The power of Duke Richard and the Church threatens to destroy them and the business success they have created. Once again, Nichol must outsmart and out maneuver those in power and her evil half-brother Fredric. Lucette and Athena display skills that their mother doesn't possess. Available in 2025.

Book 4

The Secret Awakening

The light that the *Lady* has surrounded Nichol with has extended to her daughters. The New Land, a land where women are not subservient to the church or to men, is the final destination with a port expanding trade to neighboring kingdoms and countries for the goods they produce. Available in 2026.

www.ingramcontent.com/pod-product-compliance
Lightning Source LLC
Chambersburg PA
CBHW031825310726

48972CB00005B/1155